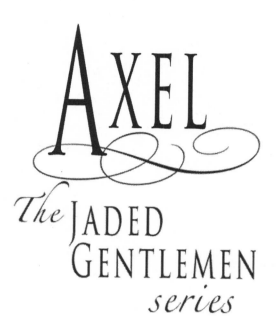

Axel

The Jaded Gentlemen

series

Grace Burrowes

Published by Grace Burrowes Publishing, 21 Summit Avenue, Hagerstown, MD 21740.

ISBN for Axel—The Jaded Gentlemen Book III: 978-1941419205

Cover by Wax Creative, Inc.

To the bench scientists, and to those who love them

ACKNOWLEDGEMENTS

Axel and Abigail's tale is a nice, big book—slightly more than 100,000 words—and the story took me in some unforeseen directions. Twining about the romance is a murder mystery, though I didn't set out to write one of those any more than Axel Belmont set out to be a magistrate. He's a botanist, for pity's sake, and all he wants is to become a fellow at nearby Oxford University.

In the Regency period, the Oxford fellow was not permitted to marry. The lovely folks at the Oxford University Information Office and the Oxford University Archives responded to my inquiries regarding this curious situation, an artifact left over from the University's medieval associations with the church. Without the University's generous assistance on this topic, I would have disappeared down the research rabbit hole, possibly never to be seen again.

I owe another enormous debt to Joyce Lamb, my editor, who is also a RITA™-nominated author of romantic suspense novels. Any boo-boos in these pages are, of course, my own, but if the plot works, if the prose sings, it's because of Joyce's keen eye, and the supporting roles ably played by my proofreaders, Sarah and Cora.

And now, on to the romance… and the roses!

CHAPTER ONE

"Any neighbor who turns up deceased in the middle of a frigid January night has exhibited the height—the very zenith—of bad form."

Axel Belmont announced this thesis to his horse, for Ivan had never been known to contradict one of the professor's opening statements.

"Said bad form," Axel went on, "would be surpassed only by a fellow who has the effrontery to complain of the inconvenience resulting from that neighbor's poorly timed death."

Even if that fellow had been summoned from his late-night glass of wine among his dearest companions, all of whom hailed from the family *Rosaceae*.

"The part about being magistrate I detest the most," Axel muttered as he guided Ivan up the Stoneleigh Manor drive, "is becoming privy to my neighbor's dirty linen. Mind the footing, horse. You are laden with precious cargo."

Precious, *shivering* cargo. Axel's estate bordered the Stoneleigh property, but by the lanes, that was still nearly two miles of slow going in fresh snow. An arctic wind did nothing to improve Axel's mood, nor did the thought of his grafts, abandoned in the warmth of his glass house not thirty minutes earlier.

He brought Ivan to a halt in the Stoneleigh stable yard, and Ambers, the Stoneleigh head groom, stomped out of the barn.

"I'll take your horse, Mr. Belmont. Very bad business at the manor tonight. Very bad, indeed."

"No argument there, Ambers. Hay for my intrepid steed. I don't know how long I'll be." An eternity of the figurative sort at least, for a man who was cold, tired, and more interested in flowers than felonies.

Axel handed off the reins and marched across the stable yard, up the snow-covered drive to Stoneleigh Manor's solid three-story façade. Despite the lateness of the hour, lamps on the front terrace were ablaze. The door opened before Axel had used the boot scrape on his oldest pair of riding boots.

"Come in, Mr. Belmont." Shreve, the Stoneleigh butler bowed. "Come in, please. It's colder than Hades out there tonight, and you'll catch your death…oh dear lord… What I meant to say, well, begging your pardon, sir." The old fellow bowed again, though he'd yet to close the damned door.

"Good evening, Shreve," Axel said, pushing the door closed. "I can see to my own coat, hat, and gloves. Where is the deceased, and where is Mrs. Stoneleigh?"

Shreve gestured vaguely with an ungloved hand. "She's in the library with the, er, with… the colonel. The late colonel." He blinked, then stared straight ahead, as if he'd heard an odd noise of the sort butlers didn't acknowledge.

"Might we have a tea tray in the family parlor?" Axel asked.

More blinking and bowing. "A fine idea, sir. Tea in the family parlor. I'll see to it at once." He'd likely forget before he reached the kitchen, not that Axel was in the mood for a perishing pot of tea.

Axel had been an occasional visitor at Stoneleigh Manor in years past, so he made his way to the study unescorted, knocked once, and let himself in.

Two impressions struck him before he'd taken a half-dozen steps into the room.

The smell of death by gunshot at close range was unmistakable—a hint of blood, metallic and acrid, and overlaying that, the faint, sulfurous stench of the discharged weapon. The second salient aspect of the room was the wintry temperature, caused by the January night air intruding through open French doors.

Axel was halfway across the room, thinking to close the doors, when a single word stopped him.

"Don't."

Mrs. Stoneleigh remained so still in the shadows beside the hearth, Axel hadn't detected her presence. She rose with a rustle of skirts and stepped from the shadows.

"If we lay my husband out in here, the room should remain unheated. Thank you for heeding my summons, Mr. Belmont."

"Mrs. Stoneleigh." Axel took her cold hand, bowed over it, and examined her as closely as manners and firelight would allow. She was tallish for a woman, though still a half foot shorter than Axel's own six feet and several inches. Abigail Stoneleigh was also pretty in a quiet, green-eyed, dark-haired way.

Because she was—had been—another man's wife, Axel's assessment of her beauty had never gone further, though if she weren't so perpetually aloof, if she ever once smiled, she might even be beautiful, not that he'd care one way or the other.

She had to be frozen to the bone.

"If I recall your note," Axel said, "you begged the favor of my presence at my earliest convenience. Hardly a summons, madam." Her penmanship had been elegant, though the groom who'd delivered the note had nearly babbled the news of Stoneleigh's death.

Axel led her over to the hearth, where a dying fire was losing the battle with winter's chill.

"I should warn you, Mrs. Stoneleigh, I am here in the capacity of magistrate as well as neighbor."

"To come at this hour was still considerate of you."

The woman's spouse was crumpled over the desk, not fifteen feet away, her only defense against the frigid air was a plain brown wool shawl, and she was offering pleasantries?

Everybody coped with death differently. Caroline's passing had taught Axel that.

He took off his jacket and draped it around Mrs. Stoneleigh's shoulders. "Why don't we repair to the family parlor? I've asked Shreve to bring the tea tray there."

Mrs. Stoneleigh's gaze swung away, to the darkness beyond the French doors. "My—the colonel would not want to be alone."

Wherever Stoneleigh's soul had gone, the life had departed from his mortal remains. Wanting or not wanting to be alone no longer came into it. Axel knew better than to argue reason at such a time, though.

"Nothing in this room,"—such as a dead body, for example—"can be moved until I've looked the situation over more closely, Mrs. Stoneleigh. I would prefer privacy to do that."

"You may have your privacy, but I'll send Ambers to stay here thereafter. I'll await you in the parlor."

As imperious as a bloody queen—a pale, bloody queen. "You don't want Shreve with the colonel, or perhaps the colonel's valet?"

"Mr. Spellmen is on holiday visiting family in Hampshire. Ambers will do. Shreve is overwrought."

While the lady was glacially calm. She also bore the faint fragrance of attar of roses, which realization had Axel longing for his glass house all over again.

He escorted her to the door, then turned his attention to the question of how a man reasonably well liked, in good health, with wealth aplenty, and no apparent vices had managed to get a bullet through his heart at close range in his very own home.

* * *

Abigail waited until the door latch clicked shut before drawing Axel Belmont's wool coat more closely around her. His garment smelled good, of fresh flowers and the green, growing scent of a conservatory, and the coat was blessedly warm from the heat of his big body.

Mr. Belmont and Gregory had always been on noddingly cordial terms, so over the years, Abby had had some opportunity to observe her neighbor.

The magistrate was pleasant to observe: tall, blond, and good-looking in the way of a man who likes to be out of doors. He was considered quite the catch, having both family and personal wealth, and he was always in demand as an escort or partner at the local assemblies. To his credit, he was devoted to his sons, Dayton and Phillip, and he was a quiet neighbor.

He'd come in response to Abby's note, in the middle of a frigid, snowy night too.

From Abby's perspective, his list of positive traits ended there. Mr. Belmont had a blunt, uncompromising quality, an indifference to the opinions of others, an inner set of convictions that made him rigid, to her way of thinking. Others referred to him as quite bright—he lectured at Oxford!—and academically inclined, for he'd published many scholarly treatises on botanical topics.

In Mr. Belmont's presence, Abby had always felt tacitly condemned for marrying a wealthy man thirty years her senior.

But what, what on God's green earth, could she have done otherwise? And what was she to do now?

Shreve appeared with the tea tray, an inordinately comforting bit of consideration. Then Abby recalled that Mr. Belmont had ordered this sustenance for her.

Nonetheless, a hot, sweet cup of tea settled the nerves, and Abby's nerves were… overwrought. She swallowed past a lump in her throat at that understatement. She could *not* have Mr. I Am Here As The Magistrate Of Doom Belmont see her discomposed.

"Shreve," she said as the butler turned to withdraw, "because Mr. Belmont will be joining me forthwith, perhaps you'd better fetch the decanter from the library."

"Will there be anything else, madam?"

He needed to be kept busy, to be given simple tasks, lest he fall to pieces.

Abby needed simple tasks too. "If you'd bring me my lap desk, please? Family will have to be notified, and I'll write those notes before I retire. When Mrs. Pritchard arrives, she can lay the colonel out in the study, provided Mr. Belmont is through. The neighbors may call Thursday afternoon between two and five, and I'll send a note to the vicar to that effect.

"We'll need the black hangings," Abby went on, though making her mind focus on practicalities was a prodigious effort. "You'll find the crepe in the attic above the gallery. Any servant still awake may have a medicinal tot of spirits, for we'll need our rest, despite tonight's upset. Draping the windows, mirrors, and portraits can all wait until tomorrow."

As could crying, pacing, and fretting. Swooning, though tempting, was out of the question.

"Yes, madam." When Shreve returned with the brandy and the writing supplies, Abby sent him sniffing and blinking back to the kitchen. Shreve had been with her husband since the colonel had come home from India eleven years ago.

The butler, unlike the lady of the house, was entitled to faltering composure.

Abby turned her focus to writing an obituary, because the local weekly would expect it of her.

Then too, she needed to remain occupied, or she'd hear again the obscene report of a gun in her own home, at an hour when all should have been seeking their beds.

Her third draft of an opening sentence was disturbed by a single, brisk knock on the door, followed by Axel Belmont striding into the family parlor. His height and his sense of purpose made the room seem small, and if Abby had resented him before, he provoked her to positive distaste now.

She rose from the sofa and shrugged out of his coat. "I trust you left Ambers at his post?" she asked, holding the coat out to her guest.

Though tonight he was *the magistrate*, not a guest at all.

Mr. Belmont slipped into the coat with the ease of a man who managed often without a valet.

"I left Ambers in the study with Mrs. Pritchard. Shall we sit? We have matters to discuss, Mrs. Stoneleigh. Matters you will find troubling. I can delay this conversation until tomorrow, but the news will not improve with time."

Gregory would be just as dead, in other words.

"My husband shot himself," Abby said as evenly as she could. She put that blunt reality on offer, not because she wanted to spare Mr. Belmont's delicate sensibilities, if any such sensibilities he possessed.

Abby spoke those terrible, bewildering words because she needed to yank the truth out of the shadows down the corridor, where it quite honestly frightened her.

"The colonel was in good health," she went on. "He had much to live for, seemed in reasonably good spirits most of the time, and yet he took his own life. What could be more troubling than that?"

* * *

Your lack of reaction, Axel wanted to retort, but when his own spouse had died, his control hadn't slipped until he'd come upon his brother Matthew, holding a sobbing Dayton after the funeral.

"Let me tell you what I've observed so far," Axel suggested. "Shall I pour?" A widower would expire of dehydration if he didn't learn to navigate a tea service.

"I've had a cup. Shreve brought the brandy if you'd rather."

"I would." Tea at nearly midnight, at the scene of a crime, seemed insufficient fortification given what Axel had to tell her.

Mrs. Stoneleigh poured him a generous portion of brandy, the glow from the hearth creating fiery highlights in her dark hair. Her movements were elegant and graceful, and that was somehow wrong.

Was she surprised by her husband's death? Relieved? *Pleased?*

"First," Axel said, after a bracing sip of good brandy, "my condolences on your loss."

"My thanks." Two words, and tersely offered. She took one side of a brocade love seat pulled close to the hearth. "Won't you sit, Mr. Belmont? The hour is late, you have to be tired, and we must discuss awkward matters. I'd rather be able to see your face."

Forthright, Axel thought, running a hand through his hair, which the winter wind had doubtless left in ungentlemanly disarray. Mrs. Stoneleigh had a way of expressing herself that made him feel as if he were trying her patience and insulting her intelligence.

All thorns and no blossom.

Axel could be blunt too. He lowered himself not into a wing chair, but to the place right beside her.

"I have reason to believe your husband was the victim of foul play." Murder being the foulest form of human *play* imaginable. "To quiet misgivings from our vicar, I will preliminarily rule death by accident."

Mrs. Stoneleigh was silent for a moment, not reacting at all.

Then she sat taller. "Sir, you will explain yourself. Please."

"The cause of death was likely that gunshot to the chest—to the heart—as you no doubt suspected." Contrary to what the Gothic novels propounded, once the heart ceased performing its function, little bleeding occurred—and Stoneleigh's heart had stopped instantly.

"I did not move the body," Mrs. Stoneleigh said, her hand going to her middle. "I knew he was dead, because I put my fingers to the side of his neck, and I saw blood spattered on the desk and blotter. I also saw the gun in his hand, but I did not... I did not *look.*"

"You were wise not to disturb the scene." Was she reacting now? Was there a slight tension around her eyes and mouth? She was mortally pale, though many English women went to pains to protect their complexions.

"You needn't flatter me, Mr. Belmont. I simply did not know what to do, other than to send for my nearest neighbor."

Who had the bad luck to be serving as the temporary magistrate—something she apparently hadn't known.

"Given the gun in your husband's hand, a casual observer might think the colonel had, indeed, taken his own life, or perhaps had an accident while cleaning his equipment."

Axel took another swallow of brandy, resisting the urge to down it all at once.

Mrs. Stoneleigh reached toward the tea service as if to pour herself a second cup, but her hand drifted to her lap instead.

"God help my late husband if, after more than twenty years in the cavalry, he was attempting to clean a loaded gun."

"True." Axel hadn't considered that perspective. "The difficulty with the theory of suicide, though, is that the gun in your husband's hand had not been fired and was, in fact, still loaded. Your husband was shot, and the fatal bullet was not fired at close range."

Axel braced himself for a swoon, some ladylike weeping, even a fit of hysterics. People took their own lives. This was tragic, of course, but in Axel's estimation, suicide was preferable to murder most foul two doors down the corridor.

"How can you tell how far away the bullet was fired?" Mrs. Stoneleigh's voice was steady, her gaze on the fire equally steady, and her very composure ripped at Axel's sensibilities. She'd been married to the man for, what, nearly a decade?

She might have been discussing the weather.

He topped up his brandy and gave her a brief explanation of the initial evidence.

"Powder burns," she summarized. "You are saying the colonel's clothes have no powder burns."

"None to speak of, so the bullet must have been fired from some distance."

"Is there more?" she asked, gaze still fixed on the flames.

"Not much." Would a second brandy refill be rude—or stupid? "The dimensions of the wound suggest a small gun was used, and from across the room. Such weapons—pea shooters—are notoriously inaccurate. They lack the length of barrel to steady the projectile toward its target, and such a small weapon seldom fires with much force."

"I've carried such guns, and you are correct. Their greatest value is in the noise they create, but somebody apparently had good aim."

Would a woman guilty of murder make such an admission? "Who heard the shot, Mrs. Stoneleigh?"

"I did. I was in my room, directly above the colonel's study, where he usually finished his evenings with a nightcap. Shreve would have heard the shot, because he was in the corridor tending to the lamps, as was his habit as the hour approached eleven. Those servants still awake below stairs heard it, as did Ambers, who was outside the stable master's quarters smoking. Ambers was the first to arrive at the colonel's side. Shreve became occupied with... escorting me to the scene."

If somebody on that list hadn't killed the colonel, then a murderer as yet unknown had also heard the shot and taken off across the snowy grounds, all footprints conveniently obliterated by the brisk wind.

"The colonel never finished that nightcap," Axel said. "I'll want to talk to Ambers, and to Shreve, sooner rather than later, and to the rest of your staff."

What Axel truly wanted was to return to the quiet and warmth of his glass house, there to work on grafts until his back ached and his vision blurred.

"Shreve is busy now," Mrs. Stoneleigh said. "He should be available to speak with you mid-morning tomorrow."

Axel was the magistrate, for pity's sake, investigating the murder of her husband in her own home. She ought to want answers more than she wanted her next breath. "What can Shreve possibly have to keep him busy?"

The look in Mrs. Stoneleigh's eyes was faintly pitying. Her expression was as close to warm as Axel had seen it, ever, then he realized the direction of her thoughts.

"When a spouse dies," she said, gently, "there is much to be done. The windows must be hung with crepe, and the portraits and mirrors in the public rooms, as well. The liveried servants must acquire black armbands, the deceased must be laid out, the coffin built, the surviving family's wardrobe must be dyed black, the hearse hired, the vicar notified, and so forth. You know this."

Axel did know this, and he resented her bitterly for making him recall that he knew it. Resentment fueled by fatigue prompted his next observation.

"You're coping with your husband's demise well, Mrs. Stoneleigh."

"Am I a suspect?" The pity, at least, was gone from her eyes.

"No." *Not yet.* "But if murder was done in this house, while others were about, then we have both a crime and mystery on our hands."

"And a tragedy," she amended. "Have you more questions, Mr. Belmont, or shall I see you out?"

"I can see myself out," Axel replied, unhappy with himself for his pique. "And again, my condolences." He rose, surprised when she did as well, albeit slowly, and walked him to the door.

"You seem fatigued," she said. "Unusually so, not merely like a man at the end of a long day." Her observation wasn't rude, but neither was it... flattering.

"I've arrived just this afternoon from my brother's home in Sussex, hailed back to Oxfordshire by Rutland's decision to nip off to Bath in the dead of winter. Phillip and Dayton chose to remain with their uncle until spring."

Unfortunate word choice—*dead* of winter—which she was apparently too much of a lady to react to.

"You are orphaned, then. I am sorry to have disturbed you when you are much in need of rest. Shall I tell Shreve to expect you tomorrow morning?"

Axel spared a thought for his grafts and crosses.

"By eleven," he replied, taking her hand and bowing over it. "Will you be all right?"

Now where had that come from, and why was her hand still so cold?

"I don't know." She seemed unaware of their joined hands, or at least unconcerned. "I've heard of people being shocked beyond the expression of appropriate sentiments, and I suspect I am in that situation. My husband is dead, and though we were not... entangled, as some spouses are, I did not foresee such an end to the day, to any of my days. The colonel was not ill, he was not reckless, he did not drink to excess..."

A minute shudder passed through her, one Axel detected only because he was holding her hand.

"I suppose," she went on, "I will realize more fully what has befallen this house when Mrs. Pritchard and I lay out my... the body."

"Mrs. Pritchard will charge you good coin for tending to that office, and she needs the money too. You are not to return to the study until the morning." Axel made it an order, which was a blunder. The father of two adolescent boys learned that giving orders all but guaranteed his wishes would be disrespected.

Mrs. Stoneleigh withdrew her hand. "I want to argue with you, but only to argue for argument's sake, not because I want to see my husband's corpse, particularly, not with a bullet..."

Another little shiver, two...

"Mrs. Stoneleigh?" Axel drew her back over to the hearth, grabbing an afghan from the back of the love seat and draping it over her shoulders. "Have you somebody who can sit with you, get you up to bed?"

"I do not use a lady's maid," she said, much the same as she might have reported eschewing sugar in her tea. "The colonel regards it... *regarded it*... Well, no. I do not have a lady's maid."

Axel endured an inconvenient stab of compassion—one that temporarily obliterated the question of her role in her husband's death. Abigail Stoneleigh was alone, more alone than a woman expected to be at the age of... twenty-eight? Twenty-nine? Her husband had died violently, and even if she'd killed him, who knew what her motivations might have been?

Time enough later to locate proper outrage if she'd done the old boy a fatal turn.

Axel took a moment to study her, the way he'd studied each and every specimen in his glass houses when he'd returned to Candlewick after weeks of absence. Mrs. Stoneleigh looked overwatered and undernourished, ready to drop leaves and wilt.

"I don't want to leave you alone."

"I'll manage." She was grimly certain on that point. "I've been managing alone for some time, Mr. Belmont. My thanks for your concern. Until tomorrow."

Axel had no authority to gainsay her, so he bowed and took his leave. He was back on his horse—why on God's good green earth had nobody devised a means of warming a saddle before a man sat his innocent, unsuspecting arse on chilled leather?—when he finally put a name to what he'd seen in Mrs. Stoneleigh's luminous green eyes the last time he'd bowed over her hand.

Fear. Mrs. Stoneleigh was afraid, but was she afraid of the murderer, or of having her part in the murder revealed?

CHAPTER TWO

A small crowd stood about in the frozen churchyard after the service, most people keeping scarves wrapped about their faces. The snow muffled sound further, in addition to the quiet required by the solemnity of the occasion.

Because nobody seemed comfortable approaching the widow directly, Axel took it upon himself to escort Mrs. Stoneleigh back to the manor, a mile's distance along a frozen, rutted lane. He let the other menfolk see to the graveside ritual, and the concomitant freezing of ears, nose, and toes.

"Shall I have a carriage sent?" he asked.

Mrs. Stoneleigh lifted back her black veil and pinned it to her bonnet, revealing eyes a little red at the rims. By daylight, she was too thin, too pale, and yet, also too pretty.

"We can walk," she said, which comported with the decision of most of the congregation. "I am much in need of activity and fresh air, if you don't mind. The past days have seen me nigh trapped in that house."

Axel tucked her hand over his arm, knowing all too well the road Mrs. Stoneleigh faced—assuming he didn't have to arrest her for murder.

"When Caroline died, I was struck by the contrasts," he said. "The house was so full of people on the day of her funeral, I wanted to bellow them off the premises, and then it was empty. Wretchedly, unendingly empty. I wanted company, and I wanted to be alone. Caroline was nowhere to be seen, and she was everywhere I looked."

"She died in winter, didn't she?"

"March. We spent the next March with my brother, but then his spouse also died." Axel's own grief had finally lessened when he had become the one who knew the path of mourning. He'd tended to the practicalities while Matthew had reeled and stumbled, and stared into an unrecognizable future.

"Aren't you supposed to tell me time will heal my loss, Mr. Belmont? That a quick death is a mercy?"

Axel suspected spouting platitudes to this woman, even as wan and slender as she was, might land him on his arse in the snow.

"Somebody has already told you what a blessing it is to have your freedom, I take it, along with all the casseroles you can eat, provided the sight of nothing but black for the next year doesn't destroy your appetite."

A chance to start over, some fool had said upon Caroline's death. *To find a fresh mount.* Axel hadn't known whether to be violent or sick, or violently sick, at that brand of comfort.

"You might consider going away," Axel suggested after they'd hiked a quarter mile directly into the wind. "Spain is a pleasant contrast this time of year, or Italy."

"And who will tend Stoneleigh Manor? Gregory left it to me, or told me he would, and I don't trust his children to care for the estate in my absence. They are much enamored of their city routines."

Mrs. Stoneleigh was Axel's immediate neighbor, and Colonel Stoneleigh had ridden Candlewick's bounds more than once in Axel's absence.

"I will keep an eye on the property for you, if necessary. For the next month or two, nothing will need much tending in any case." Travel would also allow the widow a margin of safety if the murderer was still in the vicinity—assuming she hadn't had Stoneleigh killed herself.

"That is a generous offer, Mr. Belmont. A kind offer, and I will consider it, but I would like to know who killed my husband before I abandon his house for sunshine and new faces."

"We would both like that answer." She, likely so she could put her husband's memory to rest; Axel, so he could return to the soothing embrace of his flowers, and the herbal on horticultural remedies for female complaints that would be his next publication.

After more trudging arm in arm, they passed through the Stoneleigh Manor gates. Black bunting luffed in a bitter breeze, and the head footman, a black armband pinned to his sleeve, black crepe about his hat, bowed them onto the property.

"You will tell me if I am a suspect?" Mrs. Stoneleigh asked, halfway up the drive.

By night, the house had looked settled and solid. Under gray skies, with windows swagged in black crepe, the façade was as grim as an open grave. All dead grass, dark earth, cold, and sorrow.

Mrs. Stoneleigh's question required an answer.

"You are not a suspect, as of now. I considered you, of course, because you had opportunity, living in proximity to the deceased. You had motive, being one of Stoneleigh's heirs. Shreve reports you came down the stairs in response to his cries of alarm. Unless you found a way to shoot your husband, discard the murder weapon, climb up to the second floor, and then emerge from your room and run down the stairs, you are not the perpetrator. Finally, Mrs. Jensen was going up to her room and saw you emerge from your bedroom."

Axel's relief upon interviewing the housekeeper had been considerable. For all Abigail Stoneleigh was not likable, he'd wanted her to be innocent of murder. As a result, he'd investigated her activities thoroughly.

"I am truly not under suspicion?" Her voice was low, carefully steady.

"You were concerned?" She was not under suspicion of having pulled the trigger, though she might have hired an accomplice.

Her gaze flicked over his face as they crunched along the frozen road. "Rather than sleep, I have thought and thought about the colonel's death. Shreve said the French doors were open a crack when Ambers found Gregory—Ambers came through those doors and claims he hadn't had to unlatch them."

Thus far, her recitation comported with the sequence of events as Axel had been able to reconstruct them. Shreve had dissolved into dignified tears fifteen minutes into Axel's attempts to question him. Ambers had been summoned from his interview by news of the colonel's favorite afternoon hunter cast beneath a pasture fence.

"Shreve assumed the doors were open for fresh air," Mrs. Stoneleigh went on, "because Gregory often enjoyed a pipe with his brandy, though doubtless the killer left in haste. I asked Ambers to look for fresh tracks, but he was unwilling to leave me alone under the circumstances, and the winter wind did its work quickly."

Axel could not fault Ambers's decision, for the *circumstances* had included a murderer at large, or possibly dithering about the very scene of the crime.

"We have only Shreve's word regarding the open French doors," Axel said. "Ambers told me that they were unlocked, not that they were ajar."

Shreve ought to be a suspect, along with the dapper, devoted Mr. Ambers, who'd been so conveniently smoking out of doors at the very hour his employer had been murdered. No night porter had been on duty at the front door to confirm Ambers's contention that he'd come hotfoot up the main drive either.

"You don't want to accuse Shreve?" Mrs. Stoneleigh asked.

"I do not." What man wanted to accuse *anybody* of murder? "He hasn't as clear an alibi as you. He was closest to the scene, and he had time to commit the crime, open the French doors, secret the murder weapon somewhere, then run into the corridor."

Though, damn and blast the luck, diligent searching with a strong compass magnet had not revealed a gun beneath the snow anywhere near the house.

"What is Shreve's motive?" the lady asked, as if repeating a familiar query. "Gregory left Shreve a tidy sum for years of service, but Shreve will probably keep his post with me."

Clearly, Mrs. Stoneleigh knew the contents of her late husband's will. "Lack of apparent motive is one reason I have not taken him or Ambers into custody."

"Character," Mrs. Stoneleigh rejoined, "is another. Ambers has been with us for years, as has Shreve. He and Gregory struck up an acquaintance on the passage home from India, and they were as close as servant and employer could be."

Axel and the widow toiled up the drive arm in arm, the silence between them growing chillier with each step.

"I am sorry, madam. Murder is offensive business. I am insensitive to discuss such matters with you now. I do apologize."

"Don't," she said. "I would rather have your blunt questions than Mr. Weekes' well-meant platitudes. His eulogy was interesting."

The eulogy had been blessedly short, given how cold the church was. The Stoneleigh Manor drive, by contrast, seemed quite long.

"Did the vicar's eulogy in any way describe the man you were married to?"

"As long as we're being shockingly honest, there was a resemblance— Gregory loved his hounds."

Gregory Stoneleigh had loved to strut about, waving his riding crop in time to his bloviations.

"But?"

"But Gregory had no more clue how to run this estate and care for his lands than I would have about, say, building one of your glass houses. I think he married me largely for my ability to salvage his estate."

"I wasn't aware of that." Because Mrs. Stoneleigh's attractiveness was the first thing any man would see about her—and her reserve.

She marched up the front drive, from which the snow had been cleared. "Gregory was a cavalry officer to his bones. The horses were exclusively his domain, and he doted on them endlessly. The home farm, the tenant farms, the cottages, the commerce, the crops, the cloven-hoofed stock, the dairy—they baffled him, and by the time we married, the functional parts of the estate were much in need of management."

"Stoneleigh came out eleven years ago?" Axel tried to recall the year, pegging everything in memory against his sons' ages, his wife's death, or when he'd built the second glass house.

The wind caught Mrs. Stoneleigh's black veil and batted it against her mouth. She re-secured the lace with an onyx hat pin, never missing a step.

"The colonel returned to England more than ten years ago. He lasted here some years before the income stopped covering the expenses. He wasn't about to invest his own money in the land, his Indian wealth being for his children, so he acquired me to improve the situation."

Her recitation was matter of fact, not quite bitter.

"The colonel explained this to you?" If this was Stoneleigh's entire view of marriage, the lady's lack of obvious grief made more sense.

Axel was so intent on the conversation, that when Mrs. Stoneleigh slipped on a patch of muddy ice, he nearly didn't catch her.

For a moment, she hung against him. For those few instants, she struck Axel as too slight, disoriented, and winded, rather than prickly or overly composed.

She straightened and resumed her progress. "Gregory was honest. I was desperately in need of marrying—my parents had recently perished in a house fire—and he was in need of a competent wife for his country estate. He provided well, and I saw to it he was left free to ride about the countryside—occasionally with you—while his children got on with the business of being adults."

None of the mourners walking ahead had so much as glanced back at Mrs. Stoneleigh's misstep.

"When are Stoneleigh's children expected?"

"Gervaise will arrive on Tuesday, Lavinia probably the same day, possibly a day later, but they'll stay in Oxford. Each made it plain I was not to delay the final obsequies on their behalf."

Axel had met the son—a handsome, bachelor barrister quite assured of his own consequence—but not the daughter.

Mrs. Stoneleigh stumbled again on a rut, this time pitching right into Axel.

He wrestled with the impulse to carry her to the manor, which lay a hundred yards ahead. She'd hate him for that, and yet... He kept both hands on her shoulders and studied her, not as a magistrate searches for clues, but as botanist assesses a specimen newly arrived to his care.

"You are tired. Exhausted, probably. Can you sleep?" The question was personal, even from one who had been bereaved himself, though she did not appear to take offense.

"I can sleep." She glanced away, as if she recognized the bleak winter landscape and could not place where she'd seen it before. "Some. Gregory and I were cordial, but my bed is not where I miss him."

Her husband had been thirty years her senior, and had had a daughter nearly her age. Conjugal relations between the Stoneleighs had likely been infrequent and ... subdued. And yet, the male part of Axel regretted that a man was dead and his own wife would not miss his attentions—at all.

"You missed your Caroline that way, though, didn't you?" Mrs. Stoneleigh asked. "As more than a cordial housemate? I am so sorry, Mr. Belmont. Women can cry, carry on, faint, and go into declines, but men are allowed much less latitude when bereaved."

How Axel hated funerals, all funerals, and nearly hated Abigail Stoneleigh for her very solicitude.

"I missed Caroline." He still missed her—sometimes.

"She was wonderfully lively," Mrs. Stoneleigh replied. "I envied her that boisterousness, and she seemed an ideal mother for two busy little fellows."

They reached the house, the widow leaning on Axel more than she had earlier. Perhaps she allowed his support because she was tired, or perhaps because Axel had given her a few honest words, and she'd comforted him.

Caroline had died so long ago, he should no longer need comforting, and he didn't. And yet, Mrs. Stoneleigh's condolences hurt, albeit not with the same tearing pain they might have years ago. The late Mrs. Belmont had been a healthy, strapping Viking of a woman, lusty, lively, and perfectly capable of matching her retiring young spouse measure for measure, in bed or in an argument.

Some might have considered Caroline unfeminine, but she'd been a good mate for him, and she had thrived on raising the children.

"My wife and I suited, as opposites do," Axel said, pulling his thoughts back into the present. "You and I have arrived to our destination, Mrs. Stoneleigh. I believe Mrs. Weekes has commandeered your music room and formal parlor for the buffet."

"Will you escort me there?" Trepidation flickered in her eyes as she beheld the black crepe wrapped about the front door knocker. "If I must stand around and accept condolences, at least I'll do so indoors. That sky looks like snow, and my feet are frozen. But forgive me. You are being very kind, and I am out of sorts."

"You are grieving," Axel said, quietly enough not to be overheard by others coming up the drive. "There is nothing to forgive."

The look she gave him might have been gratitude, with a bit of adroitly masked surprise.

He took her around to a side entrance—no crepe on the knocker—and let her establish herself in a corner of the music room. Folding doors between the largest parlor and the music room had been opened, and furniture moved aside to create a large open space—large enough for dancing, in other circumstances.

A groaning buffet was set up along the outside wall.

Like his brother Matthew, Axel could put away a prodigious amount of food. Maybe the local populace hadn't particularly taken to Mrs. Stoneleigh when her husband had lived, but by God, they knew how to cook for a funeral. Axel put himself together a plate and found a quiet vantage point from which to observe mourners offering their platitudes to the new widow.

As he demolished the food—why did all funeral casseroles taste the same?—he kept an eye out for possible suspects.

Mrs. Stoneleigh had been holding court in her corner for almost two hours when Axel decided the shadows under her eyes and her pallor demanded she be allowed privacy.

"Would you be offended, Mrs. Stoneleigh, if I suggested the assemblage is waiting for you to withdraw?"

"Is that how it's done? Well, I am willing to oblige." When she rose, she leaned on Axel and didn't merely take his arm for show.

Mrs. Weekes took Mrs. Stoneleigh's other arm. "She hasn't taken a thing to eat, poor lamb. Not so much as a tea cake."

The poor lamb stiffened, perhaps at being referred to in the third person.

"Wait here." Axel ducked over to the buffet and filled another plate. He crooked his elbow at Mrs. Stoneleigh, and barely waited for her to wrap her fingers around his arm. "You simply leave. You keep walking, you don't chat, don't meet anybody's gaze. Otherwise, your neighbors will shower you with their infernal, interminable kindness until you can barely stand."

The lady heeded his instructions, and within moments, he had her upstairs in her private sitting room, a plate of food before her.

"Eat," he admonished. "I'll fetch you tea, unless you'd like something stronger?"

"Tea would be lovely, with milk and sugar."

He eyed the plate, from which she had eaten nothing, and realized he was well and truly—if inconveniently—worried about her. The worry housed a goodly dose of resentment too, which probably made him convincing when he treated her to his best "do as the professor says" scowl before taking his leave.

Axel Belmont, an unlikely guardian angel if ever there was one, would stand over Abby until she consumed her portion, so she tucked into the food. He'd chosen simple fare: slices of apple, cheese, and ham, and two pieces of liberally buttered bread.

He paid attention, and not simply to the evidence relevant to a murder investigation.

Mr. Belmont had loved his wife, as had been obvious to anyone with eyes. His Caroline had loved him back, and loved their boys as well. They'd been such a happy little family, Abigail had dreaded the sight of them, the boys up before their parents when they rode out, or all four in the buggy on their way to church.

So of course, Mr. Belmont would comprehend that rich food did not digest easily on a grieving stomach. He would understand that a woman needed solitude after dealing with so many people, most of whom hadn't bothered to call on her twice in all the years she'd dwelled among them. He would grasp immediately all manner of realities Gregory would never have understood even were they explained in detail.

Mr. Belmont reappeared carrying not a delicate tea cup, but a substantial, steaming mug.

"Your tea, and I purloined a few of these." From his pocket he withdrew several tea cakes in a serviette, keeping one for himself and putting the rest on Abby's plate.

"Will you sit, sir?" The tea was ambrosial, soothing and fortifying, prepared to the exact sweetness she preferred.

Mr. Belmont flipped out his tails and lowered himself beside her. "I will remain as long as you keep eating. I am avoiding interrogation by the gentlemen around the punch bowl."

Interrogation about—? Oh.

Oh dear. Abby bit into a cold slice of apple. "For you and I to be closeted up here isn't quite proper, is it?"

He settled back, his frame filling his corner of the sofa with elegant, sober tailoring, and a perpetual scowl.

"You're a widow now. By virtue of your husband's demise, you graduate from needing chaperonage to being a source of it."

Like the tea, the apple was lovely. Belmont's brusque company was fortifying too, oddly enough.

"We are such a silly society," Abby said.

"In many ways, though you have cleared the first hurdles of losing a spouse, so some of the silliness is behind you. You're through the death, the wake, and the burial, and can get on with the grieving."

Death. Mr. Belmont eschewed platitudes and euphemisms, while Gregory had hardly ever dealt in blunt truths. All bluster and chit-chat, when he wasn't scolding some servant or other.

Or his wife.

"I keep waiting for the grieving to start." Abby considered a slice of apple, which her grandpapa had insisted was the fruit of the tree of knowledge of good and evil. "I keep waiting for tears, for sorrow, for something momentous, but all I feel is upset and… sad."

"I recall saying nearly the same thing to my brother when Caroline died. There's no wrong way to mourn. You've described your relationship with Stoneleigh as cordial, and maybe a marriage free of passion means you are spared passionate grief as well."

Must he be so philosophical? Abby set the rest of the apple slice on the plate.

"Perhaps I will sit bolt upright in bed at midnight, realize I have no spouse, and be overcome by strong hysterics." *Again.* For what Abby *did* have was a *late* spouse, who'd been murdered at his very desk.

Mr. Belmont ranged an arm along the back of the sofa, the gesture of a man not put off by an ungracious comment.

"Does the possibility of hysterics concern you, Mrs. Stoneleigh?"

Abby had many, many concerns. "One doesn't know whether to be more concerned by a temptation toward drama, or a lack thereof. I've never been a widow before. Ah, what an awful word that is: widow."

His scowl became less fierce, more irascible. What sort of man had a vocabulary of scowls?

"Widower is equally as unappealing," he said. "Then it takes on a gilded edge in the eyes of some, as a man becomes desirable for his bereaved status." This gilding had not appealed to Mr. Belmont.

"Women whose spouses have died are seldom viewed as having the same cachet as men in similar circumstances."

Perhaps because the men could and did quickly remarry. Nonetheless, this startlingly unsentimental conversation was safer ground than the floundering bewilderment that had struck Abby the instant she'd seen her husband's body.

Or the fear.

Mr. Belmont passed her a slice of cheese. "If you inherit this property, then you are a wealthy widow. Stoneleigh Manor is lovely, well run, and large, as acreages go in this area. I'd wager that among those assembled below, you will find several of the single gentlemen prompt with their condolence calls, and a few won't even wait three months."

A spark of anger flared, at Gregory, for subjecting Abby to those gentlemen and their *prompt* calls after years of neighborly indifference.

She took a bite of the cheese, an excellent cheddar. "You speak from unhappy experience."

"I do. A man cannot possibly raise his own sons without the assistance of some female who knows the children not and loves them not."

Many men wouldn't even try. "I regret that we never had children."

Mr. Belmont moved Abby's tea closer to her side of the tray. "Would you really want to be comforting a seven-year-old today, trying to explain why her papa can't ever take her riding again, or why death isn't like oversleeping?"

Abby accepted the second slice of bread from Mr. Belmont's hand, along with the knowledge that his wretched honesty was more comforting than all the platitudes of condolence put together.

"No wonder you are such an ill-tempered fellow."

He shot his cuffs, which sported a surprising dash of lace. "My sister-in-law calls me reserved, my sons describe me as professorially stern. My brother says I'm backward but dear, and my late wife called me an ass more often than you might think."

Heavenly days, Mr. Belmont's recitation provoked him to something approaching a smile.

"Your brother has remarried?" Abby posed the question with the relief of a befogged mariner whose conversational oars have bumped against dry land by chance.

"Recently." Mr. Belmont held her mug of tea out to her.

She sipped and set it down, but shook her head when he presented a slice of ham.

"You are pale as a winter sky, madam. You need sustenance."

"I need a pause in my gluttony." Abby cradled the mug close, wrapping both hands around its warmth. "I haven't eaten much lately, and my digestion is tentative."

Blond brows lowered to piratical depths. "Could you be carrying a posthumous child?"

How... presuming and sad the question was. "I could *not*." Before Mr. Belmont could stumble through an apology for that bluntness too, Abby charged on. "Oh, don't poker up. I wasn't that sort of wife."

He busied himself building up the fire, while Abby wondered what he'd make of her expostulation. He was apparently condoling the widow today, not investigating the murder, so he kept his questions behind his perfect, white teeth.

"I will take my leave of you," he said, when the fire was throwing out decent heat. "I would like to call upon you within the week, to discuss what I learned when speaking with the staff yesterday, and I want to hear the reading of Gregory's will."

So did Abby. Gregory had made promises concerning that will, but Gregory's promises were more often earnest in appearance than reliable in fact.

"The will should be read next week, after Gervaise and Lavinia have recovered from traveling out from London," Abby said, rising and putting her mug of tea down. "You have been most kind, Mr. Belmont, exceedingly kind. You have my thanks."

She did not want him to leave, and she couldn't wait to get rid of him.

"I have been merely polite," he replied. "Some would say not even that. Get some sleep, and call upon me should the need arise. I am not saying that for form's sake."

"You're not, are you? You have unplumbed depths, Mr. Belmont."

"And a murder investigation to complete."

* * *

The Stoneleigh Manor servants had congregated in their parlor, black armbands in evidence on the livery, tankards of ale or cups of tea for any who weren't stepping and fetching for the gathering upstairs. Madeline Hennessey wondered if her employer, the estimable Professor Axel Belmont, might have been more comfortable below stairs on such a day.

He'd asked her to keep an ear out for the odd snippet of talk, and Lord knew, the talk was flying. To facilitate loitering among her peers, Hennessey kept her plate full—the Stoneleigh cook had a lovely hand with the roasted beef—and her eyes down.

She could do nothing about her red hair, which got her noticed at any gathering.

"Mrs. Stoneleigh claims the colonel left me his pipes," Robert Ambers said, not for the first time. He never referred to himself as the head stable lad, he was the *stable master*. He affected a neck cloth even on weekdays, and had his clothing made in London, and according to Mrs. Turnbull, the Candlewick housekeeper, Ambers had once mentioned titled family among his antecedents.

He might be a baron's by-blow. Had the public school diction and the London tailoring of the Quality, and apparently gave orders like they did too.

"Nigh ten years of service," Ambers went on, "and he left me a perishing lot of stinking pipes."

He shot a look at Shreve, who was too old to be on his feet for hours at a time, though too conscientious to desert his post above stairs for long. That look was resentful, and commiserating too.

"Some of the colonel's pipes are quite ornate," the housekeeper observed from her seat by the hearth. Mrs. Jensen was reported to be a strict but fair supervisor, a fussy way to say she made a relentless pest of herself to the maids, just as a housekeeper ought.

Hennessey took another sip of her winter ale, a bitter brew for a bitter day.

"Did Missus say anything else?" Heath asked. He was an underfootman and had asked Hennessey to walk to services with him more than once.

She'd declined, of course. Raising a man's hopes when she was abundantly happy with her post at Candlewick would have been unkind—also a nuisance.

"We do not gossip," Jeffries, the head footman said, helping himself to more of the sliced beef on the sideboard. Jeffries was a strapping blond specimen who'd made it through the foolish years of young manhood without losing his hair or his common sense.

Hennessey had collected a few kisses from him at a harvest gathering or two. A nibbler, not the worst approach a man could take to kissing.

"Meaning no disrespect, but we can worry for our positions," Heath retorted around a mouthful of beef. "We can long to know if we'll have bread in our bellies and a place to sleep at night. Times are hard, and Missus might decide to take a repairing lease at some spa town."

To go husband hunting? Hennessey didn't know the lady well, but doubted Mrs. Stoneleigh was anxious to replace the colonel any time soon. He'd been a cold fish, full of his own consequence, and stinking of dogs and pipe smoke even when Hennessey had run into him in the Weasel.

Jeffries paused in his consumption of sliced beef long enough to shoot Heath a reproving look.

"Today is not the day to air those worries." Jeffries and Heath bore a slight resemblance—cousins, or possibly half brothers. These things happened.

"Death turns a household upside down," Mrs. Jensen observed. "And such a death as this…"

"Quite so," Ambers said, rubbing his thumb over a signet ring on his smallest finger. "A tragedy for all concerned."

The staff clearly knew the colonel had been murdered. Mr. Belmont had said nothing to the Candlewick servants, of course. Suicide was a bad, awful business, wreaking havoc with the inheritances and denying the deceased an honorable burial. A ruling of suicide would not require the magistrate—whose first love was the solitude of his glass houses—to spend hours interviewing servants, peering into desk drawers, and otherwise poking about.

Himself had grumbled about the burdens of his official duties the last time he'd invaded the Candlewick kitchen in search of sustenance, a transgression of which he was regularly guilty, much to Cook's feigned horror.

"I'm sure madam would write characters for any seeking other prospects," Shreve said, pulling on his gloves.

Nobody looked relieved.

"Mrs. Stoneleigh needs to know she can rely on us now," Mrs. Jensen said, rising from her wingchair. "We're worried about ourselves, when we all know the lady of house hasn't been faring well lately, and now this." She surveyed the various footmen and maids taking advantage of the generous fare.

Ambers was gazing out the window, holding himself slightly apart from the house staff, as usual. Whether he did this out of deference to the usual servant hierarchy—house servants being above ground servants—or because he considered himself superior to them all, Hennessey neither knew nor cared.

Ambers had once tried to *demand* kisses from her—more fool he. He'd made quite a fetching picture, writhing on the ground in his London finery.

Hennessey glanced at the clock. In fifteen minutes, she'd file out the servants' entrance with the rest of the Candlewick employees paying their respects, and wedge herself into the Belmont traveling coach for the short journey home.

Mr. Belmont had declared that his staff was not to tromp the lanes in frigid weather when reasonable people availed themselves of coaches on such a solemn occasion. The professor was a great one for declarations, treatises, lectures, and general grumbling.

Hennessey wished him the joy of his investigation. If she'd concluded anything in more than an hour of sitting on a hard chair and avoiding Heath's hopeful glances and Jeffries's subtle ones, it was that the servants were keeping secrets.

Servants did that. Their discretion was bought and paid for, also a matter of honor. This group might quietly admit Mrs. Stoneleigh wasn't faring well, but never go so far as to worry aloud that the widow looked positively sickly, and had lost too much flesh in recent months.

Heath was right to worry, and Mr. Belmont was right to investigate, alas for his roses, lectures, and much-respected treatises.

CHAPTER THREE

Axel Belmont returned to Stoneleigh Manor for the reading of the will, which to Abby's relief, did indeed, leave her the entirety of the landed estate. Gervaise inherited the London-based import business—another relief—and Lavinia received a trust to be administered by her solicitor husband.

All in order, all quite equitable.

Gervaise went trotting back to Oxford along with Gregory's solicitor immediately after the reading, Lavinia's coach following in their wake.

"I'm glad you have some family in the area," Mr. Belmont said, peering out the formal parlor window as if to ensure that family had in fact gone haring back to town. "Even if they're staying elsewhere and only for a few days."

"Lavinia is dear." Lavinia was particularly dear in small doses, and she was a dear unwilling to bide under a roof where murder had been done. "Was there something else you wanted to discuss, Mr. Belmont?"

"I have more questions for you, though we should sit, because this might take a while."

"My private parlor is warmer," Abigail said, turning to go.

Mr. Belmont's hand on her arm stopped her. "You're not eating and probably not sleeping." His blues eye held the concern of a man who had explained to a seven-year-old that death was not the same as oversleeping.

"I'm managing, Mr. Belmont. You need not be anxious." Because if he continued looking at Abby like that, she might... lose her wits, run barefoot across the snow, drink every drop of spirits in the house. As she'd lain awake night after night, she'd concocted a long list of things she must not do.

Startle at every sound the house made as it creaked its way through the interminable hours of darkness, for example.

Abby shrugged out of Mr. Belmont's grasp and led the way to the smaller, cozier room closer to the back of the house. A wood fire—extravagant, that—burned in the hearth, while Shreve added water to a vase of roses.

"Gervaise sent them," she said, when Mr. Belmont—the botanist—leaned in for a whiff. "He knows they are my favorite, and I will never again enjoy the scent of lilies."

The scent of funeral casseroles was equally disagreeable, along with Gregory's infernal pipes. In recent months, the pipe smoke had been enough to put Abby off her feed entirely.

The sight of Shreve hovering by the door didn't agree with her lately either. Ambers, she'd been able to mostly avoid, and she kept the door open when she met with Mrs. Jensen these days too.

"Funeral lilies aren't my favorite," Mr. Belmont said. "Trim up the stems on the roses daily. Change the water, don't simply add more, and they'll be happier by the window, where the temperature is lower and the light stronger. Shreve, would you be so good as to bring Mrs. Stoneleigh the tea tray and some sustenance, and for myself, pencil and paper?"

"Of course, Mr. Belmont. Madam, anything else?"

"Thank you, no," Abby replied, not wanting to delay Mr. Belmont's interrogation one moment more than necessary. She moved the roses to the table near the window, lest the professor do that himself, and took the rocking chair she'd had brought down from the nursery years ago.

Mr. Belmont took the nearest corner of the settee. Behind him hung a painting of hydrangeas arranged in a purple crock—one of only four paintings in the entire house Abby had chosen—the flowers the same lustrous blue as Mr. Belmont's eyes.

"We might as well begin with the handsome, charmless barrister," Mr. Belmont said, crossing his legs at the knee. "Gervaise benefited greatly from his father's death, so he had motive to commit murder. How well do you know him?" The magistrate's pose was relaxed and Continental, a neighbor paying a call, not an inquisitor starting on a martyr.

And yet, Abby knew his pose was likely the only thing relaxed about him. She earned a few moments' reprieve from answering when Shreve returned with the tea, sandwiches, sliced apples, and a small offering of tea cakes.

Abby poured Mr. Belmont a cup of tea, recalling when he'd brought her a mug to savor in private.

"You will have it that we don't stand on manners, Mr. Belmont, but talk murder over our tea and crumpets?"

"You are refreshingly direct, Mrs. Stoneleigh."

He wanted this over with too. The realization brought Abby a drop of comfort in an ocean of heartache and anxiety. Who had killed Gregory? *Why?* When, if ever, would she be able to eat and sleep normally again?

She passed over his tea. "Would it surprise you to know you have also been called refreshingly direct, Mr. Belmont?" Blunt as an andiron, according to Mrs. Weekes, unless he was discussing his blooms.

"I would be astonished," he replied gravely.

They had shared a joke. Abby was almost sure of it. She dropped her gaze, but not before she saw the flare of humor in his eyes. Next she might be tempted to flirt with him.

Flirt?

With *him*? She wouldn't even know how.

"I don't know Gervaise well," Abby said, preparing her own serving of tea. "He was already through with his terms when I married Gregory, and well established in London's legal community. The import business will make a suitable inheritance for him, for he seldom leaves Town. It's said he never represents a party unless he believes his client to be innocent."

Mr. Belmont stirred his tea slowly, deliberation apparently part of his nature. Abby knew from churchyard talk that he didn't simply direct gardeners to see to his roses. He personally tended the plants in his glass houses, and published scholarly botanical treatises too.

Axel Belmont was probably closer to his roses than Abby had been to her own husband.

"Murder is usually motivated by greed, revenge, or passion," Mr. Belmont said. "Gervaise doesn't strike me as particularly greedy, or passionate, and I cannot discern what revenge he might have taken on his aging father."

"Gregory was hardly doddering." Though he'd no longer been a man in his prime. Abby had never seen him unclothed, but she'd noticed the tremor in his hands of late, a quaver in his voice where command had once been. Gregory had been tall, but in the past year, that height had taken on the stooped quality of advancing age.

"Eat something, Mrs. Stoneleigh."

For form's sake, Abby arched a brow at Mr. Belmont's peremptory tone, but then reached for a scone. Her digestion was off, though no worse than usual.

"With butter, madam, if you please."

She let her hand fall and hoped her stomach wouldn't growl. "You are not my nanny. What else would you like to know?"

"Tell me of Lavinia." Mr. Belmont slathered a scone with butter, slapped it on a plate, and passed it over.

They were to be *very* informal then. "She is the friendlier of the two." Abby's stomach did growl, drat the luck. "Lavinia wed the year after I married Gregory, and has two small children. She dotes on them and on their father, Roger, a successful solicitor who should manage Lavinia's bequest quite competently."

Or... was Roger a solicitor who only *appeared* successful? "Roger has sent the children here for an occasional summer," Abby went on, "and the children seemed to love their holidays." She had certainly loved having the children underfoot, while Gregory had barely tolerated them. "Roger would be called high-strung were he a female, and I think he's relieved when the children are elsewhere."

And their mother with them, though Abby munched a luscious, buttery bite of scone rather than admit that.

"Any other family?"

"Gregory had a cousin or two, older fellows. Gervaise could tell you more about them. They sent Gregory the occasional letter. I recall a few old chums from the army too, some of whom were mentioned in the will. Mr. Brandenburg, his London factor until recently, was a business acquaintance of long standing, but he's gone to his reward."

"Do you have Gregory's correspondence?" Mr. Belmont asked, picking up the second half of Abby's scone and holding it out to her.

He was relentless, like one of those thorny climbing roses that took over all in its ambit.

"I have his letters," she said, accepting the scone. How had Mr. Belmont's children avoided acquiring dimensions comparable to market hogs? "I suppose you'll want to see every note and rough draft? At times Gregory and Mr. Brandenburg were weekly correspondents."

"My brother, who has brought numerous felons to justice, has cautioned me against undue haste in my investigations. Nonetheless, the murderer doesn't seem inclined to step forward and announce himself, so I'd best have a look at those letters."

"A woman can fire a gun, Mr. Belmont." And what were tea cakes with chocolate icing doing on that tray? "I do not recall asking Mrs. Jensen to stock our larder with sweets."

"I sent them over." Mr. Belmont was not apologizing for that presumption either. "When Caroline died, Day and Phil developed a fondness for chocolate. I enjoy it myself."

Abby chose a confection and held it out to him. Someday she might be capable of saying the words *when Gregory died* without wanting to clap her hands over her ears and run shrieking from her own home.

"My thanks." Mr. Belmont took the sweet from her hand and set it on a plate.

"The treat provides greater pleasure if you place it in your mouth." Abby demonstrated with her own tea cake. For the first time since the colonel's death, she was almost... enjoying herself. Not in the sense of merriment, but in the sense of feeling on her mettle, despite an unsolved murder, bad digestion, and an utter lack of energy.

Feeling somewhat safe too, as long she had Mr. Belmont to spar with—lowering thought.

He watched her devour her sweet, his scowl thunderous. Perhaps he was feeling on his mettle too.

"Have you family, Mrs. Stoneleigh?" he asked when he'd dispatched his tea cake.

"How is that relevant?"

"Greed," he said, quartering an apple with the silver paring knife. "You are now personally wealthy; hence, your heir's circumstances have improved."

He held out a section of apple on the point of the knife.

"I don't know as I have an heir." Which was sad, and also Gregory's fault, though Abby hadn't pressed him on the matter. She'd learned not to press him on any matter.

She plucked the apple from the knife.

"The Regent will be happy to serve as your heir of last resort. Have you no family whatsoever?"

"Third cousins, perhaps?" Abby bit into the apple, thinking. "When I was a girl, my grandfather took me to Yorkshire to meet some cousin of his. He was a delightful old fellow, the Earl of Helmsley. His lordship grew flowers over every arable parcel of his estate, or so it seemed to a child. I recall two girls and a boy, his grandchildren. I was older than the girls, but younger than the boy, and he was a boy—nasty business, boys of a certain age, you know? I cannot recall their names."

"The last Earl of Helmsley," Mr. Belmont said slowly, "died this past summer under house arrest for attempting all manner of mischief against his sisters. The title has lapsed, and the estate reverted to the crown long enough to be passed out to some war hero—a duke's by-blow, I believe. The flowers were famous throughout the realm in their day, though the gardens have long since been neglected."

"You know this, how?" Abby asked, because really, what need had a rural squire for such gossip?

"I read the papers, and I have an abiding interest in ornamental horticulture."

Mr. Belmont also lied when it suited him, though not well. He must have a towering *passion* for his flowers to know this sort of trivia.

"I do not read the papers, much less the society pages. What was your next question?"

"Have you any lovers?"

* * *

"Why do you ask?"

Color stained Mrs. Stoneleigh's cheeks, and Axel was relieved to the point of gladness to see a normal reaction from her.

Duty alone could force him to put such a question to a recent widow. "You might lack the ability to end your husband's life, but you are an attractive woman, and a man intent on spending the rest of his life with you, on this large and thriving estate, could act rashly."

Attractive was a parsimonious word for her beauty, but she'd take offense at anything more honest. She resembled a pale, blown rose, all the more lovely for the delicacy of her appearance.

She munched a chocolate tea cake into oblivion. "You insult me by suggesting I would play false a husband who provided for me generously when I had neither grandfather nor parents to look after me. You compliment me as well, implying somebody would desire my company enough to kill for it."

"I am not withdrawing the question." And she was stalling rather than answer directly.

"I do not now," she said, picking up another tea cake, "nor have I ever, had reason to stray, Mr. Belmont. What on earth would be the point?"

Not a clear no, and since when did erotic pleasure require a *point*? Axel poured himself more tea to buy a moment to consider her prevarication. He'd lifted the silver teapot and served himself half a cup before he caught her watching him.

Helping himself to a lady's tea tray.

"I beg your pardon." He sat back, chagrinned at this small, pathetic evidence of his widower status.

She didn't smirk, she didn't even smile. "Perhaps you'd top up my cup as well?"

He obliged, as a memory assailed him. He'd come upon Colonel Stoneleigh on a morning hack, hounds trotting at the horse's heels, Ambers several respectful yards behind on a nervous hunter. By way of small talk, Axel had asked if Mrs. Stoneleigh enjoyed riding out, and the colonel's ruddy face had wrinkled with distaste.

"She's the delicate sort," he'd said. "Easily overset, always flying into the boughs. A man wants to start his day with some peace and quiet. Can't be cosseting the weaker sex at all hours, can we?"

Mrs. Belmont might be pale, but easily overset had been husbandly exaggeration from one who was himself given to tempers at the local pub and in the hunt field.

"Back to the topic, Mrs. Stoneleigh." Axel set the teapot down, then realized he'd only bungled further. "Oh, very well." He added milk and sugar to her cup, then passed it to her.

"Thank you, Mr. Belmont. I cannot recall when I last was served a cup of tea as I prefer it, but for your fussing on the day of the funeral. My husband was far too liberal with the sugar. You will have to call more often."

Axel Belmont did not fuss, except when among his roses. Was she teasing him? Flirting? Or maybe—sad thought—realizing that life without a spouse could be grindingly lonely?

"About your lovers?" Axel prompted. "You may have none now, but I want you to keep a list of fellows who come calling, and the ones who seem particularly solicitous or curious about your finances."

"Gregory has—had—an old friend several miles east of here." She took a sip of her tea, closing her eyes for a moment as if inhaling fortitude along with the fragrance of a mild gunpowder. "Sir Dewey Fanning. They served together, and as you heard, Sir Dewey is the recipient of Gregory's collection of hunting horns. He'll likely come to call any day—hang protocol, for Sir Dewey is a bit of a mother hen—and several other old army chaps might come around as well. You don't need to know about those fellows, do you?"

Half the regiment would soon be camping on her doorstep, Axel suspected, though where were *her* friends who'd *hang protocol* to be at her side?

"I do need to know about those fellows, Mrs. Stoneleigh, and why are you frowning?"

Worse than frowning, he'd caught her blinking at her tea cup in a manner that made a man eye the door and hope his handkerchief was clean. She set down her tea cup, rose, and went to the window.

"Would you frown, Mr. Belmont, were I to order you to name your potential intimates for my perusal, lest one of them be guilty of murdering your spouse?"

He would eject her from the premises. "Valid point, but my brother assures me that dalliance, while a predictable element of grief, is not usually suspicious. You want to take note of those fellows who are subtly beginning the courting dance."

"I see."

He approached her, wanting to *see* her eyes when the conversation turned difficult—also wanting to look her in the eye when he apologized.

"I have offended, and I regret that. Is this transgression greater than my usual lack of tact or delicacy?"

She stared out at the snowy landscape, though she likely did not see the gray stone walls marching over the bleak pastures and fields.

"I am… knocked off my pins, Mr. Belmont. I found myself thinking this morning that we hadn't enough chairs in the formal parlor, because we'd need one for Gregory when the will was read. I expect Gregory to come in to breakfast, kiss my cheek, and tell me how his ride went while he fixes my first cup of tea with twice as much sugar as I prefer. I hear a door slam and think he's back from the kennels… but he isn't, and he never will be again."

"You can't prepare for those ambushes." Nor could Axel have prepared for the urge to comfort this woman with an embrace. "Knocked off one's pins is a good way to describe the ordeal you face." Axel settled a hand on her arm, then moved back to the hearth, out of the range of hysterics and temper, both.

Though if ever a woman had justification for a bout of dramatics, Mrs. Stoneleigh did.

"The first year is the hardest," he said. The second was hardest too, in a way, and the fifth as well. "The first spring, the first summer holiday, the first Christmas, the first time you observe all those small rituals alone that you used to observe together."

Outside the cozy parlor, flurries danced down on the bitter wind. In deepest winter, Axel had gloried in the hours required in his glass houses, while Caroline had complained about having the boys constantly underfoot and her husband nowhere to be seen.

"You know you are making progress," he said, "when you can recall the bad things honestly."

"I beg your pardon?"

Telling her this was not disloyal, it was honest, and Abigail Stoneleigh deserved at least that. Axel had the sense that nobody else, not the widows in the churchyard, not Mrs. Weekes, not anybody, would explain this aspect of grieving to her.

"Six months after Caroline died, I admitted to myself while fishing with the boys, how blessedly quiet it was without their mother along. A fellow could hear himself think and catch some fish, though the very thought made me feel like a cad. I realized then that one day, one distant, unimaginable day, the grief would become manageable."

Mostly.

Mrs. Stoneleigh resumed her seat, and Axel settled beside her, as much fortification as he could safely offer.

"When I am relieved not to have to smell Gregory's blasted pipes, that is not a bad thing?"

Poor woman. The entire house still reeked of the colonel's fondness for tobacco.

"It is not. Have a sandwich." Axel chose one for her, and she took it without any fuss or posturing—a relief, that.

"I will have to think on this, though we are far, far from the topic of our murderer."

Or her lovers. "We are. Are you comfortable turning the colonel's correspondence over to me, or shall I read it here?"

She made a face, probably finding the prospect of Axel running tame in her halls distasteful.

"Why not sort through it here and take with you what you want to read in detail?"

"That will suit, but as for the estate books, I'd best look at those on premises."

Another grimace, this one around a bite of sandwich. "In some ways, Mr. Belmont, that is more presumptuous than asking about my personal life."

Her love life, given how women typically viewed sexual intimacy. "If somebody has embezzled from your accounts, Mrs. Stoneleigh, then they had a motive to murder your husband."

An uncomfortable thought intruded: They had a motive to murder Mrs. Stoneleigh now too, if she was about to discover the embezzlement.

"You are so sure you are correct about the means of death, Mr. Belmont, all you concern yourself with is the motive."

Gregory Stoneleigh had not died of a heart seizure or an apoplexy while cleaning his weapon. He hadn't had the grace to die of a plant-based poison either, which Axel was uniquely positioned to have detected.

"I saw your husband's body, and yes, I am convinced he died of a gunshot wound to the chest. I had quite the frank talk on this very point with Gervaise Stoneleigh, and asked him to make inquiries regarding any suspicious aspects of the import business."

"Gervaise will make those inquiries regardless. Thoroughness runs through his very veins."

Axel's impression of Gervaise Stoneleigh was one of brisk, unsentimental competence. The younger Stoneleigh wouldn't leave to chance what diligence and effort could make certain.

A fine quality in a barrister—also in a murderer.

"Have you more questions, Mr. Belmont, or shall I show you to Gregory's correspondence?"

"One more question." Axel rose, and his hostess stood with him, which put them close enough he could see fine lines of fatigue fanning out from her eyes. She might have hidden them with cosmetics were she more sophisticated or less honest female.

She might also have emphasized her grief with cosmetics, but she had not.

"Ask, Mr. Belmont. I can't imagine you've anything remaining your arsenal to shock me with."

"Did Gregory have a mistress?"

* * *

Mr. Belmont was relentlessly inappropriate, but also fearless, and thus when *he* asked Abby the questions she'd been pushing aside since Gregory's death, she came closer to answering them.

"I did say a woman's hand can pull a trigger, did I not? But why would a mistress shoot her protector?" At least some of the sleep Abby had lost had been spent trying to come up with that answer.

"Because that protector was leaving her? Because he'd cast her aside for another, got her with child and denied his own progeny, given her diseases? Because he'd been unkind, or lost his temper and injured or disfigured her? A woman can have many reasons for hating a man with whom she's been intimate."

Blunt speech indeed, and yet, it proved Mr. Belmont had been thinking the case through, and that was reassuring.

"Hell hath no fury?" Abby recalled being furious, early in her marriage. Then she'd learned to keep busy and out of Gregory's way. "You must also ask: Would I be so jealous as to put someone else up to killing Gregory if he disregarded his vows?"

A wife committed adultery, a man disregarded his vows. The law and society both considered it so, though most wives doubtless took a different view of the matter.

"You don't strike me as a woman…" *Given to passion.* Apparently, even Axel Belmont would not put that sentiment into words. "As a woman given to violent impulses."

Before her marriage, Abby had been very passionate. She'd argued politics with her grandfather, philosophy with her father, and the rights of women with her mother. She'd been infatuated with the son of another bookselling family and even had girlish designs on that fellow's future. Her fondness for the fellow had blossomed in the midst of many heated debates over literary matters.

"I honestly don't know if Gregory was unfaithful." Abby hadn't wanted to know. "He'd pop into Oxford every few weeks, and light-skirts abound there, for the university boys and the unmarried faculty, both. Gregory liked to go to Bath each quarter or so, and he and Sir Dewey went into London on occasion, or up north, shooting in the summer. They were always off on some lark. My husband and I were cordial, but… I don't know how to answer you, Mr. Belmont."

In too many instances, Abby simply did not know how to answer the magistrate's questions, and that probably made her look like a very bad wife indeed.

Gregory might not argue with that characterization—he'd found much about her to criticize. The longer he was gone, the less Abby cared what her husband had thought of her, and the more she succumbed to the simple fear that whoever had killed Gregory might come for her next.

* * *

Mrs. Stoneleigh pulled open the desk drawers and produced two bags of tobacco, three pipes, and some pipe-cleaning supplies—all of which Axel had come across the night of the murder and replaced in the desk. Another drawer yielded bundles of correspondence.

Her hands were not quite steady as she passed him the letters.

He'd never enjoyed being magistrate, and he was coming to loathe the job now. "And the estate books?"

"I keep those in my office. Come along."

They returned to her office, as she called it, where she crouched before the shelves beside her desk and heaved up a bound ledger from a lower shelf.

"I keep the books myself. You are welcome to look at the ledgers here, or take them with you."

"I'll start with the letters," Axel said. "This would seem to be the most private place to work." Also the most comfortable, and the only part of the house he'd seen so far that belonged to his hostess. The roses would like it here too, simply because the air did not reek of pipe smoke.

"You'll not be disturbed. Make yourself at home, and I've wanted to ask, when will you take possession of your mares?"

His... mares. Stoneleigh had bequeathed him a damned pair of yearling mares.

"I'd honestly forgotten them. I can fetch them early next week." An idea popped into Axel's head, one having to do with Mrs. Stoneleigh's pallor, the passing tremor in her hands, and too many years of not being a very good neighbor to her. "Would you be willing to accompany me on such an errand?"

She lifted the vase and sniffed at the roses, the gesture artlessly lovely.

"Isn't that a little like going riding with you, Mr. Belmont? I am in first mourning and barely allowed to set foot out of the house for the next two months or so, save to go to services or see family and very close friends."

Or to humor a magistrate whose investigation had brought no answers thus far?

Axel liked his idea the longer he thought about it, and he did not like the idea of her becoming a prisoner in this house on behalf of a husband who'd regarded a lady's maid as an extravagance.

"And what a pleasure that will be," Axel said, "to sit alone and watch the snow fall, then melt, then fall again. We'll merely walk the mares from your stable to mine, and we can accomplish this without even using a proper road if you're concerned about public opinion. I hardly think seeing the colonel's bequest executed constitutes gross disrespect for the dead."

"I suppose not."

Axel didn't press for a definite yes, having learned a few things in the years of his marriage.

Instead he offered a slight bow. "Until next we meet."

Mrs. Stoneleigh disappeared in a swish of black skirts, leaving Axel to absorb himself for the next two hours in the artifacts of another man's life. Gregory had kept up a rambling and occasionally illegible correspondence with several old friends—late-night applications of brandy seldom improved penmanship—and he heard occasionally from his children. Nothing stood out as evidence connected to murder.

Shreve appeared, wheeling a tea cart before him. "Beg pardon, sir. Madam thought you might be getting peckish, and suggested luncheon would be in order."

Sandwiches had been stacked in a tower beside a dish of sliced pears. A vented tureen savored of hot barley soup. Chocolate tea cakes graced a candy dish. "Madam is thoughtful," Axel said. Surprisingly thoughtful, for a woman whose husband had accused her of requiring constant cosseting.

"She is that." Shreve fussed with trays and rearranged linen. "But, Mr. Belmont?"

"Shreve?" Stoneleigh's own wife may not have known if he'd had a mistress—what wife wanted to confront such a fact?—though Stoneleigh's butler likely would.

"About Mrs. Stoneleigh." Shreve's gaze remained on sliced pears arranged in a pink bowl.

Axel kept his tone level when he wanted to shake the old fellow until his jowls flapped.

"I can keep a confidence, unless it points to somebody's guilt in Mr. Stoneleigh's death."

"Well, as you are the only neighbor coming and going from the estate," Shreve began, a blush creeping up his neck, "and as duty alone prompts me to speak, I am breaching all protocol to mention this to you."

"I am listening." Axel had also prepared lists of further questions, for both Shreve and Ambers, though at Mrs. Stoneleigh's request, Ambers had taken several horses to Melton for sale.

"Madam isn't doing well, sir. She barely eats, and I know she's suffered a grievous shock, but one must eat."

"One must, though these things take time." The words were ashes rather than a source of warmth to a grieving heart, and yet, they were true.

Shreve lifted the lid over the soup tureen for the third time. "If it were only that, Mr. Belmont."

"Out with it, Shreve."

"She doesn't sleep, and she's taking laudanum, which madam has never done before with any frequency."

"Many people medicate their grief." The mention of laudanum sparked alarm and anger. Why wasn't the woman's physician calling on her, or had that fool prescribed the poppy to a widow when she was enduring the most vulnerable and isolated weeks of grief?

Shreve drew himself up. "Madam leaves the candles burning at night on every floor, walks the house for hours, then collapses in her bed near dawn, only to rise shortly thereafter. Her digestion is most delicate, her strength ebbing. She is not coping well."

Axel considered the woman who'd spoken with him at such length earlier in the day: polite, gracious, cooperative, and capable of humor and humanity if not exactly warmth.

Not that *he* had acquired the knack of warmth on social situations.

He compared that woman with the widow who'd greeted him at the crime scene: composed, calm, physically cold, and something else plucked at his awareness, like brambles snagging at his sleeve…

Afraid.

"I'll deal with it, Shreve. For now, I suggest you run out of laudanum, or at least make sure the supply is limited, and do likewise with the decanters."

"But sir, I wouldn't want…"

"Shreve," Axel said gently, "Madam knows you are grieving too, and she will not hold it against you if the decanters aren't immediately refilled, or the medicinals run low. Falling asleep with the candles lit is dangerous, and she doesn't need for this place to burn to the ground."

Shreve's sigh should have fluttered the curtains. "I will see to it."

Axel ate in silence, considering his options and his duties, which had lately multiplied, much to the detriment of his progress with the herbal.

Mrs. Stoneleigh was without family, and she needed to be taken in hand. She was grieving, frightened, and living in the same house where her husband had been murdered, while the murderer was still at large.

Axel had heeded the neighborly summons, he was investigating the murder as best he could, but was he being a *gentleman* when the damsel was clearly in distress?

And of those three duties—neighbor, investigator, and gentleman—which mattered the most, and where did that leave the other two?

CHAPTER FOUR

"Did you find anything in the letters?" Abby asked as her mare plodded along beside Mr. Belmont's gelding.

"I pulled out a half dozen or so, but no. They're exactly what you'd expect from an older gentleman's family and cronies. I've written to a few of his regular army correspondents and commanding officers, making general inquires, but I don't expect much in reply. Sir Dewey has an exquisite hand, while the colonel's penmanship declined with the lateness of the hour, apparently."

"Sir Dewey is a gentleman in every particular." A handsome gentleman too, about the same age as Mr. Belmont. "One wonders how a fellow so given to aesthetics coped in the military. Every room of his home is lovely and filled with exotica."

"Lives alone, does he?" Mr. Belmont glanced back at the two mares, who were behaving themselves on their lead lines. They'd probably eat buttered scones at his command and not even dare to colic thereafter.

"Sir Dewey dwells alone," Abby said, "though with a regiment of servants from his days in India. He and Gregory always enjoyed one another's company. They could tell stories on each other for hours."

The same stories, though. Over and over, which must have been tedious for Sir Dewey.

This outing was not tedious. The sun shone blindingly bright on the snow, and Mr. Belmont sat with the ease of a cavalryman upon his horse, a great, black beast given to admonitory snorts at nothing.

"Do you ever wished you'd served?" Abby asked, as one of the mares took exception to a dark patch of ground.

"My brother and I were both left with children to raise while the Corsican was wreaking his mischief. I could not see taking up arms to save the world while depriving my offspring of the company of their only surviving parent. *Settle now, you two.*"

The mares settled while Abby's mount tripped on a frozen rut. "Easy, Pumpkin."

"Pumpkin?"

"Why not Pumpkin? She's chestnut, Gregory named her, and she knows that's her name. Upon whose back do you sit?"

"Ivan the Terrible." Mr. Belmont looked a bit sheepish at this disclosure. "He's not terrible, but as a lad, he was a handful. I must confess that today's excursion serves an ulterior motive, Mrs. Stoneleigh."

"Confession is said to be good for the soul." Though Abby did not want to hear *his* confession, nor did she want to return to Stoneleigh Manor, particularly.

"I'm kidnapping you," Mr. Belmont said, in the same tone he might have predicted more snow, or an early lambing season. "You will be my guest for the nonce, until I can make progress determining who killed your husband."

Abby hadn't seen this coming, but then, in her present state, she could hardly see the coming of the next dawn.

"I am in your custody?" The notion should have been foul rather than reassuring. The sight of Candlewick, a quarter mile ahead at the end of the drive, was very reassuring indeed.

"You are certainly not in *my* custody. You're enjoying a repairing lease at the home of a concerned neighbor."

The horses clopped along, while Abby tried to locate anger, indignation, or even some mild dismay.

"I would rather you had consulted me." Not that Abby would have had anything sensible to say. Now that she was on Belmont land, this kidnapping all but a fait accompli, she was... more relieved than anything else.

How telling—and pathetic—was that?

Mr. Belmont wanted for tact and charm, he had no finesse with social niceties, and his neighboring over the years had been casual at best, and yet, Abby would feel safer under his roof than her own.

She would *be* safer under his roof. "If you think I am in danger, Mr. Belmont, then I suppose a short visit might be for the best. I trust you have a housekeeper in residence to put a patina of propriety on this repairing lease?"

Their horses came to a halt in the stable yard, and along the eaves of the coach house, icicles hung like so many glistening sabers.

"Mrs. Turnbull quotes her Scripture better than Mr. Weekes cites his, she's been known to emasculate presuming footmen at a glance, and my boys fear her setdowns worse than they fear my own. She'd chide me sorely for using the word emasculate in a lady's hearing too."

Abby liked unusual words, a relic of her days growing up in a bookshop. She hadn't heard *that* one spoken aloud before though.

Mr. Belmont remained in the saddle as the eaves dripped and Abby's chin grew numb.

"No 'To blazes with you, Mr. Belmont'?" he said. "Or 'This is an outrage,' and 'How dare you? Of all the nerve.'" A list—Mr. Belmont apparently favored lists and organization.

"You aren't doing this to upset me," Abby replied, "and I've already told you I wish you had consulted me. Regarding future decisions that affect my welfare, please see that you do. As magistrate, you are probably within your authority to do this, and nobody will gainsay you, save perhaps Gervaise."

Then too, the ride over had exhausted Abby. She was simply too tired and cold to muster a show of resistance. Cold in her bones, in a way that had little to do with the weather.

A groom trotted out to take the mares, and Mr. Belmont swung down. He came around to Abby's mare and glowered up at her.

"Mr. Belmont?"

"I cannot believe the colonel was so lacking in gallantry he neglected to offer assistance when you mounted and dismounted."

The colonel had been utterly lacking in gallantry, once he'd become Abby's husband. She put a hand on each of Mr. Belmont's shoulders and eased off the horse.

Pumpkin took one step to the side, pitching Abby into her kidnapper.

"Steady on." Mr. Belmont had Abby by the waist, but as she stepped back, she bumped into the mare, who sidled over again, knocking Abby chest-to-chest into Mr. Belmont.

"We'll change her name to Bumpkin." He stepped away from the horse, guiding Abby to follow him as if he were her waltzing partner. "You truly won't rail at me, will you?"

His scent—fresh flowers, scythed grass, and wool today—wrapped about her, as did the sure knowledge that Axel Belmont dreaded feminine hysterics and had done his gentlemanly duty nonetheless, such as he conceived that duty.

"I'm to dissolve into histrionics because you kept me from falling on my... derriere?"

"For absconding with you." He tucked Abby's hand over his arm and steered her toward the snowy garden. "For being high-handed, thoughtless, inconsiderate, you know the list. My late wife kept it close at hand lest I forget my transgressions."

"The list." What did a woman long dead have to do with a murder investigation? "I suppose you had some of my things sent over?"

"I gave Shreve no choice."

"He doesn't do well with a great deal of choice." Not many men did, in Abby's experience. "Do you really think someone might try to hurt me?"

Please scoff, which you do well. Please inform me I'm being dramatic for no reason, and grief makes women hysterical.

"I think, on your present course, you are well on the way to neglecting yourself, madam. My housekeeper will cosset you within an inch of your life, and you will bear up as best you can lest she redouble her efforts."

Abby stopped walking and dropped his arm. "Explain yourself, Mr. Belmont."

"You have more or less stopped eating," he began, even as he held the door to a back entrance for her. "You do not sleep, you pace at all hours, then take enough laudanum to fall asleep, leaving candles burning on every floor of the house. If you burn the house down, or waste away to a shadow, you could well accomplish whatever the murderer's initial goal was, all the while making it harder for *me* to do *my* job."

Clearly the difficulty of Mr. Belmont's task as the king's man trumped any petty consideration such as Abby's continued existence.

She had the lowering suspicion he was sparing her pride. "Shreve peached on me."

"Probably put up to it by your cook and Mrs. Jensen," Mr. Belmont temporized.

"Once it becomes known I reside with you," Abby said, as she was led into a large, cozy kitchen, "how will you keep me safe, how will you force me to sleep, how will you ensure I eat every bite on my plate?"

Mr. Belmont started undoing the frogs of her cloak. "I can at least encourage you to look after yourself properly and make it harder for you to get to the laudanum. My staff will abet me, or they'll be sacked."

"You forgot to mention the brandy," Abby said, lifting her chin rather than smack his hands away—competent hands they were too. "And the opium, the rum, and the gin. Godfrey's Cordial will do in a pinch. What do you take me for, Mr. Belmont?"

"I take you for a newly widowed neighbor," he said, slipping off her cloak and hanging it on a peg near the hearth, then seeing to his own greatcoat.

"You are too tall."

"My apologies." He bowed slightly, as if he heard this complaint frequently. "My oldest nephew will soon be as tall as I am, and you will likely be making his acquaintance. I will inform him in advance of his transgression."

Abby passed Mr. Belmont her gloves and bonnet. "I met him at services this autumn. He's the son of your brother, Michael?"

"Matthew," Mr. Belmont replied. "Christopher and Remington, Matthew's two oldest, are at university. They are frequently here on weekends, cleaning out my larder, putting the laundresses to work, and sleeping round the clock. The youngest nephew, Richard, has remained with his father, Dayton, and Phillip in Sussex."

What must it be like, to have nephews and sons to share back and forth, a sibling to visit? Surely such family came in handy when a woman could no longer feel safe under her own roof?

"And in this way, Matthew's new wife will grow to love your whole family immediately?"

"She already does." Mr. Belmont sounded not smug, and certainly not playful, but simply very certain.

The kitchen smelled good, of cooking, stored spices, hanging joints, and a blazing wood fire. Abby was abruptly famished and thirsty, as well as exhausted, but then, she'd been exhausted for months.

"Your new sister-in-law sounds like a lovely woman." A brave woman.

"She is, but Matthew saw her first, and we've ever been gentlemanly with one another in that regard. Then too, I have long had my eye on an Oxford fellowship, and one finally seems to be coming my way. Holy matrimony is not in my plans. Let me show you to your room, and perhaps you'll want a bath before luncheon?"

Mr. Belmont would treat his prisoner well, some consolation for putting up with his high-handedness.

And Abby wasn't truly his prisoner. If he believed her to be a murderess, he'd have tossed her into the storeroom at the Wet Weasel without a thought.

"You will order me a bath, Mr. Belmont?"

"A nice, long, hot, lazy soak, with a glass of wine, perhaps a French novel, some scented soaps."

"What on earth are you going on about?"

He shrugged broad shoulders as he led Abby up into the front of the house. "A good, long soak always soothes my spirits, though I take the papers or an herbal into the tub with me, rather than anything so frivolous as novels."

"I am fascinated to hear this." Abby tried to sound disdainful, but ended up sounding only bewildered. Perhaps men truly did treat widows differently, or this man did. Academics were permitted a few crotchets along with their studious natures.

"I'll send you a maid, and by the time you've had your bath and joined me for luncheon, your things should be here and need putting away. Mrs. Turnbull will present herself to offer the staff's welcome and inquire as to your specific needs and preferences. The more of those you have, the more delighted she'll be. A list would be well advised."

"You have matters well in hand, Mr. Belmont." Not exactly astounding. Most successful kidnappers probably had some notion of planning.

"I've lived in close proximity to an adult female. Ladies like to know where their effects are, and to arrange them just so, regularly."

Now he did sound smug, and climbing a second set of stairs had left Abby winded.

She braced herself on the newel post, a carved tulip of all things. "You have lived in close proximity to precisely one adult female that I know of. Do not, pray do not, think that makes you an expert on the gender or on me, any more than living with Gregory made me an expert on you or on the male gender in its benighted entirety."

Rather than stand nattering in the corridor another minute—or succumb to the slight vertigo plaguing her—Abby swept past Mr. Belmont, passed through the only door ajar, and closed it firmly in her wake.

* * *

"So how does this work?" Mrs. Stoneleigh let Axel seat her at luncheon and crossed her arms over her chest.

Her somewhat ample chest, for all her slender proportions.

"How does what work?" Axel lifted the lid from a serving tray and passed her a bowl of vegetable soup, followed by hot rolls and butter.

She ignored the food, while Axel tried to ignore the hint of color in her cheeks—delicate pink, reminiscent of campions in spring.

"How does this business of being your prisoner work? Particularly when I am in mourning."

Oh, *that*. She was back in her green velvet riding habit, which, thanks to her negligent staff, had yet to be cast into the dye vat of eternal woe.

"My staff can dye your frocks for you. As for the rest, please do not leave this house without letting me know your exact destination, and do not leave the property without my escort, or an escort approved by me."

She snapped her serviette across her lap. "My presence will be disruptive for you. I inspect my acres regularly, meet with Mrs. Jensen, and so forth."

Disruptive was an understatement, but Axel had settled on this course when confronted with the notion that Mrs. Stoneleigh's decline might be because she feared becoming the murderer's next victim.

Which thought had stopped all progress on his herbal, and damned near resulted in a nasty slice to his right index finger at the grafting table.

"I can accompany you on those errands, Mrs. Stoneleigh, or send somebody along."

"You will find my routine surpassingly tedious." Either that thought, or the aroma of the soup steaming before her pleased her.

Who would have guessed she had such a beguiling, mischievous smile?

"Please do eat, madam. I cannot start on my soup until you at least make a pretense of consuming yours."

"Somebody pounded manners into you," she said, taking a dainty spoonful of broth. "For all you kidnap your neighbors."

She put her spoon right back down, so Axel buttered a roll—liberally—and passed it to her.

"Madam will note that I'm on my best behavior. This is my first kidnapping, you see."

No smile, but she did tear off a corner of her roll. "In truth, I am not very social, and Gregory preferred a retiring life. I love to read though. I'll probably become eccentric."

"Eat your soup, Abigail." But for his children, Axel would have blundered past eccentric long ago. He was comforted by the knowledge that Matthew might have succumbed to the same fate, but had also been saved by the necessity of raising Axel's nephews.

"Now there," Axel's guest said, "you have again made a decision affecting me without consulting me. I do not appreciate it, *Axel*."

The daft woman thought his name on her lips would serve as a scold. "My apologies, but you are a guest in my home, and I am the king's appointed kidnapper in this shire, so I ask you for the privilege of informal address when sharing an informal meal."

"My own husband usually referred to me as Mrs. Stoneleigh, but then, Gregory was old-fashioned," she replied, dipping a corner of her roll in her soup and nibbling at it. "When you and I are private, I see no harm in informal address, but you should have asked."

She was right of course, and she was also eating.

"I beg your pardon." Axel would probably be doing that a fair amount, unless he discovered she'd conspired in her husband's death.

Which, increasingly, he hoped he would not be doing.

"You are attached to the university, are you not?"

Not small talk, but rather, an interrogation. Mrs. Stoneleigh's kidnapping—or the prospect of refuge from her own home—had apparently improved her spirits.

"I do most of my teaching in the autumn. Plant physiology, morphology, and reproductive anatomy. With my next publication, and some generous donations in the right pockets, I hope to become a fellow. The sex life of the flower is surprisingly worthy of study."

Mrs. Stoneleigh's spoon clattered to her half-empty bowl, which she set aside. Axel had lost the habit of allowing servants to hover at his elbow at the midday meal, fortunately for the lady's composure.

"Further, unending apologies." Axel set his empty bowl aside too, though he could have done with seconds. "One loses the knack of social discourse when adolescent boys are the most frequent companions at mealtimes."

"And do you educate them regarding the reproductive life of the flower at table, Professor?"

"Occasionally. One doesn't want to waste an opportunity when the boys are sitting still." Axel lifted the lid from the ham, which sat at his right over a chafing dish. "May I offer you some ham?" He carved off a thick slice—enough to occupy Dayton for three consecutive minutes—and tipped it onto the lady's plate.

"Is this your idea of luncheon, or are you going to an effort on my behalf?"

The good daily silver was on the table, suggesting the staff had gone to an effort. Mrs. Turnbull and Cook were thick as thieves when it came to the household's pride.

"I eat well, and I eat a lot. Matthew is the same, but the true gourmand in the family is Christopher. He's on the rowing squad, recently turned eighteen, still growing, and never still for long."

Axel heaped potatoes and peas on his guest's plate, which still left plenty for him. "No apples, please."

He paused, the serving spoon poised above the apples. "You don't care for them?"

"I like them well enough."

"But you don't like them to touch the other food, because they are sweet, and the rest of your plate is not."

She was almost-smiling again. "Something like that."

"What are you thinking?" Axel asked, starting on his own slice of ham.

She speared a microscopic bite of pork. "Gervaise reminds me of you."

"He is a well-favored, successful, and reasonable man. I will choose to be flattered, despite dear Gervaise's choice of profession."

Mrs. Stoneleigh's nibble of potatoes could best be described as minuscule. "He's also ruthless, and practical to a fault."

"A barrister cannot afford to be sentimental, but do I understand you account me ruthless?"

The peas she merely pushed about with her fork. "You kidnapped me."

"I see you enjoy the potatoes," Axel said. "We add sour cream and a blend of garden spices along with the mandatory full tub of butter."

"The food is wonderful, though yes, you and Gervaise both have the ability to do what must be done. You are not sleepwalking."

Matthew's youngest, Richard, had gone through a sleepwalking and a nightmare phase after his mama's death.

"What does that mean?" Axel carved himself a second slice of ham, because he intended to spend the afternoon out of doors. The ham of course needed a complement of potatoes to be properly appreciated.

"Gregory was asleep," Mrs. Stoneleigh said, turning the stem of her wine glass. "He would ride out most mornings, unless it was pouring, and come back to join me for breakfast. I would ask how was his ride, and he would tell me his gelding was a little stiff to the right, or one of his hounds ran riot after a hedgehog, and so forth. He could ride right past a collapsed wall on his own property and not see it. His ewes might have gone calling en masse on your tups, and Gregory wouldn't see that either. He was asleep."

"Preoccupied?"

The lady finally deigned to put three buttery peas on her fork. "*Unaware.*

Maybe he used up all his awareness staying alive in India, and a gentleman of his years was entitled to focus on only his hounds."

No, he was not. Axel spooned stewed apples into a fruit bowl. "Try them. Cook enjoys the desserts most of all. Because the boys are away, her genius grows frustrated. My only hope of maintaining her spirits is to regularly threaten to sack her."

Mrs. Stoneleigh assayed a spoonful of apples. "Your children must grow to great heights to have room for all the food you stuff into them. These spices are marvelous."

Stewed apples, with cinnamon, cloves, and walnuts, were comforting on a cold winter afternoon.

"My mother had a recipe for muffins that used the same spices," Axel said. "I associate cinnamon and cloves with rainy days spent in the kitchen stealing batter and playing cards with my brother. Matthew's preferred fragrance comes close. I think he has it blended in Paris."

"You are very close to this brother of yours."

And yet, Axel and Matthew lived nearly a hundred miles apart. "Having no other siblings might have that result. When we're through with our meal, I planned to check on my brood mares, though it's far from foaling season. Would you care to walk with me?"

He wasn't nearly done interrogating her, and—bracing thought—she likely wasn't done interrogating him either. The apples had disappeared from her bowl posthaste, though.

"A constitutional would suit," she said. "Your mares are in your south pasture, if I recall?"

Dayton and Phillip might not have known that much. "That part of the property has the most reliable water," Axel said, rising and holding her chair.

"You could easily put in a cistern and a windmill pump on the western pastures. The breeze is seldom still, and you have better drainage on that side and more shade as well."

"Hadn't thought of that." Neither had Axel's land steward, who'd been managing rural properties since before the Flood.

When they reached the back corridor, Axel took her cloak off a peg, settled it around her shoulders, then began to tie the frogs.

"Axel Belmont." She had closed her eyes.

"That is my name. Axel Lysander Horatius Belmont, of all the pretensions."

"I am capable of dressing myself."

He dropped his hands and stepped back, though her *point* eluded him.

"This was a habit with your wife, I take it?" Mrs. Stoneleigh's gaze was understanding, and resentment blossomed, not at her, not even at her understanding, but at a past that still had the power to ambush the present.

"A habit, yes."

She held out his coat. "A lovely, domestic gesture. Sweet."

Ye gods, sweet. What else had she said? That Axel was *awake*, and close to his brother, which had made him uncomfortable because her observations were accurate and based on very little evidence.

Abigail Stoneleigh was awake as well, though what had life with the colonel done to such an intelligent, alert spirit? She'd both looked at Axel and *seen* him. Seen the widower, the papa, and the professor.

Had she seen the man?

Axel had long since given up wishing for a woman to focus on him that closely. Far easier to be overwhelmed with raising his sons, delivering his scholarly lectures, running his estate, popping down to Sussex to see his brother. Far more pleasant to unravel the mysteries of the rose, or the wonders of what Americans called witch hazel.

"You are silent, Mr. Belmont," Mrs. Stoneleigh said.

They'd left the snowy garden and were crossing the paddock immediately behind the stable. All without Axel offering a word of conversation.

"Shall I chatter on about the weather?"

He dropped her arm to leap across a rill of snowmelt encrusted with ice. He straddled the water and planted his hands on her waist, swung her over it, then grasped one of her gloved hands to pull her up the opposite bank.

The lady was too slight, and riding habits were not ideal attire for marching about the countryside. He'd wanted her to take some fresh air though, to regain the campion-pink flush to her cheeks.

"The weather is a dreary topic this time of year," she said. "I like the quality of your silences, for the most part."

"What of Gregory?" Axel asked, keeping Mrs. Stoneleigh's hand in his, for now they were on a rutted bridle path. "Was he quiet or noisy?"

"He fretted about his bitches when they were about to whelp, or his mares come May, but when he got to brooding, it was mostly about the past. He was old enough to have lost many friends along the way."

"One doesn't like to think of that aspect of a long life. My parents were barely forty when they died."

Where in the perishing, frozen hell had that admission come from?

Mrs. Stoneleigh squeezed Axel's hand. "That is young. No wonder you and your brother are close."

"Blazing, bedamned perdition." Axel came to an abrupt stop a dozen yards from the edge of a wide field, where eight shaggy, sway-bellied horses placidly regarded the approaching humans. "It is damned February, and that is a goddamned foal in my field."

He'd vaulted the fence and left Mrs. Stoneleigh standing on the snowy lane before he recalled that one didn't curse in the presence of a lady.

Well… *blast.*

CHAPTER FIVE

"I have correspondence to tend to, and my prison cell has a well-stocked escritoire," Abby said. "Enjoy your bath, Mr. Belmont."

"You are my guest," he replied, before Abby could reach the stairs. "You have my thanks for your assistance with the foal. Few ladies would have managed as well."

Abby started up the stairs at a brisk pace, though the walk across the Belmont fields had renewed her exhaustion. Then too, thanks from Axel Belmont would surely put her to the blush, and her dignity could not bear that insult.

A marmalade cat leapt up the steps ahead of her and waited on the landing, almost as if the beast knew what an effort mere stairs had become. The cat followed Abby up to her sitting room, a cozy space adjoining her bedroom.

"I don't even know your name," she said to the cat, who appropriated a spot on the sofa.

"That's Lancelot."

Abby jumped half out of her boots at the voice from the bedroom, though it was a female voice.

"Show yourself, please."

"Mr. Belmont says your fire is to be kept blazing," said a young lady emerging from the other chamber. "A tea tray is on the way with plenty of biscuits. The Belmont menfolk are ever so fond of their biscuits."

The maid, a mature, sturdy, red-haired woman rather than girl, was clearly fond of the Belmont menfolk. The porcelain vase she carried held a single red rose, and that she placed on the desk.

"A tray won't be necessary." Finding a seat had become imperative, however. Abby took the chair behind the escritoire, despite proximity to the window making that a cold choice. The rose—a big, gorgeous specimen just shy of full bloom—would look pretty in any location.

"Mr. Belmont said you'd refuse a tray, and we're to ignore you. Lancelot will help you with the cream, the shameless beggar. We're to serve you cream rather than milk on the professor's orders." The maid added wood to the fire—not coal. "Would you be having a nap after your tea, ma'am?"

God, yes. "I had thought to work on my correspondence."

"Mr. Belmont's mood is never improved by his correspondence, not that he's a cheery soul to begin with. You might consider getting into your dressing gown, and if you find your eyes growing heavy, you can catch a lie-down at your pleasure."

Abby knew well what manner of maid had been dispatched to attend her. If Axel Belmont was the general in command of the entire estate, Mrs. Turnbull was his trusted lieutenant, all smiles and polite suggestions one dared not thwart.

This maid was his gunnery sergeant, adept at handling both raw recruits and smoking cannon, all while appearing to defer to the commissioned officers.

"What is your name?"

"I'm Hennessey, though the footmen call me Carrot, because of my hair. Will you need anything else, ma'am?"

Abby could get herself out of a riding habit, and her own dressing gown was draped over the privacy screen visible in the bedroom.

"Nothing, thank you. What time is dinner?"

"Country hours. Six, more or less, depending on Mr. Belmont's schedule. He'll try to be punctual as long as you're here."

Abby yielded to temptation. "He's not normally punctual?"

Another maid appeared in the doorway, a large tray in her hands.

"You may come in," Abby said. "I'll ask you to close the door on your way out, lest we lose all the heat from the fire."

The second maid set the tray on the escritoire, popped a curtsey and withdrew.

"Mr. Belmont loses track of time when he's in his glass houses," Hennessey said. "And he'll worry over the new foal, of course, and this magistrate nonsense takes a toll as well."

In other words, Abby was not to overtax her host with a pesky, unsolved murder. "I'll ring should I need anything further, Hennessey."

Another curtsey, and Abby had blessed, delightful solitude in a home where no felonies had been or would dare to be committed. A riding habit was perhaps the easiest garment for a woman to get herself into and out of unassisted, so Abby changed into her nightgown and dressing gown.

The bed beckoned, but she helped herself to a cup of tea and a ginger biscuit, because she'd eaten only as much as she'd dared at luncheon. Ginger biscuits aided digestion, something a botanist would know.

Mr. Belmont had certainly known what to do with an unexpected foal.

Abby took her tea to the bed, then brought the rose to the night table as well. She climbed under the covers and closed her eyes, hoping for sleep.

Instead her memory presented her with the image of Axel Belmont, standing hands on hips over a damp foal shivering in the snow. Tracks in the snow suggested the filly had been born at least an hour past, and yet, the mare was still trying to lick her baby dry.

Much foul language had ensued while Mr. Belmont had begun casting off his clothing, tossing it at Abby as if she were his valet. He'd stripped off everything above the waist, then knelt and used his shirt to towel the filly dry.

The snow had been bloodstained, the cold air had crackled with Mr. Belmont's profanity, and yet, his ministrations to the filly had been gentle and thorough.

He'd been oblivious to his own nudity, while Abby had been unable to look away. She'd stood a few yards off, holding his clothing—a heavy bundle of fine tailoring—and marveling at the sight of a healthy adult male without his shirt.

Gregory in the full bloom of youth would not have looked as Mr. Belmont had—lithe, powerful, impervious to the cold. Axel Belmont's torso, shoulders, and arms were a mosaic of muscle and movement, a testament to the Creator's eye for beauty.

Mr. Belmont had cursed as he'd rubbed every inch of the filly's coat dry, but Abby had given thanks for the very sight of him. Had a valuable animal's life not been at stake, that gift would never have come her way.

When the filly had risen to nurse—assisted by Mr. Belmont and his blue-tinged encouragements—Abby had scolded him back into what clothing had not been ruined. He'd complied readily, alas, apologizing all the while for the necessity of disrobing on such a damned cold day.

Lying in the cozy bed, a fire crackling in the hearth, Abby slid her nightgown up to her thighs and closed her eyes. Axel Belmont without his shirt was a sight she'd never forget and certainly intended to savor now that she had privacy to do so.

She touched herself, as she learned to over years of pouring over naughty books, and more years of solitudinous wifehood. She was widowed now, and this solitary pleasure was even more her right than it had been when Gregory was alive.

In Axel Belmont's house she was safe from whoever had killed Gregory, and whatever evil Gregory might have invited into his life.

While Abby was helpless to defend herself against the image of Axel Belmont, kneeling bare-chested in the snow as he alternately cursed and pleaded with a new life to fight its way to the coming spring.

* * *

"The filly is thriving," Axel said, dishing up eggs for his breakfast companion, "though livestock is probably not the topic a host should embark upon with a guest at breakfast."

Buttered toast, the crusts cut off, came next. Two slices, because if Axel put one slice on Abigail Stoneleigh's plate, she'd eat only a half.

She poured herself a cup of tea, stirred in sugar and cream, then sat back and closed her eyes, the cup held before her, the steam rising around her like High Church incense.

"I did worry about mother and baby," she said. "I take the running of Stoneleigh Manor seriously, and horses are worth a pretty penny. I must compliment Mrs. Turnbull on my comfortable bedroom. After a night under your roof, I'm exceedingly well rested."

Mrs. Stoneleigh had spent a night under Axel's roof sleeping like the dead, as it were. He'd checked on her twice, the first time thinking to offer a game of chess after their evening meal, the second...

Papa's instincts, maybe. A man's curiosity, more likely. Axel had cracked the bedroom door enough to ensure the coals had been banked and hearth screen was in place, then decided that the bed curtains ought also to be drawn.

Which was either overly conscientious of him, or very... presuming.

He set the plate before her and took his seat at the head of the table. "You are a new widow. You must rest as much as you please, and my staff will not comment, lest Mrs. Turnbull scold them before I can turn them off for their own safety. Eat your eggs."

Mrs. Stoneleigh heaved out the sigh of long-suffering women everywhere, then took a sip of her tea.

"Eat, Abigail." *Please.* She picked up her fork, and Axel admitted to relief.

"You never considered remarrying?" she asked, taking a bite of eggs.

He'd ordered a cheese omelet with chives, garlic, and other seasonings, and Cook had done the hens proud.

"I considered the notion a time or two. My aspirations are academic, so reason prevailed."

She bit off a corner of her toast. "Reason?"

"The problem was simple lust, or loneliness, or a troublesome combination of the two. One needn't remarry to deal with either difficulty. You will no doubt have to guard against such temptations yourself in the coming months."

She regarded him with—could it be?—another half-amused smile over a second forkful of eggs.

"Ladies are not supposed to be greatly troubled by the first of those ailments," she said. "I don't believe a gentleman is supposed to allude to it either."

Good God, he was out of practice with polite women. Caroline was probably howling with laughter from some celestial perch.

"Ladies are quite susceptible to the loneliness," he said. "Most men know how to exploit any confusion between lust and loneliness, I am ashamed to admit. More tea?"

"Please. Have you no friends, Mr. Belmont?" she asked, when he'd passed her the refilled tea cup.

What fool had sought some verbal sparring over breakfast? Axel fetched the basket of fruit from the sideboard and began tearing the peel from the ripest orange.

"My brother is my friend," he said, the words oddly satisfying. "I am cordial with all my neighbors, and a few others whom I regard as friends." All of those friends knew not to visit too frequently in late winter, when Axel preferred to lavish time on the specimens in his glass houses.

And ignore the fact that Caroline had died in early March.

"Eat, Abigail, and no more of this Mr. Belmont nonsense over breakfast. You will sour my delicate digestion."

She stilled, a corner of the toast pointing toward her open mouth.

"That's the way. You take a bite, chew, and swallow, then repeat." Her company was more diverting than the morning newspaper, also more worrisome.

She set the toast down. "If you say, 'good girl' I will not answer for the consequences, Mr. Belmont. My own mood is less than sanguine, in case you hadn't noticed. Which reminds me, I will need to send a note to Mrs. Jensen."

He'd noticed her pale complexion. He'd noticed she needed to eat. He'd noticed that she slept as if cast away, but a simple walk across the fields had tired her.

"You need more frocks?" he asked, putting half the peeled orange on her plate. More frocks meant a longer stay under his roof, possibly.

Mrs. Stoneleigh was abruptly absorbed with her remaining piece of toast. "I have need of some personal effects, and Mrs. Jensen can send along a bottle of laudanum."

The substantial meal in Axel's belly lurched disagreeably. "No laudanum. I will divert you with cards, music, scintillating repartee, or good literature. If you insist, I will play my damned violin. I will bore you to sleep with discourses on the successful grafting of roses, on which topic I am a noted expert. I will walk with you, or read damned Scripture by the hour, but no blighted—"

"Stop lecturing. You are incapable of scintillating repartee. If you truly think I am at risk for abusing the poppy, then have her send over a single dose."

Now, when Axel wanted to pitch crockery in all directions, Mrs. Stoneleigh was dispatching her eggs.

"You are well rested, a hint of color graces your cheeks, your eyes are clear, and you do not seem to be in any obvious pain." Axel knew, he'd known as a boy, how need for the drug turned a reasonable person into a begging, screaming, incoherent wreck. Thank God that Caroline had understood and accepted his position on this at least. "No laudanum."

"I am not in obvious pain, because some suffering is personal, and not evident to the almighty male eye. I am not asking for an entire bottle, and I am not obliged to remain here as your prisoner."

She dabbed at the corner of her lip with her serviette, the movement confoundedly dainty.

"Mr. Belmont. *Axel*," she went on, "you were married, you are the father of two children. Can you not conceive that my husband's unexpected death might have disrupted the regular occurrence of certain bodily functions that occasionally cause a woman discomfort?"

Before Axel's eyes, her countenance flooded with color, right up to her hairline. Whatever her supposed indisposition—

A drop of raspberry jam marred her otherwise clean plate. Raspberry was a staple in every woman's herbal, useful for...

"One dose," Axel said, turning her plate so the orange sections were closest to her. "I will watch you take it, and you will not ask for more."

She tipped up her empty tea cup, studying the dregs, ignoring the succulent fruit.

"You make pronouncements as if your word is law, but on other issues, you can be reasoned with, somewhat. What is it about a medicinal dose of laudanum that bothers you so?"

Axel knew what it was to interrogate, to fire off questions in search of truth. He'd put enough questions to Abigail Stoneleigh that she was due a few of her own, though tomorrow, he'd be taking a breakfast tray in the glass house reserved for his roses.

He went to the window, which looked out on a bleak, snowy landscape. In the distance, the broodmares were heavy, dark shapes, heads down against the winter wind.

"My mother," Axel said without turning, "died of an intentional laudanum overdose the very night after my brother's wedding. She'd been addicted for years, but we didn't see that final maneuver coming. My father was gone a little over a year later, dying essentially of a broken heart—or guilt—though he managed to hang on long enough to see me engaged."

"I am sorry." Axel hadn't heard her move, but she was beside him, a gentle hand on his shoulder. "Gregory told me that in India the whole issue is openly accepted. There are places for addicts to go and consume themselves to death, places where opium is offered like tea or coffee. Their society shrugs, and tolerates the whole tragedy, which he seemed to think was far more sensible."

"Ours shrugs and ignores it."

She rubbed the middle of Axel's back in circles, drawing the tension from him. In winter, Caroline had applied her scented lotions to his back, soothing the dryness caused by cold weather.

"How old were you when your mother died, Mr. Belmont?"

Whatever difference did that make? "Sixteen. Matthew was seventeen, nearly eighteen, marrying a woman who was in need of an immediate husband for the obvious reason. Our mother opposed the match, and when it went forward over her protestations, she took her own life."

Mrs. Stoneleigh dropped her hand. "Your poor brother and his poor wife."

"And my poor father, and on and on. I do not generally speak of this." He did not *ever* speak of this part of his past.

"Of course not. You'd rather ask near strangers whether they've taken lovers or have unpaid gambling debts." She poured another cup of tea, added cream and sugar, and brought it to him. "We need not discuss this further."

The tea was good. Comforting, and prepared exactly as Axel preferred. "You still want your dose?"

"I do. By this afternoon, my back will be in stitches. I doubt I'll come down to dinner tonight. I do not normally *speak of this* either. I try not to even think of it, if you must know. Shall we sit?"

Axel held her chair, realizing that his expectation—his near wish—that breakfast degenerate into an argument was to be thwarted. He was confident life without a female in the house was a more peaceful existence than the alternative, but Abby Stoneleigh had refused to prove his hypothesis true.

Yet. "Your back pains you?"

She flicked a glance at him, inherently feminine, nothing he could read, then dabbed her finger in the drop of raspberry jam and licked the tip.

"Midwives have told me a child could improve the situation, but that solution seems both drastic and unrealistic now."

Axel had known exactly when Caroline's menses were bearing down on her, because she'd go from laughter to tears to bellowing mad in the course of an hour. Then, without warning, she'd be up in bed, sweet, sleepy, and achy, willing to cuddle for hours, apologizing for the previous three days of dramatics.

He'd comforted her as best he could, feeling privileged to do so.

"You are lost in thought," Axel's guest remarked. "Reminiscing?"

"If you can call it that." He finished his tea in a single gulp and stood. "My apologies for being a poor breakfast companion. I'm off to finish perusing your ledgers, and I will retrieve your medicinal tot. If I am back in time for luncheon, will that serve?"

She rose before Axel had a chance to hold her chair. "You will be careful at Stoneleigh Manor?"

"Do you caution me for a particular reason?" He was revisiting the scene of a murder. Of course he would be careful, and he would ensure every lock on the property was changed too.

"Whoever killed Gregory," she said, "seems to have known his schedule intimately, and knew how to enter and depart the premises undetected. That suggests the murderer was a familiar, possibly somebody on staff, or a frequent visitor. They might even have had a key."

Which meant Abigail Stoneleigh was afraid of her own staff, and not without reason. *Well, damn and blast.* Axel would hire more than one locksmith to expedite the job.

"Before I depart for Stoneleigh Manor, would you like to visit the new foal with me?"

Because every indisposed woman longed to tramp through the cold and snow to see an awkward, gangling bit of livestock whose acquaintance she'd already made.

"Fresh air appeals," Mrs. Stoneleigh said.

Axel ushered his guest to the hallway, settled her cloak about her shoulders, and stepped back rather than tend to the fastenings beneath her chin. He did, however, take her arm as they crossed to the stable yard, pleased she'd make the outing with him.

A fellow incapable of scintillating repartee liked to know that his company, however prosaic, yet held some attraction for a woman who might well have told him to go to blazes.

* * *

"You're worried about your brother."

Matthew Belmont's new wife settled into his lap, which eased all of his worries. He and Theresa had been married only a handful of weeks, and with each passing day, Matthew's ability to recall his years of widowerhood faded.

"Axel sends felicitations." Matthew set Axel's letter aside and wrapped his arms around Theresa. "He reports that Remington and Christopher appeared to enjoy their recent visit and nearly waddled back to their studies."

"And?"

Theresa had a way of caressing the nape of Matthew's neck that positively wrecked his concentration. Positively and most agreeably.

"And Axel has a murder investigation on his hands. His immediate neighbor was shot dead, and for reasons my brother isn't being entirely forthright about, the widow is now visiting at Candlewick."

Theresa appropriated a ginger biscuit from the tea tray on Matthew's desk, took a bite, then held it up for Matthew to do likewise. No biscuit had ever tasted better, and Axel claimed ginger settled a woman's digestion in the early months of pregnancy.

"Do you fear Axel has taken a murderer under his roof?"

"A lady who conspired to commit murder, perhaps. I'm more worried that Mrs. Stoneleigh is conspiring to commit... marriage."

The matter wanted discussion, so Matthew rose with his wife in his arms, gently deposited her on the sofa, and took an armchair across the low table from her. Theresa had bloomed since their marriage. She no longer wore only drab colors, her smiles had acquired a hint of devilment, and her affectionate nature had become *inventive.*

Alas, Matthew's affectionate nature had failed to lock the library door.

"Axel is lonely," Theresa said, rising to fetch the bowl of biscuits.

She offered them to Matthew, who took three. Affection, at the rate Matthew and his spouse expressed it to each other, was a delightfully taxing aspect of married life.

"My brother is… I hesitate to use the word, but it fits: vulnerable. He wishes us well on our nuptials, then dispatches his sons for an extended visit here. I'd wager Axel has spent his days since returning to Oxford in his glass houses, eating from trays, when he eats at all, soil staining his fingers, and little sprigs of greenery peeking from his pockets. He's always been widow-bait, but now that I'm married…"

Re-married, though Matthew's heart didn't feel that way. Conjugal union with Theresa was the institution as it was meant to be enjoyed.

"Widow-bait, Matthew?"

"Richard coined the term, though he was referring to Nicholas Haddonfield."

Theresa helped herself to a second biscuit. Her dresses were high-waisted, but because Matthew's marital enthusiasm for his wife—and hers for him—had already resulted in conception, the dress was snug across the bodice.

Distractingly snug.

"When last I saw Nick, he struck me as restless," Theresa said. "He's waiting for the social Season to start, so he can begin bride-hunting, and yet, he's enjoyed his time here in Sussex."

Nick Haddonfield, though an earl's heir, had spent the last two years working as a stable master on the neighboring estate. The post had provided a reprieve from the matchmakers and allowed Nick to keep a close eye on a younger sibling.

"I have a confession, my dear," Matthew said, getting up to lock the door. "I have been naughty."

Theresa set down half her biscuit and dusted her hands. "I do so adore your naughty streak, Mr. Belmont."

"I suggested to Nick that if he'd pay a call on Christopher and Remington, I'd be most appreciative."

The way Theresa watched Matthew cross the library suggested another kind of appreciation all together.

"Candlewick is in Oxfordshire," she said, scooting closer to the middle of the sofa.

Matthew dropped to the carpet and positioned himself between his wife's knees. "So it is, and I have yet to warn my brother of this suggestion I made to our Nick." He insinuated a hand beneath his wife's skirts, where lovely memories abounded. "Mrs. Belmont, promise me you will never take up the Continental fashion of wearing drawers."

"Drawers would be a waste of time," she said, fingers going to Matthew's cravat. "One would end up taking them right back off again. You will write to Axel today Matthew, and alert him to Nicholas's impending visit."

Matthew closed his eyes and for the hundredth grateful time, memorized the contour of Theresa's bare knee against his palm.

"Of course, my dear. *Later.*" Much, much later.

* * *

Axel returned from his morning with the Stoneleigh ledgers bearing a sack from Mrs. Jensen and a brown glass bottle with an inch or so of liquid in the bottom. He also brought a list of questions for his guest.

"If you are up to further interrogation over the noon meal," he said when he found Mrs. Stoneleigh in the library, "I'd like to ask you about Stoneleigh's finances."

"I'll manage." She rose from the sofa, her movements a little stiff, a little careful. When they were seated in the breakfast parlor, steaming bowls of chicken soup before them, Axel considered a bit of small talk might be in order.

Though not witty repartee—never that. "What did you find to do this morning?"

"I finished putting away my clothing, acquainted myself with the layout of your house, investigated your stillroom, replied to the notes of condolence I've received so far, copied Gregory's obituary for Sir Dewey, and stared at the same page of some book or other for several years."

How well Axel knew that last activity. "What preoccupies you?"

He asked the question out of curiosity, but also because Mrs. Stoneleigh had started on her soup.

"With your staff off to market, this morning is the first time I've had real solitude since Gregory died, and I find myself… He was here, on this earth for nearly sixty years. He got up one morning, rode out as he always did, spent the morning in the kennels, stopped in at the Weasel for his customary pint, perhaps chatted up the vicar, Sir Dewey, who knows who else… A typical day, and then he's gone forever. No more Gregory Stoneleigh."

She put her spoon down, took a measured breath, and rose. "Excuse me."

Well, hell. Axel caught up to her at the door, foiling her escape with a hand on her wrist. She'd spent the morning brooding, and he'd forgotten this was market day. Not well done of him, to leave her without any company at all.

"Go ahead and cry. It won't be the last time."

"I'll be fine," she said, staring at Axel's cravat even as he drew her into his arms.

"You will,"—unless the murderer went after her too, or Axel had to arrest her—"but your husband's life was ended too soon and wrongly, and that is sad enough to make any wife cry, or it should be."

Her weight settled against him, too slight, too angular, for all her endowments. "Our soup is getting cold. You'll chide me if I don't eat." Then, more softly, "I hate to cry."

Gregory Stoneleigh's widow went down to defeat silently, shuddering against Axel in slow, drawing sobs that cut him like a winter wind. He held her and stroked her hair, smoothed his hands in circles on her back and nape, hoping simple proximity and touch comforted her.

Holding her, he had time to notice exactly how her bones were too prominent under his hands, though she fit him; her body lined up with his such that he could rest his chin at her temple and take all of her weight against him.

He snatched a linen serviette off the table for her to use as a handkerchief. "Do not apologize for crying, or letting the soup get cold, or anything else."

"Then shall I apologize for seeking my room?" She drew back, but didn't entirely leave Axel's embrace. "After such a performance, you can't expect me to sit at table, can you?"

"After such a performance, I know you need sustenance more than ever. Will you join me in the library if I put some of this food on trays?" Every morsel of it, in fact.

"I will, though you must not badger me to eat. I seldom have much appetite at times like this."

Times like...? Axel recalled her furious blush over breakfast.

"I don't badger, I merely suggest." And occasionally lecture. He was capable of exhorting in a pinch, and admonitions were also within his reach. Axel stepped away from her and rummaged in the sideboard for trays, then set about assembling two full plates, cutlery, and glasses of wine.

When they reached the library, he kept the conversation superficial, reporting on which neighbors had collected hounds from the dispersal of the colonel's kennel and how the staff fared at Stoneleigh Manor.

"Shreve is a dithering sort, isn't he?" Axel asked, as he set the trays on the low table before the sofa.

Abigail went wandering across the library, though doubtless she'd inspected the entire room.

"I used to joke to Shreve that Gregory didn't need a wife when he had such devoted help on his staff. Shreve took his duties very seriously within the manor, and Ambers was Gregory's trusted shadow out of doors."

Ambers, who had dodged or cut short Axel's every attempt to interview him since the day after the murder. Matthew had said to avoid any show of haste, though, to allow the miscreant a false confidence that no arrest would be forthcoming.

"Eat your lunch, Abigail, or I will chide you for it."

She peered at a sketch Axel had done of swamp roses beside a still pond. "Was that a suggestion? I don't believe it was."

Better, for her to be chiding him. She wandered back to the sofa, situated herself behind her tray, and speared a braised carrot on the end of her fork.

"I'm a papa. Perhaps scintillating repartee eludes me because I've had to develop such a sure touch with my scolds and chides."

Abigail did not make faces at her vegetables before consuming them, unlike Axel's offspring.

"You expect me to be grateful that I won't have children, Professor?"

Ah. Of course. "You may yet have children. You are young."

"Not that young," she said around at bite of carrot. "I will mourn for anywhere from one to three years, two at least, at which time I will be thirty. Thirty is old for a woman, quite old to start a family."

She ate more when Axel disagreed with her, and on this topic, he could offer a genuine difference of opinion.

"If you truly wanted a child, you could marry next week and have a baby by Christmas, God willing. Once you become a parent, though, time itself alters. One minute you're singing every last lullaby you can recall in hopes the little blighter will go to sleep, the next you're lecturing him about proper deportment at university. Fortunately, when my boys go to university, they'll be only a couple of hours away."

Until such time as Axel became an Oxford fellow himself.

"Unless they choose Cambridge, Professor Belmont."

"Eat your beef, Abigail, and do not commit such sedition in my house again. Cambridge, indeed."

She cut off the smallest bite of beef. Dayton and Phillip would have regarded sharing a meal with Abigail Stoneleigh as a form of torture.

"Speaking of young men," Axel said. "I've mentioned that two of my nephews are in Hilary term and may join us of a weekend. Do not neglect your potatoes, Abigail."

She put her fork down. "Another suggestion?"

A plea, did she but know it. "You are uncomfortable?" She'd eaten about half her food, and that only because Axel had pestered her.

"Increasingly. Not much of soldier, am I?"

"You are a widow. Shall I bring the laudanum to your room?"

"Please." She winced as she rose, so Axel slipped an arm around her waist and led her to the door.

"Humor me," he replied, anchoring his arm more firmly around her.

"Another suggestion. What a helpful fellow you are."

"You are teasing me. Were you this disrespectful to your late husband?" Whose ledgers they hadn't so much as mentioned.

"Gregory had clearly defined expectations of what ladylike deportment entailed. I learned to meet those expectations."

"Do you regret marrying him?" Axel asked, when they reached her door.

She shrugged free of his arm. "Of course not. My parents and most of their possessions had perished in a fire. My grandfather had died only weeks earlier of old age or a wasting disease. Gregory had been one of Grandpapa Pennington's business associates, and thus I'd had a passing acquaintance with him for years. The colonel's offer of marriage was all that saved me from the workhouse, and I would have married him if he'd kept me in his kennels."

What a ghastly admission, not because it whispered of reasons to kill a man, but because it reflected so miserably on the late colonel.

"Abigail, sometimes I am relieved my spouse is gone. I loved her as well as I could, but in the end, she was suffering terribly. One finds peace, eventually, in being honest, and I'm honestly glad Caroline's suffering ended. I'll not chide you for honestly resenting that Gregory was a disappointment."

A disgrace to his gender more like.

Abby nodded once, then slipped into her room, quietly closing the door behind her.

What in the hell was wrong with the young men of England, that a self-important, fifty-year-old cavalry veteran had been the only option for a woman as lovely as Abigail Stoneleigh?

And when had Axel begun to think of her as not simply pretty, but lovely?

CHAPTER SIX

A long, laudanum-laced nap did nothing to restore Abigail's spirits, though the thought of all the books in Axel Belmont's library was modestly cheering. Mr. Belmont owned a variety of novels, and Gregory had scoffed at fiction.

Women were to read improving tracts, sermons, and recipe books in addition to the Book of Common Prayer and the Bible.

Sometimes I am relieved my spouse is gone. A woman whose husband had been murdered did not dare admit to the same sentiment. Axel Belmont's honesty had been so welcome, such a relief, Abigail had nearly hugged him for it.

And yet, she'd also been happy to doze through the dinner hour, and sorely hoped Mr. Belmont had sought his own chambers for the late evening hours rather than the warmth of the library.

The library door was a few inches ajar, and a murmur of masculine voices drifted into the corridor. For a moment, Abby was thrown back to all the times she'd heard Gregory and Sir Dewey chatting similarly, all the times she'd waited, hand poised to knock, until the conversation had found a natural lull, for Gregory had not tolerated unannounced interruptions.

"I haven't any real suspects yet." That would be Mr. Belmont. "More brandy?"

"If you please." Another man spoke, his voice as cultured as Mr. Belmont's, maybe a little smoother. "What about the wife? You say she inherited the property, and is decades younger than the deceased."

Liquid sloshed, glass tinkled. "She didn't inherit any more than the son or daughter did. Two reliable witnesses placed her on the next floor up when the shot was fired."

"She could have hired it done." The other man was idly speculating, while Abby's heart had begun to thump against her ribs. "Thirty years is a great age difference, even in these opportunistic times."

The corridor was chilly, but Abby could not have moved if her life had depended upon it—which, if Axel Belmont still considered her a suspect, it might.

Damn him, though. Damn him for his feigned solicitude. *Do not neglect your potatoes, Abigail.*

"If Mrs. Stoneleigh wanted her husband gone, why wait eight years into the marriage?" Mr. Belmont mused. "Why use a gun, when poison would have been tidier? She's not a stupid woman."

Abby wasn't a smart woman, to have been so thoroughly charmed by Axel Belmont's gruff attentiveness.

"Have you ruled her out or not?" the other fellow asked.

"I have," Mr. Belmont said, causing Abigail to sag against the wall in relief. "And I haven't."

What?!

"Is she pretty, Axel? Your grieving neighbor who must share your roof?"

"Mrs. Turnbull would toss you over her knee for impugning the honor of the house, and if there was anything left of you, I'd take a turn thereafter. Mrs. Stoneleigh is quite pretty." Pretty was a problem, based on Mr. Belmont's tone. "She's also not entirely forthcoming, hence my hesitation."

Oh no. Oh no, oh no, oh no.

"Why not seduce her? You'd get your wick trimmed and learn her secrets."

"Mrs. Turnbull deserves a go at you for that remark alone, Nicholas. I will not seduce a female under my protection," Mr. Belmont replied, his voice, of all things, amused. "Particularly not in the king's name. You seduce her. No, on second thought, don't you dare. She's grieving, alone, and in no condition to endure your casual trifling."

Who was this man? And how on earth had Axel Belmont concluded that Abby was keeping secrets?

The door opened the rest of the way without warning, and she was confronted with more human male than she had seen in one body. This Nicholas person stood at least six and a half feet tall, every inch of him bound in muscle. Worse—much, much worse—his blue eyes were full of unholy humor.

While discussing murder?

"Won't you join us?" He took her by the wrist and drew her into the library's warmth. "You haven't the temperament for murder, Mrs. Stoneleigh. Only a truly calculating female would recall to eschew her perfume when she's bent on eavesdropping."

"You smelled my—?"

"Nicholas Haddonfield." He bowed with easy grace, a blond curl flopping over his brow. "At your service. The scent of roses becomes you wonderfully, especially in this household."

Mr. Belmont's expression was far less welcoming. Abby could see him wondering how long she'd been listening, hearing no good about pretty, secretive murder suspects.

"Don't look at the professor like that," Mr. Haddonfield said, leaning brazenly close. "Makes him think you like the broody, academic type, when I am certain I can convince you that a golden god such as my lonely little self would be more to your liking."

"Nicholas, for pity's sake," Mr. Belmont said on a sigh. "Mrs. Abigail Stoneleigh, may I make known to you Nicholas Haddonfield, Viscount Reston, though you will also hear him referred to in less-flattering terms. His familiars refer to him as Wee Nick. Nicholas, my neighbor, Mrs. Abigail Stoneleigh, whom you will not pester."

"Good evening." Abigail bobbed a curtsey, still dumbstruck by the man's sheer size and more than a little impressed to be in the presence of a title— while wearing her nightgown and robe, no less.

"You'll warm up to me, particularly if the professor can charm you into a tot of brandy."

Mr. Belmont gestured with the brandy bottle. "Mrs. Stoneleigh?"

Mr. Haddonfield took the bottle, poured a finger, and passed Abby the glass. "A mere nip, to keep the chill away."

Abby did not want a *nip*, she wanted to take a bite out of both men where it counted.

"Ignore him, madam. Nicholas thinks he's being helpful by giving you time to fashion an excuse for eavesdropping."

Abby nearly dashed her brandy in Mr. Belmont's face. "Are you fashioning an excuse for your suspicions, Mr. Belmont? You're all polite concern over a meal, while suspecting me of murder most foul?"

"All murder is foul," Mr. Haddonfield interjected. "My condolences on your husband's death. I am ever fond of husbands, because the women they marry can no longer bother me with their conjugal aspirations. Let us talk of murder, which is more fascinating than my marital prospects."

Axel Belmont's fists went to his hips. "Nicholas, you make light of Mrs. Stoneleigh's loss at your peril."

The threat was sincere. Viscount or not, giant or not, Axel Belmont's guest could find himself thrashed to flinders on Abigail's behalf. And yet, the professor did not deny that Abby was still a murder suspect.

"My apologies, Mrs. Stoneleigh," the viscount said. "I mean no disrespect. I will bend my considerable brilliance to assisting Professor Belmont in apprehending the felon. What does Matthew think of this situation?"

Matthew would be Mr. Belmont's brother.

"Does all of England except the victim's own widow have a say in this investigation?" Abby asked.

Axel took her glass from her—Abby was not in the mood for spirits—and set it on the desk. "I hesitate to pursue this topic in Mrs. Stoneleigh's hearing."

Because the professor did not want to distress her, or because he did not trust her? Abby could not read him, though he could apparently read her.

"Pursue it," Abby said, stalking to the estate desk and taking the seat behind it. "Perhaps I might share a few of those secrets I've been keeping."

* * *

The lady unwittingly confessed to keeping secrets—plural—and Axel's heart sank.

"I beg your pardon, Mrs. Stoneleigh," he said with a bow in her direction. "I should not accuse you of secrecy, so much as of reticence."

She wrinkled her nose at this wilted specimen of an apology. Axel would not have been surprised if she'd begun rifling his desk drawers in retaliation for his suspiciousness.

"I assume Lord Reston is in your confidence, Mr. Belmont?"

Matthew's spy was trying to look harmless, though Axel had raised boys and wasn't fooled.

"Despite appearances to the contrary, Nicholas has earned that privilege. I literally trust him with my firstborn."

"And his second," Nick said, settling onto the sofa, "at the same time, and the boys adore me, as do most sensate creatures. Come join me." He patted the spot beside him. "Ladies wandering around in their nightclothes provoke my every friendly instinct." Abigail remained right where she was, behind Axel's nice, big, solid desk. Her nightclothes covered her far more modestly than evening attire would have, and her air of indignation should have frozen Nick's presuming balls off at thirty paces.

"Nicholas," Axel said, *pleasantly*, "I realize you are in anticipation of London's annual bacchanals, but you will behave, lest I take you in hand. Mrs. Stoneleigh is a lady, and bereaved."

She was also, apparently, amused by Nick's witty damned repartee.

"Take me in hand, Professor?" Nick replied. "I've heard of this taking in hand. Day and Phillip do not speak highly of it."

"Exactly. Now, pay attention, and I'll sketch in a few more details regarding the mystery of Gregory Stoneleigh's death." Axel started from the beginning, reviewing the contents of the will and what he knew of Gregory's habits and associations.

Abigail sat across the room, as regally as if she'd been in presentation robes rather than nightclothes, shawl, and slippers. She'd picked a fine time to begin availing herself of a widow's relaxed view of the proprieties.

"Follow the money," Nick said, after listening to Axel's recitation. "Gregory Stoneleigh does not appear to have been a philanderer, and he was also singularly lacking in enemies. That rules out passion and revenge, and leaves greed. He was wealthy?"

"That's one piece of the puzzle," Axel replied. "Abigail, you said Gregory married you in part to acquire a manager for the estate, and he wasn't about to put his own money into the place. What money?"

"The estate banked in Oxford," Abigail said, running a pale finger around the rim of her glass. Nick had served her from one of the Jacobite set, the inscription—*audentior ibo*—translating loosely to *I shall go more boldly.*

"Gregory would come back from some horse auction," she said. "Ambers would have a new pair of hunters for the stables, though Gregory would not use estate money to procure his horses. He traveled with Sir Dewey frequently and did not ask me for funds from the household accounts."

Nick posed the obvious question. "Where did Gregory's money come from?"

"From his import business," Abigail said. "From the rents on his London properties, from investments, I assume."

And none of that income had been reflected in the ledgers Axel had seen. "I'll ask Gervaise for the appropriate records, but some funds had to have been kept here in Oxford." And yet, no correspondence from any Oxford bank had been among Stoneleigh's letters, nor had any ledgers referred to Oxford accounts other than those Abigail used.

She rose and set her untouched glass on the sideboard. She was a graceful woman, and Axel had missed bickering with her over dinner.

"What else did you want to ask me, Mr. Belmont?"

Did you conspire to kill your husband, and if so, how will I bring myself to arrest you for it?

"Tell me about the bookkeeping for the estate in earlier years," Axel replied. "You said when you married Gregory, the estate was sliding into debt. I can't see why that would be. Your land was in fair condition when Gregory took it over years ago, and you've been prudent in its management."

If Axel's compliment registered with her, her expression didn't show it. "I can only tell you what I found when I married Gregory, and that would be the accounting equivalent of chaos. Gregory would go on queer starts. He wanted one of our streams to have retaining walls on both sides for part of its length, the better to train his hunters on water obstacles. Masons and stone take money, as do trips to the quarry, teams, wagons, and so on. His little project was exorbitantly expensive, and he began it without so much as estimates in hand."

His little project had also been ridiculous. Hunters were best trained over natural terrain in the company of experienced campaigners.

"When did you learn how to manage the ledgers?" Axel asked. "You could not have been but nineteen or twenty years old when you married."

Though Axel had been managing Candlewick by that age, or trying to.

"My father believed I would someday, with my spouse, take over the

Pennington family businesses. My earliest memories are of sitting on Papa's lap while he showed me how to use the abacus."

"What did your father do?" Axel's children would never have sat still long enough for such instruction.

Abigail tidied the glasses on the sideboard, then used a handkerchief to polish one of the decanters.

"Papa and Grandpapa started with a printing shop in Oxford," she said, moving on to the next decanter. "To that my father added a bookshop, the year I was born. The bookshop did very well, or so I thought, because we were near many of the colleges. When I was a girl, Papa bought the property next door to the bookshop and turned it into a coffee shop and tea room. I thought he was quite successful at all three."

"But?" Nick and Axel asked at the same time.

She dusted off the last decanter and lined them all up just so. "But he died in debt, and I inherited next to nothing. Gregory explained that all had been mortgaged, the better to afford tutors, lessons, and frocks for me."

But no dowry? A merchant who could purchase entire businesses had set aside nothing for the daughter he adored?

"You put no value on the frocks," Axel said.

She moved on to the hearth, using the broom on the hearth stand to sweep ashes back against the screen. Axel wanted to caution her not to get her hems dirty, but she held them aside with one hand.

"Why buy me a Broadwood piano for my sixteenth birthday when Papa could not sustain the businesses he'd owned for years? The ledgers all showed healthy balances and regular sums set aside for savings. Gregory's description of Papa's finances made no sense to me, but then, I was devastated to lose my parents so shortly after Grandpapa Pennington's death."

Another mystery, then, except paternal pride might be the entire explanation.

"Impending financial ruin inspires many men into an irrational determination to maintain appearances," Nick observed.

Another possibility fit the available facts: Stoneleigh had connived to marry an heiress. Axel had no evidence to disprove that theory—and none to support it. Abigail's parents had died nearly a decade ago, and relevant financial records were likely long gone.

"I didn't know you played piano," Axel said. Most women of any means played *at* the piano.

Abby's next project was a fern growing in a suspended pot near the globe. The plant enjoyed the light from the bow window and some warmth from the hearth, but it did tend to dry out. Abigail tested the soil with her finger, then used her handkerchief to wipe the dirt away.

"I used to play by the hour, but Gregory found my skill lacking," she said, using a water glass to give the fern a drink. "I read voraciously too, when I was younger. I came down here thinking to raid the library shelves."

"And instead," Nick said, wiggling his eyebrows, "look at the treasure you found."

"Without doubt, I am the luckiest of females."

"She's warming up to me, Professor," Nick said. "You can hear her growing fondness in her very words."

What Axel had heard was sadness, old puzzlement, and longing—and not for more silly banter. He rose and crossed to the bookshelves.

"What manner of story would you like? Something improving or something entertaining?"

He ignored the highest shelves, the ones bearing his collections of erotica and poetry. Every academic had such a collection, after all.

"A novel, if you have any."

"If I have any?" Gregory Stoneleigh's widow had much to learn about enjoying life. "I suppose you think only exponents of that lowly institution on the River Cam enjoy recreational reading? If I have any…. " He waggled his fingers at her, gesturing her to his side.

"Sir Walter Scott," Axel began, "Jane Austen, Mrs. Radcliffe, whom Day and Phillip have both read, but you must not own I told you that. Fielding, a goodly helping of pastoral poetry, and the mandatory Byron, though that hardly qualifies as verse in the opinion of many. What is your pleasure?"

She perused the shelves, her expression carefully composed, as if this choice, rather than Axel's suspicions regarding her husband's death, was more likely to reveal latent criminal tendencies.

"Austen," she said reaching for a book, only to have her hand collide with Axel's. "I beg your pardon," she murmured as a blush crept up her neck.

Austen was a fine choice for a blushing widow in evening dishabille. Axel took Abigail's hand and slapped the book against her palm.

"Excuse my clumsiness," he said softly. The best he could do, with Nick listening to every word.

"I might be needing a book myself," Nick said from the sofa.

"Try the Bible," Axel retorted. "Take it up to your room and start with Genesis. Don't come down until you've finished Revelations."

"Already read that one," Nick replied. "I like the Song of Solomon best. Caught my eye when I was a wee lad. Shall I light you up to your room, Mrs. Stoneleigh?"

Axel wasn't half done questioning her, but she was already paging through the tale of Mr. Darcy's fall from arrogance.

"Nicholas will behave," Axel said, "or you have my permission to bludgeon him with the book."

She considered her tome. "It's a slim volume, and bound books are very dear."

"You wound me, madam," Nick said, rising and picking up a carrying candle. "I'll behave, Mrs. Stoneleigh, because I am a gentleman and too tired to do justice to a flirtation with you—for now."

"You will behave," she said sternly, "because I expect it of you, sir."

Nick beamed at her. "I am in love. She understands me."

"Bother you," Abigail muttered, preceding Nick from the library, Miss Austen at the ready.

The widow was safe with Nicholas, or as safe as she wanted to be. Axel gave the fern another drink and wondered where a fellow learned the knack of witty repartee.

Nick came back to the library a few moments later—too few moments for much mischief to have occurred.

"I do not see a bright red handprint on your cheek," Axel said. "I conclude you are working on a stealthy seduction rather than overwhelming the lady with your appeal."

A dalliance might do Abigail Stoneleigh good. All of Axel's scolding had yet to put roses in her cheeks, or win a true smile from her.

"I doubt she has much familiarity with trifling," Nick said, collapsing onto the sofa and tugging off his boots. "You could help her with that. She's too damned pale."

"She is pale." Axel had grown accustomed to Abigail's pallor, and the woman was grieving, after all.

"Tell her to stop using the damned arsenic." Nick yawned and propped his stockinged feet on the low table. "My step-mama wouldn't let my sisters use it."

"Arsenic?" Axel settled in beside Nick, who had half a regiment of sisters. Axel was familiar with every cosmetic use of plants, but knew nothing of what else might lurk on a woman's vanity.

"The ladies use arsenic to give their complexions that lovely, ethereal quality," Nick said, closing his eyes. "Genuine grief apparently has the same result."

"She does miss the old fellow." *Axel hoped.* "Tell me, Nicholas, how is my brother? And how are my sons?"

"I had to leave," Nick said. "Matthew and Theresa are besotted, and she has that secret glow of the breeding woman. Loris and Thomas are in the advanced stages of the same condition on the next property over, and the whole shire stinks of marital bliss. Move down."

Axel complied, shifting to the end of the sofa, only to find Nick's feet in his lap, while the considerable length of his friend lounged along the rest of the sofa.

"Your fatigue is catching up with you." Axel pulled an afghan from the back of the sofa. He tossed the blanket over Nick's face, letting Nick arrange it further.

"This sofa,"—Nick closed his eyes—"must be conveyed to me in your will.

Or if I die first, you must bury it with me so I might have it in the afterlife, like the pharaohs of old from whom a god such as myself is doubtless descended."

Damn and blast. From the mouths of marriage-shy viscounts. "I should look at their wills."

"Whose?"

"Abigail's parents. She believes they died deeply in debt, but her upbringing was the finest, and her father's businesses were to appearances thriving." And her father would have recently inherited whatever her grandfather had left behind, too.

Nick opened his eyes. "Appearances have little to do with finances, particularly among the aspiring class. Will you seduce her? I think she likes you."

"Nicholas, you grow tedious. She doesn't like me." Especially not after hearing Axel's speculation regarding her guilt, or those secrets—plural—*which she had not shared.* "She might respect me. We were not well acquainted prior to Gregory's death, and we're both pleasantly surprised to find each other human."

"Oh, right. Admit it, Belmont. You left Sussex and traveled nearly a hundred miles in the dead of winter to escape the foul miasma of marital bliss under your brother's roof."

"I'm not jealous, Nicholas, and neither are you. We're happy for Matthew." *Mostly.*

"Overjoyed," Nick said. "Why don't you bring that decanter over here, and we'll drink to Matthew's glorious benighted happiness."

Axel fetched the decanter, which was merely what a conscientious host and a good friend would do, after all.

* * *

"So what will you do with your day?" Abigail asked her host. They were alone in the breakfast parlor, something of a relief.

"I thought I'd call upon Reverend Weekes, maybe visit Sir Dewey Fanning, get off a letter to Gervaise, and nose about at the Wet Weasel. Have you an errand you'd like me to dispatch?"

Abby chose a slice of toast from the rack on the table, and Mr. Belmont pushed the butter toward her. The crust was golden perfection, the toast still warm.

"I'll be content to remain close to the house today." Abby slathered her toast with butter. Gregory had preferred delicacy on the female frame, while Axel Belmont apparently liked to see a woman enjoy her food.

The raspberry jam was another delight of the Belmont table, so Abby added a portion to her toast.

"I have letters of condolence to acknowledge," she went on, "and I'd like to explore your library."

"Help yourself to any volume that catches your fancy, of course." Mr. Belmont poured her a fresh cup of tea and plucked an orange from the bowl on the table. "Nicholas will probably sleep late. He had a hard day of travel yesterday and was no doubt keeping Town hours before that."

"About Nicholas."

Mr. Belmont put aside the orange, several inches of curled rind already trailing from the fruit.

"What about him?"

"Did you...?" Abby's host was being inscrutable, and he was dashed good at it too. "You did not intend... That is, you didn't ask him..."

"What exactly are you dancing around, Abigail?"

She got up and went to the window, where a weak sun was trying to find openings in a gathering overcast.

"His lordship implied he was available to comfort me, though he was delicate about his insinuations, and I might have misconstrued them. You didn't put him up to that, did you?"

Silence, which Abigail took for an affirmative, then she heard a chair scrape.

"Comfort you, *how*?" Mr. Belmont asked from immediately behind and to her left.

"As a man comforts a woman." Or was supposed to comfort her? "In bed."

"Were you offended?"

They had the most peculiar conversations. "I ought to have been, but I was not. Not very. He might have meant nothing by it." Or he might have been encouraging Abigail to dally with Axel Belmont. She hadn't been sure, and thought perhaps his lordship preferred her to remain confused.

"I will certainly warn him off—if you wish me to."

Mr. Belmont did not sound angry. Not with his friend, not with Abigail even if she'd been considering a liaison under Candlewick's very roof, and Gregory barely gone a month.

"You haven't answered my question, Mr. Belmont." Abby hadn't asked the question that truly plagued her. Would a magistrate who suspected her of colluding in her husband's murder test her loyalties by dangling temptation at her elbow?

"Did I procure Nick's services for you? Do you really think I would?"

What Abigail thought was that nearly a decade of marriage to Gregory had given her no sense of how to handle men in the wider world, and certainly no ability to handle this man.

"I've offended you." Or perhaps she'd amused the professor, or foiled his nasty strategy. "I'm sorry, but you seemed so sure I would develop such associations now that I am a widow, and I am at sea in so many ways. I do not know how these things are done. I did not mean to give offense."

Mr. Belmont turned her gently by the shoulders.

"If I thought you sought that kind of consolation, Abigail, I would hardly set Nick upon you. I love the man dearly, and he's accounted a good time by the ladies, but you deserve better than a mindless romp."

He dropped his hands. What would he do if Abby told him that, indeed, she sought that kind of consolation? Axel Belmont wouldn't offer a mindless romp, not to her, not to anybody.

He would be mindful, very, very mindful. Just as he'd mindfully arrest her in the king's name if he suspected she'd arranged Gregory's murder.

He drew her chair back. "Eat your breakfast, Abigail. I'll tell you about Nick, and maybe you'll forgive him."

She sat and took up her toast, though the entire exchange had raised more questions than it had settled.

"Nick is at war with his papa, the Earl of Bellefonte." Mr. Belmont resumed peeling his orange. "The earl wants Nick to marry and produce the requisite heir. Lord Bellefonte is rumored to be in failing health, but Nick isn't ready for domesticity. He has fought for ten years against the inevitable, and his father's patience is at an end. When the Season begins, Nick will be on the hunt for a wife."

"I do not understand the male of the species," Abby said, savoring the combination of butter, toast, and raspberry jam. "Your friend gives every appearance of adoring women, but can't be bothered to find one special woman for himself."

The orange squirted juice all over Mr. Belmont's fingers. "Perhaps having a fondness for all women does not allow for loving only one."

"You loved your wife." Abby needed to believe this about him, though she and Gregory had not loved each other. She'd been grateful, she'd been dutiful, she'd prayed for Gregory's soul—but she hadn't loved him.

"I was a young man," Mr. Belmont said, "who'd found a woman willing to bear my children and all that entailed, so of course I was enamored of Caroline." He ripped the last of the peel away from the orange and tore the fruit in half. "She was well-situated, pretty, passionate about life, and not so diminutive that I felt like an oaf when we danced."

Half an orange landed on Abby's plate. "You married her because she did not make you feel like an oaf?"

He picked off the pith from his half, while citrus and awkwardness perfumed the air.

"I was a good catch. Not titled, but wealthy and biddable. Reasonably presentable in evening attire."

He was stunning, in his way. "Biddable?"

"A fine quality in a husband. I'm sure your mama told you how to encourage it in the colonel." His half of the orange lay in tatters on his plate.

"Whatever are you talking about? Gregory was my husband, the head of our household. Of course he wasn't biddable and by the time I married him, my mama was laid in her grave.

Mr. Belmont studied the mess on his plate. "If Caroline wanted something badly, she knew to ask me for it... when the exercise of certain marital privileges was much on my mind. I was *biddable*."

How had they ever got onto this topic, and more to the point, how could they pretend they'd never discussed it?

"I know nothing of this kind of manipulation between spouses, Mr. Belmont. If Gregory asked something of me, I tried my best to accommodate him, and I'm sure he made similar efforts. The behavior you describe... It had no place between us."

Abby had taken less than a year to establish what her spouse needed from her—an orderly, quiet home; a well-run country estate; companionship between his jaunts to the grouse moors, Melton Mowbray, or London.

Nothing more, and nothing less.

"You make Stoneleigh sound like a paragon, Abigail. I rode out with the man enough to know he was given to pomposity, self-absorbed, and rigid. He could be jocular, but he was becoming an arrogant old martinet."

Well, yes, but fortunately, being an arrogant old martinet was not grounds for murder.

"He was a fine man," Abby shot back. She hadn't truly known Gregory Stoneleigh, any more than his housekeeper or head gardener had known him. Even his children, after early years in India, had been sent back to England to finish growing up.

"We are having an argument," Mr. Belmont said, patting Abby's hand. "I haven't argued with a woman for years. Are you enjoying this altercation?"

The orange had got the worst of it. "I am loath to admit it, but I am. I did not argue with Gregory." *Not ever.*

"Look at the fun you missed. I argued with Caroline from time to time— one didn't take her on lightly—and while I disliked the altercations, I enjoyed patching things up afterward."

"And you call yourself biddable. Caroline was lucky."

"So was Gregory. Now that we are friends again, would you like to visit the filly with me?"

Friends. An invigorating notion, when Abby suspected Mr. Belmont would arrest such a friend without a qualm. They were soon crossing the back gardens, though any trace of sunbeams had disappeared behind the clouds.

"That sky does look like snow," she said. "Don't tarry in the village, if you please."

"Will you worry about me, Abigail?"

She liked hearing him say her name, part challenge, part... friendship. "I will worry about *me*, lest I be snowbound with Lord Reston of the easy virtue."

"You tell him no, and he will desist. If he doesn't, protect yourself accordingly with my blessing."

"Protect myself? Not to cast aspersion, but I wonder if *you* could protect yourself from his lordship when he's in a temper."

"Nicholas never lets himself get into a temper, and you can protect yourself in the manner of women."

Abby crunched along beside him between bare hedges and dormant roses. "This must be something else my mama neglected to tell me, along with how to keep my husband biddable."

"A man can be rendered utterly harmless by a knee to his stones, and from you, he'd not expect it." Mr. Belmont's tone was lecturing, as if the next topic were propagation of fruit trees in winter. Had Abby not spent time with her nose in various naughty tomes, she would have had no clue regarding the male anatomy under discussion.

When they reached the stable, Mr. Belmont fussed over the little filly, then stopped by the stall of the viscount's enormous mare—Buttercup, by name. The mare greeted Mr. Belmont as if he were a long-lost friend, wiggling her lips against his cheek.

"Ivan will be jealous." Abby was jealous, not of a horse-kiss to Mr. Belmont's cheek, but of the easy affection between man and mare. Of a marriage where spouses were free to argue with each other, of women who knew how to protect themselves from importuning viscounts.

She was a wealthy widow, and yet, she felt impoverished.

"Geldings don't get jealous," Mr. Belmont replied, "but they do get impatient. Wheeler, I'll take Ivan now. Come along, horse, and we'll escort Mrs. Stoneleigh back to the house."

Ivan the Not Very Terrible toddled placidly behind his master, while flurries danced down from the sky.

"I doubt I'll be back for luncheon," Mr. Belmont said, halting his horse by the mounting block before the front steps.

Maybe he'd had that kind of marriage too. The kind where spouses kept each other informed of their whereabouts. Gregory had often simply departed for "Melton," or "London," with little notice and fewer details, rarely even specifying his date of expected return. He'd more than once told Abby he was off to check on the import business's activities in Town, only for Brandenburg, the London factor, to send inquires as to when the colonel's next visit would be.

"I'm accustomed to eating alone," Abby said. "Be off with you."

She patted Ivan's shoulder and aimed an I'm-just-fine smile at Mr. Belmont. The sooner he left, the sooner he'd return, and the notion of a supper tête-à-tête with the viscount was not to be borne.

A knee to the.... *Well.*

Mr. Belmont brushed a kiss to her cheek and swung into the saddle. "See that you eat, whether you're alone or in company. Keep a list of all the condolence notes you receive, especially from impecunious bachelors. Take Mr. Darcy up to bed for a nap if you're so inclined."

"Yes, sir. At once, Mr. Belmont. Of course. Now shoo, before I turn into an ice sculpture."

He turned his horse away from the mounting block, then cantered off down the frozen driveway, but not fast enough to hide the glimmer of a smile in his eyes.

CHAPTER SEVEN

Axel might have stopped in at the Wet Weasel for his midday meal, but Ivan, doubtless longing for his cozy stall and a heaping pile of hay, instead brought his rider home for luncheon after the interview with Weekes.

"I wasn't expecting you," Abigail said. "Was Mr. Weekes not home?"

She was the picture of domestic bliss on the library sofa, her feet curled under her, a cream-colored shawl about her shoulders, the everyday porcelain on a tea tray before her.

"You've been cavorting with Mr. Darcy," Axel said, closing the library door. "Better him than Nicholas. Weekes was at home to callers, though I've discovered a capacity for mendacity in our vicar."

"Tell me," Abigail said, patting the sofa beside her. "Even Mr. Darcy's charms have their limit, though he writes a compelling letter."

She wanted scintillating repartee *and* compelling letters, while Axel wanted to unburden himself concerning the interview with Weekes. He took the place beside her, unwrapped the linen from the pot, peered inside, and enjoyed a blast of fragrant warmth against his cheeks.

"Weekes is apparently in his study at all hours," Axel replied, pouring a cup, adding cream and a dash of sugar, and passing it over to Abby. "He puts it about that he's working on his sermons, but he's in truth napping and reading novels."

"Gregory would have been scandalized by a man of the cloth reading novels." She took sip of her tea, rather than expound on that point. "He always served me tea at breakfast, and it was horridly sweet. This is perfect."

Coming in from a cold, windy ride to a cozy library and a cozy woman with whom to discuss the morning's developments was indeed, perfect. The tea was hot, the shortbread flavored with cinnamon, and Nicholas was nowhere about.

Axel poured a second cup for himself, pleased that Abby would allow him the privileges of a host—or a friend.

"Weekes also lies about his biscuits. He claims his visitors consume the lot, all but two, when in fact, the good vicar is leaving a trail of crumbs all over his side of the hearth. Do you recall the name Cassius Pettiflower?"

Abby set her tea down and uncurled her feet from beneath her. She wasn't wearing slippers—those were warming before the hearth—and her stockings were good, sturdy, black wool.

"I haven't heard that name for quite some time. Cass was a dear, and I had girlish aspirations in his direction, but when my parents died in the fire, it's as if Cass disappeared with them. You'll spoil your lunch if you eat all of that shortbread."

"I'll expire of hunger if I don't. Weekes received a letter from Mr. Pettiflower a month or so after your marriage to Stoneleigh. Vicar recalled the letter because of the unusual name and because, being a bibliophile, Weekes knows of Pettiflower's bookshop in Oxford."

"Friendly rivals, I suppose you'd call the Pettiflowers. If Grandpapa didn't have a book somebody wanted, we'd send them over to Pettiflower's establishment, and the Pettiflowers did likewise. Cass's parents were getting on, and he was assuming more and more responsibility for the business. He and I had taken to walking out after Sunday services, and I thought my parents approved of him."

Axel dusted his palms together, wishing he didn't have to report the next part. "Pettiflower called at your parents' bookshop repeatedly after the fire, hoping to find word of you. He was told you didn't want to see him. When he found out you were biding with your late grandfather's business associate, he sent three bouquets of condolence, and you never acknowledged them. He wrote to Weekes out of concern for you, but by then you'd married Stoneleigh."

Abby rose and wandered to the sideboard, where a single rose in a crystal vase sat amid the decanters.

"Nobody told me Cass had called, and I did stop in at the bookshop, though not during business hours. The colonel did not approve of my traveling into Oxford, but I wanted to be where my parents... where I'd been happy. Perhaps the colonel was being protective."

"That rose has wicked thorns," Axel said, abandoning the sofa. "Be careful."

She'd tilted the rose, the better to sniff it. The bloom was a bold, showy red, the fragrance on the sweet, spicy side—a fine specimen from across the room—but the thorns had been a sore disappointment.

"Don't all roses have thorns?" Abby asked, touching a petal.

"On some the thorns are mere gestures, on others they'd stop even the hungriest deer from browsing. You believe the colonel was being *protective* by turning away one of your few friends when you were bereaved?"

She drew her shawl more closely about her. Was she less pale, or did the lighting in the library flatter her at this time of day?

"The colonel was prone to focusing on an objective, which is a fine quality in a cavalry officer, but then he'd remain fixed on his goal even when all sense begged him to desist. I learned to stand clear of him when he was on a tear. Full mourning meant no callers, to a man who prized protocol."

Full mourning should have meant *no hasty marriage*, by that same reasoning.

Axel took her hand, pleased to find her grasp warm, and led her back to the sofa. "Stoneleigh became fixed on marrying you, apparently. Weekes managed to spare the ginger biscuits long enough to convey a discreet dislike for your late spouse."

An intriguing realization in the middle of a murder investigation—even the local pastor had not liked Stoneleigh.

"Gregory could be difficult, but again, I attribute that to both his advancing years and to an officer's decisiveness."

Axel passed her the second-to-last piece of shortbread. "Weekes said Gregory's temper was well known among the locals. He was not welcome on darts teams at the Weasel, and he'd been known to tear a strip off Ambers at the hunt meet for something as minor as a smudge on a stirrup iron."

"And yet," Abby said, "when Gregory bestirred himself to attend services, he could be the soul of congeniality in the churchyard. Should you alert the kitchen that you're home for lunch?"

"They know," Axel said, dunking his shortbread in his tea. "They have eyes and ears everywhere except the glass houses, where they dare not interrupt me for anything less than news of the king's death—and even that is risking a severe scold."

"I've been thinking, about the servants."

Well, damn Darcy for an indifferent companion. "You were supposed to be absorbed in your book, madam."

"Have you questioned Ambers?"

Not nearly enough. "I have, but let me finish my report on Weekes." Something in the library was different, something besides the presence, slight fragrance, and cozy company of a lady.

"I won't like this report," Abby said, finishing her tea. "I do like that you tell me, though."

"Weekes chided me for being a poor neighbor to you, and he was right. We've lived side by side for years, and I've never invited you and Gregory to supper."

"Gregory said country people have estates to run, and socializing is different in the countryside. In town, we were always calling back and forth, dropping by, or sharing Sunday dinners. Here… first I was in mourning, then I was trying to get the estate put to rights, and lately, I've been… tired."

Lonely too, though Axel had only lately come to recognize the symptoms when they stared at him from his shaving mirror.

"I should have taken more interest in my nearest neighbor, but as Weekes pointed out, I take little interest in anybody unless they can talk horticulture. In any case, Weekes reports that Ambers often drives you to services, and that he deposits you on the church steps precisely on the hour, then returns to your side before the last organ note dies away."

"He's attentive. I suspect Ambers is a gentleman fallen on hard times. I sometimes wish he weren't so attentive, but one adjusts."

Another single rose drooped slightly from a bud vase near the window, as if leaning toward the fern for a chat. Axel had brought in the latest collection of hothouse blooms not two days earlier, but some varieties simply did not do well off the vine.

"You tell yourself Stoneleigh was protective and Ambers attentive. You were led to believe that rural neighbors neglect each other, and in this, confound the luck, your nearest neighbor was complicit, but it's also possible Stoneleigh wanted you isolated and without friends."

She peered into her empty tea cup, and Axel reached for the pot.

"No more tea, thank you. You're saying Gregory was possessive."

A polite word for treating a wife like the chattel the law said she was.

"At best he was odd," Axel said. "Not in a good way. Why did you separate my bouquet into single stems in different vases?"

A third lone rose sat on the desk. The effect was different from massed blooms, and Axel's staff would not have altered his choices regarding the flowers without his permission.

Regarding his flowers, he was both protective and possessive.

"Roses are my favorite," Abby said. "They are beautiful, fragrant, varied, and hardier than one might think. I like their thorns too, because one doesn't underestimate a flower that can pierce one's very flesh. I wanted to look up and see roses from wherever I sat, not have them all huddled together in that cold, gray window. Yours are particularly cheering, because I might not see another rose until high summer."

"Stoneleigh never brought you flowers?"

A heavy tread overhead confirmed that Nicholas had left his bedroom—just in time for luncheon.

"I've told you, Mr. Belmont. My husband and I were not sentimentally entangled. Roses are the height of sentiment, an extravagance, a gesture of such—what?"

"I am angry with your late spouse," Axel said, bringing the rose from the desk over to the tea tray. "Caroline once said, but for my flowers, she'd attribute no worthy feelings to me at all. I could convey with my posies all the awkward, tender, intimate things a young husband ought to express with words, according to her. When she was ill, she charged me with creating the perfect rose."

How generous she'd been, at the last, to give Axel leave to while away years in his glass houses, when all through the marriage she'd begrudged him his "hobby."

Abby broke the last piece of shortbread in half and held out a portion to him. "So you disappeared into your glass houses, becoming a near recluse who might have been welcome on a darts team but couldn't be bothered to show up. You don't linger at services either—when you go—and you use the lack of a hostess to excuse your unsociability. No wonder it took a murder to allow us closer acquaintance."

Axel was saved from replying to those thorny observations by Nick's arrival to the library.

"Somebody ate all the tea cakes," Nicholas said. "No matter. Mrs. Stoneleigh, good morning, and a pleasure to start my day in your company. I will content myself with the sweet boon of your presence. Move over, Professor. I've flirting to do."

Axel stayed right where he was. "If you'll give the bell-pull two tugs, the kitchen will know we're ready for luncheon. You may join us, if you'll promise to sit across the table from Mrs. Stoneleigh."

"The better to gaze into her lovely eyes," Nick said. "I'm in good form today, don't you think?"

No, Nick was troubled about something, having hidden in his room until Axel had returned. Abby didn't appear offended by Nick's blather, though neither was she impressed.

The interruption was for the best. Axel had been about to apologize for overly familiar behavior at the mounting block earlier, though perhaps no apology was needed. He'd offered Abigail only the merest gesture in the direction of a kiss, after all.

* * *

Perhaps magistrates went about kissing ladies they suspected of conspiring to commit murder. Abby had meant to ask Mr. Belmont about his parting gesture, but then Nick joined them at luncheon, and any hope of sensible discourse disappeared before the soup had been served.

"You're off to visit Sir Dewey?" Nick asked, as Mr. Belmont served pear torte from the head of the table.

"He's the next logical interview. Elbow off the table, Nicholas."

The viscount remained as he was, handsome chin propped on his palm, elbow *on* the table.

The pear torte smelled divine, full of spices, a hint of spirits, fresh baking… Abby's appetite was returning, and if she took only a small portion of everything served, her digestion was improving as well.

The dish Mr. Belmont set before Abby held at least three times what she could comfortably consume.

"What questions do you have for Sir Dewey?" Abby asked.

"He might know something of the colonel's finances," Mr. Belmont said. "He should be able to shed light on military connections, as well as on friends or enemies made on these walking tours, shooting trips, visits to London, and other journeys. He'd note any peculiarities of the colonel's demeanor in recent days, such as snappish incidents in the hunt field."

"Sir Dewey doesn't ride to hounds," Abby replied. "He claimed the tropics left his blood too thin for cold-weather sport."

"Ask him why he kept company with Stoneleigh in the first place," Nick said. "If the colonel was difficult on a good day, then why bother with the old blighter at all—meaning no disrespect to present company—much less travel with him repeatedly?"

The two men exchanged a not-in-front-of-the-lady look.

Oh, for mercy's sake. "I don't think the colonel and Sir Dewey were lovers," Abby said.

Nick's spoon clattered to his bowl.

"My grandfather imported books from all over Asia," she went on. "I was in the shop at all hours, and I found the books I wasn't supposed to see, the ones Grandpapa kept on the shelves behind the counter."

Mr. Belmont's brows came down, as if the bite of pear on his spoon had become day-old porridge before his eyes. Was her host wondering if she'd found the treasures on the highest shelf behind his desk?

Indeed Abby had, and Mr. Darcy had been shamefully neglected for more than an hour.

"Upon what,"—Mr. Belmont set his fork down—"upon what evidence do you base your conclusion?"

"Sir Dewey was never affectionate with Gregory, never touched him at all that I can recall. They argued frequently, though Sir Dewy was never uncivil. Their original connection was business, I think, and then shared army memories, but they…"

Both men were studying Abby, dessert apparently forgotten. "I think Sir Dewey was fond of me," Abby said. "Not in an inappropriate way, but I suspect part of why he tolerated Gregory's company was out of pity for me."

She'd needed that pity too, and all morning, as she'd meandered from Mr. Darcy to exotic, forbidden woodcuts, Abby's joy in renewed proximity to books had been bounded by a growing anger. Reading had been her greatest pleasure, her means of coping with all trials, and Gregory had scolded, scowled, and tut-tutted it from her grasp within the first year of their marriage.

"Sir Dewey felt pity," Nick said, pushing a nearly empty bowl a few inches away. "For you."

"For my situation," Abby said, regretting that she'd opened her mouth.

"I'll ask Sir Dewey to chronicle his whereabouts the night of the murder," Mr. Belmont said. "Nicholas, you will excuse us. Mrs. Stoneleigh must see me to my horse."

Nick reached for the uneaten portion of Abby's sweet. "The professor is preparing to lecture you about your propensity for honesty at the table, Abby dearest. Without his sons to keep him on his toes, his sensibilities have become delicate."

"I'm sparing the lady any more of your nonsense," Mr. Belmont said, "and aiding her to get a breath of fresh air. Until dinner, Nicholas."

Nick half rose when Abby stood, saluted her with a spoonful of torte, and winked. "The professor takes great pride in his lectures. Try to look impressed."

Abby smacked Nick on the shoulder as hard as she dared, which violence apparently met with the professor's approval.

"We're not going to the stable," Mr. Belmont said, when Abby had donned a cloak, scarf, and gloves—all black, but warm enough. "My glass houses are the only place where I can be certain no helpful viscounts or conscientious staff will eavesdrop, and you and I need to have at least one difficult, private conversation."

Abby trundled along at his side across the snowy gardens, the wind plucking at the ends of her scarf.

"Are you arresting me?"

"For God's sake,"—he stopped and tucked her scarf back over her shoulder—"I am not arresting you. You are at Candlewick to rest, to recover from the shock of your bereavement, to have some companionship as you adjust to your loss, dubious though the present offerings might be. Come along, or Nick will see us tarrying here and scold me for keeping you out in the foul weather."

He stomped off, not waiting for Abby to fall in step beside him. His tracks across the snow made a straight line toward his glass houses, which sat nearer to the manor than the stable did.

Abby came along. If her marriage had taught her nothing else, it was to obey an order when given by a man who was in the grip of strong emotion.

* * *

Abigail Stoneleigh was a guest, not a detainee of the crown, and Axel's first order of business was to clarify that point.

"Around this way," he said, leading her to the stable side of the first glass house. The interior walls were wet with condensation, which meant even where plants did not block the view, nobody outside would see what happened within.

Exactly as Axel preferred it. He unlocked the door and ushered Abby through, then closed the door behind them, turning the latch. The wind would snatch at the glass and shatter the door if the latch wasn't secured on every occasion.

"To be inside here must be such a relief," she said, unwinding her scarf and stashing her gloves in a pocket. "That scent—green, growing plants, flowers, rich soil... it's a safe smell."

Caroline had never cared for the smell of dirt. "Safe, how?" Axel hadn't bothered to button his coat or put on his gloves. The warmth and scent of the glass house barely registered with him anymore.

Abigail remained where she was, between two rows of potted roses, most of which were devoid of blooms but sporting lush foliage.

"If plants can thrive," she said, "then all will be well. Everything depends on the plants. The beasts would have no fodder, the sheep no grass, the birds no nests, without plants. We'd have no wool, no meat, no vegetables, no flowers, without the plants. No paper, no books, no wooden furniture, no linen, cotton, spirits, or shelter save for what we could fashion of stones. If you safeguard plants, you safeguard life itself."

She uttered not a lecture, but a sermon. Axel wanted to kiss her, and write down every word she'd spoken, though neither endeavor was the reason for this visit.

"These are my failures," he said, gesturing to the roses on her right. "I experiment in here. In the other house, I propagate for my own pleasure, and for commercial purposes. I am modestly successful in the flower trade."

He could live splendidly on what his flowers earned. Only Matthew knew that. One didn't farm for profit according to the gentry version of high stickling, one rented tenancies and complained about the tenants.

Axel had dismissed that approach as balderdash within a year of his marriage.

"One suspects you of shrewd business instincts," Abby said. "These plants are marvelously healthy. Why are they your failures?"

Axel explained about the unpredictable results of crossing varieties, the patience required to make even slow progress toward a perfect specimen. Years of devoted recordkeeping and plant tending, observation and experiment, failure upon failure, all for the smallest advance.

"The thorns are quite small on this one," Abby said as they rounded the end of the table. "Do you consider it a success?"

"I won't know unless or until it blooms, and I see if the trait breed true," Axel said. "My very best grafting stock, for example, a fellow whom I refer to as the Dragon, has beastly thorns, but everything I bind to him thrives. Any progress is encouraging, but so often, gain in one sense means loss in another." He and the late Empress Josephine had commiserated by correspondence on that very point.

The glass house was Axel's favorite place to be, as if he were one of the roses, not the botanist. He could breathe here, he could sense in what direction light came from. A good place to have a difficult conversation with his guest.

"You mean," she said, "you can reduce the size of the thorns, but then the blooms will also be smaller, or you'll lose the fragrance, or the plant never grows more than a foot high?" She sniffed one of the few blooms on the failure table. "This one looks very robust, and it's larger than the others. Did you not prune it back as far?"

"I did. The damned thing grows like a weed, which would be a fine quality if it didn't also smell like a weed sunk in brackish water. About what you overheard last night."

"You aren't arresting me, but I'm a suspect," Abby said, turning to face him.

Between the rows of plants, Axel had left only enough room for a person to pass without disturbing the foliage. He and Abby were close enough to embrace, close enough that he could see improvement in her appearance.

She wasn't as pale, as tired, or as gaunt as she'd been at the time of her husband's death.

"I will discover who killed Gregory and why," Axel said. "You can't feel entirely safe, you can't move forward in all the ways that matter, unless I find those answers. I will not fail you."

He'd surprised her, and he'd surprised himself. A magistrate should solve a case because justice was a fundamental tenet of societies bound by the rule of law. Justice was a fine old concept, but in this situation, justice meant finding answers for Abigail Stoneleigh.

Not for the crown, not for the community, not for the ailing king. *For her.*

"But you suspect me. I did not kill my husband, Mr. Belmont."

"Of course you did not. I thought about this all the way to the vicarage and back. I do not kiss murderesses."

"You kissed me."

The humidity was making her hair curl, turning a tidy coiffure heedless of its pins.

"So I did, and you did not object. Do I need to apologize for that kiss?"

Wind rattled the glass panes, though the structure was sturdy. Axel had designed it himself and was accustomed to winter's threats.

"You need to explain," Abby said, moving down the row. "If these are your failures, where are your successes?"

"I haven't any successes, only hopes, and those are at the next table. Nick is a friend."

"He's also something of a hope, I'm guessing. Your friend is troubled by the prospect of marriage."

"Every man should be. What I said to Nick—that I think you're keeping secrets—is the truth. You did not confide to me how frightened you were to remain at Stoneleigh Manor, where your husband had been murdered. That fear is reasonable, and yet, you tried to hide it."

"And failed, apparently. I know you better now, but we were barely cordial previously, and I've never been a widow before. I don't know how one goes on with the magistrate when one's husband has been murdered."

Fair question. The magistrate wasn't entirely sure how to go on either.

"I didn't want Nick to get the wrong idea," Axel said, as Abby paused before a swamp rose pining for its home. "That one will revive in spring. I hope. Some wild varieties give up in here, others thrive."

Axel wanted Abigail Stoneleigh to thrive.

"So you will add me to your collection of hopes," she said. "I am well read, or I was, and I'm good for amusing lonely viscounts, but my energy is lacking. I'm prone to staring off into space when I recall my husband was killed in his own home, but you expect I'll come right with enough sunlight, nourishment, and care. Good of you, Mr. Belmont. That still doesn't explain your kiss."

Such thorns she had, and she was entitled to them. "Weekes surprised me, or insulted me, I'm not sure which. Shall we sit?"

By imperceptible degrees, the glass house had become comfortable for at least one human specimen in addition to all the plants. An old rug pilfered from the attic lay before one of the hearths. A spare table doubled as a desk, a rocking chair that rocked unevenly had migrated from the nursery.

Abby took that rocker, while Axel took the chair at the table. She unbuttoned her cloak, while he… formulated a lecture.

"I was concerned Nicholas would think I was taking advantage of you," Axel said, though he hadn't articulated the concern to himself until he'd been halfway to the vicarage. "I was concerned he'd leap to conclusions about your virtue and my honor. I voiced my suspicion of you mostly to reinforce my role as magistrate in Nick's mind. I do not suspect you of having any responsibility for your husband's death."

This too, had become clear on the way to the vicarage, while the rosy scent of Abby Stoneleigh had yet been fresh in Axel's mind.

"So you cast guilt in my direction, rather than let your friend think you're attracted to me?"

Attracted to her? He wasn't at—well, he was. Somewhat.

"I tried to appear disinterested, in command of all the evidence, and competent as an investigator. I'm sorry for my words. If I had any basis upon which to suspect you of colluding in Gregory's murder, I'd send you to Weekes's care while making the case against you."

She sat back, the quality of her composure at once the same as, and different from, what Axel had observed the night of the murder.

"You suggest I might be both a suspect and not safe, else you'd send me home."

"You had no motive to kill your spouse," Axel said. "I've puzzled over this and puzzled over this. You genuinely bore the colonel no ill will. You accepted him for the overbearing old martinet he was rapidly becoming. He left you a sort of freedom, even as he isolated you, and you fashioned a meaningful and not unpleasant life. Whoever killed your husband took risks—of significant injury from the colonel's loaded gun if nothing else. You have no motive to take such risks."

She wrinkled her nose. "I was meek, so I can't be guilty."

"You're *good*, so you can't be guilty," Axel said, scooting his chair close enough to take Abigail's hands. "You're also intelligent. If you had decided to do Gregory mortal harm, you'd have been clever about it, made it look like a heart seizure, an apoplexy, a bad fall from his horse. You had all the opportunity in the world—for years—but no motive. You did not kill your husband."

She used her gloves to swipe at her cheek. "That helps, though if you ever hint, for any reason, that I might do such a thing, I will apply my knee in a location you won't enjoy."

She'd warn him first—warn him again.

"Abigail, I am sorry. I'm not a magistrate by natural inclination, nor am I social by inclination. Nicholas's arrival has surprised me, though I doubt he'll stay for long. This is apparently the season for surprises."

"Not every surprise is bad, Mr. Belmont. You surprised me at the mounting block."

Axel had probably surprised the Deity Himself, as well as the servants gawking from the windows and Ivan the Sluggard.

"I was concerned Weekes would think your biding at Candlewick irregular. He instead thanked me for taking matters in hand, and said Mrs. Turnbull would put you to rights in no time. Your pallor and poor health were remarked upon after Gregory's service. Mrs. Weekes even referred to you being in a decline prior to your husband's death."

And so thoroughly had Axel neglected the activities expected of a wealthy bachelor—no mistress, no regular visits to London, no regular calls on comely widows—that, abetted by Mrs. Turnbull, he'd apparently acquired the qualities of a chaperone himself, at least where a widowed neighbor in poor health was concerned.

A man aspiring to the celibate reputation of an Oxford fellow should have been pleased.

"I'm a shopgirl by rights," Abby said, "not some baron's daughter or earl's niece. My reputation ought not to concern much of anybody, but it concerned you."

"I ought not to have kissed you."

The rocking chair came to an abrupt halt. "If you apologize for kissing me, Mr. Belmont, for a harmless little peck on the cheek in the broad light of day, I will show you that I am capable of doing violence to a man after all. Do you know how often I've been kissed?"

Not often enough. Axel's years of marriage preserved him from the folly of making that observation.

Abby shoved to her feet. "When Gregory came to me on our wedding night, he explained that excessive passion was a young man's affliction. He would not plague me unduly as a spouse, though he expected wifely decorum at all times from me. I was not to flirt with, encourage, mislead, or bat my eyelashes at any other man. I recall the list, because I possessed none of those skills, and still don't."

She was angry. Any botanist knew that spindly foliage could be a function of stress to the roots, and thus Axel rose as well.

"Abigail, it won't—" He'd been about to say, *It won't happen again*, to assure her, unequivocally, that he esteemed her too much to allow his gentleman's manners to be waylaid by another casual slip, another reflex left over from years of married life.

Abby would unman him if he said those things.

He snapped off a pink bud from the nearest of the hopefuls. "You are entirely deserving of kisses, as many as you like of whatever variety you please. I was married for years, and Caroline and I agreed early that we would not part in anger. We kissed at that mounting block more times than I can say, and for the most part, it meant little. An old habit, but a comforting one. I'm sorry Stoneleigh was such an ass, sorry he neglected you in the ways only a husband can care for a wife."

Her eyes flashed with relief, as if she'd needed, badly, to hear another man convict the colonel of stupidity and neglect.

Axel could do better than that. Much, much better.

CHAPTER EIGHT

"Kisses are like roses," Mr. Belmont said. "You cultivate them, learn their nuances, and they'll flourish abundantly."

He stood at Abby's elbow, the pink bud in his hand. He tucked the stem into the lapel of Abby's cape, and abruptly, Abby wanted to cry. Those meaningless gestures at the mounting block were more than she'd had with Gregory. Axel Belmont, as a shy, young husband, had known to offer his wife those kisses, to bring her flowers.

"Who else has seen your hopes and failures, Mr. Belmont?" Had his late wife joined him here? Did he come here to be close to her memory?

Truly, Abby would cry, or smash this entire glass house, if she reflected on how much she wanted to stay away from Stoneleigh Manor. Not because it was the scene of a murder, but because it had been the scene of her marriage.

The callused pad of Mr. Belmont's thumb brushed Abby's chin, then his palm cradled her check.

"I will ask this time," he said. "May I kiss you? This is not a kiss born of old habit, not a mere peck on the cheek. This kiss is a consolation and a pleasure, Abigail, and it belongs only to us."

A kiss of loss and hope, grief and comfort, combined. Abby closed her eyes, the better to hoard the sensation of Axel's hand against her jaw. Those hands tended delicate roses, they wielded the knife that cut the graft free from its home.

His boots scraped the plank floor, the scent of him and a sense of heat came nearer as soft warmth pressed against her mouth.

She opened her eyes, ready to complain that that hadn't been nearly enough of a consolation for years of—

He did it again, touched his mouth to hers, another warning salvo. "A kiss involves two people, Abigail."

A kiss also involved patience, generosity, tenderness, and courage. By slow, almost courteous degrees, Abby learned that more than lips were involved. A kiss could grow like a vine, to involve tongues, breath, weight, embrace... Even her heartbeat was affected by the time she stood, her arms around Axel Belmont's waist, her cheek resting against his chest.

"No wonder Gregory was concerned that I'd stray."

She *should* have strayed, should have found a way to pluck such a glorious intimacy from some quiet garden and pleasure herself with it regularly. Except, unlike her other indulgences, a kiss could not be solitary.

Axel's hand glossed over her hair. "You are angry, Abigail."

Furious—and bewildered. Gregory hadn't wanted her kisses, but he hadn't wanted her to share them with anybody else either.

"There's much I don't understand," she said. "You think you know somebody, live with them for years as husband and wife, speak vows with them in good faith, forsake all others..."

Another caress to her hair, devastatingly tender. "And then they're gone."

All manner of emotions tangled around Abby's heart. She was *glad* Gregory was gone, because selfish old martinet was apparently a kind description of her late husband. Dog in the manger, hypocrite, liar...

And yet, she was glad to be in Axel Belmont's arms too. He desired her—she understood that clearly enough—and he was comfortable letting her know it.

She rubbed her cheek across the wool of his coat. "Who else comes here, to your glass house?" Where all was order, fragrance, warmth, and light.

"No one. The staff knows I'm not to be disturbed here. My brother might follow me in uninvited, my sons will knock and wait to be admitted if they've a problem to discuss privately, but the glass house is my *sanctum sanctorum*. If you bring Mr. Darcy here, Nicholas will not interrupt."

Abby dropped her arms, because Mr. Belmont had been waiting for her to be the one to end the embrace.

"Is this why you want a fellowship at the university? Because you can teach others to work with roses the way you do?"

He began buttoning up his coat. Abby brushed his hands aside and took over.

"A college fellowship is a lifelong dream, but first I must complete my book. There's an order to these things, and scholarly publication figures in that order. What will you do with yourself this afternoon?"

Abby would nap, and dream of kisses. She'd explore that shelf behind the desk in the library, she'd... sit here, amid the beautiful, thorny roses, and be angry at her deceased spouse.

"Read," she said. "Return another dozen notes of condolence, rest." Wonder who killed Gregory. Wonder *why*. Wonder if she'd ever feel safe at Stoneleigh

Manor again.

"Then I'm off to call on the gallant Sir Dewey. I have the only key to this house, Abigail. If you lock up after me, nobody else can get in, and I'll warn you to be very certain you've latched the door when you leave."

He'd check when he came back, that's how conscientious his care for these roses was.

Abby kissed him on the mouth, though her lack of skill was evident, because she got him off-center and had to correct her aim. He growled, or chuckled—she wasn't sure which—and endured her fumblings thereafter, but apparently wasn't interested in being further ravished in his own glass house.

"I'm sorry," she said. "I presumed, and you're clearly not—"

He took the scarf from around her neck. "You should be sorry, for I'm in no condition to sit my horse. The longer I stand about in here, indulging your curiosity and my animal spirits, the less likely I am to keep my appointment before spring. We will talk, Abigail, though conversation is not among my natural talents. You are to rest, read, raid the larder, and keep a list of those notes. You are not to fret."

He was lecturing her as he wrapped her black wool scarf about his neck. The black wool contrasted with his blue eyes gave him a buccaneering air.

Abby grasped the placket of his coat and rested her forehead against his shoulder. "I will fret."

"Not about a single kiss, you won't. You're a widow. You bestow kisses where you please, though I'd rather you favor Mr. Darcy with your attentions than Nicholas."

He kissed her nose, tossed the end of her scarf over his shoulder, and marched out the door. The latch turned with a definitive click, though Abby wondered at Mr. Belmont's determination to secure the premises.

His roses dwelled in a glass house. Anybody intent on gaining entry needed only a stout rock or length of wood to bash through the walls, and the roses would soon expire of cold.

* * *

"She doesn't know how to kiss," Axel informed his horse as they walked—*walked*, in deference to the crowded conditions behind Axel's falls—down the Candlewick drive.

"The woman was married for years and has not an inkling how to kiss."

Abigail had nearly jumped a foot when Axel had touched his tongue to her lips, but then, by God, she'd been enthusiastic about the possibilities.

"Gregory Stoneleigh was either a monk or a fool, or prone to left-handed pleasures."

The warmth of Abby Stoneleigh's kiss plagued Axel most of the way to Sir Dewey's estate, and that gave a man with university aspirations pause.

When the German priesthood had abandoned its Catholic associations for the Lutheran faith, in many cases, the woman identified in one census as the priest's "housekeeper" was identified in the next as his "wife." The Oxford fellows doubtless had comparable arrangements, discreet liaisons, and convenient friendships that allowed a nod in the direction of the required celibacy without causing too great an inconvenience to the fellow.

"I hadn't given the matter much thought," Axel admitted—to his horse—as they trotted up Sir Dewey's drive. "I am not, however, a gelding."

Something of a revelation, though not bad news, exactly. Not if Abby Stoneleigh took to being a widow the way she'd warmed to Axel's kisses.

"These thoughts are ungentlemanly." But they were human, in a way that spending season after season alone in a glass house could never be. "Leaves me wondering about Stoneleigh."

When Ivan had been taken by a groom, Axel was shown to a tidy, cozy library. Books lined some of the shelves, but Sir Dewey also apparently collected scent bottles and snuff boxes. A brass samovar held pride of place on a handsome teak sideboard, and the entire library was subtly scented with sandalwood.

In contrast to the brass, teak, and exotic treasures, an old mastiff lazed on a rug by the fire, raising its head when Axel entered the room. Unlike the Stoneleigh Manor library, not a single weapon was on display. Not matched fowling pieces over the mantel, nor handsome pistols mounted on the wall, nor ivory-handled knives under glass.

"Easy, Crusader." The butler, a young, dark-skinned fellow, spoke loudly to the dog. "We've a guest. No need to trouble yourself."

Nonetheless, the beast heaved to its feet, padded over to sniff at Axel's boots, then returned to the rug with a heavy sigh—a beautiful Turkey carpet, for an old dog.

"Greetings, Mr. Belmont." Sir Dewey rose from behind a massive desk, hand extended. "Pay Crusader no mind. His days of bringing down quarry are long past. A tea tray, Pahdi, and perhaps it's time Crusader went for his constitutional?"

"Very good, sir." Pahdi bowed slightly and withdrew.

"Crusader is largely deaf and most assuredly blind," Sir Dewey said, "and yet he takes his guard duty seriously. One never knows when a brigand might slip into my library of a winter afternoon. Shall we sit, Mr. Belmont?"

Sir Dewey looked to be about Axel's age, his smile that of a cordial host, comments about brigands in the library notwithstanding.

He folded his lanky frame into a wing chair and gestured for Axel to do likewise. "I can guess why you've come."

Axel's host was sandy-haired, trim, perhaps an inch over six feet. His complexion was slightly weathered, his bearing military, his features patrician, and his smile engaging. Women would consider him handsome, while men would pronounce him good company on a morning ride.

"I wish this were a purely social call," Axel replied, meaning it. "I have unresolved questions relating to Gregory Stoneleigh's death, and thus my visit is in an official capacity."

Axel did not use the word homicide, the preliminary ruling being death by accident.

"The whole business is a damned shame," Sir Dewey said, a hint of the Borders in his words. "I understand Stoneleigh was in his own home, more or less enjoying a nightcap by himself."

Gossip being the most reliable news service, Sir Dewey probably knew the exact time of death and what the deceased had been wearing.

Also that Stoneleigh had been murdered.

"I am sure the gun in Stoneleigh's hand did not kill him," Axel said. "That is about all I know for certain."

And that Abigail Stoneleigh was a woman in need of kisses.

"Suspects?" Sir Dewey steepled his fingers, as if prepared to solve the crime himself. Typical English gentleman, absolutely convinced he was the measure of any task, regardless of his lack of skill or training.

"We can get to possible suspects,"—when Axel damn well pleased to provide Sir Dewey such a list. "I was not as well acquainted with Mr. Stoneleigh as some, and I'd like to ask a few questions. You were his closest friend."

The dog affled in its sleep, chasing a dream thief, or perhaps running riot.

"I was probably Gregory Stoneleigh's only friend. He was a good fellow, but he could be difficult."

Abby had begun to admit as much. "I seldom saw that aspect of his behavior, and I lived next door to him for more than a decade." Though Stoneleigh could be a perfect ass to his groom.

"The loss of temper was never serious," Sir Dewey said. "Ranting and fuming, the same behaviors I saw from every officer I served with in India. Conditions there can strip away anyone's veneer of civilization, and when one returns to England, rebuilding that veneer is trying."

Sir Dewey seemed to have managed well enough—to appearances. "You served with the colonel in India?"

A soft tap on the door heralded Pahdi entering with a tea tray. When the butler had put the tray on the low table, he bid the dog—quite loudly—to come.

Crusader regarded Pahdi with an I-am-disappointed-in-you gaze most canines perfected before weaning. Sir Dewey pointed to the door—"Now, Crusader," in stern tones—and the dog slunk from the room.

"I have become much like Crusader," Sir Dewey said. "Resentful of any change in my routine, reluctant to leave my cozy hearth."

"Crusader had best go for his constitutional now," Axel said. "The wind is picking up, and the sky promises misery."

Sir Dewey poured out, then pushed a plate of scones toward his guest.

"If it's that nasty out, then eat up, Mr. Belmont. Cook is more sensitive than that old dog. She's Scottish and passionate about her baked goods."

Investigating was nutritious work. No wonder Matthew, with his prodigious appetite, enjoyed it.

"You were asking about India," Sir Dewey said, stirring neither milk nor sugar into his tea. "I was there for ten years, and for a few of those, I shared a post with the colonel. I did not serve under him, which allowed us to be friends."

"That would not have been possible otherwise?" The fragrance of the tea was exquisite, a gunpowder delicately laced with true jasmine, not its lesser cousins. Either Sir Dewey had been born to wealth, or his years in India had been lucrative.

"Some officers lead by charisma," Sir Dewey said. "Particularly the ones whose units see frequent battle. Others, like Gregory Stoneleigh, lead by discipline, by the certain knowledge that whatever enemies their men face, those enemies are less to be feared than one's commanding officer. Stoneleigh and I argued about that a great deal."

"Stoneleigh's wife claims she never argued with him." And Axel believed her.

"How is Abigail? I saw her after the service, and she looked to be bearing up, but when I spoke with her, she was... murmuring the platitudes, while longing to be elsewhere."

"She is managing." Was Sir Dewey smitten with the lady, and *thus motivated to murder her husband?* "She enjoys my hospitality at present. Remaining at Stoneleigh Manor with the murderer at large was hard on her nerves."

Oh, what the hell. No need to offend Sir Dewey's cook. Axel split a scone and applied butter and jam to both halves.

"Gregory had no clue what a treasure he'd married when Abigail Pennington accepted his proposal. He and I argued about that too."

"Can you be more specific?" *And might you share your cook's recipe for scones?* Abby would love these with a late-afternoon pot of tea—as would Axel.

"Gregory kept his wife virtually a prisoner at the manor," Sir Dewey said, cradling his tea cup in his hands. "He never took her calling, and he sent Ambers along when she went to church to see that she barely had time to exchange pleasantries. He treated her like a child or doughty aunt, incapable of managing her own affairs. All the while, he relied on her to keep Stoneleigh Manor running like a military garrison, even when he went off shooting for weeks at a time, or spent half the spring in London, ostensibly looking over Mr. Brandenburg's able shoulder in the import office."

All without Stoneleigh's nearest neighbor remarking the situation. Axel took a sip of tea, though nothing would wash down a sense of guilt.

"You chided Stoneleigh for his behavior?"

"For a time. Then I realized I was making no impression, or possibly making Abigail's situation more difficult. One doesn't interfere between man and wife, so I learned to keep my mouth shut."

Alas, a magistrate had not the same privilege. "Are you in love with Stoneleigh's wife?"

"I am a gentleman," Sir Dewey replied, without particular heat. "I might admire a friend's spouse, Mr. Belmont—I hope my friends marry admirable people, in fact—but such admiration would be my private privilege. I would not trouble the lady by expressing my sentiments."

Spoken like a true soldier, or a very good liar. "You bore Mrs. Stoneleigh tender sentiments."

"I esteem her," Sir Dewey said, topping up Axel's tea cup. "Abigail had neither brother, nor cousin, nor father to intervene with a negligent husband. I will admit to being protective of her."

Not a hanging offense. Any *good* neighbor should probably have admitted to the same.

"Were you and Gregory close enough that you might have insights into his finances?"

Sir Dewey peered at his tea. The service was exquisite, with what looked like peonies hiding golden dragons amid pink blossoms and pale green foliage. The impression was one not simply of wealth, but also refinement. This was Sir Dewey's *everyday* service, and probably worth more than Axel would spend on a new horse.

Sir Dewey downed the tea in one swallow. "Sitting for hours over cards, or sharing the miles on the Great North Road, surprising topics come under discussion."

"Please elaborate."

"Gregory doubted his children were actually his," Sir Dewey said, pouring himself more tea. "I'm drawing conclusions based on casual comments, the occasional almost-nasty remark offered when a fellow should have gone up to bed an hour ago. Several hours ago."

Axel knew the type of comment, having made a few himself, and had heard plenty from others. Even some from Matthew, whose gentlemanliness bordered on excessive at times.

"What did Stoneleigh let slip regarding his finances?"

"His finances came from the import business. He left the manor mostly in Abigail's control. The property would be hers after he died, so her stewardship or lack thereof would be her eventual reward, according to Gregory."

Sir Dewey paused to swirl his tea, spilling not a drop onto the saucer.

"While in India," he went on, "Gregory made good connections for a man thinking to turn a profit on imports. After he came home, I maintained those contacts for my remaining years in India. Gregory benefited initially from similar connections made decades ago by the founder of the import business, old Mr. Pennington."

Well, of course. Abigail had to have met Stoneleigh through family dealings of some sort, about which Axel had failed to ask her in any detail.

"You and Gregory were business partners, Sir Dewey?"

"We were at one time, and when I was associated with the business, we did modestly well, but only that. When I returned to England, my interest in things Asian did not accompany me. I wanted my horses, my acres, peace, and quiet. If I never see another cashmere shawl or hear another peacock again, I will die content."

Despite Sir Dewey's professed lack of interest in Asia, the sideboard was teak, the tea service likely Chinese, and if the library wasn't perfumed with sandalwood, Axel would swear off scones for life.

"You and Gregory argued about the business?"

After a soft tap on the door, the dog ambled back into the room and sat at Sir Dewey's knee, while the door was drawn closed by a silent, unseen hand.

"We argued bitterly," Sir Dewey said, tugging gently on the dog's ear. "I yet felt a certain sympathy for Stoneleigh, so I relinquished my shares, and we got past our commercial differences. The business grew profitable as exotica came more into fashion, and that allowed Gregory to live as he pleased."

With no real friends? With a wife whom he described as a mentally unstable poor relation while he used her as an unpaid land steward?

"Why would Stoneleigh have chosen a very young woman for his wife, one without dowry, family, or consequence of any kind?" And if the import business was profitable, and some share in it had been part of Abby's inheritance from old Mr. Pennington, then why would she think the estate bankrupt?

Why—rather—would Stoneleigh have *allowed* her to think that?

"I have wondered about Stoneleigh's choice of bride myself," Sir Dewey said. "Particularly given his treatment of Abigail through the years of their marriage. I conclude Gregory was motivated in part by gentlemanly concern for the lady, because her circumstances became difficult when her parents perished in a fire, and in part by his version of loneliness."

"You're suggesting the union was a matter of expedience on both sides?" Was the murder another example of expedience?

The hound put his grizzled chin on Sir Dewey's knee.

"Not purely expedience," Sir Dewey said, stroking the dog's head. "Gregory was prey to the impulsiveness that affects some men when they hear a fine brood mare is for sale. He's coveted her privately and wants to possess her. He starts thinking about which stud to put her to, how soon he can breed her back, what he'll do with the foal she's carrying, and before he's even got up from the table, he's won half the races at Newmarket—if only he can fetch the mare home."

Stoneleigh's inane scheme to landscape his stream came to mind, no estimates, no materials on hand, no schedule, no plan.

"He then pets and fusses her for a while," Axel said, "until another mare comes up at auction."

"Like a child with a puppy," Sir Dewey said, petting his old dog, "or a new toy, and then it's on to the next."

"A wife is not a plaything." Axel had grasped that much even at the age of eighteen.

Sir Dewey tossed the dog a corner of scone and rose. "Abigail is a wealthy, comely young widow. That isn't all bad."

For whom? "I suppose not," Axel said, rising as well. "You've given me much to think about. Please feel free to call on Mrs. Stoneleigh at Candlewick. Her comments regarding you were flattering, and deep mourning without any family about is difficult."

Sir Dewey turned, hands behind his back. "I hope Abigail does not enjoy your hospitality because she is a suspect? I would take exception to that, Belmont. Either you arrest her on sufficient evidence, or you allow her the liberty due every law-abiding subject of the king."

Axel chose to be honest—mostly. "Both Shreve and Mrs. Jensen put Mrs. Stoneleigh above stairs when the shot that killed Gregory was fired. I found no sums missing from her account books that suggest she hired murder done by a third party. She had no motive, because she was equally well fixed whether her husband lived or died."

Other factors Axel kept to himself: Abby had had years to do away with her husband if she'd taken him into violent dislike, and she would not have botched the job if she'd decided to end Stoneleigh's days. Then too, time would likely have seen to Gregory's demise if he continued to ride hell-bent after the hounds in all weather.

The lady was truly innocent—thank all the kind powers.

"I am relieved to hear she is free from suspicion," Sir Dewey said, keeping to his place by the window. "I will call upon her forthwith to express my condolences, if she would not view such a visit as an imposition."

In the months after Caroline's death, time had dragged, every day had hurt, and only duty to Axel's children and hours in the glass houses had kept him sane.

"When one loses a spouse," he said, "one can struggle, feeling one ought to grieve in some proper sequence, according to protocols concocted by gossip and custom. I've told Mrs. Stoneleigh that isn't so, and she'd welcome a visit from a friend."

A gentleman's honor required that Axel proffer this invitation. He was bound for Oxford if all went according to plan, while Abby... Abigail deserved every possible option a widow could have.

Right up to and including a wealthy, handsome English gentleman who had esteemed her greatly for years, been a good neighbor to her, and probably claimed endless stores of scintillating damned repartee.

Though as Axel once against sat himself in a damnably cold saddle, a question plagued him about the handsome Sir Dewey: Why would a man who professed to crave the warmth and comfort of his elegantly appointed hearth upend his routine repeatedly to hare all over the realm during the cold and wet of the shooting seasons, and in less than congenial company, too?

* * *

By the time darkness approached, desultory flurries had organized themselves into a snowfall. Abby sat in a rocker by the fire in the library, the candles unlit, her book face-down in her lap. She'd read out in the glass house for hours, an orgy of reading, and she was almost halfway through the tale of Mr. Darcy's reformation—or Elizabeth's.

The gloom in the library soothed, a rest for her tired eyes.

She'd done this many times as a girl, read the day away, forgetting time, place, cares, and worries.

Why had she let Gregory take this pleasure from her? She'd done an excellent job with the estate, and that was all he should have asked of her. Her free time should have been her own.

"Are you sleeping in that rocker?" Axel Belmont asked, bringing a branch of candles into the library and setting them on the mantel.

"I am thinking, and hiding from Nicholas."

"He's out in the stables, having returned from a sortie to the Weasel," Mr. Belmont said, seating himself on a hassock. "Has he been insufferable?"

"Trying." Or amusing. Nothing in Abby wanted to kiss Nicholas Haddonfield, not the way she wanted to kiss Axel Belmont again, and yet Nick appeared available for kissing while Axel Belmont's attentions were a more complicated prize.

"Will you be offended if I take off my boots?" he asked, tugging hard on one heel. "My feet will take at least until Easter to thaw."

"You will not offend me. Nicholas came fairly close." Abby wanted Axel to know this, but also wanted to air her reaction as a measure of comparison. Were widows expected to enjoy mindless flirtation and endless innuendo from available men?

"I apologize on Nick's behalf," Axel said, as the second boot came off. "Did you slap him?"

"Slapping him won't do any good. I think his affliction is grief."

"My nephew Remington once said something like that," Axel replied, arranging his boots side by side. "Said the loss of bachelorhood must be grieved by men the way loss of a husband is grieved by women. Did Nick at least apologize?"

Axel was tired, but the firelight also suggested that even as he aged, he'd be an attractive man. His looks were interesting—scholarly Saxon landowner one moment, a Viking impervious to winter the next.

"Nick apologized in his fashion." By leaving, by going for a ride in the bitter weather, when he'd recently ridden up from Sussex.

"May I offer you a brandy, madam?"

Abby hadn't wanted to presume by offering her host a drink in his own home, but she also wanted to put off learning what Sir Dewey might have contributed to the murder investigation.

"I am now a widow, in that small subclass of ladies who take spirits on occasion with impunity."

Axel handed her a drink and took his back to the hassock a few feet away. They sipped in companionable quiet, the tranquil hiss and crackle of the fire the only sound.

"If I ask you a question," Abigail said, studying the firelight reflected in her brandy, "will you promise not to laugh?"

"I will not laugh." Instead, he smiled. Mostly with his eyes, mostly at his drink, but Axel Belmont had smiled.

"How did you kiss your wife?"

The smile became sweeter, sadder, more reflective. "Frequently. I like kissing. One tends to forget that, after a few years."

He was comfortable with this affection for kissing too, which was odd in a man who coveted the celibacy of an Oxford fellow and the exclusive company of thorny horticulture.

"You kissed her frequently, in the manner you kissed me earlier?"

Abby could not be in this library without being aware of what lay on that top shelf behind the desk. Eastern texts, explicit in their illustrations, depicted postures and pleasures that had fascinated her as an adolescent in her parents' bookshop.

They fascinated her still, as did Axel Belmont's kisses.

CHAPTER NINE

"When Caroline and I married," Mr. Belmont said, "she probably had more experience kissing than I did."

He took off his stockings and draped them over the tops of his boots. The familiarity was that of a man comfortable in his own home, one who seldom entertained, and did not regard present company as easily shocked by a man's informality.

The sight of Axel Belmont's bare feet and loose cravat was more interesting to Abby than even the impossible poses suggested by his erotic woodcuts. He rose and toed on a pair of slippers warming by the hearth, then returned to his hassock.

"Did that bother you, that your wife had experience?"

"Of course not. I was hardly a duke, that titular succession required excesses of premarital purity in my spouse. Being a university scholar, I wasn't without experience myself. My sons will tell you I'm a man of shockingly egalitarian principles, despite the results of those sentiments in the hands of the French. No fellow of eighteen wants to face a cringing virgin on his wedding night. But, back to kissing..."

He'd corresponded with the Empress Josephine on the subject of roses. One of her letters—thanking him for his suggestions—was framed over the sideboard. Academics could be ferocious in their own way, truth taking precedence for them over national boundaries and even wars.

And now Axel likely wanted to discuss murder, or roses, while Abby was preoccupied with images of smiling women who could spread their knees impossibly wide.

"Between spouses," he said, rubbing his right foot with his two hands, "there develops a vocabulary of kisses. I'm sure you and Gregory had yours—the good-morning peck on the cheek, the glad-to-see-you buss upon homecoming, that sort of thing."

"I'm not asking about those kisses." Had Caroline ever rubbed his cold, tired feet? "I kissed my wife however the mood dictated." He paused to sip his brandy. "There were playful kisses, seductive kisses, voracious kisses, thank-you kisses, but I suppose they were all intended to be I-love-you kisses."

The very last description Abby would have expected from him, and yet, his answer pleased her.

"All of them?"

"I did love Caroline, and my facility with words of that nature was frustratingly limited, at least from her perspective. I don't think I'm answering your question." He uncrossed his ankle from his knee and slid his foot back into its velvet slipper. "What did you really want to ask, Abigail?"

"Why did you kiss me?" As Abby had inspected rose after rose—hope after hope, and failure after failure—the whys of Axel Belmont's kiss had plagued her.

"Ladies first," he said. "Your motives are of interest to me as well."

"Why must motive always fascinate you?"

Up went one blond brow.

"Curiosity," Abby said, with the sense that she was reciting in a tutorial session. "Loneliness." A loneliness of the heart and body, so deep and abiding, Abby had begun to think it her normal state. Affection had played a role in their kiss, for Axel Belmont had endearing qualities visible mostly in close quarters and at fleeting intervals.

He kissed her on the mouth. A friendly, brandy-flavored greeting of a kiss.

"What was that for?"

"This shouldn't be a serious discussion, Abigail." He repeated the kiss. This time he lingered, so Abby could enjoy the simplicity of the gesture, the soft, warm sensation of his mouth touching hers. Her hand slipped around the back of his neck, her fingers stroked the damp locks that fell over his collar.

Kisses were about pleasure, Abby thought, as a delicate whisper of tongue eased across her lips. About life being good and dear. About connection with that goodness, and the sheer physical delight any human ought to glory in from time to time.

"Not serious," he said, softly. "When you're enjoying the firelight and the company of a woefully informal gentleman at the end of a long, cold day, kisses ought not to be serious."

Mr. Belmont sat back, when Abby would have kissed him again.

"Your spouse smoked pipes," he said. "He might have been self-conscious about inflicting unpleasant breath on you. One should be considerate of one's spouse."

He topped off Abby's glass, then his own and switched seats, so he was beside her and his feet propped on the hassock.

Gracious... And yet, Abby was far from affronted. If anything, she wanted to snuggle closer. To him, to his kisses, to his unapologetic brand of gruff warmth.

"If you're preparing to have an attack of manners, Abigail, I don't think lectures and scolds will do much good. I've been a bachelor raising boys for too long, and the niceties were never very firmly in my grasp to begin with. Academics are allowed a few eccentricities. If I've presumed too egregiously, I could send you to Weekes, but I'm unwilling to return you to Stoneleigh Manor yet."

The idea of Stoneleigh Manor, empty save for nervous servants, echoes of violence, and memories of misery, appealed not at all.

Though neither did the notion that the estate Abby now owned was drifting without her managing presence.

"I did ask you about kissing." She'd been asking about loneliness, about other people's marriages, about so much of which she'd remained in ignorance while a wife.

He patted her hand. "So you did, and I am ever prone to lecturing. Let me tell you about my chat with Sir Dewey, who holds you in fearfully high esteem."

Nicholas chose that moment to interrupt—without knocking—and went straight to the brandy decanter.

"Colder than the ninth circle of hell out there, and a man must decide between breathing freely or freezing his face off. Thoughts of smiles from my dearest Abby were all that warmed me."

Nick's hair was tousled, his cheeks ruddy, and the gleam in his eyes suggested he might sit in Abby's lap.

"We're discussing Mr. Belmont's interview with Sir Dewey," Abby said. "You will please stop flirting long enough for a serious conversation."

"In the presence of a pretty woman, I never stop flirting. I see we're being scandalously informal."

"I'm preparing Mrs. Stoneleigh for that day when the nephews descend from Oxford. If this is informal, they will turn the household barely civilized. Sit down, Nicholas, and give us the benefit of your thinking."

Nick eased himself into a wing chair with the sigh of a weary horse flopping into deep straw at the end of a day's journey. He pulled off his boots and propped stockinged feet on the other side of the hassock, cradled his drink in his lap, and closed his eyes.

Being a widow had unexpected aspects, to say the least, but the very informality of the moment gave Abby a sense of being esteemed and accepted— admitted to a secret society on the far side of strict decorum, a more sensible place, and less lonely.

"Say on, Professor," Nick murmured. "Did Sir Dewey confess to murder most foul, and can he account for himself the night of the murder?"

"I don't know," Axel said. "His staff would lie for him, so I saw no point asking and enflaming his curiosity. Doubtless he'd say he was tucked up in his library, working at his ledgers as any nabob ought to be."

Nothing in Sir Dewey's interview came as any surprise to Abby, but she was disappointed nonetheless. She'd wanted him to have a solid alibi—darts at the Weasel, a short trip down to London, anything to put him beyond suspicion.

But then, she wanted everybody to be beyond suspicion and the murder to never have happened—though regaining the status of Gregory Stoneleigh's wife in exchange for that of his widow also held no appeal.

No appeal at all.

* * *

Wasn't this just lovely?

Nick had left Sussex intent on escaping the miasma of marital bliss afflicting his friends there, and now, in the household of the most confirmed bachelor Nick knew, in the dead of winter, romance was blossoming.

Coming in from the stable, Nick had had a stray dog's view through the library window of Axel Belmont and Abby Stoneleigh kissing. The sheer wonder of their intimacies, the savoring and tenderness, had nearly turned Nick around for another slog to the Weasel.

Except he'd been to the Weasel and had news to report.

"You'll talk to Sir Dewey again?" Nick asked.

"Very likely, and Shreve and Ambers and Mrs. Jensen, at least."

Axel clearly didn't want to. He wanted this investigation to be over—death by accident, as the preliminary reports had stated—but the woman sitting next to the professor would not have peace until Axel brought some fool to justice.

"I asked a few questions at the Weasel," Nick said, as if nosing about the local watering hole had been his avowed purpose for riding two miles in bitter weather.

"You had a few pints too," Axel replied. "And flirted with Polly Nairn."

Polly, in truth, had made a good attempt to flirt with Nick. He'd barely been able to muster a wiggle of the eyebrows for the poor woman, though he'd left plenty of extra coin for her efforts.

"I had one pint. The publican's winter ale is not the Weasel's finest recommendation. You will be pleased to know that all the shire is relieved to have Mrs. Stoneleigh taken in hand by a responsible household."

"This again," Abby muttered, twitching at her shawl. "I am not some waif shivering in a church doorway."

That would be a charitable assessment, compared to what Nick had heard. He exchanged a look with Axel, whose expression across the hassock was, *Get on with it.*

"You are high-strung, my dear," Nick said. "Easily overset. Everybody knows this. You are delicate. The colonel had his hands full with you, which is why he never took you calling. The death of your grandfather and your parents in quick succession dealt a blow to your nerves from which you never recovered, hence your reclusive nature. Mrs. Turnbull and her minions are tasked with hauling you back from the brink of a complete breakdown."

The twitching stopped. "I'm a witless wonder, while I ran that estate, even when my husband was larking around the grouse moors for weeks at a time? When he'd disappear to London, to do God knew what with God knew whom? I can't tell you how often he claimed to be in London, though if I sent him a note care of Mr. Brandenburg, even my most urgent queries often went unheeded."

"You needed solitude," Nick went on, for Polly had been very sure of this point, "and the colonel needed respite from the demands of your company. The Stoneleigh staff was simply too loyal to admit the burden your care placed on them."

Abby rose and set her drink on the end table. "Stoneleigh Manor has a full complement of servants, and yet I had no lady's maid. What hysterical wreck manages without her lady's maid? I had no nurse, I had no companion, I never drank to excess, never raised my voice. Why would people be so cruel?"

"Not cruel," Axel said, staring at his slippers. "Misguided. I don't get the sense anybody bears you ill will, Abigail. They are repeating a fancy woven long ago, embellished with convenient facts."

She stood before the fire, a pillar of outraged consternation. "What facts? I ran my husband's property. I kept ledgers, I tried to compensate for the worst of his follies without antagonizing him. I dealt with squabbling servants, directed the steward regarding eight tenant farms. I gave up my reading, I stopped sketching, I stopped playing the piano—"

"You became eccentric," Nick offered, at least by the standard of country folk who expected the gentry to be... genteel.

"I became the wife Gregory Stoneleigh wanted," Abby said. "He saved me from the poorhouse or worse, and I was determined to be a good wife to him."

One could not be a good wife to a selfish idiot, though Nick hardly knew how to convey that sentiment respectfully.

"Sometimes," Axel said, "when somebody has a shortcoming—an inability to express fine sentiments or appreciate art, for example—rather than admit that shortcoming, they attribute it to those around them. My nephew Christopher vociferously castigates his brother for being late, when in fact, Remington is generally punctual, but Christopher, the elder brother, loses track of time."

In his example, the professor had apparently offered Abby a measure of comfort.

"My father was always losing his spectacles," Abby said. "If my mother misplaced her reticule once every two years, she never heard the end of it from Papa. Gregory wasn't eccentric, exactly."

Nick could help with this, for the professor had seized on a telling point. "Stoneleigh had no friends, save Sir Dewey," Nick observed. "He had odd tempers. He traveled frequently, though we're not sure why and haven't even confirmed his destinations. He never took you along, his finances are a mystery, he was not close to his children, and he supposedly ran an international import business, but couldn't be bothered with his own acres. *He* was difficult, demanding, and eccentric."

That Abby had to be convinced was sad, also a tribute to how determined she'd been to be Stoneleigh's "good wife."

"I've seen your quarters, Abigail," Axel said, his tone ominously gentle. "You have no cheval mirror, only a small hand mirror in your bedroom. Gregory had two cheval mirrors, one in his bedroom, one in his dressing closet. He was never less than perfectly turned out, while I'd guess you haven't had a new gown in two years."

Abby's expression said the new gown had likely been five years ago. "Gregory said an excessive interest in one's own appearance led to vanity."

"Gregory always went about in fashionable attire, and apparently visited London tailors from time to time," Axel pointed out. "Gregory had a valet, you had no lady's maid. How were you to manage?"

"I rang for a maid to deal with my laces when I wasn't wearing jumps," Abby said. "I wasn't raised with a lady's maid, so I thought little of it. Gregory said small economies were the basis of greater luxuries, and I do like my privacy."

Gregory had said a bloody damned lot to his young, grieving bride. Somewhere in the midst of his dictates, Abby had misplaced the distinction between isolation and privacy.

"You are not eccentric, Abigail," Axel said. "But the more I learn of your late husband, the more I believe he was hiding something from all and sundry, including you."

A conclusion Nick could drink to—so he did.

* * *

"I'm investigating two murders," Axel said to Nick.

Another day had been spent in a freezing saddle, haring about the shire. Another day when Axel had been warmed by the thought of Abigail Stoneleigh reading by the hour in his glass house, in his library, in her sitting room.

He ought to move his collection of erotica to the estate office, but Abby would notice an abruptly empty shelf or two in the library. She was a bookseller's daughter to her very bones, much to his surprise and delight.

"My bachelorhood is about to be murdered," Nick said, lighting the branch of candles on the piano. "Get out your fiddle, Professor. My manners have grown ragged lately, and my spirit needs soothing."

What Nick needed was an hour sampling the tender charms of Polly Nairn. Axel suspected half the reason his nephews frequented Candlewick was to ogle

Polly's bosom and practice their fledgling flirtation skills.

"Nicholas, you cannot be made to marry. Stop sulking and resign yourself to courting, or tell your papa you aren't ready to take a bride."

Though Nick *was* ready. The man was so lonely he'd intrude on any friend, brave any weather, to avoid the bridal search awaiting him in London.

Men could be such fools when it came to matters of the heart.

"Where do you keep your fiddle?" Nick asked, raising the cover over the piano keys. "One never sees you practice, and yet, your skill remains sharp."

Like kissing apparently, some of the knack remained after the opportunity to flourish one's expertise had passed.

"If Mrs. Stoneleigh is resting, your pounding and my scraping will disturb her."

Nick sat at the piano while Axel poured two brandies. The consumption of spirits in his household had increased considerably, but then, so had the availability of interesting company.

"I do not pound, you do not scrape," Nick said, leafing through a bound volume of Beethoven. "What are your intentions regarding the fair Abigail?"

The role of knight protector suited Nick, much as Axel resented the question. Like the good academic Axel aspired to be, he considered the query as dispassionately as one sip of brandy allowed.

"I intend to keep Abigail safe, and to aid her to regain health that was apparently slipping from her grasp." Axel also intended to kiss her again—another surprise.

"Abby reminds me of a barn cat," Nick said. "One promoted to pantry mouser in the depths of winter. All this ease and comfort appeal strongly, as does the warmth of the hearth, though she's bewildered by it too, and cautious."

Well, yes. Abigail's kisses savored of bewilderment, also of wonder.

"Good evening, gentlemen," said the lady herself, standing in the library's doorway. "I hope I'm not intruding."

Nick rose and bowed. "My dear, you could not possibly intrude, because you are ever present in my thoughts. Axel has news to report from his day's labors, but after dinner, we must inspire him to find his violin. He will rise in your esteem beyond all bearing when you hear him play."

Abby wrinkled her nose. "I esteem Mr. Belmont quite highly enough for his hospitality, his botanical accomplishments, his tireless efforts to find justice for my late spouse, and his unwillingness to bother a new widow with clumsy flirtation."

Axel wanted to stick his tongue out at Nick, but settled for pouring a third brandy.

"Nick plays the piano well." Not as well as he flirted, damn the luck.

Abby stared at her brandy. "As a young lady, *I* played the piano well. My grandfather insisted that everybody should be competent on a musical instrument. He said we couldn't read all the time, or we'd ruin our eyes."

"About your grandfather."

Abby, rather than take the corner of the sofa Axel had mentally consigned to her keeping, took the place beside Nick on the piano bench.

"Grandpapa Pennington was a dear," she said. "He understood people, as a good shopkeeper must. He knew what his customers would enjoy and delighted in providing it. I can't tell you the number of times he lent a book to some elderly patron, asking her to read it for him so he'd know to whom to recommend it. He said he hadn't the time to read, though that was a lie, for he read every night. He was engaged in shameless kindness."

"Books are not intended to sit about on dusty shelves," Axel said, opening the sideboard and extracting his violin case. Young wives with endless imagination and aching hearts were not intended to molder away on remote country estates either.

He set the case on the sideboard and opened it.

"Won't you play for us?" Nick asked.

"Not now. The instrument will only go constantly out of tune until it's physically warm. After supper, perhaps I'll run through an air or two, but for now, I have something to give Abigail—from her grandfather, as it turns out."

Axel left his violin breathing like wine on the sideboard and extracted a bound volume from the top right desk drawer.

"Cassius Pettiflower sends his warm regards," Axel said. "When your family died, and the shops were sold, the staff came across this volume and asked him to give it to you. Pettiflower kept it, hoping to pass it to you in person. I suspect he held on to it for sentimental reasons."

Abby took the volume cautiously, as if it had thorns or teeth to bite her. "What is it?"

"Your grandfather's journal." Axel wished he'd waited, wished he'd done something to prepare Abby for this moment. One didn't simply tuck an instrument under one's chin and start sawing away, after all.

She opened the book and did exactly what Axel so often did in his glass house, she sniffed.

"Sandalwood." She ran a finger down the page, though the writing was fading. "Grandpapa said the scent made him feel dashing."

She blinked and sniffed again, though not at the pages. Nick passed her a monogrammed handkerchief—white silk, based on how it caught the firelight.

"What did Pettiflower have to say, Professor?" Nick asked, as Abby dabbed at her eyes and clutched the journal to her heart.

Axel glowered at Nick, for what was the urgency about a few rude questions between strangers, when Abigail was in tears?

"Tell us," Abby said, taking up her corner of the sofa. "Cass would never dissemble before the king's man."

Nick took the place at Abby's side, which was just as well. Axel felt a towering need to hold the woman's hand, put an arm around her, or perhaps smash his brandy glass—another specimen from his treasured Jacobite collection.

He took the wing chair instead.

"Pettiflower corroborated the vicar's rendition of events." How Axel wished that was all he had to report. "Pettiflower wrote to Abby, and his letters came back unopened. He sent flowers, those unacknowledged. He had to apply to his vicar to find Stoneleigh's home parish and could thus write to Weekes."

"I don't under—" Abby set her grandfather's journal on the end table. "I don't understand *why*. Why would a good friend have been kept away from me when I'd lost both parents and my grandfather in a succession of weeks?"

Nick crossed his arms, muscles flexing. By firelight, the genial, blond viscount looked fleetingly capable of murder himself.

"What else did you learn, Professor?" Nick asked.

"Pettiflower had spoken with Abigail's father, who'd given tentative approval of a match. Anthony Pennington asked that Pettiflower not propose for another six months, because Abby's papa didn't want Abby to feel as if she'd snapped up the first offer to come her way. She was not yet twenty, and she was an heiress."

Nick rose. "Well, of course. Greed will out. What sort of heiress?"

The truth Axel had to convey was all thorns, no fragrance, no lovely bloom—also not entirely a surprise.

"Abby's father had looked into the Pettiflower finances, and Pettiflower, being of a mercantile bent, did likewise with his prospective in-laws. Pettiflower was willing to support Abby's parents in their old age, but what he found astounded him."

"I'm astounded," Abby said, her grip on the journal fierce.

Hours later, Axel was still, more furious than anything else. He sat forward, gently pried the journal from her grasp, and passed her his drink.

"Pettiflower's mother is one of thirteen," Axel said. "His father one of eight. He has relatives keeping shops all over Oxford, with their fingers in many different enterprises. His information is better than Bow Street and a team of solicitors could gather with unlimited time and funds. Your parents were well beyond comfortable, your grandfather was wealthy."

"You were an heiress twice over," Nick said, stalking back to the piano bench. "I could toss this piano through the window I'm so angry on your behalf, Abby. If Stoneleigh weren't already dead—"

Precisely. "Here is a motive for murder, or the beginnings of one," Axel said. "Stoneleigh committed a great theft, a swindle, at least, and if Pettiflower knew of that, he had a motive to take Stoneleigh's life."

"Because the colonel took my future, my fortune, my books," Abby said.

Murdered them, more like. Murdered Abby's innocence, the crime an ongoing violation of decency that cried out for an explanation—and for justice.

"Does Pettiflower have an alibi?" Nick asked, closing the lid over the piano keys.

"The night of the colonel's demise, Pettiflower was with family, having dinner, guests at the table." Then too, Pettiflower had had years to avenge his intended's fate, but he'd instead written a single letter, minded his shop, and gone on with life.

As a gentleman ought when a lady has categorically dismissed him from the suitor's lists.

Pettiflower's alibi had been the company of his own family—his prospective wife, her parents, his parents. All of them enjoying a meal that by rights Abby might have planned with him, had Stoneleigh not worked his evil.

"I am angry," Abby said. "I am furious, enraged. If I had learned what you've just told me—"

"Which is why Stoneleigh kept you locked in your tower, surrounded by false rumors of delicate nerves, and no less than eight tenant farms to keep you occupied," Axel said. "If you had intimated that family wealth had gone missing, then your questions would have been dismissed as fanciful imaginings. This answers at least one question."

For the first time, Abby looked at him. She had put her tears aside, perhaps to be renewed in private, and her gaze held both betrayal and determination.

"If any man, ever, thinks to keep the truth from me again," Abby said, "he will do so at the cost of his safety. I love words, Mr. Belmont, I love elegant prose and the exquisite turn of phrase. For the loathing that grips me now, I have no words. I have no, no... I haven't *anything* adequate to convey my sentiments. Death for Gregory was a mercy, compared to what I'd do to him."

"Perhaps somebody saw to the matter for you," Axel said. "We at least know where Gregory's money came from. His wealth came from your inheritance. Now we need only determine where it went."

"At present, I leave that puzzle to you gentlemen, and you will excuse me," Abby said. "I'll take a tray for dinner, though don't expect me to eat a bite, and don't presume to scold me for it. My grandfather's journal wants reading."

Axel rose and held up the unfinished drink. Abby downed it at one swallow, replaced it gently on the sideboard, and departed the library on a soft swish of her hems, the journal clutched against her chest.

"She'll cry hysterically," Nick predicted, abandoning the piano. "And yet, I have the sense you pulled your punches, Professor. There's more, isn't there?"

There was more brandy, fortunately.

"Investigating this murder will turn me into an obese sot," Axel said, switching seats to take Abby's corner of the sofa. "Pettiflower knew which firm of solicitors handled the Pennington estate."

"Lawyers," Nick said, coming down beside Axel. "Now comes the truly nasty part."

"The import business—not the printing press, the bookshop, or the tea shop—was handled by Handstreet and Handstreet. Pettiflower has relations who no longer use them, and said the firm has become, in the hands of the present generation, the type to not ask too many questions. The family solicitors responsible for the shops were Nehring and Son, a fine old firm Pettiflower could highly recommend."

"Stoneleigh was a fine old cavalry officer too, I'm sure."

"When did you get so skinny, Nicholas?"

"I'm in a premarital decline. I saw you kissing the fair widow, my friend. At least close the curtains before you dispense that sort of consolation."

The consolation in that kiss had gone both ways. "You've taken to peeking in windows, Nicholas. Should I be concerned?"

"Cheer me up with talk of murder, please. We're taking trays in the library so you can play me out of my megrims."

Axel would play his violin for the woman upstairs, who was mourning the murder of her dreams at the hands of a greedy old man, for purposes Axel had yet to divine.

"The entire Pennington estate," Axel said, "for the grandfather and both of Abby's parents, was handled by the Handstreet lawyers, the same firm that was responsible for the import business dealings here in Oxford."

"While another pack of mongrels dealt with the London end of things," Nick said, yawning. "Probably more of the same in Portsmouth, or Liverpool... But why would Handstreet—a firm charged with business matters—get involved in chancery issues such as the Pennington estates? You said the Nehring firm was already in place and known to the family."

Between the brandy, the earlier long, cold ride to Oxford and back, and the seductive warmth of the fire, Axel was falling asleep. He rose, though a scoot and a shove were needed to win free of the sofa's embrace.

"I don't know why the colonel's business firm took over the settlement of the deceased couple's affairs," Axel said. "But I intend to find out. Doubtless, the Handstreet solicitors will attempt to thwart my investigations, and demand that I produce some sealed document confirming the colonel's death and the need for an inquest."

Nick slouched lower into his corner of the sofa. "Let's visit the lawyers together. I'll produce my left fist and my right fist, throw around the title, drop some coin in the hands of a few ferret-faced law clerks. This will be good practice."

Axel's investigative instincts, numbed halfway to frostbite by the day's outing, stirred.

"Practice, Nicholas?"

For a moment, Axel thought Nick had dozed off. The fire crackled softly, and the violin warming on the sideboard called to Axel's spirits.

"My papa is dying, Ax. I don't know what to do."

Bloody perishing hell. "Nicholas, I am so sorry. When papas get to dying, there's often not a damned thing one *can* do." Axel pressed a hand to Nick's shoulder, moved the brandy bottle nearer to Nick's elbow, and went off to order supper trays—and another bottle of spirits.

CHAPTER TEN

Abby could read no more of her grandfather's journal. The handwriting was faint in places, her head throbbed, her eyes ached, and the hour had grown late.

A soft tap came at her bedroom door, disturbing a mental state too riotous to qualify as brooding.

That gentle knock was the gesture of a man who wanted to be able to say over breakfast that he'd come by to check on his guest, but hadn't wanted to disturb her slumbers.

Abby pulled the door open and found Axel Belmont holding a white rose in a pink porcelain bud vase.

"You are awake." The professor spouted a metaphor, did he but know it.

Abby stepped aside. "Come in."

He ought not to set foot in her bedroom, and not because the hour was late and they were unchaperoned. Unchaperoned apparently did not signify, when a woman's late husband had made sure all and sundry thought her prone to hysterical fancies.

Axel eyed the journal in Abby's hand. "Abigail, I am sorry."

"I don't want your pity." She dragged him by the sleeve into her room and closed the door before all the fire's heat escaped into the dark and drafty corridor. "I want to kill Gregory Stoneleigh several times over, I want to thank the person who pulled that trigger, and I don't care if that makes me a monster."

Axel set the rose on her night table. "You are not a monster. You have been monstrously wronged. I'll get to the truth. That, I vow to you."

The covers had been rumpled as Abby had tossed and turned her way through her grandfather's pages. Axel began making the bed.

"You might not find the answers," she said, setting the journal on the desk, well away from the hearth. "I almost don't care who killed Gregory. I care that

Gregory likely squandered every shilling my family worked their entire lives to acquire. I care that Gregory lied to me, repeatedly, for years. I care that I was made to feel grateful to him, *grateful*, every waking moment, season after season, when he—"

She'd whipped back toward the hearth to find herself face-to-face with Axel.

"Curse if it helps," he said. "Bellow down the rafters, rant, hurl the breakables. You're entitled."

If Abby ran cursing into the night, Axel Belmont would find her. That thought alone preserved her from the frightful impulse to strike him. His crime was to tell her the truth, and yet, violence coursed through her.

"Do you know what the worst part of a fire is?" she asked. "A fire takes lives. So do disease, war, and old age. Fire takes everything else too—your dearest treasures. Not money—money can be replaced—but your great-grandmother's recipes written in her hand, the sketches done by a great-uncle who emigrated to Canada and was never heard from again. The sentimental anchors that tell you who your family is, who has loved you, and for how long."

Abby was crying, again, when she'd thought all her tears had been shed. "Fire destroys the very place you thought would be your refuge when your loved ones were gone. Fire eats up your memories and turns them to ash; it consumes everything, your past, your hopes, your home. And there was Gregory, all solicitude and concern, stealing even my right to grieve."

She'd been nearly shouting.

Axel brushed his thumbs over her cheeks. "Then grieve now, for grieve, you must."

His touch was... everything unexpected, and everything good. Gentle, unhurried, intimate. Abby closed her eyes and turned her face to his palm.

"I hate Gregory Stoneleigh." The words gave her a sad kind of peace. "I hate him with a passion I didn't realize I was capable of."

"Good. Hate him as passionately as you need to, for as long as you need to."

She opened her eyes, and held Axel's hand to her cheek. His gaze was steady, fierce, and approving.

Hatred was exhausting, though the force of Abby's antipathy had been a revelation. How dispirited had she become? How weak, that a betrayal of this magnitude had been necessary to rekindle her temper?

Tomorrow she would look like a harridan. She'd make herself eat, make herself go down to breakfast, or possibly luncheon. She'd swill tea, scold Nicholas, and start planning her return to the estate she now owned in fee simple absolute.

Tonight... tonight she would run wild.

She kissed Axel Belmont, grateful that Gregory's sterile, avaricious version of marriage hadn't imbued her with even this skill.

"I will never refer to him as my spouse again," Abby said. "He was my jailer, an assassin preying upon innocence. Don't stop kissing me."

For long, quiet moments, Axel obliged. As he'd once indicated, he possessed an entire vocabulary of kisses. Sweet, soft, savoring, *comforting*, daring—kissing was not a silent endeavor either. Mouths touching and learning each other, arms embracing, had a whispered music Abby had never heard before.

She followed that whisper, tucking herself close enough to feel the evidence of Axel Belmont's arousal, and like a fire finding a fresh breeze, her emotions shifted.

Axel drew back. "Abigail, we must not. You'll regret—"

"I have many, many regrets," Abby said, resting against him. "I will have them for years, as you have your regrets. I want you now, Axel Belmont. I want all of you there is to want, with all of me that remains to do the wanting."

Little enough though that was. Axel couldn't know how little, nor could he know how badly Abby wanted to give it to him and him alone.

His hand, slow and warm, caressed her hair. "I will not take advantage of—"

"That is the most wrong, misguided argument you could make. I desire you, you desire me. I'm a widow. Will you presume to know what's best for me, to tell *me* what I want or need? To judge when I'm competent to make a decision, and when I'm not?"

Oh, the terrible pleasure of hoisting an intelligent, honorable man on the twin petards of logic and respect. Axel could not deny her without disrespecting her wishes, as she'd been so brutally disrespected in the past.

"I won't beg," Abby said, kissing him again and nudging a knee between his thighs.

"You should never have to beg," he muttered against her mouth. "Not ever, Abigail. Do you understand me?"

She understood that he'd relented, that despite the convoluted, male flights along which honor might speed in the morning, her desire for him would be gratified now. This was a victory, against Gregory, but also against grief, and against losses so intimate, Abby could not have shared them with even the man about to become her lover.

"Begging does not serve," Axel said, easing back from Abby's embrace. "Not until we're under those covers, not a stitch of clothing between us, our mutual dignity in a panting heap on the floor. Then you may beg me all you please."

He locked the door, but his lecture was not complete. "Haste does not serve. If you are determined to take this bold step with my humble and obliging self, though it complicates all and solves nothing, though it confounds both reason and decorum, though Nicholas will be most—"

Abby unbelted her dressing gown.

"Lectures will not serve," she said. "Do you need assistance undressing, Mr. Belmont?"

He held out a hand. "You may undo my cuffs. Dexterity at this hour eludes me."

Abby's room was warm. She'd been pacing, reading, fuming, and crying behind her closed door for hours. She shrugged out of her dressing gown, draped it over the chest at the foot of the bed, and took Axel's hand in both of hers.

She kissed his knuckles, for the sheer pleasure of rewarding his surrender— also for the newfound delight of unnerving him. He had experience, of course, but Abby was convinced his experience was far from recent.

His sense of his own desirability had been a casualty of the failures and hopes in the glass house, of parenting, botany, time, and benign neglect.

She dropped his cuff-links into his palm.

"Get into bed, Abigail. I can't have you taking a chill."

Abby glowered at him, though in her heart she was beaming. Axel slipped his cuff-links into his watch pocket, pinched the bridge of his nose, then stared at the ceiling.

"*Please*, rather. Abigail would you *please* consider, at your leisure of course, getting into the bed, so that in all my frail conceit, I might be spared the burden of concern for your welfare? A gentleman never imposes on a lady, particularly not when in her very bedroom, contemplating intimacies so precious and unexpected that the same gentleman, against all dictates of rational—"

How she loved to hear him babble. Abby hopped onto the bed, which had that lovely, cozy, half-made feel because Axel had straightened the covers earlier.

The room had a privacy screen. Axel disappeared behind it, and the sounds of water splashing and fabric rustling came next. Abby yanked off her nightgown and fired it in the general direction of the foot of the bed, then scooted beneath the covers.

So that's how this is done. She hoarded up the simple sequence of a mutual seduction, one small increment of knowledge against all the ignorance she'd been enshrouded in over the years of her marriage.

Axel emerged from the shadowed corner, naked from the waist up, the firelight gleaming against his damp chest. He held his boots, shirt, waistcoat, and cravat in his arms and deposited the lot in a pile on the chest.

"Do not scold me for failing to hang up my clothing," he said, setting his boots near the door. He banked the fire next, casting the room in damnably thick shadows.

Abby had wanted to see him, had wanted to glory in every inch of him, exposed once again for her delectation, but perhaps that wasn't the done thing on a first encounter, or perhaps ladies never expressed—

Woodcut images of smiling women, their knees spread, their bodies exposed for the mutual pleasure of both—or several—parties, came to mind.

To blazing hell with what ladies did and did not do. With Axel Belmont, at least, Abby need not be a lady. She need only, finally, be herself.

Axel sat on the bed, his back to Abby. "In the past, I have been ridic—*chided*, rather, for excessive modesty," he said. "I am not... I am not—"

Abby rose, pressed her bare breasts to his back, and wrapped her arms about him. The contact was warm, friendly, pleasurable, and shocking—probably to them both.

"You bring a few bruises and memories of your own to this bed," she said, kissing his shoulder. "I could not be here with you otherwise. Be as modest as you please, Axel. I could never trust myself with a strumpet of a man."

Those broad shoulders relaxed. "The things you say, Abigail."

She liked hugging him this way, liked exploring the odd contour of male chest hair, muscle, ribs, and even nipples without being able to see any of it. She paused on a happy sigh, in charity with a life that a half hour ago had seemed endlessly bleak.

The bleakness would encroach again, but this night would give Abby at least one torch to hold up against that darkness.

"Is madam quite finished having her way with my person for now?"

Madam was barely getting started. Abby let Axel go, though. He couldn't get his breeches off as long as she was plastered to him.

"Have I told you, Mr. Belmont, how much I admire your patience?"

He stood and faced the bed, his breeches loose about his hips. Abby climbed under the covers and realized he was waiting for her to dart a glance his direction. He pushed his breeches off, paused for a deliberate, unblinking moment, then bent to toss them onto the pile on the chest.

Anger and bravado had inspired Abby to proposition Axel into intimacies, as had a sense that if she did not seize this moment, she might become the woman Gregory had tried to paint her—spineless, retiring, fragile, and dull.

With one small moment of naked silence, Axel had recast the nature of the encounter. A gentleman would never impose on a lady, but a lover, a bruised veteran of his own private battles, could offer his trust.

And in that moment, much to Abby's relief, the shadows on her heart receded. Her deceased family, the murder investigation, marital betrayals, and fortunes squandered ceased, for a time, to hold sway in her mind.

Widows were permitted to dally discreetly, that was a universal truth, whether Miss Austen had ever acknowledged it as such.

"Come to bed," she said, holding out a hand. "Please, rather. Axel Belmont, won't you please come to bed?"

The mattress dipped, and for the first time, Abby found herself sharing a bed with a lover.

* * *

Truly, Axel's academic calling was genuine, if he could not recall the last time he'd been intimate with a woman. He'd given up house parties years ago— polite orgies for the most part, and a high price to pay for a peek at some viscount's conservatory, or an earl's gardens.

He would never forget this night with Abigail.

He'd withdraw, of course. He'd become frightfully adept at withdrawing. The boys had come so close together, he'd been determined Caroline would not be burdened with another pregnancy until she was demanding more children of him as only Caroline could demand.

Axel sank onto the bed and, as naturally as he pulled on a favorite riding jacket, drew Abigail into his arms.

Caroline had told him—ordered him—to remarry, one of the last orders she'd given him. Remarry and be happy. Don't grow old, contrary, and blind in those damned glass houses.

"Should I be doing something?" Abby asked.

She should be changing her mind.

"I'm considering my strategy." Though Axel hadn't a strategy. Distracting Abigail from the heartbreak he'd served her wasn't a strategy. Obliging a new widow on her first reckless tear wasn't a strategy either. "I function well within clearly articulated rules."

Abby wiggled around to peer at him. "No, you don't. Whoever told you that was wrong. You function well when given a task and left complete latitude to decide how to execute it. Your estate thrives, and nobody tells you how to go on with it. Your boys are perfect gentlemen, if their behavior in the churchyard is any indication. You raised them without any guidelines save your own common sense. Your botany is entirely your own undertaking. Rules, indeed. I am in bed with a daft man."

She wasn't... she wasn't wrong. She was warm, and naked, and so clearly happy to be in this bed. Axel wanted to savor that, and yet, he wanted *her* too.

Desperately.

"Lecturing is apparently contagious," he muttered. "My sons have warned me this is so. Enough lecturing, then." *For once.*

Axel rose over her, arranged himself on all fours, and commenced a spree of kissing that felt so miserably overdue, he nearly spent on Abby's belly when she brushed her fingers over his cock.

Haste would not serve, but restraint would kill him.

"You want me," she announced.

"Do I detect a note of glee in your voice? Perhaps smugness is the more accurate term. You're the prose lover in this bed, and—merciful God, Abigail...."

She had the most beguiling way of wrapping her fingers around a man's sanity. Caroline had been all reckless dispatch, a woman intent on her goals. Axel had been expected to aid that objective, and be content with what pleasure he could manage for himself along the way.

Abigail was the curious sort. She had deucedly good coordination too, tangling tongues as she stroked him and explored his most vulnerable attributes.

"Men are so oddly constructed," she said, fondling him gently. She was bold but careful, and diabolically thorough. "I love touching you."

Had Abigail raised her knee, she could not have dealt a greater blow to the composure Axel was determined to maintain, even under intimate circumstances. Every man should hear those words—*I love touching you*—spoken in those exact, purring tones, and yet, Axel never had. Not from his wife, not from the casual liaisons from years past, not from the well-practiced women who catered to strutting, insecure university boys.

"Your touch conveys your delight, Abigail. I can *feel* your joy to have me in your grasp."

Not simple desire, which could be so much selfishness. He'd merely kissed her, and yet her joy in the moment—in him—was as much a source of warmth as the fire in the hearth or the covers surrounding them.

"You know you make a fetching picture in your breeches," she said, palms brushing over his fundament. "I like to watch you walk away. I am shameless."

She was balm to a widower's soul.

This time, when Axel kissed her, he added a caress to her bare breast, and that—most fortunately—slowed her plundering of his wits.

"I like that," she said. "You give me the warm shivers when you do that. The loveliest warm shivers."

Not, "Again." Or, "Harder." Not, "Stop that!" Or, his least favorite, "Will you *get on with it...*?"

So Axel shaped, caressed, tasted, and nibbled, until Abby was squirming and sighing beneath him. The warm shivers were apparently as contagious as lectures.

"Now, Abigail? In choosing the moment of joining, your complicity would be appreciated." Not her direction, not her permission. They would be accomplices in mutual passion.

What a novel concept. Axel poised above her, enduring the fascinating sensation of Abigail's tongue applied to his right nipple, while a moment of bereavement assailed him, for a very young husband who'd tried his best.

For a young wife who'd not lived long enough to learn what Abigail already knew. Mutual pleasure was the best pleasure, and in the last hour, Axel had been ruined for anything less.

Abby became perilously inventive with her mouth.

"Perhaps you didn't hear my question," Axel whispered, pushing gently at her sex. "Now, Abigail?"

"Mmm."

He teased, he feinted, he reveled in a joining that didn't consist of the lady taking him by the hand, shoving him along, and then flopping back to the mattress as if her obligations for the entire evening had been met, and somebody should ring to have the coach brought around at the top of the hour.

"You are a devil," Abby said, biting his shoulder. "You are the worst, most delectable devil. You could do this all night, couldn't you?"

With her, Axel was capable of feats of loving heretofore unknown to mortal man. Never had the reproductive organs of one male and one female been as slowly, carefully, or pleasurably introduced to each other. Instead of the tired parents' marital hornpipe, joining with Abby was a pavane of bliss.

The fit was exquisite, and Abby did Axel the great courtesy of remaining still until they were fully joined.

She stroked her hands down his back, then cupped his backside. "The *feel* of you, Axel Belmont... The sheer, glorious feel of you. You can't know... I want to move, to thrash out my gladness that we are close like this."

She would soon have him in tears.

"We'll move together." He started slowly, because they did not know each other intimately, and yet, with Abigail, the rhythm was just there, a gift to each other born of mutual attention and genuine regard.

The thrashing phase came soon enough, and Axel obliged his lady without limit. Abigail's passion was magnificent in its spontaneity, and nearly lethal to Axel's self-restraint. When she was panting beneath him, her fingers lazily disarranging his hair, he realized that part of him was waiting on his marks.

Old habits died hard, if at all, and yet, he didn't ask.

"You are such a fraud, Axel Belmont. Such a terrible, shameless fraud." Abigail's tone was drowsy and pleased, but her words sent unease through passion Axel could barely limit to a simmering boil.

"I'm a fraud?"

"You trot about the shire, tending to the king's justice, or you spend hours muttering to your roses. I can tell you've spent years with your violin too, but all the while, you are the dearest, loveliest man. I don't even have the words to tell you what I want, and yet, you know. That generosity, that attentiveness... You are nothing less than a wish come true. I suspected you would be too, but not like this. Nothing, not the most exquisite, explicit book in the world, could have prepared me for this."

She kissed his temple, undulated luxuriously beneath him, and the intermission was over.

Axel set those extraordinary words aside to be admired, sniffed at, and examined later—he could show her *very* exquisite, explicit books—and bent himself to the bodily admiration of the woman in his arms.

He'd had sex with enough women. For a time after Caroline's death, he'd been a monk, then he'd been overtaken by a need to assure himself of his continued functioning. Some of those excursions had been pathetic, but some had been pleasant, a few had been very pleasant.

But this... with Abigail... this was a new kind of intimacy, and he was enthralled. Axel didn't simply see to her pleasure. With his body, he worshipped her, and in her arms, he felt worshipped in return.

Her satisfaction came easily the next time, a long, sweet, rolling thunder of bliss moaned against his ear, followed by a sigh against his chest, as natural as spring breezes wafting past wild daffodils.

The experience was beyond words, beyond…

"Now you," Abby said, patting his bum.

How he adored the sensation of her touch on his backside. How he blossomed with renewed desire at her gentle pats and quiet murmurs.

"I'll withdraw." A promise, to her, to himself, to his scholarly ambitions, and to common sense. Children should be conceived with at least a commitment between their parents, with love of some sort, and a respectful—

"No lectures. Move, Axel. You move so beautifully, but I lack your stamina. You've loved me too well."

He moved.

He held off as long as sanity allowed, then longer still, because he did not want this interlude to end, and because Abigail was *with him* in a sense new to his experience. The tender edges of that newness wanted exploring, and yet, desire demanded satisfaction too.

He withdrew—barely—and poured his seed onto Abigail's belly. She held him ferociously tight, not easing her grip until Axel found the strength to raise himself up on his arms.

"I left my damned handkerchief in the pocket of my breeches." Proof he'd been ambushed by Abigail's overtures.

"Use mine," she said, brushing his hair back. "I don't want you to leave this bed a moment sooner than you must."

He nearly collapsed back on top of her, brought down like flying game by her sleepy sentiments. Only the certain knowledge that the maids would know if he made shift with the linens could have driven him from the bed.

Abby fumbled for the handkerchief on the night table, and Axel sat back. The moment was oddly intimate, for he'd barely allowed her a glimpse of him earlier. She lay on her back, knees spread, shadows flickering across her pale thighs, Axel's seed glistening on her belly.

And kneeling between her legs, he was exposed to her too. From neck to knees, with the scent of spent passion in the air, Axel had never been with a woman so casually naked.

"What?" Abby asked, holding out her handkerchief. Such a delicate article was hardly adequate for the job, and yet, Axel managed. He tended to Abby first, then to himself, using some of the rose's water to dampen the cloth.

Abby made no move to cover herself, nor did she look away as Axel dealt with their ablutions. Pity for Caroline assailed him, so demanding, *and so unsure of herself.*

"Earlier," Axel said, folding the handkerchief and setting it under the rose's vase, "I said something to you about others attributing their own shortcomings to us."

"The log in your own eye, rather than the speck in your brother's?" Abby murmured as Axel arranged himself beside her.

"Something like that. Remington being accused of tardiness by the brother who is, in fact, more lacking in punctuality."

"I recall. You are wondrously warm, Mr. Belmont, a human recommendation for chilly winters and long, cold nights."

He tucked an arm around her waist. "I might have overstated my capacity for bodily modesty."

For even the Oxford fellow's version of celibacy too. But then, the past hour had sent Axel's every concept of himself into the waste bin, a random heap of vines, leaves, twigs, and roots that had once been a recognizable plant.

Not a very happy plant though, not a great, blooming, robust specimen.

Abigail's passion, by contrast, was an open, generous, unguarded gift. For the first time in his life, Axel felt as if he'd made love with a virgin. The gift of her desire and closeness had been all his, and only his, a perfect rose.

Perhaps the man who'd made love with Abigail had been something of a virgin too. A dreaming virgin, who might bring his lady a few more lovely blossoms on long, cold winter nights.

CHAPTER ELEVEN

The first sight to greet Abby's eyes in the morning was the little white rose on the night table. The fragrance was delicate but distinctive, so she could lie amid her covers and breathe in sweetness, mulling spices, a tangy hint of cider, lush summer meadows... and Axel Belmont.

Weak sunlight filtered around the edges of the bed hangings that some considerate botanist had drawn closed on three sides. Abby pushed back the hangings on the window side of the bed, revealing morning sun, though she'd probably missed breakfast.

Ah, well. Allowances would be made. She'd been up late reading, having a tantrum, and...

Making love with Axel Belmont.

Somebody tapped on the door—not *his* tap.

"Come in."

"Morning, missus," Hennessey said, pushing the door open with one hand, while the other balanced a tray. "Mr. Belmont left orders we weren't to disturb you, but I was afraid your fire might go out."

No, in fact, Abby's fire had been rekindled. "I've slept as much as I can for now, thank you, Hennessey. Something smells good." Abby's appetite had apparently awoken along with the rest of her.

"Cinnamon toast," Hennessey said. "The footmen will give up their half days for extra servings of Cook's cinnamon toast, or so they claim."

Abby sat up as Hennessey set the tray on the side of the bed. The dishes were porcelain with purple flowers patterning the glaze, and a bouquet of violets graced one corner of the tray.

Violets stood for modesty. Any girl who'd grown up with her nose in books knew the language of flowers.

"Mr. Belmont has asked that I act as your lady's maid, if you need one. I have three sisters, which probably qualifies me as well as anything could."

A rose, a lady's maid, violets... small considerations to some women, but to Abby, sumptuous offerings. She would have traded them all to know how, exactly, a woman faced the man who'd shown her what pleasure between consenting adults could be.

"Will I disturb you if I build up the fire?" Hennessey asked.

"Of course not. Is that peat?"

"Mr. Belmont does experiments, and this winter's fancy is comparing the heating properties of coal, wood, peat, and I don't know what else. All this science is for his glass houses, of course. We test his theories here in the manor house, and any benefits go to the flowers. He'll be very much at home among the other professors at Oxford. They doubtless compare experiments with each other the livelong day."

The cinnamon toast was... ambrosial. The bread had been sliced to a generous thickness, then fried in some sort of batter, complete with spices more complicated than simple cinnamon. Sugar and melted butter adorned the whole, and a bowl of pears completed the feast.

And yet... Hennessey had mentioned *Oxford*. Axel's ambition was not news, but the reminder dimmed Abby's joy.

"When do you expect the professor to remove to university?"

"After he's published his latest herbal, though he's been working on it ever so long. Shall I come back to lace you up?"

"That won't be necessary, thank you. I mostly wear jumps. Please give Cook my compliments on the cinnamon toast. It restores the soul." A steady diet of such meals would help a lady fill out her dresses too.

Hennessey gave the room a visual going-over, popped a curtsey, then withdrew.

Abby treated herself to two cups of gunpowder tea and an entire slice of cinnamon toast, but left the second slice for some deserving footman or boot boy. Since joining the Belmont household, she'd done little besides eat, sleep, and read—also cry—and yet, she was feeling... better.

Not simply better as a grieving widow gradually recovers from the shock of her husband's death, but better than she had for weeks, possibly for months. Her digestion was settling down, her energy was coming back, her temper was reappearing in fine style, and soon... she'd be well enough to return to Stoneleigh Manor.

Every rose came with a complement of thorns, a reality even Axel Belmont hadn't been able to change.

* * *

"The law conspires against a man's honor," Nick said. "The widows know it too. You have a small window in which you might console the dear lady without repercussions, and she'll thank you for it. That's not taking advantage, Professor, that's merely—"

Axel drove his fist into Nick's gut.

Because Dayton and Phillip occasionally had a go at the old man—all in good fun, of course—Axel knew how to deliver a blow without trumpeting his intentions about the shire first.

He and Nick were in the stable, so if Nick wanted to oblige with return fire, no breakables were endangered. Right now, Axel would enjoy throwing a few punches. Or a lot of punches.

He'd forgotten how passionate lovemaking could put a man back on his mettle and renew his spirits in all regards... or perhaps this was a new discovery.

"Ouch, dammit," Nick groused. "I suppose I deserved that."

"You are not to procure on behalf of the lady, Nicholas. She bides here newly bereaved, and the neighbors already regard her in a pitying light, at best. Then too, I wanted to hit something solid and worthy of my ire."

"Happy to be of service, and at least you didn't rearrange my handsome phiz. Damned lawyers are enough to turn any reasonable man violent. What will you tell Abby?"

Axel had yet to discover those particular words, for they'd be difficult to say. "I've not the slightest—the lady approaches."

In her black cloak, Abby stood out against the snowy garden like a raven winging free against the winter sky. Was her walk more relaxed? She hadn't bothered with a bonnet, hadn't bothered with a scarf. She didn't even look cold, and the sight of her warmed Axel in places too long neglected.

The center of his chest, his hands, his throat, the middle of his back.

Behind his falls.

"The lady thrives in your care," Nick said, leading his mare into a loose box. "She's like one of those droopy, sad, horticultural specimens you get from Cathay or Persia. They arrive half dead, not even a rose to the casual observer. A year later, all is blossoms and exotic perfume."

Nick exaggerated, but not by much.

"Mrs. Stoneleigh, good morning." Axel took the lady's hand and bowed over it. "You're looking well." She looked shy, delectable, rosy-cheeked, and entirely lovely. "You will not remain well if you insist on braving the elements without gloves or a scarf."

Nick emerged from Buttercup's stall. "Forgive him. He's been to see the lawyers and is thus in more of a foul humor than usual. I can cheer him up with a sound thrashing, if you like. Might cheer myself up too. In fact, I think a little friendly pugilism is just the thing to settle the manly humors on a brisk winter morning."

Abby commenced scratching Ivan's withers rather than meet Axel's gaze. "You've been to see Handout and Whoever?"

The horse loved to have his withers scratched, while the middle of Axel's back had developed an infernal itch.

"To no avail." Except... the early morning ride into Oxford had removed Axel from the temptation to look in on his guest again, to linger at breakfast in hopes she'd come down for the meal when he'd ordered that she wasn't to be disturbed.

Wasting time with the lawyers had saved Axel from making a complete fool of himself, in other words.

"They wouldn't talk to us," Nick said, unhitching Ivan the Shameless from the cross-ties. "You're ruining a good horse, Abby dearest. Stealing his last pretensions to dignity, and making me jealous."

Abby dropped her hand and beamed at Nick, who'd doubtless been tossing metaphors at Axel instead of punches.

"I'm also getting my hands dirty, which a lady never does. Why wouldn't the lawyers talk to you? Mr. Belmont is the magistrate, and you're prone to violence around lawyers, I take it."

As a younger man, Axel might have taken his horse from Nick, shoved the pathetic creature into a stall, and muttered about checking on the roses. Nick was, after all, well equipped to explain to Abby the frustrations of their outing to Oxford.

Axel was a professor, which in the ordinary course required some facility with explanations.

"Handstreet told us that he owes his clients a duty of confidentiality," Axel said. "Without an order signed by a judge, or a power of attorney signed by you, he wouldn't discuss particulars of the estate settlement."

Abby patted Ivan's retreating quarters, then aimed a smile at Axel, a naughty, delightful smile, such as should have melted not only several acres of snow, but the glass houses Axel so treasured.

"Handstreet waved about a power of attorney," Nick said, leading Ivan to the stall nearest the mare and foal. "One that purported to have your signature on it, Abby mine. On the strength of that document, we were politely shown the door."

"I might have signed such a document," she said. "Papa told me never to sign something I didn't understand, though. Not a contract, not a bill of sale, not a receipt for goods unless I'd checked the tally myself. Papa had learned from Grandpapa a great respect for the written word, and yet... I did not cope well after the fire. I was told there wasn't an estate to speak of, so I might have been less then entirely cautious."

Abby's smile acquired the equivalent of black spot, going all tentative and wan about the edges. She'd been told *by Stoneleigh* she had no estate to inherit, the blighter.

"Nicholas and I will pay another call on the Handstreets," Axel said. "I told you I'd get to the bottom of your situation, and my every instinct insists Handstreet is hiding important information. For one thing, the same firm does not represent the heirs and the estate, and yet Handstreet would have it so."

"When a lawyer wants to hide something—" Nick said, shaking his head.

"His own arrogance will be his undoing," Axel retorted. "He waved his almighty power of attorney right under my nose, and a botanist is an observant sort."

"What did you see?" Abby asked.

Axel saw that she'd been ready to accept defeat, simply because a pair of arrogant weasels in solicitor's plumage had brandished a piece of paper.

"I saw that your so-called signature was witnessed by Shreve and Ambers," Axel said. "I saw that either your signature has changed a great deal in recent years, or it was forged on their power of attorney."

"When did you—? You saw my signature when I sent for you the night Gregory died, and you recall it that well?"

Axel recalled the pleasure of Abby's sighs warming his ear, the novelty of her breasts pressed against his back, the devastation in her eyes as she'd described the horror of a household victimized by fire.

He recalled all of it, also the lovely, looping script rendered by her own hand.

"The professor is a force to be reckoned with," Nick said, rubbing his belly. "Ask any scholar unprepared to recite in lecture at university. Do you suppose Cook has noticed our return? A midday meal might revive my spirits."

Abby found it necessary to study the mare and foal, despite the fact that the foal was indelicately attending to her own midday meal.

"I was hoping Mr. Wheeler might see me over to Stoneleigh Manor," she said. "I'm in the mood to get back on the horse, so to speak."

"Abby, my own sweetest turtle dove, under no circumstances—" Nick began, which prompted Axel's elbow, all on its own accord, to drive itself into Nick's ribs.

"If you're inclined to pay a call on Stoneleigh Manor," Axel said, "I'll happily escort you. I've a few pressing questions for Ambers and Shreve, assuming Ambers has returned from Melton. I'm sure Nick has correspondence to tend to in our absence."

Abby's gaze went from Nick to Axel, as if she'd never seen two gentlemen conveying the exact same quotient of innocence quite as effectively. Nick did not want Abby returning to the scene of a murder without protection—very reasonable of him, though Nick failed to grasp how ordering Abigail Stoneleigh about could precipitate disaster.

Axel did not want Abby to have any excuse to leave Candlewick one moment sooner than necessary. His desire—his duty, rather—to keep her safe was also quite understandable.

"I'm off to greet my roses for the day," Axel said. "Abigail, perhaps you'd like to join me?"

Nick sidled out of elbowing range. "I might like to visit these roses. It's not every day that a botanist published on three continents—"

"Nonsense," Abby said, lacing her arm through Axel's. "You simply want to flirt and pester and cheer me up. Dear of you, Nicholas, but I'm in good spirits. I started the day with a bouquet of violets and a serving of Cook's cinnamon toast to brighten my morning. The professor's escort to the glass house will be more than sufficient, thank you all the same."

Axel might have smirked at Nick, but Nick merely winked as Abby half dragged Axel out into the blessedly cold winter air.

* * *

Abby had collected her handsome specimen, but now what was she to *do* with him?

"Have we etiquette for this situation?" she asked, as they made their way toward the glass house.

"Of course. You ask knowledgeable questions as I introduce you to each of my roses. When a botanist shows you the great honor of personally acquainting you with his crosses and hybrids, of reviewing with him his failed experiments, and even examining his unexpected results, you are bound by decency to humor his every lecture and digression. I can't tell you the number of dukes and nabobs in whose conservatories I've been trapped, longing for a glimpse of a famed orchid, which of course is the last item on the itinerary. Amateurs are ruthless."

Widows could be ruthless too. "I woke up thinking of you. *Feeling* you."

Axel stopped outside the first glass house and produced a key, then stared at it cradled in his bare palm.

"One hardly knows what to say, Abigail."

"Apparently one doesn't say what I just did. I'm not asking about botanical etiquette. I'm asking about…"

He thrust the key in the lock and gave it a sure twist. "About dallying?"

Was that what they'd done? Merely dallied? "Yes, about dallying. I honestly hadn't expected to embark on the liberties pertinent to my widowed status quite so soon."

She sounded professorial to her own ears—or nervous. Maybe lecturing *was* contagious.

Axel led her into the warmth and verdure of the glass house, then latched the door behind them and tucked the key into his watch pocket.

"Have you regrets, Abigail?" he asked, surveying rows and rows of plants.

Most were potted, sitting on tables, away from the ground's chill. A few were so tall as to rest on the floor, their canes brushing the glass ceiling.

"I have so many regrets," Abby said, unbuttoning her cloak. "I regret my entire marriage. I regret that I gave up my books, my piano, my writing, my—"

Axel was peering at a thorny bush, studying it closely, his fingers trailing along a green shoot.

Abby had been married, and for years, she'd made her priority the study and interpretation of Gregory Stoneleigh's silences and asides, his postures, and his gestures. Axel Belmont was listening to her, and his listening had a cautious quality, as if he expected her to burst into recriminations at any moment.

She took his hand and kissed his palm, which tasted faintly of metal and leather. "I have no regrets at all where you're concerned, Axel Belmont. I dreamed of you, when for the past few weeks, all I've dreamed about were gunshots, the scent of stale pipe tobacco, disappearing footprints in the snow... I dreamed of your warmth, your weight. Good dreams that I hope to revisit during my waking hours."

He drew her into his arms, or Abby hugged him as close as winter clothing allowed. Their embrace was mutual, of that she was certain.

"I lack... I lack, of all things, flowery speeches," Axel said, his cheek resting against Abby's temple. "Thank you for those generous sentiments. I like to hear them. Last night, after you fell asleep, I remained with you, simply listening to you breathe."

He put worlds into that admission. Wonder, pleasure, not a little surprise.

"The violets were lovely. The scent of that white rose is as complicated as the blossom is simple. Is it one of your crosses?"

Whatever the etiquette of dalliance, that question was appropriate between Abby and her lover. Axel explained the intricacies of breeding roses, of balancing scent, disease resistance, appearance, longevity of the bloom, and even the rare ability to bloom more than once in a season.

All the while he led her from plant to plant, he held her hand, patted her knuckles, tidied her hair. By the time they reached the end of the second row, and Abby had been introduced to his sturdiest drafting stock—the Dragon— she had to kiss him.

"You have so much passion in you," she said, resting against him several glorious moments later. "You're like a carrying candle, and I can light my own taper from your warmth. You wait years for one of your crosses to produce the offspring you long for. You document everything. You learn entire languages simply so you can correspond with botanists in far-off lands."

"If one knows Latin and French, Spanish and Italian aren't that difficult."

While English probably defied Axel frequently outside the lecture hall. He'd unbuttoned his greatcoat, which allowed Abby to press close. Despite his dispassionate tone, their kisses and proximity had created a blooming interest behind his falls.

And that was... that was worth waiting years for too.

"Gregory was a disgrace." Abby pulled away and took a seat in the rocker before the hearth. "I need to say this, so please don't muddle me with more of your kisses yet."

"My kisses muddle you."

"Don't tease me either. My grandfather was very learned, and his passion was books. All kinds of books, even the naughty ones. To him, books were a kind of holy relic, standing against death, ignorance, war, despair. He gave his books away as quickly as he collected them, saying that books needed to be read and loved. My father was passionate about commerce. He adored seizing a business opportunity and making it thrive as your flowers flourish. He was generous with advice and would back an interesting venture the same way you'll cross two roses for the sheer curiosity of it."

Axel sat on the worktable, out of touching range, but precisely positioned for Abby's visual delectation. His blond hair was tousled, his cheeks slightly reddened by the cold, and he looked at home here. This was his classroom, his library, and his conservatory, all in one place.

Perhaps it might even be his boudoir, if a lady were enterprising enough.

He looked around, as if seeing the damp glass walls, the thriving roses, the worn rug for the first time.

"I love my roses. I love the mystery and beauty of them, their many medicinal properties, and even how fleeting their beauty is."

He'd never said those words aloud, probably never even thought them. Abby was so sure of this, she felt as if he'd given her another fragrant white bloom.

"Gregory was a caricature of an adult man," she replied. "He dawdled about, riding the same acres, kissing the same hounds, smoking the same pipes, year after year. When Sir Dewey took him shooting, I always felt better. I could think clearly, I could tend to the estate with more energy. My digestion settled, as much as it ever does."

She fell silent, though apparently today was a day for voicing previously unacknowledged sentiments.

"Abigail, you do realize Gregory swindled a fortune from you, not only your love of reading or your sketching?"

"I was an heiress, and he found lawyers willing to connive in his swindling."

"I suspect he forged your signature on a power of attorney. That goes beyond conniving to felonious behavior."

Victimhood reared its weepy, forlorn, powerless head. Again and probably not for the last time.

"I don't need that fortune, Axel. I have made Stoneleigh Manor into a thriving estate, I can live sumptuously on its proceeds. I would like answers though."

He pushed off the table. "You want to know where the money went. So do I, and I want to know who killed your—who killed Gregory Stoneleigh."

"I don't care about the money, but I care about the *why*. Gregory was one of Grandpapa's business associates, though I believe Grandpapa had sold him all but a few shares of the import business. Why did Gregory have to steal my entire inheritance? Why lie to me? Why not court me properly? He might have achieved the same result."

"No, he would not have." Axel turned one of the enormous clay plots sitting on the floor, one that held a small tree—and he turned it easily. "You have good judgment, Abigail, and you would have chosen Pettiflower over Stoneleigh, given half a chance. You were given no chance whatsoever."

He surveyed the tree, which now caught the light at a different angle.

You have good judgment…. You were given no chance whatsoever. From him, those words comforted.

"Were you planning to work in here this afternoon, Axel? I can ask Nick to take me over to Stoneleigh Manor."

His gaze as he studied the tree said that yes, he longed to spend hours among his roses, but his smile… oh, his smile was a rare, precious bloom.

"Nick is not the magistrate, so he has no authority for questioning Ambers and Shreve. I have promised you answers, and some of those answers lie at Stoneleigh Manor. To Stoneleigh Manor we shall go, after we've tended to sustenance."

With that, he kissed her. Truly, properly, wonderfully kissed her. "I dreamed of you too, Abigail. All the way into Oxford, all the way home, through bitter wind, on the snowy highway, while resisting the urge to thrash those lying scoundrels, I dreamed of you."

He put the key to the glass house in her hand and gestured her toward the door. The kiss, the key, the flowery words… in Abby's heart, springtime beckoned. After a long, miserable, lonely winter spent half asleep, ailing in spirit, and out of sorts, springtime finally beckoned.

* * *

Axel was reasonably certain that within the next three years, his glass houses could produce a rose without fully developed thorns, to much polite acclaim from his fellow rose enthusiasts.

Who would then smirk behind their brandies and mutter pityingly in their conservatories about Belmont's latest oddity.

Axel routinely cut the thorns from roses he took into the house. He could achieve in a few moments mechanically what years of experimentation might not yield. Success required more than a simple stripping of the rose's defenses, however.

And yet, the thornless rose within Axel's theoretical grasp would have no scent. Its blossoms would last less than a day once cut. They would be puny, and lack both color and a pleasing shape.

Riding over to Stoneleigh Manor, he sorted through his situation with Abby as he might have considered potential crosses.

Solving the murder was necessary, for the sake of duty and honor, but also so that Abigail would feel safe in her own home.

Parting with Abigail's company on any terms had grown problematic, and yet again, for her sake, creating a safe path to widowed independence was clearly what honor required.

Conducting a liaison across the property line bore the promise of obvious pleasures, but also great awkwardness. Did a fellow send a note, seeking the boon of afternoon tea on Tuesday, and hope for the favor of a reply? Did he live in anticipation of a visit from the object of his longings?

Did he boldly invite her to inspect his latest, robust pink blossom?

What about when that fellow removed to town for weeks at a time to wallow in academics and... celibacy? Why would Abigail—after years of marriage to a negligent, felonious, martinet—tolerate such an arrangement?

"You're very quiet," Abby said, over the crunch of horses' hooves on the snowy lane.

"My late wife often remarked on my propensity for quiet. Are you nervous, to be returning to Stoneleigh Manor?"

"Yes."

Axel hadn't wanted Abigail to pay this call, and yet, he knew she must.

"I will be on the premises with you at all times," he said. "If you experience the least frisson of unease, the slightest hint of a possibility of a worry, you scream, and I will charge hotfoot to your side. The tiniest spider, a glimpse of a mouse, a suspicious noise that turns out to be the pantry mouser above stairs, and I'll fly to you, brandishing my pistol before you can take your next breath."

Abigail turned her mare through the Stoneleigh gates, which still bore their swaths of crepe, though white snow had collected in the black folds and creases.

"I love it when you tease me, Professor."

Who was teasing? "I will interview Ambers in the colonel's study. You will gather up more clothing, or lecture the footmen, or do whatever you need to do. I'd also like to speak with Shreve."

"In the colonel's study? That's diabolical." Abigail apparently approved of diabolical.

"My brother Matthew suggested it by letter. He has much more experience in these matters."

Matthew had more experience in matters involving the ladies, who'd always found him charming, and he had more experience in matters of murder. Advice in either regard would have been welcome, but Axel had found the words to solicit Matthew's opinions regarding only the murder.

Ambers was not in evidence in the stables, so Axel escorted Abby around to the man's quarters, a tidy two-story cottage far more commodious than what Wheeler enjoyed. A maid answered the door, looking flustered to find both the magistrate and her employer on the stable master's front porch.

"Please send Mr. Ambers up to the manor at his earliest convenience," Abigail said. "And do set your cap on straight, Miller, lest Mrs. Jensen get to scolding."

The maid remained in the doorway, alternately dipping curtsies and gawping, while Abigail marched down the steps, Axel trailing behind her. When he linked arms with her to escort her across the garden, she came to a halt.

"I tell myself it's merely a house—*my* house now. Not a very pretty place, with all that black hanging about the windows."

"Black doesn't flatter you either," Axel said. "I'm glad you don't insist on full mourning when you're at Candlewick. You might consider putting in flower beds along the front walkway. Lavender borders work nicely where the drainage is good, heartsease does well in spring and autumn—"

She'd started walking, towing Axel along. Caroline had frequently ignored him when he'd begun on horticultural musings.

"I like delphinium," Abby said. "Your eyes are that blue, sometimes. When you kiss me."

"You've peeked? Abigail, I'm mortified." Also pleased.

Axel had peeked too, though apparently not at the same moments. He'd watched her face as pleasure overcame her, mentally compared the curve of her lashes against her cheek to the curve of a rose petal at full bloom. Desire echoed through him at the memory, despite the cold, despite his need to wring answers from Shreve and Ambers. "I was an utter virgin regarding kisses, Mr. Belmont. I suppose one doesn't peek?"

She'd been a virgin in other ways too—a virgin to shared pleasure—but had she been a virgin in the simplest sense of the word?

"Are we in a hurry, Abigail?" For the idea that Stoneleigh hadn't consummated the marriage *in any sense* made Axel want to stop, stand still, and simply ponder.

"I want to be done with this, Axel, but every step we take closer to that house, the more angry I grow. I can still hear him: *A lady doesn't call attention to herself. A lady is modest at all times. A lady never seeks to put herself or her own needs forward, but thinks always of others.* Gregory said a shop girl trying to masquerade as gentry must be grateful for a little well-intended guidance."

"You married a right bastard, Abigail. A true gentleman does not presume to correct a lady." Or use foul language before a lady.

"I do so enjoy your facility for honesty. Let's get this over with."

Axel led her up the steps, which some fool had neglected to shovel free of snow, and opened the door for her. She swept through, sparing the black-clad knocker not a single glance.

The foyer was deserted—no butler, porter, or footman to be seen.

"I was right to do this," Abby said, untying the black ribbons beneath her chin. "The staff is not dealing well with Gregory's passing, and they need to know I haven't forgotten them."

The mirror over the sideboard was sashed with black, also finely coated with dust. Axel resisted the urge to assist the lady out of her cloak, though he did hang it on a peg for her before seeing to his greatcoat.

"I sent no warning of our impending visit." Matthew had advised that a sneak attack yielded more productive interviews. "You might find the servants gambling for farthing points over a tipsy hand of whist below stairs."

"Which I, of all people, do not begrudge them. I want to start sorting through Gregory's belongings, and ridding the house of as much of it as I can. If I recall the reading of the will, there were specific bequests. Ambers was to have Gregory's collection of pipes, Shreve his snuff boxes. First, I want to see the study."

"To whom did he leave his weaponry?" The whereabouts of the household firearms mattered when a lady was feeling insecure. Other than the relics on display in the library, Axel couldn't recall a gun cabinet on the premises.

"Gregory owned only small arms," Abby said, running a finger through the dust on the mirror, "and those mostly left over from his cavalry days. The fowling pieces in the library are merely for display."

"What about when he went shooting? Did he use Sir Dewey's firearms?" Matthew claimed that guns had quirks and characteristics, and successful hunting usually required knowledge of a specific firearm.

"I don't know." She cast a glance down the corridor, from which no helpful footman or housekeeper emerged.

"Shall I go with you, Abigail?"

"No, thank you. In my own home, among my own staff, I should be comfortable enough. Perhaps you might alert the servants that company—that *the owner* is on the premises?"

Emotion quivered through her voice. Anger, very likely, possibly fear beneath that, and maybe, far below the reach of conscious thought, excitement at the prospect of turning this oversized hunting lodge back into a gracious country estate.

They were alone, and Axel knew not what to say that would fortify her against those conflicting sentiments. He lifted her hand and pressed a kiss to her cold knuckles.

"All you need do is scream. One good cry of dismay, a shout will do. I'll be down that corridor like a hawk on a field mouse."

"A lady never creates needless drama." Abby kissed him on the lips—a right smacker that promised woe unto the man who protesteth such familiarities under the lady's own roof—and then she marched off toward the study.

Not five minutes later, Axel interrupted a rousing argument over late-morning tea in the servants' parlor. He'd climbed halfway up the footmen's stairs when a terrified scream rent the air.

CHAPTER TWELVE

Axel was down the corridor faster than a plummeting hawk, his arms around a distraught Abigail.

"Gun," she panted, gaze fixed on the open door to the study. "He has a gun. A man, in there—" She waved toward the study, her whole body trembling. "There's a safe, and a gun, and you can't go—"

"You lot," Axel barked at the servants assembling at the top of the steps. "See to Mrs. Stoneleigh."

He thrust Abby in Mrs. Jensen's direction, stole a look into the study, then strode in, swiped the gun off the sideboard and set it on the desk.

"You wait right there," he instructed Shreve, who looked ready to wet himself, "or I'll arrest you before you twitch in the direction of the door."

Shreve had given Abigail an awful fright, and for that alone, he should be arrested, questions of murder and thievery aside. Axel went back to the corridor, where servants in various stages of unliveried dishabille remained gawking.

"Mrs. Stoneleigh was understandably upset to find an unexpected situation at the scene of her husband's demise," Axel said. "You may return below stairs."

The lot of them remained unmoving.

"You may return below stairs *now*."

"Please do as Mr. Belmont asks," Abby said. "Thank you all for coming to my aid."

Mrs. Jensen, a formidable, aging blonde with a hint of pumpernickel in her speech, drew herself up.

"I can remain, if madam would like."

The footmen, maids, and assorted others were clearly willing to remain as well. *Now* they showed loyalty to their mistress?

"I was simply startled, and I'd forgotten today was half day," Abby said.

"Mr. Belmont will summon help if it's needed. Before I leave the premises, I'll impose on Mrs. Jensen for a chat."

"Of course, madam." The housekeeper cast Axel a sniffy glance, then herded her charges in the direction of the stairs.

"I'm fine," Abby said when her staff had departed. "That's Shreve in the study?"

She sounded fine, but she was adept at *sounding fine*. She was once again the pale, self-contained creature Axel had encountered the night of the murder.

"Shreve has swooned by now," Axel said. "The damned nerve of the man, giving you a fright like that. You'll assist with this interview, if you're up to joining me in there. All you need do is look bereaved and affronted, which one supposes you are, though you should also ask any questions that come to mind."

He held out a hand, a presumption—a hopeful presumption, because he needed to touch her.

Abby studied his outstretched palm as if it held a blue and purple rose. "You want *me* to ask Shreve questions?"

"Of course." Involving her in the interrogation was the only reasonable means of keeping her by Axel's side. "That was a fine specimen of a scream, Abigail."

She grasped his hand. "I've been saving up, apparently."

They lady preceded Axel into the study, head held high. "Shreve, you have a deal of explaining to do. Mr. Belmont is by nature a patient and fair man, but the circumstances are most troubling. Set aside any notion you harbor of dissembling, or the gallows could await you."

"M-madam." Shreve bowed. "Of course, m-madam."

"Mrs. Stoneleigh, perhaps you'd like to have a seat?" Axel gestured to the desk at which Stoneleigh had died. Abby settled herself behind it with all the aplomb of a judge taking the bench.

Shreve remained by the side board, a wall safe gaping open behind him.

"What's this?" Abby moved the gun aside and peered at a sheet of vellum. "You intended to leave the colonel's employ?"

Axel locked the French doors—lest Shreve think to take the fresh Oxfordshire air of a sudden—then accepted the paper from Abby.

"The date is nearly two weeks before the colonel's death," Axel said. "What were you about, Shreve?"

Shreve cleared his throat and put his hands behind his back. He resembled one of Axel's university scholars preparing to launch into a lengthy, articulate recitation about a reading assignment the boy hadn't so much as glanced at.

Abby ran a pale finger around the nacre inlay on the gun's handle. "Mr. Belmont is patient and fair, while I am newly bereaved, and reputed by all and sundry to be nervous and given to dramatics."

"I respectfully beg madam's leave to disagree," Shreve said, rocking forward. "At every turn, we tell those fools at the Weasel that you are the steadiest, kindest, most reasonable mistress, that you are the soul of solicitude and understanding, and—"

"And thus your protestations reinforce their every suspicion to the contrary," Axel said. "Put your coat on in the presence of a lady, Shreve. Why did you give notice?"

Abigail had latent talent as a thespian, for she aimed the gun in the direction of the French doors and sighted down the barrel, while Shreve fumbled into his jacket.

"The colonel was growing difficult," Shreve said, when he'd buttoned up with shaking fingers. "Increasingly difficult, and I am not the only staff member to remark this. I'm two years beyond the age at which the colonel had told me I might have my pension, and thus I felt justified in stepping back from my post."

Plausible. Abby confirmed that much with a glance, and set the gun down. "Why do you suppose the colonel was becoming difficult?"

"Advancing years? Too much time in the tropical sun as a younger man? His temper was growing shorter, he was forgetful but wouldn't acknowledge it, and he... One doesn't want to speak ill of the departed."

Abby resumed her perusal of Shreve's letter of resignation. "Does one want to hang by the neck until dead for a murder one didn't commit?"

Axel had no evidence to tie Shreve directly to the murder, and Shreve had no apparent motive. The butler had also had so much opportunity over the years, that for him to have killed Stoneleigh in the middle of a full house and by means of a loud gunshot made no sense at all.

Nonetheless, Shreve sagged, bracing himself with a hand on the sideboard. "The colonel had begun throwing things. His snuff boxes, even his pipes."

Abby set the paper aside, as if it had developed a rank odor. "He loved those dratted pipes. The lot of them are willed to Ambers. The snuff boxes were to be yours."

Were to be... before Shreve had been caught in the grip of felonious impulses.

"I was not stealing, madam. Please believe me. I simply had not been able to locate the combination until today—half days come only once a week, you know—and I wanted you to decide what to do with the safe's contents if I could get it open."

Axel believed him, up to a point. A man who'd serve for many uncomplaining years beneath the heel of an arrogant martinet hadn't the daring necessary for theft. Such a man would, though, be motivated to retrieve his letter of resignation from the safe if he hadn't found it in more predictable locations first.

"The colonel died a good month ago," Axel said. "It took you that long to open the safe?"

"I could not find the combination, Mr. Belmont. I fault myself for that, but I could look for it only during the odd hour on the odd day, and I was growing desperate. Mrs. Stoneleigh's health is reported to be improving, and we hoped she might return to us here. Once that happened, I'd have little opportunity to retrieve—to open the safe."

"To retrieve your letter of resignation," Abby said, "because you wouldn't mind working for me in the colonel's absence."

Shreve had the sense to remain silent.

"Where was the combination?" Axel asked.

"Under the colonel's blotter."

"I looked under the blotter the night of the murder. Nothing there." Axel had rifled the entire desk, sorting through papers, two pouches of tobacco, pipe paraphernalia, old letters, and other orts and leavings of a man's life.

"I do apologize, sir. I meant, on the under*side* of the blotter. Once or twice when I delivered the colonel his nightcap, I caught him writing on the underside of the blotter. Most odd, but I'd forgot about it until the, um, present situation arose."

Timid, sensible, and diplomatic. "How long have you known about this safe?"

"The colonel said he'd had security measures installed prior to taking possession of the estate," Shreve replied. "On the subcontinent, one typically had a safe or two, for obvious reasons. Unrest was lamentably common."

"So you've known about this safe all along," Axel said, "and you kept the information from the magistrate investigating Stoneleigh's murder—a murder that took place in the very same room as the safe?"

"Mr. Belmont, I mean you no disrespect," Shreve said, "but Stoneleigh Manor belongs to Mrs. Stoneleigh now. Should the contents of the safe devolve to the discredit of madam's deceased spouse, then it is for her alone to say how relevant those contents are to your investigation."

"A lovely sentiment," Abigail said, "though woefully self-serving, Shreve. Mr. Belmont, I will leave you to examine the contents of the safe, your discretion being utterly trustworthy."

She rose, while Axel resisted the urge to applaud her performance.

Shreve bowed. "My resignation is, of course, yours to accept, madam."

"I'm sure Mr. Belmont will have more questions for you, Shreve. Your fate lies in his capable hands."

Abby moved toward the door, leaving the letter of resignation tucked under the gun on a corner of the desk, and the etched blotter wrong side up, like an unearthed rune stone.

"I'll be in Gregory's suite, Mr. Belmont."

Not by yourself, you won't. "Would you object to the company of footmen while you're about your tasks there?" Axel asked.

He did not dare order this woman to do anything, and his pleading skills were lamentably rusty.

"I'll need assistance if I'm to box up the colonel's belongings for the poor. Shreve might help as well, assuming he remains at liberty."

Shreve nearly collapsed against the sideboard, while Abby made her exit.

"You'll not hang," Axel said. "Not for murder, but bear in mind we have more than two hundred capital offenses here in Merry Old England. Why didn't you tell Mrs. Stoneleigh about the safe when you had the chance? She bided here for a fortnight after the colonel's death, and you were the fellow who suggested she be removed from the premises."

A suggestion Axel had been reluctant to heed... at the time.

"I was honest with you then, Mr. Belmont, and I shall be honest with you now," Shreve said, straightening. "Madam was not doing well. She hadn't been doing well for some months. Mrs. Jensen saw madam nearly faint any number of times. The chambermaids saw evidence of a bilious stomach. We considered that Mrs. Stoneleigh's poor health was one of the factors weighing on the colonel's disposition, in fact."

Abby had been tired, pale, and underweight when she'd arrived at Candlewick. Weak, not precisely ill.

"What were her symptoms?"

"One doesn't want to be indelicate."

Axel took the place Abby had vacated behind the desk. He let silence build, one of Matthew's first recommendations for conducting a proper interrogation. Silence was the best friend of the king's man, and Axel had a talent for holding his peace, as it happened.

"Madam appeared to occasionally suffer the bloody flux," Shreve expostulated, blushing furiously. "She was losing her appetite. We feared a wasting disease, but the colonel was not fond of physicians, and one hesitated to speak up."

Lest one be pelted with a snuff box and turned off without a character. What a charmer Stoneleigh had been behind the walls of his own castle.

The back of the blotter was covered with tiny, nearly indecipherable figures in tidy columns. In the right-hand corner were two rows of digits separated by dashes.

"Did the colonel even know of his wife's ailment?"

"One cannot be sure. The colonel and Mrs. Stoneleigh had separate chambers, though to be fair, the colonel was generally solicitous of his wife's well-being. He fixed her tea at breakfast, he never smoked in her presence, he tolerated no disrespect of her among the staff, not that we would have disrespected her."

Oh, a damned knight in hunting pinks, was old Gregory. "This is the combination to the safe?" Axel asked, pointing to the top row of figures.

"Indeed. I had some difficulty determining the proper directions, but it's right-left-right-left, like a platoon embarking on a parade march."

"Then what's this second row of figures?"

"I've assumed those are the combination to the second safe."

"What second safe?"

* * *

Had Axel Belmont not been on the premises, Abby would still be in the corridor outside the study, shaking with fear. She might have had a heart seizure, she'd been so terrified.

What remained was rage—a great, undifferentiated mass of rage aimed at Gregory Stoneleigh, whose perfidy expanded the longer he was dead.

Beside the rage, choking it tight at the roots, was, incongruously, gratitude.

Axel Belmont *had* been on the premises, only a scream away, and had insisted on accompanying Abby on this errand. His arms around her had made safety real and trustworthy in the space of a moment. She would find the words to convey her gratitude to him, and his dignity would simply have to endure her honesty.

For now, she needed to begin evicting Gregory's ghost from her house.

"We'll need boxes," she told Jeffries, the head footman. "The staff gets first crack at the colonel's clothing, then everything remaining can go to the church. The same with the boots and shoes and shirts and... all of it."

Gregory's chambers still bore the sweet, tobacco stink of his pipes, so Abby had opened a window. Now the air was cold, still cloyingly acrid, but the fresh breeze kept her from being sick.

Jeffries was an attractive blond fellow above middling height, though he and Abby had typically communicated through Shreve. He shifted from foot to foot, refusing to meet Abby's gaze.

"What?" Abby asked, pausing in her peregrinations around Gregory's bedroom.

"The colonel wore London tailoring, ma'am," Jeffries said, maintaining his position near the door. "Fine workmanship, excellent cloth."

The second footman, another tall, handsome specimen, this one named Heath, ventured to speak without being addressed.

"Much of it's quite new, Mrs. Stoneleigh. Quite... new."

They were trying to tell her something, and not simply that they'd had a look inside Gregory's wardrobe.

"The lot of it is also quite odoriferous," Abby said. "I can wear none of it, and Mr. Stoneleigh's immortal soul might benefit from charitable dispersal of his effects. You two look to be nearly the same height as the colonel."

Heath shot a desperate glance at his superior.

"Nobody would think the worse of you if the clothing were sold, ma'am,"

Jeffries said. "Fetch a pretty penny too, and who can't use some extra coin?"

Abby's first thought was that they were worried about the solvency of the estate that employed them, but in the next instant, gazing at two earnest expressions, revelation struck.

They were concerned *for her.*

"Gentlemen, Stoneleigh Manor is on quite solid footing." Abby spoke the truth, thanks to a shop girl's mercantile instincts and her willingness to work hard. "I'm selling off the hounds and horses because I don't care for fox-hunting, not because we can't bear the expense. I'm parting with the books in the library because they reek. I'm selling the display of guns and knives because they were purely ornamental."

Also downright ugly.

"Now, when the hunt season will soon draw to a close," she went on, "is the time to reduce the size of the stables. Your positions are secure. Please convey the same sentiment to the rest of the staff."

Relief filled Jeffries' eyes, while Heath went so far as to smile. "Will do, missus. Shall I fetch those boxes?"

Abby might have said yes, except Axel had asked her to keep the footmen near. Asked her, not ordered, not assumed, not demanded.

"The boxes can wait, but everything in this room will go either to charity or to the staff. The bed hangings will stink for years, the carpets as well, even if we beat them daily for a month. As if the pipes weren't bad enough, I also detect the odor of canines. One despairs of these rooms ever being habitable."

And yet, they had the best view of the pastures and the home wood.

"Might I suggest incense?" Jeffries said. "My brother works for Sir Dewey, and sandalwood is frequently burned in Sir Dewey's library on the theory that it helps deter creeping damp."

They were deep in a discussion of how best to air out Gregory's rooms when Shreve appeared in the doorway, looking, small, old, and anxious.

"Mr. Belmont has bid me to make my farewell to you, Mrs. Stoneleigh. He suggests I pay an extended visit to my sister in East Anglia, provided you accept my resignation."

The footmen's expressions went blank, while Abby's relief was enormous.

"I'm sure you miss your sister very much," she said. "And you can't depart until we've packed up Mr. Stoneleigh's snuff boxes for you to take along. You'll want to make your farewells at the Weasel and in the churchyard, and choose a departure day when the weather bids fair."

She could say that, because when her errands at Stoneleigh Manor were complete, she'd return to Candlewick. She would not have to face Shreve's sad gaze after today.

"Madam is most generous, but the snuff boxes... I've never taken snuff."

The snuff boxes were valuable, about half of them inlaid with semi-precious stones commonly found in India. The bequest in addition to a pension might be considered extravagant by some.

Extravagant, or intended to buy silence.

Abby never wanted to lay eyes on a snuff box again. "We will make a list of the colonel's personal effects—cuff-links, cravat pins, watches, anything of value in this room. The staff will each choose items from the list, one at a time, until nothing remains. The snuff boxes will be yours, Shreve. Ambers will have the pipes, but the rest will be shared among the entire staff, right down to the boot boy and the tweenie, as... as mementos of the colonel's regard for those who served him loyally."

Oxford probably had more pawnshops than London, Portsmouth, Yorkshire, and Brighton combined. When Abby considered the cracked hand mirror in her bedroom, she could think of no more fitting fate for Gregory's little treasures. The staff would know how to get good coin for them too.

"Madam is most, exceedingly generous," Shreve said, bowing. "I will take my leave, with heartfelt thanks, and unending wishes for madam's continued well-being."

He was doubtless off to relay the news of this windfall below stairs, but Abby had had a taste of interrogation and wasn't about to let him go that easily.

"You can accompany me to the housekeeper's sitting room," she said, "and answer a few more questions along the way. Jeffries, Heath, you will begin the inventory of the colonel's effects, find boxes for anything the staff doesn't want, and for heaven's sake, open the balcony doors and the rest of the windows. Airing these rooms will take an eternity."

She left the footmen to their tasks, and preceded Shreve to the head of the main stairs.

"First question, Shreve: Was there anything else you did not share with Mr. Belmont that you wished to impart to me first?"

They were alone, Shreve was in Abby's debt, he'd been given leave to flee the scene, and he had no motivation to lie. Still, he glanced about, as if the portraits had ears, or as if he'd promised himself that this question—*if asked*—he'd answer honestly.

"Madam should put the same inquiry to Mr. Ambers."

Ambers had been very much Gregory's creature. Abby crossed her arms. Shreve blushed a shade that would become one of Axel's more robust roses.

"Madam might ask Ambers where the colonel went," Shreve said, "the first Wednesday of every month, without fail."

A mistress? "Where do you suppose he went?"

"Oxford, based on the length of the appointment. If the colonel was unable to go, Ambers went alone."

If Gregory went on horseback, Ambers would go to attend the horses, presumably.

"Why would Ambers go alone?"

Shreve looked as if he'd prefer to hurl himself down the staircase. "Perhaps to pay for the other party's time?"

A mistress, then—may heaven keep the woman, whoever she was—but why hire a mistress when a young, all-too-accommodating wife resided on the premises?

"Anything else?"

"No, madam. If I do think of something, might I presume to write to you?"

The look in his faded blue eyes was a shock. Hopeful, worshipful even. Abby was abruptly glad he'd be removing to East Anglia, for such devotion might, indeed, have motivated murder.

"You're better off writing to Mr. Belmont regarding particulars of the colonel's death, though I hope you'll send along a note at the holidays and assure me of your continued happy retirement."

Shreve brightened. "Certainly, madam. Yuletide greetings by post are a fine old English custom."

Well no, they were not, not that Abby knew of.

He followed her down the stairs, rather like one of the hounds Abby had evicted from the manor the day after Gregory's death. To her great relief, Axel was coming up from the kitchen as she would have gone below stairs to chat with Mrs. Jensen.

"Shreve, if you'd have Mrs. Jensen meet me in my office, please?" Abby asked. "And safe journey. My thanks for your years of service to the colonel... and to me."

Shreve bowed so low as to expose the very top of his shining, pink head, then took himself off.

"Damned if he isn't smitten with you," Axel muttered. "Matthew warned me there's no predicting the course of an investigation."

"Shreve can be smitten in East Anglia," Abby said, mentally stripping the walls of Gregory's blasted hunt scenes. "We'll manage without a butler henceforth, or I can promote Jeffries to the position. While you interview Ambers, I'll speak with Mrs. Jensen. The house is falling into a state, which will not do. Before one embarks on a redecoration, a house must be at least clean."

Something she'd said had Axel smiling with his eyes, while his mouth remained a solemn, straight line.

"Don't you want to know what was in the safe, Abigail?"

"I'm sure you have that all in hand, Mr. Belmont, though please ask Ambers where the colonel went the first Wednesday of every month without fail. If the colonel could not attend this errand, Ambers went in his stead. Shreve's guess is Ambers went to pay for 'the other party's time.'"

Axel took her by the arm and escorted her—rather hurriedly—into the second parlor. The room was Abby's favorite of the public chambers, all green and cream, soft velvets and framed cutwork, though today it was also chilly.

"What's different about this room?" Axel asked, closing the door.

"The air doesn't stink, for one thing. I redecorated it, for another. I asked Gregory's permission, and he refused me. By then I'd been married well over a year, and I'd realized my husband had little patience for details. I presented him my monthly ledgers, which always balanced to the penny, and Gregory had no idea that instead of potatoes, I'd bought a few pounds' worth of fabric."

"Resourceful," Axel said. "Resilient, and talented with a needle. Is that your cutwork?"

"I did that the first time Gregory went shooting in Yorkshire with Sir Dewey."

Axel studied the frame, one of the many treasures Abby claimed to have "found in the attics."

"Chestnut wood has a beautiful grain," he said, "but Abigail, when did you plan to tell me that Gregory was poisoning you?"

CHAPTER THIRTEEN

Abigail sank like dropped fruit onto an elegant little green chair by the cold hearth.

"Poisoning me?" The words came out in a whisper while her right hand went to her middle. Her left gripped the side of the chair, as if her seat might slide out from under her otherwise.

"You had no suspicion?" Axel asked. "Not the least inkling?"

She shook her head, while Axel wanted to kick something.

"I might be wrong, Abigail." Except he wasn't. He'd questioned Mrs. Jensen, who as housekeeper was also the first defense at Stoneleigh Manor against illness.

She'd confirmed Shreve's assertion that Abby had suffered bouts of severe bowel trouble, along with a waning appetite, lack of energy, increasing pallor, and occasional faintness. Peppermint tea had become Abby's choice unless the colonel would be served from the same pot.

"He had no opportunity to poison me," Abby said. "We took breakfast and dinner together, usually. Sometimes luncheon as well. We ate the same foods, more or less, though of course not from the same plates."

"Those meals *were* his opportunities, Abigail. Shreve said the colonel often fixed your tea."

She wrinkled her nose. "And never got it right. A dash of sugar, I told him, over and over, and invariably, he'd heap sugar into each cup, then stand over me, smiling, until I had no choice but to——"

"But to consume poison. Your health doubtless improved when he went off shooting. Did the colonel ever suggest you use arsenic to maintain a pale complexion?"

She jerked to her feet, the movement putting Axel in mind of the night of the murder.

"No, he did not. Cosmetics were for vain women, in his estimation. I'd enjoyed good health until this past year. My spirits always improved when Gregory traveled, and when he came back from Melton last spring, I was predictably… dispirited. Over the summer, my mood did not improve. I began to have problems."

Not arsenic then, or not undiluted arsenic, thank God. Gregory had chosen a slow poison, and those were the least effective. Had Abby's symptoms comported with known botanical toxins Axel might have suspected something sooner, but lethal plants tended to kill quickly and with dramatic effect.

"How do you feel now?" For what mattered to Axel most—even more than finding Stoneleigh's killer—was that Abby live to enjoy her widowhood, that she be well and happy and whole.

She looked around the room, her first successful rebellion against her husband's tyranny.

"I feel tired much of the time, and as if I'm observing myself live a life I'd never planned. Foggy, forgetful, little appetite, though my outlook and my health seem to be improving the longer I'm widowed."

Normal grief there—Axel hoped—and an indication that whatever poison had been attempted, Abby was recovering rapidly.

"Any other physical symptoms?"

She took down the cutwork and used a corner of the draperies to dust the glass and frame.

"My appetite is coming back. I'd attributed that to your scolding and your cook's skill, but my own cook has no lack of ability. I was simply… not well."

Cutwork required using a tiny pair of scissors to nibble and snip away at folded paper, until what resulted was more light and air than paper. Axel wanted to pitch Abby's little creation against the hearthstones and wrap her in his arms for the next year. The colonel had been snipping away at Abby, at her health, her spirits, her very life, and the contents of the safe had revealed his motive for doing so.

Axel took the seat she'd vacated, a ridiculous little perch for a man his size.

"When was the last time Gregory spent the entirety of a hunt season here at Stoneleigh Manor?"

"Not until this year, not as long as we'd been married. I'd hoped he'd go north for the shooting as August approached, but no luck. I assumed Sir Dewey had refused to accompany him, or perhaps Gregory had tired of all that haring about. Gregory made a few trips to London, but he was never gone for more than a fortnight."

During which brief intervals, Abby's abused body would have struggled to recover from weeks of poison.

She rehung her cutwork, adjusting the frame exactly plumb.

Axel wanted to thank the person who'd killed Gregory Stoneleigh, also to break something. He fell back instead on his classroom skills.

"I've a few suggestions, Abigail, if you will tolerate a small lecture?"

"Very small. Violent hysterics have become an attractive possibility, Mr. Belmont."

Axel rose and studied the painting over the mantel, when he wanted instead to take Abby in his arms.

"I've found that in matters of plant toxicity, the body often knows what antidotes are most appropriate. Though your health does appear to be improving, if you crave peppermint, swill peppermint tea without limit. If an odd preference for ginger marmalade befalls you, have it at every meal. Trust your gustatory instincts, and you might come right very quickly."

Abby wrapped her arms around him, which helped... a little. "I've been sleeping much more at Candlewick than I ever did here. Sleeping better too."

Dreaming even. Axel took comfort from that. "Our investigation has grown more complicated, Abigail. Matthew says that's an encouraging sign."

"You're not encouraged. You miss your roses." She withdrew and took a seat on the green velvet sofa, though her black velvet skirts against the green sofa was a jarring combination. "I'm sorry, Axel. I wish Shreve had presented you with a signed confession, and you could leave me here, tossing Gregory's effects and ripping his damned hunt scenes from the walls."

She was *sorry*; Axel was damned glad she was alive, but those words would not aid her to regain her composure.

"You chose the art in here?" Over the sideboard hung a still life of polished red apples in a green crockery bowl with a sheaf of yellow chrysanthemums in the foreground. Above the fireplace in a simple wood frame, a cat napped on a hearthrug near a wicker knitting basket, a fire blazing in the background.

"I conspired with Lavinia. I chose the art in Oxford, had the paintings sent to her from the shops, then had her send them here as examples of her work. Gregory could not deny me the right to display them. He even took one of my selections to hang in the alcove outside his apartments—another portrait of a napping cat, of all things. I'm very fond of the hydrangeas that hang in my office. I cannot believe my own husband..."

She trailed off, her gaze going to the cat above the mantel. Abby's choice of art had been prosaic, comforting, and well-executed. As rebellions went, the paintings were a brilliant place to start, though the parlor was as yet dusty, cold, and unused.

And Axel needed to be away from this place where yet more of Gregory Stoneleigh's evil had come to light.

"You have a conservatory," he said. "Suppose you show it to me."

"Hadn't we better spend the time questioning Ambers? I'd like to know where Gregory went on those regular appointments."

She'd probably like to establish a pension for any woman who'd spared her Gregory's attentions, and doubtless Ambers was waiting at that moment in the servants' hall for Axel's summons.

But Matthew had said that haste was the enemy of a successful investigation, and Axel needed to consider what he'd learned over the past two hours.

Questioning Ambers again could wait one more day. "A conservatory can take years to put to rights, Abigail. Best let me have a look now. We haven't much more light."

And Axel didn't want to put her through another upsetting interview with a servant. Let Ambers leave the shire or worry himself into a confession, if a confession there was to make.

Which Axel doubted. Again, Ambers had no obvious motive, and years upon years of much better opportunity than late one January night in the colonel's own home, drat the luck.

The conservatory was a cavernous waste of cold, damp, and poorly sealed glass, an altogether dreary place at the back of the house. Most estates would fill their conservatories over the winter months—conserving delicate species in cold weather being the intended use of same. Save for a few potted ferns and an anemic banyan tree, the Stoneleigh conservatory was empty.

Not a rose, not a damned pansy, to be seen.

"I'll make you some sketches," Axel said. "A deal of work is needed to set this place to rights."

In the gathering gloom of an advancing winter afternoon, a shadow passed through Abigail's eyes. Axel had said something amiss, or she'd recalled the latest of the revelations resulting from Stoneleigh's murder.

Axel paced away from her, lest he wrap her in his arms and never let go. "You think somebody killed the colonel to protect you?"

"Shreve was smitten, you said as much."

"Shreve did not kill Stoneleigh." Axel was not quite as confident of this conclusion as made himself sound. "Shreve had years to end the colonel's life. He could have slipped a sleeping powder into the colonel's brandy then held a pillow over his employer's face, nobody the wiser. He could have added a fast poison to his hunting flask. I've heard of poisons from the Amazonian jungles that will drop a man in his tracks with a single dose. Shreve spent years in India, where he would have been exposed to all manner of exotic violence and strange potions."

Abby gently untangled fern fronds, creating a mess of disintegrating leaves on the conservatory floor.

"You acquit Shreve not on the basis of motive, but because he had too much opportunity and did not avail himself of it, but I became unwell only in the past half year."

Axel turned her by the shoulders. "I vow I will solve these puzzles. I will not rest until I find you the answers you need to feel safe in your own home. I promise you this, Abigail."

She slipped her arms around his waist and leaned into him, and while she felt lovely and warm in Axel's embrace, her silence suggested he'd yet again said something wrong.

* * *

Was it wrong to wish Axel Belmont's version of solving a lady's problems did not also involve a vow to return her to her own property? Not simply assurances, or casual promises, but a *vow*?

Abby pondered that question as her mare plodded back to Candlewick, side by side with Ivan.

"You're quiet, Abigail," Axel said. "Shall I tell you what was in the safe?"

Bother the safe, which had appeared to hold nothing more than a gun, papers, and ledgers. Abby wanted to push Professor Magistrate out of the saddle and into the snow, there to commence kissing him witless until spring.

She was upset of course, to have learned that Gregory had been trying to kill her—*kill* her—but she was also confident that her health was returning. Like one of the professor's roses, proper attention was putting her quickly to rights.

Axel Belmont missed his roses; Abby would miss Axel Belmont. "What was in the safe?"

"Some answers, and more questions."

"The usual, then."

"I've wondered where the colonel's funds came from. Traveling in comfort is not cheap, purchasing a stable full of prime hunters, maintaining a large kennel, kitting oneself out in London finery season after season... Stoneleigh treated himself to a very gentlemanly lifestyle, and yet, the import business, from what Gervaise has written, showed only a modest profit. Brandenburg kept scrupulous records, and as long as that fellow was extant, the import records were all maintained in order."

"Have you found my family's fortune?"

"I found accountings from three different Oxford banks, Abigail. Your cash reserves have increased... enormously." Axel named a figure that, like much in recent days, Abby could not entirely comprehend.

"I'm back to being an heiress."

"You are an independent woman of substantial means, one of the rarest blooms in the English garden."

Not necessarily one of the happiest, considering how she'd come by her wealth.

"Could this money be proceeds from the import business?" Gervaise was due the entire sum, if so.

"The import business accounts are in London, and Gregory's will included a 'rest, residue, and remainder' clause, meaning anything not specifically bequeathed to another party was left to you. The sum documented in that safe is too great to have been accumulated importing peacock feathers and jade paperweights."

The horses turned up the Candlewick drive. The manor house sat a quarter mile away, a lamp already burning on a post near the mounting block. No black crepe, no knocker swathed in black… No tainted memories of a marriage based on evil and greed.

"Next," Abby said, "you will tell me of a labyrinth of darkened passages beneath Stoneleigh Manor leading to a smuggler's cave or pirate treasure."

"I dare not answer that, despite Oxfordshire's landlocked position, when we have no idea where the second safe is nor what its contents might be. What we've learned today is that you've had a near miss, assuming your health continues to improve."

He would speak of this, for which Abby was both grateful and… not.

"A person using slow poison has to be willing to watch their victim die by inches," she said, because Axel would not put that into words. "But what if we're wrong? What if I was simply enduring a bout of ill health?"

Her question was met with silence, broken only by the sound of the horses crunching along the drive in the direction of the stables. The sun was all but gone, the world had turned to the frigid blue-gray twilight found only in deepest, snowy winter.

When they reached the stable yard, Abby nearly slid off her horse straight into the snow, so great was her fatigue. Axel caught her in his arms and held her in the space between the horses.

"I'll find the truth," he said, kissing her cheek.

Abby rested her forehead on his shoulder. "You can find every answer there is, Axel, and nothing you discover will make me want to set foot on that property again. I nearly died there. I was… growing more ill by the week, bleeding from the wrong places, unable to sleep, losing flesh. Gregory said I mustn't seek attention for common female ailments or overindulge a nervous tendency. These little indispositions pass…"

She was beyond tears, beyond even hatred, though not beyond fear. Axel's scent soothed her. His scent and his simple, generous embrace.

"Be patient," he said. "You're like a soldier who's survived a bitter battle. The artillery has fallen silent, the cavalry charge is over, the infantry has done its worst. You're still standing, but as you absorb the devastation around you, and learn of one friend after another taken by the enemy, your well-being is embattled all over again. Time helps, and that you have."

For a man who lacked flowery speeches, Axel Belmont sometimes had the right words nonetheless.

Abby gave herself one more moment to borrow his strength, lean against him, and be comforted by his nearness, and then made herself stand back.

"A toddy in the library appeals," she said. "And perhaps a tray in my room. I didn't make much progress with Grandpapa's journal last night, and I don't think I'd make good company at dinner."

"Come," Axel said, flipping Ivan's reins over the horse's head and doing the same with Abby's mare. "I can't think where Wheeler has got off to, but we'll find somebody to put up the horses, and get you that—"

He'd started leading the horses into the stable, but came to a halt at the sight of a substantial gray gelding in the cross-ties.

"That is Hermes. By God, I'd know that handsome rump anywhere, and that is my brother's favorite mount to the life."

* * *

"Has Nick come back from town?" Matthew Belmont asked when Axel had returned from lighting the pretty widow up to bed.

The pretty widow who'd apparently turned an increasingly unsocial academic botanist into a surprisingly attentive host, if Axel's behavior at dinner was any indication. For his younger brother's sake, Matthew was pleased.

Axel went straight to the sideboard and poured two neat brandies. "Nick will likely spend the night in Oxford, renewing old acquaintances as it were."

Corrupting Matthew's sons in the process, no doubt. Ah, well, what was university for? Matthew had decided to tarry first at Candlewick rather than surprise the boys with a visit.

"I could have sworn I heard the front door closing," Matthew said. Through the library windows, he'd also seen Axel, hatless and coatless, staring into the darkness beyond the lamps illuminating Candlewick's front terrace.

"The front door did close." Axel brought Matthew a drink. "I was taking a bit of air, admiring the night sky."

Matthew tried a sip of his drink rather than comment. The closer he'd ridden to Candlewick, the lower the clouds had descended, until only a thin band of light had remained to the west. The sunset had been spectacular, but no stars would be visible in the night sky.

The wintry air would subdue a man's… unruly imagination readily enough.

"You should marry her." Matthew settled back on the sofa as Axel came down beside him.

"Marry? Abigail?" Axel sounded as if Matthew had suggested crossing a potato with an orange.

"Of course, Abigail." Mrs. Stoneleigh, to her neighbors. Her *other* neighbors.

Axel set his drink on the end table, beside a porcelain vase holding a single white rose.

"The lady and I are not that well acquainted, Matthew."

The professor was a terrible liar, always had been. "You were an awfully long time lighting her candles."

"Shut your mouth. We exchanged a few pleasantries, is all. Abigail's day was exceedingly trying, and her health remains delicate."

Kissing could be very pleasant. Theresa had suggested Matthew investigate the situation in Oxfordshire—and perhaps the murder as well.

"Now you're the chatty type, Professor?"

"Must I beat you, Matthew? I'm younger, quicker, and I spent the entire autumn with all five of our offspring taking turns at me."

"I'm older and more devious. I spent the autumn resting my ancient bones and honing my tactics."

Instead of an elegant mass of blooms on the piano, flowers had been placed about the library in smaller bouquets and single buds. This scheme was a departure from what Matthew usually found at Candlewick, though the effect was pleasing.

More work though, for Axel considered the positioning of every blossom he brought in from the glass houses, much as he pondered every point and supporting thesis in his well-attended lectures.

His magistrate's reports would be works of documentary art, as were the herbals he published.

"You honed your courting tactics," Axel muttered. "Now your wife has put you up to seeing that my foot is caught in parson's mousetrap as well."

Theresa had merely said that she was worried about Axel, all alone in the middle of winter, and wouldn't it be lovely for Christopher and Remington to see their father for a short visit?

Matthew had sent them back to university less than a month ago.

"Theresa said you deserve to be loved." This fraternal conversation would have been extraordinary before Matthew's recent remarriage. Now, what made it extraordinary was that Axel hadn't yet resorted to fisticuffs.

A man of few and well-chosen words, was the professor. "Caroline loved me."

"She did. She also put you off marrying again."

Axel leaned forward and pulled a hassock up, then tugged off his boots and put his feet on the hassock. Matthew did likewise, brotherhood having its privileges. Marriage had not, and never would, change that.

"Why would you accuse Caroline of putting me off marriage? You're not by nature obnoxious for the hell of it, one of your many endearing qualities."

"I loved her too, because she made you more or less happy, but Caroline was a damned lot of work on a good day, and a walking megrim for the unsuspecting male betimes."

The relief of putting that sentiment into words was nearly fifteen years overdue.

Axel took a leisurely sip of his drink. "'A damned lot of work.' What does that mean, coming from you?"

"Coming from me," Matthew said, pushing his brother's feet aside with his own and appropriating the middle of the hassock, "whose first wife was also a trial in her own fashion. Point taken, but don't prevaricate. We're discussing your future here, not my past."

Axel gestured with his glass. "Say on. I am too tired to properly thrash you."

Too tired or too in love? "Matilda was a far from perfect wife, but did she ever announce to the assembled dinner guests that if the bull died, she could simply turn her husband loose among the heifers, and they'd all come into season?"

"Matilda was not... given to indelicate humor."

"Did Matilda ever pitch her wine in my face in front of the same guests?" Matthew inquired pleasantly.

"Matilda did not get so easily tipsy as Caroline did."

Tipsy. Hah. "Did Matilda ever tell me, in front of the same guests, I'd better not linger over my port, or I'd once again find myself sleeping in a guest room for the rest of the month?"

"We had a particularly difficult evening. You can't judge Caroline for those small lapses."

Matthew patted his brother's knee. "I judged her a hell of a lot of work. They aren't all like that."

Axel closed his eyes and rested his head on the back of the sofa. He was maturing—not yet aging, and he was a good-looking fellow. A tired, good-looking fellow with a penchant for thinking everything through down to first causes and last details. Caroline had been right about that—also right to ask Matthew to look after Axel in the event of her death.

"Caroline was good for me," Axel said. "She towed me out from behind your shadow, out from under the grief of our parents' deaths, out of my own tendency to brood and sulk."

Caroline had also doubtless provided Axel that list of positive attributes within a year of the marriage.

"You've always needed a lot of privacy. That isn't brooding and sulking. Another woman won't take your privacy away from you."

Axel peered at his drink. "Caroline hadn't yet reached her majority when we wed, and she had me in hand in a matter of weeks."

She'd yanked Axel loose from his rose bushes, in other words. "You're no longer eighteen. You simply explain to your lady that you like time to yourself. You choose a woman who can comprehend that, not the first woman to flash her bubbies at you."

"Caroline wasn't the first."

"And you weren't her first," Matthew said, setting his drink aside. Axel was lightning quick when in a temper.

"Just how do you know *that*, Matthew?"

Matthew remained silent, braced for the first punch.

"The dear lady never could keep her mouth shut." Axel's smile was wistful rather than sad. "Unless she was in the mood to make me guess at my latest transgression."

"Matilda was furious with her," Matthew said, by way of consolation. "Said it was the most vulgar thing she'd ever heard a woman brag about, and I should tell you to set Caroline aside. Coming from Tilly, that was a brilliant display of hypocrisy, but protective of you for all that."

"Your wife cuckolded you, mine led me around by my parts and made sport of me to other women in the family. You wonder why I'm not leaping back into the marital affray when I can instead have the pleasure of academic company, and the rousing intellectual challenge of Oxford university life. Dean Clemens says one of the colleges is about make me an offer, Matthew."

Good God, not this again. Axel had been maundering on about a fellowship at Oxford since he'd put off full mourning.

Time to circle back to the relevant points—or pour more brandy. "Oxford doesn't deserve you, and Caroline didn't have a very well-developed sense of marital privacy. Mrs. Stoneleigh, obviously, is cut from a different cloth."

"Matthew, for all Abigail has confided some surprising particulars to me, I can't help but feel she's still not being entirely honest."

Good for her, if she was making Axel work to earn her trust. "Women are canny. They have to be. When they trust a man, his power over them approaches life and death, and from what you said before dinner, Abigail Stoneleigh came perilously close to death at her husband's hands."

"Gives a fellow pause, and probably gives the lady pause as well." Axel stood and gathered up his boots. "Just how bad was Caroline?"

Matthew wanted to say she'd been bloody awful, particularly when she'd been at the wine and was in a mood, but if a man's memories were all he had, one had to tread lightly.

"For all her faults, she loved you."

"And I loved her, more than I knew at the time, but Matthew, nobody loved Abigail. For eight years, she managed on her own—no parents, no siblings, no children, and a spouse whose capacity for evil would make the devil blush. Stoneleigh subtly maligned her, robbed her when she was at her most vulnerable, denied her any friendships, and alternately abandoned her and left her no privacy... that was before he tried to poison her.

"The notion of remarriage holds limited appeal for me," Axel went on, "but for Abby... I can't see her ever taking such a risk again. Marriage to Stoneleigh nearly killed her. A prospective suitor with little charm doesn't waltz his way past a trauma like that."

Axel had clearly assessed the challenge such a suitor would face, though.

Matthew could write that much heartening news in his first letter to his wife.

But like a pair of young horses, the professor and the widow would trot back and forth on separate sides of the pasture fence, snorting and pawing, tails over their backs, but neither one was willing to take a leap for the sake of a shared future.

Fortunately, Matthew knew exactly how that felt and with the help of his new wife, had learned a few things about how to open gates.

CHAPTER FOURTEEN

"You left them *alone*?" Matthew asked, glowering at the closed door.

Axel took his brother by the arm and led him away from the Candlewick family parlor.

"Marriage has made you forgetful, Matthew." Also damned happy. The glow of contentment radiating from Matthew would have illuminated both glass houses on a moonless night. "I *asked* Sir Dewey to call on Abigail. Condolence calls are paid to the bereaved, not to the magistrate investigating the murder resulting in the bereavement."

Matthew's fists went to his hips, which display put Axel in mind of the male peacock, preparing to strut the bounds of his territory.

"The murder was barely a month past, Axel. Sir Dewey is rushing his fences."

"Sir Dewey is saving me, and quite possibly you, several freezing miles on horseback. When he's made his bow to Abigail—who needs the distraction of his company—we can ask him a few questions."

"Questions?" Matthew uttered the word the way university scholars spoke of freshly baked rum buns in the dead of winter.

Axel moved off down the corridor, lest Abby catch him trying not to eavesdrop.

"Did Sir Dewey know of the safe?" Axel began. "Why didn't he mention it, if so? Does he know where the second safe is? What's his explanation for the magnitude of Gregory Stoneleigh's wealth? Where exactly did they go on these shooting excursions? Were he and Gregory lovers?"

Matthew stopped short. "Hadn't thought of that. That's quite good. That will throw him right off stride, and then you can follow up with the question you really want him to answer. Which would be…?"

Are you in love with Abigail Stoneleigh? Except Axel had already asked that one, and received a perfectly gentlemanly response.

"You're the brilliant investigator. How about you think of the brilliant questions?"

Though Matthew was stepping down as magistrate by midsummer, before a blessed event could steal all of his attention not already reserved for his wife and children.

"Why not ask him if he killed Gregory Stoneleigh?" Matthew asked.

"Of all people, Sir Dewey had no motive. He's a nabob, for one thing. He tolerated Stoneleigh's crotchets, for another, such as a man bent on uxoricide can be allowed mere crotchets. Then too, nobody can place Sir Dewey on the premises that night."

And Sir Dewey did not strike Axel as a man fond of violence. Unlike Stoneleigh Manor, Sir Dewey's abode boasted no displays of crossed swords, mounted pistols, or gory scenes from the hunt field.

"Only a scholar would refer to killing one's wife as uxoricide," Matthew retorted. "Sir Dewey could have hired the murder done. Put Ambers up to it, or even Shreve."

If Ambers had done murder, he was certainly malingering at the scene of the crime when all sense should have sent him off to the Continent.

Axel had led his brother to the library. Here, Axel could picture Abby curled on her end of the sofa. He could rearrange the bouquets he'd chosen for her that morning. He could cast longing glances in the direction of his collection of erotica, which in his fantasies he shared with her.

Abigail liked books, and she liked *him*, as far as he could tell.

Matthew yanked the bell-pull.

"What in the perishing hell are you ringing for? Luncheon was less than two hours ago."

"If we're to entertain Sir Dewey, some food and drink are only hospitable."

Sir Dewey was at that moment sitting before Axel's best everyday service, and a tray doubtless piled with tea cakes, scones, jam, butter, clotted cream... fruit. Anything Axel's cook could conjure that Abby might enjoy nibbling on.

"You cannot possibly be hungry," Axel said.

"And you cannot possibly long for your glass houses."

They shared a moment of fraternal accord that only looked like mutual exasperation.

"Am I interrupting?" Sir Dewey Fanning sauntered in, all fine tailoring and lean good looks. Axel wanted to kick him right in his handsome teeth, doubtless a symptom of having neglected the glass houses.

"Sir Dewey, greetings. May I make known to you my brother, Matthew Belmont, late of Sussex. Matthew, Sir Dewey is a neighbor of several years standing."

Sir Dewey's bow balanced geniality and dignity. "I understand you are an experienced magistrate, Mr. Belmont. I'm sure you'll give us the benefit of your thinking regarding the situation at Stoneleigh Manor."

Oh, for God's sake. Kicking was too good for such blatant graciousness.

"Perhaps we might discuss that very topic?" Axel said, gesturing to the sofa. "I have a few more questions for you, if you have time to oblige me."

Sir Dewey flipped out the tails of his dark blue riding coat and took a seat. "Inquire away. If I know the answer, I'll gladly share it. I must say, I'm greatly relieved to see Mrs. Stoneleigh looking so much better."

"Better?" Matthew asked, taking the armchair nearest the fire. "I gather she was not at her best at the funeral?"

"Even before that, she was... fading. Losing flesh, growing pale. Several times I saw her steady herself when she'd risen too quickly. Clearly, the professor's care and cosseting have helped put her back to rights."

If Axel attempted to cosset Abigail beyond basic hospitality, she'd unman him.

"Your visit is much appreciated as well," Axel said, taking the other armchair. "I'd hoped Weekes might put in an appearance, but he has yet to brave the elements."

Or tear himself away from Mrs. Weekes's baking abilities, while Matthew had ridden nearly a hundred miles in the depths of winter, left his new bride and his children, to come to his brother's side.

The tea tray arrived, to which Matthew applied himself with predictable assiduousness, leaving Axel free to interrogate their guest.

"Why, exactly," Axel asked, as Matthew troweled butter onto two scones, "did you leave the import business, and did Sir Gregory buy out your interest? And please help yourself to the offerings on the tray."

If Matthew left any.

Sir Dewey selected a scone, then fixed himself a cup of tea, his movements leisurely.

"I see where you're heading with this, and I agree with you," he said. "The business bears closer inspection, being a source of revenue, debt, and entanglement with various third parties. So... I decided to extricate myself from the partnership before I had even left India, and had been corresponding with Gregory to that effect. I implemented the decision shortly after my arrival here."

He took a bite of scone. Axel waited in silence, as Matthew dabbed jam on both scones—rather a lot of jam.

"As to why I left the business," Sir Dewey continued, "that will necessitate a descent into indelicacies. One can make a pretty penny by importing the trivial exotica that appeals to the monied classes—silks, paisley shawls, peacock feathers, incense, and so forth. Sir Gregory was increasingly drawn to importation of the aspects of Eastern culture that appealed to the prurient."

"He *imported* erotica?" The hounds-and-horses, pipe-smoking cavalryman across the way hadn't seemed the type. He hadn't seemed the type to plot his wife's murder, or to defraud an innocent young woman either.

Sir Dewey dusted his hands over the tea tray. "One must experience India to comprehend its nature. It's at once the most spiritual and the most profane society I've ever seen. Much that's ordinary is made sacred—cooking, growing flowers, cogitating. Erotic matters are similarly elevated to a form of worship, even while they are also pursued in their most crude and uninspired forms. I did not concur with Stoneleigh that profit was an adequate reason for presenting only the crude and uninspired aspects of this paradox."

In other words, Sir Dewey did not want to be caught trafficking in naughty pictures—no sane English knight would.

"A culturally enlightened viewpoint," Axel said. "Would Gervaise Stoneleigh know what manner of business he's inherited?"

Sir Dewey rose, taking a tea cake with him on a perambulation about the library.

"I can't say how successful Gregory was at developing his suppliers, so I don't know what manner of business it had become. I know only that Gregory was confident of the demand and was determined on his course. Gregory would also have maintained an inventory of fans, feathers, shawls, carved ivory, incense, and so forth. Those items are profitable year in and year out."

"But Gregory wasn't an exceptional businessman, was he?" Matthew pointed out around a mouthful of scone.

Sir Dewey sniffed at the little white rose, the one Axel had positioned at Abby's end of the sofa.

"This fragrance is... this is intoxicating. I wonder if you'd part with a specimen for my own conservatory, Professor?"

Get your nose away from Abigail's rose, you bastard. "Of course. That one's quite hardy though not the most robust bloomer. About Stoneleigh's business skills?"

Sir Dewey popped the tea cake into his mouth and peered at the music stacked on the piano.

He even chewed *handsomely*.

"Gregory apparently did well with his imports, but he made impulsive decisions too. He'd get fixated on some fanciful scheme—importing tigers from India to populate European menageries, for example—and no amount of reason would sway him. I'd had enough of that, and of his rapacious view of provincial trade. I did not need Gregory's coin, so the better part of friendship was to sever the business relationship."

"Could Stoneleigh have lost money at his business?" Axel asked.

Sir Dewey circled back around to the tea tray and resumed his position on the sofa, while Matthew remained unhelpfully busy with the scones.

"Of course he'd suffer setbacks. In that sort of business, you purchase your inventory six months before your customers purchase it from you. If you acquire goods few are interested in, then you're out of luck. A ship can go down, a war can break out and destroy your caravan, or you can pay substantial bribes to one minor raja, only to have his brother overthrow him and demand yet more in protection money."

"Sounds exciting." Matthew said, choosing for himself the chocolate tea cake Axel had been considering. "Perhaps the better question is how did Gregory expect to make money at it?"

"Easily," Sir Dewey replied, taking the only other chocolate tea cake. "The business was initially old Mr. Pennington's, and he brought Gregory into it only during Gregory's last few years in India. Pennington had the local contacts, and out of respect for Pennington, people did business with Gregory in his stead. When Gregory left India, my job was to maintain those contacts, which function I was happy to perform, provided Gregory dealt honorably with them."

Axel settled for a lavender cake. "You're saying he didn't?"

Sir Dewey's shrug was eloquent. "Toward the end, payments supposedly went astray, goods in trade back to India were of inferior quality. I had questions."

"So you got out," Matthew concluded. "Seems like the prudent thing to do, and particularly well advised given how Gregory treated his wife."

"Oh?" Sir Dewey held the last bite of tea cake before his mouth. "Do I want to hear this?"

"No," Axel said, "but it will confirm your decision to leave the business, as Pennington had apparently all but done before you. Gregory's marriage was based on fraud and greed." He outlined the basis of his financial investigation thus far.

No need for Sir Dewey to know Abby had nearly died at her spouse's hands. No actual proof for that theory either, though Axel had taken a few moments to scour the Stoneleigh herbal and larders for anything that might have served as a poison.

"Seems if anybody had a motive for killing Gregory," Sir Dewey mused, "it would be this Pettiflower fellow. What exceedingly rotten luck, to have one's fiancée whisked to the altar on someone else's arm just after she inherits two fortunes."

Exceedingly rotten for Abigail.

"I haven't considered Pettiflower a suspect," Axel said. "He had years to hold Stoneleigh accountable and has since plighted his troth with another young lady. Pettiflower is also quite well-fixed himself and can account for his whereabouts the night of the murder."

"Another false start?" Sir Dewey mused, choosing an orange tea cake this time. "Well, so much for my brilliant insights."

"Had Gregory any means of keeping papers secure that you know of?" Axel asked, because Matthew was too busy ruining his supper. "Any place on the Stoneleigh premises for storing valuables?"

"In the study where he met his end, behind the painting of the hounds, you should find a safe. Rather obvious location, if you're looking for such a thing. I'm surprised Abigail didn't tell you of it." The third tea cake met its fate. "Finding the combination might be some effort if she doesn't know where it is, but Gregory did love that monstrosity of a desk. I'm guessing if you take it apart, you'll find a false bottom, a false back, someplace to stash what a man doesn't dare entrust to memory. Gervaise might know of where the combination is, or Shreve."

Clearly, Sir Dewey was overqualified as a candidate for the magistrate's post.

"Shreve has resigned his post," Axel said, "and will shortly depart for the family home in East Anglia. Only the one safe? Stoneleigh Manor is quite large."

"I know of only the one, though Gregory had a suspicious streak. Englishmen who survived in India were well advised to develop a polite, distrustful nature. Gregory might have had multiple safes on the premises, or at his business locations. Too bad you can't interview old Brandenburg."

Matthew, affecting an innocent puzzlement worthy of Mr. Garrick, sat back in his armchair. For all the man ate nearly constantly, he never seemed to have crumbs on his cravat or jam on his chin.

Life was simply unfair in some regards.

"How is it," Matthew asked, "you know of a safe, when the whole idea is that one secrets valuables in same? Not very secret if one's friends and servants know of it, is it?"

"I probably wasn't intended to know of it, but I occasionally dropped in on Gregory at the odd hour, and once came upon him before the open safe. Unless I knew the combination, knowledge of the safe's location alone hardly breached Stoneleigh's security, did it?"

"Suppose not," Axel said. "Nor are you a man who needs to raid somebody else's stash of valuables. Have you anything else to add to what we know at this point? The situation grows frustrating for Mrs. Stoneleigh. She cannot feel secure in her own home with a killer still at liberty."

The situation was also damned frustrating for Axel.

Sir Dewey's brows rose, the first hint of agitation Axel had seen from him.

"She is safe, she must know that. Gregory seldom let her go farther afield than the churchyard, which is hardly where a woman would develop deadly enemies."

"When a man is killed in his own home," Matthew said, "at an hour when others are likely to be about, such a killer is willing to take risks. A footman might have come along at any moment to tend to the fire. Stoneleigh could have rung for a second nightcap. Mrs. Stoneleigh might have stopped in to wish her husband pleasant dreams."

Gone was the pleasant brother, and in his place sat a shrewd investigator—

one who had Sir Dewey's full attention.

"We're not dealing with a felon who carefully planned his moment," Matthew went on, "and if the killer needed something from that safe, then he could well come back looking for it. The security of the household is imperiled until the perpetrator of the crime is brought to justice."

"And yet, Mrs. Stoneleigh cannot remain here at Candlewick indefinitely," Sir Dewey said, rising and tugging down a blue waistcoat embroidered in gold paisley patterns.

Axel rose, for a host ought to when a guest prepared to take his leave—or cut short an interrogation.

"Sir Dewey, you must agree that Mrs. Stoneleigh's well-being takes precedence over all other considerations. I have an obligation to the king to solve Stoneleigh's murder, but nothing less than honor itself requires that a bereaved widow be kept safe."

Sir Dewey's gaze lingered on the nearly empty tea tray. "There's talk at the Weasel, you know. Nothing malicious, but not the sort of talk anybody likes to hear regarding a lady."

Matthew plucked the last lavender tea cake from the tray before getting to his feet. "Talk about Mrs. Stoneleigh?"

"She's thriving in Mr. Belmont's care," Sir Dewey said, "or in Mrs. Turnbull's. Most are of the opinion that the professor should add her to his permanent collection of hothouse fancies."

Doubtless, that was putting the sentiment euphemistically.

"Let any man who so maligns a woman tried by grief apply to me," Axel said, wanting to slap a glove across Sir Dewey's elegant mouth. "I'll instruct him most—"

"*Axel,*" Matthew said, a bit too heartily. "The good folk simply mean you should marry her."

* * *

"I am almost through with Grandpapa's journal," Abby said, leaning in to sniff a lovely pink blossom. "I want to savor the pages remaining, though they document a man in fading health. He and Mr. Brandenburg had some grand adventures as younger men."

Axel had been in his glass house long enough to have taken off his jacket and turned back his sleeves, likely in preparation for a long afternoon of rearranging his potted trees. His hands were dirt-stained already too.

"I'd like to read that journal, Abigail."

He'd taken her in his arms without Abby needing to ask, and when he'd turned loose of her, Abby hadn't clung, though she'd wanted to.

"I'll leave it with you when I return to Stoneleigh Manor."

Axel turned away abruptly, as if the stout, thorny bush beside him—the grafting stock he referred to as the Dragon—had whispered unexpectedly.

"I cannot guarantee your safety if you return home now, Abigail. The killer is at large, and possibly more motivated than ever to do you harm."

They needed to have this argument, but did they need to have it now?

"I have never seen a rose with as many thorns," she said. Great, nasty, sharp prickles studding the stems at close intervals. "You think Shreve is the killer?"

Axel took off a thorn by virtue of simply peeling it aside. "He could be. He was early on the scene, and somewhat in the colonel's confidence. Bequeathing a valuable collection of snuff boxes to a servant doesn't make sense to me."

He gently peeled another thorn aside.

"Shall I help?" Abby asked. "I can work on this side while you take that one?"

"I remove only a few at a time. Each lost thorn creates a wound, and every wound is an opportunity for disease to seize hold of the plant. But for the thorns, this is a vigorous fellow, and he takes grafts magnificently."

Abby had interrupted the work that mattered to Axel. Investigating murder was a matter of duty, but these roses were his passion.

"Tell me about grafting." She could ask later if Sir Dewey's second interview had yielded any insights.

"Shall we sit? Grafting is a simple process, the breeding not much more complicated. I can make you a few sketches. A devotee of the rose needs mostly patience and persistence to succeed, and a bit of luck."

What did a magistrate need to succeed? Or a man?

They repaired to the area before the hearth, the warmest part of the glass house, also the side of the building away from both the manor house and the stables. The second glass house sheltered this exposure from view, not that anybody should be peeking.

One could not be tense in this place. The soft air, the fragrance of the plants, the quiet, the lovely foliage all conspired against worry.

One could be sad, though. Like the blooms here, Abby's dalliance with Axel would apparently be a fleeting pleasure. Lovely beyond description, but too soon over.

"Did Sir Dewey upset you?" Axel asked as Abby took the rocking chair.

He took the seat at the table, but turned the chair, so he and Abby were nearly knee to knee.

"In a way, yes. He said I seemed to be bearing up well, which I took for a genteel acknowledgment that I'm recovering my health. He couldn't very well say I look happy to be widowed, but he was concerned for me."

Axel looked at his hands, the fingers of which were stained brown with dirt, though around his right thumbnail, the cuticle was green.

"His concern upset you? He was knighted for bravery, Abigail, and he's wealthy."

"If you try to matchmake, that will upset me more."

The next thing Abby knew, soft lips were pressed to hers. An apology, perhaps. "You are in mourning. Did you know that the law regards any child born to a widow for a year after her husband's death as her husband's legitimate issue?"

The breeder of roses was making a point of some sort. "Children do not take a year to be born." Abby knew that. Any adult woman knew that.

"They take something under ten months in the normal course. Some come in less than nine months. Lawyers do not give birth, so we can ascribe their error to ignorance. Nicholas thinks the law allows a new widow a period of sexual permissiveness without penalty, or a time when she might take measures to conceive an heir for her deceased spouse through expedient means."

Another kiss, which only muddled Abby's ability to follow whatever profundity the professor was preparing to launch at her.

"I don't want Sir Dewey," Abby said, trapping Axel near with a hand to his nape. Sir Dewey was another soldier, and Abby had been married to one of those already, with disastrous results. "I want you, and I know I should not have disturbed you here, but soon I will return to Stoneleigh Manor—I must, Sir Dewey alluded to talk—and you will take up your duties at Oxford, and all will be—"

Axel was out of his chair before Abby grasped his intent. He scooped her from the rocker and carried her to the worktable.

"Do you know why I went tearing into town yesterday, ready to wreak havoc on lying solicitors and fraudulent ghosts?"

Abby's bum landed on the worktable, and Axel stood between her spread knees. "So you wouldn't have to face me over breakfast, the maid bringing the fresh teapot, and all that, that... intimacy between us."

His hands, warm and callused, traced the sides of her neck, his thumbs brushing over her cheeks.

"You are daft if you think I was avoiding you, Abigail. I had to walk past your door to leave my room. A drunk forgoes his gin, a lotus-eater his opium, more easily than I passed your door. I fixed my gaze on the newel post at the top of the stairs, the one fashioned in the form of a closed tulip blossom. This put in my mind the image of the male breeding organ happily prepared to fulfill its intended office. I marched down the corridor, one hand on the wall, my eyes closed, until I passed your door. I'm lecturing."

Babbling, more like. Abby was so pleased with Axel's disclosure, she urged him closer with a hand on each sleeve.

"I dreamed of you again," she said. "Wicked, wonderful dreams." The best dreams, some of which she suspected weren't dreams, but rather, memories. Axel's hands tracing over her back and shoulders, the rhythm of his breathing as she lay in his arms.

His kisses were wilder here among the lush green plants. He hauled Abby to the edge of the table as easily as if she were a potted peach tree, and wedged himself against her. Desire punched through her, a sharp prick of pleasure and longing.

"My skirts," she muttered against his mouth.

He drew back far enough to press Abby's forehead to his shoulder. "Now, Abigail? Here? Are you sure? One wants to be considerate, and I was less restrained previously than—"

He'd been *passionate*. Wonderfully, unashamedly, passionate, and so had Abby.

"You are more yourself here than anywhere else," she said between kisses. "You're happy, we have privacy, and the roses won't mind."

Axel apparently did not need convincing. Abby's skirts were soon frothed above her knees, his falls were undone, and bliss beckoned with every stroke of his fingers over her intimate flesh.

"Can you come like this?" Axel whispered.

"Mmm." Which meant she could. Thanks to her own curiosity, books, persistence, and a stout lock on her bedroom door.

And then she did. Axel knew exactly when to cease his caresses and instead drive two slick, blunt fingers into her heat. What he did with those fingers inspired Abby to soft moans, clinging, bucking, and to insights—when she could again think—into why the artificial phallus figured prominently in some of the erotic woodcuts that had made the least sense to her previously.

Axel's kisses gentled, and he kept his fingers hilted inside her.

"If you move," Abby said, "at all, the merest twitch, I will not answer for the consequences."

His smile was devastatingly sweet and beyond naughty. He wiggled, he twitched, he teased, he drove her up and over every inhibition, until Abby was braced back on her hands, panting, her hair coming undone, and her body that of a happy, well-pleasured stranger.

"We are not finished," she said. "Nobody leaves this glass house without finding his pleasure, Axel Belmont."

"Your bottom—"

She grabbed him by his cravat. "When you lecture me, I grow amorous. Lecture me about my bottom, why don't you?" She gave his derriere a firm squeeze.

"Do that again, Abigail. As hard as you like."

She squeezed, he pushed forward, and anything resembling thought fled Abby's grasp. She'd tried to learn the mechanics of breeding roses by studying a manual earlier in the day, and found the whole business too sexual.

The seed rose wept a sticky exudate when ready to receive the pollen rose's offerings; the pollen rose was stripped nearly naked of petals, the better to present the precious pollen for collection.

Those words and images collided with Axel's steady, relentless loving, and submerged Abby in a pleasure bordering on insensibility. She felt the moment of Axel's surrender, felt the instant when their joining grew so intimate that they became a single entity, suspended in a limitless, perfect passion for each other.

As the incandescent pleasure faded to a hot glow, and then something gentler still, Axel did not leave her. Abby had the sense he *could* not. Words tried to coalesce in her mind.

Unique. Precious. Hold me. Help. *Axel.*

Love.

Axel kissed her brow, stood tall, and wrapped his arms around her shoulders.

Was this how the bud felt when torn from its own stem and wrapped tightly to the sturdy graft stock? Utterly bereft of identity save for the sheltering generosity of the rooted plant? Willing to reach past the most wicked thorns if a glimpse of the sun meant the joining could become perpetual?

Axel kissed her again, left cheek, right check, mouth, then he gently withdrew. He stroked himself almost contemplatively, as if unsure where the experiment might lead, until his head tipped back, his neck corded, and on a soft exhalation, his desire came to its natural conclusion.

Resentment wedged against the pleasure and wonder in Abby's heart, for that final, silent pleasure should have been shared with her, not withheld in the name of prudence and consideration.

Axel used his handkerchief, then resumed his previous posture, arms around Abby, his warmth once again sheltering her from the cold. The resentment faded, warmth seeped through Abby's limbs, and rest beckoned. She leaned against her lover, and surrendered to peace.

CHAPTER FIFTEEN

Time in the glass house had on several occasions produced for Axel a species of euphoria.

Late at night, working quickly with newly cut rosebuds to preserve them from drying or unnecessary trauma, time often faded. The silence, the delicacy of the work, the pleasure of bringing together two different species to create something stronger... Axel could lose himself in that process until the rising sun alone brought him back to mundane reality.

His grafts were notably successful, and he'd wondered if making the cuts and binding the plants together by night wasn't part of that success. Making love with Abby had cut him, cut him to his soul, and left him bleeding and new and more at a loss for words than ever.

He'd loved his wife, and he still in some regard loved Caroline's memory. They'd been young together. They'd started a family together, fought hard with each other though not always well, and in the short space of Caroline's illness, they'd grieved together too.

Nothing, not any of that profound, unremarkable, precious marital history had prepared him for the lovemaking he'd shared with Abby Stoneleigh. He was not sore, he was *wounded* by the intensity of the intimacy they'd created.

Abigail, by contrast, had never looked lovelier, her dark braid over her right shoulder, her lips rosy, her complexion flushed, her gaze...

The moment required words, the right words, and Axel hadn't any to offer. Even *no* words could be wrong, because clearly, Abigail was prone to fancies, such as that he'd avoid her over the breakfast table, for God's sake.

"If you take a tray at dinner," he said, "I will go into a decline."

With a brush of her hand, she dropped her skirts over boots, garters, stockings, and pale thighs. Axel would miss the sight of those thighs in particular.

"It's not always like this, is it?" Abby asked, scooting off the table and pushing Axel's hands away from his falls. She did him up, while he watched and mentally bundled together evidence, intuition, and courage.

"I've wondered about something, Abigail."

"You wonder all the time." She smoothed his cravat, which was probably torn in three places. "I like that about you. Your imagination is seldom still. I'm the same way, probably because I read too much growing up."

Axel led her to the hearth, took the rocking chair, and pulled her down into his lap. Some scooting and rearranging of skirts was needed, but they got situated comfortably.

How to approach this? "I've been wondering about the colonel's will. He was lax about many things, but the will was thorough and detailed."

"He was evil. Of course he'd leave me Stoneleigh Manor, because he expected to outlive me. So generous of him."

Abby was getting over the first, most vulnerable burst of rage, then. Settling in for a siege of well-earned bitterness.

Axel kissed her temple, a gesture of gratitude for allowing him to approach his inquiry from an oblique angle.

"Gregory provided for Lavinia and Gervaise," he said. "He made specific bequests, established pensions for those approaching retirement. All very tidy."

Axel's own will was that tidy, and Matthew's was probably a work of lawyerly art.

"You are reminding me that I'll need a will—I haven't one, you know—and I must decide what to do with my newly re-acquired wealth. I can't think about that now.

I want to nap." She scooted about most distractingly. "I must nap, in fact."

A desk and a chair in the glass house made sense, but moving a bed in here…?

Axel would find a way. He'd built this glass house to come apart, expand, reconfigure, and disassemble, after all.

"Nap soon, listen now. Stoneleigh made no provision for after-born heirs." This had bothered Axel the way a new tooth makes the gum sore. For some time, a child might complain of discomfort for no apparent reason, the gum irritated, the mouth tender. Then a sharp point visibly protruded from the child's gums, and the misery made sense.

Though of course, nobody warned the little fellow's father of that progression.

Abby nestled closer. "After-born what?"

"When a man dies, his widow might have a child following his demise. As thorough as Stoneleigh—or his lawyers—were regarding the rest of his estate, as young as you are, he would have made a provision for after-born heirs."

Abby ceased twiddling the air at Axel's nape. Axel ceased breathing, for he could barely comprehend the magnitude of the trust she'd shown him.

"I've told you Gregory and I were not... entangled. He was getting on, thank God, and he spared me, that is to say, we didn't—"

"I was your first." Axel kissed her with all the wonder and sweetness of that revelation, and with a hint of smugness too. "I was also your second."

The sensation in his heart was like moving down the rows between his failures, all of which he yet loved in some fashion: failure, embarrassment, near miss, disaster, near success, failure... and then coming upon a bloom so beautiful, so impossibly perfect, the fresh wind, good earth, gentle sun, and beaming stars had to have conspired with the most sparkling showers in its conception.

"I was your first lover, ever, Abigail, and you did not tell me, because you rightly supposed I would not have availed myself of your affections had I been aware of your virginity."

Axel wanted to weep—for sorrow, that Abby would waste such a gift on him, and for joy, that he had been so privileged. Once in his life, he'd been somebody's first, and he'd not, apparently, bungled that.

For he *had* been her second too. The experiment had been replicated with verifiable results, writ indelibly in his heart.

"We can talk about that later," Abby said, "though you allow me to raise another question. I'm not... When I was younger, I wasn't horrid to look at, I was willing. Gregory was my husband, and at the time I was prepared to be dutiful."

Axel grasped her question and realized as well that she hadn't had anybody else to ask, doubtless another intended result of Gregory Stoneleigh's campaign to keep his wife isolated and ignorant.

"You wonder why Gregory didn't exercise his marital rights?" This question—or rather, Gregory's intimate indifference—likely accounted for Axel's earlier sense that Abby had been hiding secrets. What new widow wanted to admit to a near-stranger that her husband hadn't consummated the union?

Abby hid her face against Axel's throat, emotion shuddering through her. Anger, relief, or some combination too rare to name?

"Maybe the colonel could not consummate the vows, Abigail. Either he did not desire women, or he had no functioning in any regard. Illness can do that, injury, certain medicinal substances if used excessively are said to obliterate desire. Age certainly takes a toll."

The tension in her relaxed. "It's not an answer we'll find. You were my first, Axel Belmont, if you need to hear the words. You were my first, and I consider that an excellent step in the direction of revenge against many bad memories. This chair is digging into my back."

You were my first.

How was he supposed to let her go after such a confession? Axel stood and deposited Abby on her feet. While they remained in a loose embrace, he mentally tried to assemble a little speech about gratitude, and obligations—hers to him, and his to her—about children, and a place of respect in the local community. A mention of, oh, maybe years of shared pleasure might be a nice addition—

She patted his bum, and all topics and subheadings flew from his grasp.

"I came out here to tell you something," she said. "I nearly forgot, so overwhelming is the passion you visit upon me. Do you know how much that pleases me?"

"Only *nearly* forgot, Abigail? You damn with faint praise."

Another soft pat. At that moment, as far as Axel was concerned, Oxford University could remove itself to the western reaches of Persia, as long as Abigail kept stroking his fundament.

"Ambers has penned his resignation," Abby said, yawning. "The stable is being reduced with each sale of a hunter, and he intends to look for work at a larger establishment after the hunt season ends next month. With many thanks for all the years of employment, he must regretfully notify me of his intent to seek another post come April. He went prosing on at some length—the man has beautiful penmanship—but I won't be sorry to see him go."

The words she quoted were prosaic, nearly a formula of polite leave taking, but Axel could feel a shift in her, and not merely because they'd copulated like two people trying to put the passion of an all-night orgy into twenty minutes of lovemaking.

"You think our last suspect has decided to leave the scene, and thus you'll be safe at Stoneleigh Manor."

In Axel's mind, in his bones, in his heart, he wanted to bellow at her that she was wrong. That Ambers wasn't the killer, that all the arguments that excused Shreve from guilt also excused Ambers, and that Ambers's reasoning made sense—the Stoneleigh stables no longer belonged to a huntsman.

"He hasn't left yet," Axel said, tucking a lock of dark hair behind Abby's ear. "Give me some time to talk to the man, look for the second safe, and otherwise attempt to finish my investigation. I cannot abide the notion you aren't entirely secure in your own home."

Abby slid from his embrace. "Sir Dewey was very polite, but he hinted that if I'm not free to return to Stoneleigh Manor, I have only to apply to him, and he'll force the matter. I gather there's talk at the Weasel, and probably in the churchyard."

Kicking was too good for the gallant Sir Dewey.

"People will always talk, and if they talk long enough, and I listen well enough, that talk might result in a murder solved. Give me a little more time, Abigail."

She plucked a yellow leaf from the peach tree and tossed it into the dirt around the roots.

"You won't give this up."

For her sake, no, he would not, but neither would he badger her. "I will ask you to think the situation over. You needn't decide anything at the moment. Join me at the worktable, and I'll show you how to make a good, strong graft, and maybe even how to create a new breed of rose."

She peered at him, as if waiting for him to say something more, but exhortations about killers and gossip and conception occurring in a glass house would not aide Axel's cause when he wasn't entirely sure what his cause was.

"You want more time," she said, brushing his hair back from his brow. "I can give you more time, Axel, but not forever. Stoneleigh Manor is what I have to show for years of hard, lonely work, and I won't let anybody or anything take that from me—that too. I'm not a coward."

"Most assuredly not."

He took her hand and launched into one of his oldest and best-rehearsed lectures, about how to make a successful graft of two different species, a process which required patience, calm, and the ability to apply a razor to two innocent roses.

* * *

"During the entirety of Caroline Belmont's marriage to my brother," Matthew Belmont said, "she might have spent as much time in a glass house with Axel as you have on this one afternoon."

Abby found Mr. Matthew Belmont an exceedingly pleasant man—irritatingly pleasant, in fact.

She'd come to the library to work at her embroidery near the rose she thought of as hers, the little white blossom with the powerful fragrance. For a parlor rose, the species had stamina in a vase, and the scent…

She wanted a perfume of that fragrance, to remind her of how Axel Belmont's care had brought her back to life.

"The late Mrs. Belmont had a household to run, and small children to raise," Abby said, knotting off her thread. Her eyes ached, her head hurt, and her neck pained her. By contrast, the sensations lingering between her legs were the stuff of rare, rapturous books.

"Caroline called the roses his mistresses," Matthew replied, selecting from among the pieces on the piano's music rack. "Will you play with me, Mrs. Stoneleigh? We have another half hour before we go in to dinner."

Axel had come in from his glass house five minutes earlier. He'd stuck his head in the library door and told them not to wait supper on him.

"My musical skills are rusty, Mr. Belmont." Abby had practiced some since she'd joined the household at Candlewick, but the journey back to proficiency would be long and full of wrong notes. The library's Broadwood was lovely, while the piano at Stoneleigh Manor hadn't been tuned for several years.

"My skills are rusty on a good day." Matthew lifted the cover from the keys. "Unlike Axel's. Oblige me nonetheless. I want to impress my wife with these duets when I return to Sussex—my wife and our children."

Abby did not trust Matthew Belmont. He was good at solving crimes, she'd caught him studying her far too closely on more than one occasion, and he loved Axel without limit.

He was preparing to meddle, in other words.

Abby set aside her embroidery and joined Matthew at the piano. He was big, solid, warm, charming… and not Axel.

"Mozart?" she asked, squinting at the music.

He moved a branch of candles closer, so the music was easier to read. "Your orders, Mrs. Stoneleigh, are to soldier on, regardless of stumbling among the bass or tenor infantry. If we adopt a plodding tempo, I might survive the first movement. Shall we?"

He was competent, but even Abby's rusty skills exceeded his efforts, and thus she kept pace easily. His hands bumped hers, he hit some awful wrong notes, and long before the movement was over, Abby had been reduced to laughter.

Exactly as the wretch had intended, doubtless.

"You are talented," he said, as they came to the final cadence. "You will be an able accompanist should my brother deign to get out his violin."

Let the meddling begin. "Speaking metaphorically?"

"I hope I am."

"I love books, Mr. Belmont, and because books were largely denied me during my marriage, I've examined this library the way a starving child studies a thriving bakery on a bitter day. I also grew up more or less in a bookshop, and have some idea what the classic tomes are in each subject area. Axel Belmont owns one of the most complete and extensive private botanical libraries in the realm, if not in the world. My guess is, he's read every page of every pamphlet and book, committed much of it to memory, and could teach all of it if given the opportunity."

"Your guess would be correct. When other little boys were playing at knights of the round table, Axel was collecting plants in the home wood."

"Botany is his passion, and nobody should take that away from him." Not now, not when he was close to the recognition he deserved for all his years of work.

"I love my sons," Mr. Belmont said, folding up the Mozart and returning it to the stack. "Does that mean I cannot also love the daughter my wife brought to me by marriage? For I do. I already do, and did from the day I met the girl. I love our unborn child, without even having given that child a name."

Logical meddling had to be the worst variety. Abby rose from the piano bench and pretended to study the titles behind the enormous desk. One shelf above her were volumes no decent woman read in company, but before her eyes were herbals.

Medicinal Uses of Common Garden Spices by Axel Belmont.

Exotic Medicinals for the English Garden by Axel Belmont.

Intoxicant and Poison Plants Common to England and Their Antidotes by Axel Belmont.

Axel Belmont was an intoxicant.

"Because I enjoy this library," Abby said, "I see the volume of correspondence that comes in here. The professor communicates with learned minds all over the world, in several languages. He could manage Kew if he were so inclined, but I doubt he'll move that far from his own acres."

Abby hadn't been snooping, she'd simply observed what was in plain sight.

"Axel thinks academic life will make him happy," Mr. Belmont said, abandoning the piano bench.

"Academic life will make him feel useful," Abby said. "Studies such as the ones he's completed will save lives, and he's working on a woman's herbal now. That matters, Mr. Belmont. The medical men can't be bothered with such a topic, and the medical women, such as anybody still acknowledges that term, couldn't get widely published."

Mr. Belmont had come closer, so he and Abby were nearly nose to nose.

"Caroline never once defended Axel's work," Mr. Belmont said. "She was jealous of the glass houses and referred to them as his little hobby. She could not grasp the importance of being able to tell a poison dose from a medicinal one. She knew only that her husband grew distracted at company meals, because somebody made a casual observation about never being troubled by mosquitoes when weeding their lemon verbena."

Mr. Belmont's eyes were a lighter blue than Axel's, his voice was more cultured, and for that reason, when he turned up fierce, the effect was more surprising.

"I am only recently widowed, sir. I have grieving to do, a hunting lodge to make into a home, an estate to manage. I haven't seen London since my father took me more than ten years ago. I haven't even been to the sea coast, when every self-respecting widow is allowed a few weeks of staring pensively at the roiling surf. While the professor's botany is of great significance, I barely have the energy for my own concerns, and I am in no condition to—"

From the corner of her eye, Abby detected movement.

Axel, looking resplendent in country gentleman's attire, stood just inside the library door. His smile was slight, and dear.

"Apparently, your energy is sufficient unto the challenge of putting a presuming brother in his place. Don't let me stop you. That was a fine lecture in the making. Has anybody offered you a drink, Abigail, or is my brother too busy demonstrating a lack of manners?"

Axel prowled over to the sideboard, and Abby did *not* allow her gaze to linger on how lovingly his doeskin breeches clung to his… anatomy.

"I'll have a brandy if you're pouring," Matthew said. "Can we inspire you to get out your violin after dinner? I suspect Mrs. Stoneleigh would be a fine accompanist."

Mr. Belmont knew when to stop meddling—or pretend to stop.

Axel poured a half inch of spirits and passed Abby the glass. Her digestion was improving, but she wasn't in the mood for spirits. The brush of Axel's fingers, however, settled her nerves nicely.

Though how much of her tirade had he heard, and in what light had he taken it?

Axel served his brother a larger portion, then took his own drink to the desk and began flipping through the fresh stack of mail on the blotter.

Abby resumed her place at the end of the sofa and picked up her embroidery, while Matthew Belmont returned to the keyboard and began a soft, lilting melody at variance with his earlier pounding and stumbling.

"Will Nicholas join us for dinner?" he asked.

"Nicholas rarely misses meals," Axel said, separating the mail into two piles. "Abigail, some of these letters have been sent over from Stoneleigh Manor. Condolences, I suppose, and this one is from the Earl of Westhaven."

Abigail knew no earls, though Gregory's military connections had been voluminous. She rose to retrieve her portion of the mail, but remained by the sofa rather than cross the library.

Axel was regarding a piece of correspondence, and what a handsome picture he made. He'd probably written most of his learned treatises at that desk, with his publications marching along their shelves behind him, his rebellious crystal at his elbow, his erotica benevolently hiding two shelves up. He'd look much the same as he aged, though his eyebrows might grow more fierce.

"Oxford has a fellowship for me," he said, staring at a creased sheet of vellum. "I may have my choice of two, assuming I can make my bow before a handy bishop, and recall enough Scripture to appease academic protocol. My duties would begin in the autumn, if that will allow sufficient time for me to conclude my present projects, please advise, et cetera."

The moment took on a painful significance. This was the day Abby's dreams had been born, and the day they'd died. The luscious, ripe, longed-for fruit of academic legitimacy hung mere months away from Axel's grasp, after years of striving and patience. His thornless rose was about to bloom.

While the true nature of widowhood loomed clearly at last: all the freedom in the world, freedom to be lonely, irrelevant, forgotten, and eccentric.

"I'm happy for you," Abby said, saluting with her drink. "The position has been well earned, and they will be lucky to have you. You'll make botanical scholarship a jewel in Oxford's crown, and students from all over the world will study with you."

He stared at the letter, while his brother brought the little song to a close.

"Sometimes," Matthew said, gesturing with his drink as Abby had, "we get the recognition we deserve. I'm proud of you."

Matthew Belmont's pride was also obviously sincere. The look he shot Abby was harder to read.

Axel set the letter in the middle of the desk, his gaze going to the white rose. "That blossom has held up well, but I detect a bit of a droop about the outer petals." He left the desk—and the letter that assured his future—and lifted the vase from the end table, bringing the blossom to his nose. "The scent's fading, and nothing smells sadder than a blown rose. By tomorrow, this specimen will have wilted past recognition."

"Fortunately, you have others," Matthew said, peering at the letter on the desk. "Many others."

"Few like that," Axel said. "Its blossoms are rare and precious this time of year, at least on the stock I've cultivated thus far." He passed Abby the rose, water dripping from its stem onto the carpet. "Perhaps you'd like to press this one, Abigail. Most blossoms are best preserved before they begin to fade."

Abby hadn't yet decided if that last pronouncement was a lover's farewell, when Nicholas joined them, his demeanor fatigued rather than flirtatious for once.

"We're celebrating," Matthew said. "The fellowship Axel has sought for years has been offered to him. He's to choose between two different positions, and study his Scripture in anticipation of the requisite clerical folderol."

"Speaking of protocol, everybody has a drink but for my dear little self. I will rectify this oversight, and toast the professor's success."

Axel remained before Abby, holding the rose out to her while Nick busied himself at the sideboard.

"It won't last another day?" Abby asked, accepting the rose.

"By morning, the fragrance will be gone, the petals falling. Best to take it now and press it between the leaves of a stout book."

Abby inhaled the fragrance, and detected a faint, stagnant odor beneath the beautiful scent.

"Mr. Darcy remains above stairs," she said. "I'll put him to use and be down in time for dinner."

All three gentlemen bowed her on her way, and she curtseyed in return, the rose clutched in her hand. The first tear fell before she'd reached her bedroom door, though by then, she was also clutching her rose so tightly, she'd drawn a drop of blood from her palm too.

CHAPTER SIXTEEN

Everything in Axel wanted to chase after the woman who'd left her embroidery discarded on his sofa, though a man who thrived on solitude had to accept that a woman could occasionally want privacy herself.

"I'll be removing to London in the morning," Nick said, gaze on the closed library door. "If you're about to break the heart of a lovely woman, merely for the privilege of playing nanny to a lot of university boys, I don't want to be around to see it."

"The weather might prevent your departure, Nicholas," Matthew said from the piano bench. He had the knack of *looking* musically talented, of applying his fingers to the keyboard with great authority, and breezing past the wrong notes as if they were all in dashing good fun.

"Hang the weather," Nick muttered, downing his drink at once. "Axel, you cannot become an Oxford monk."

"Scholar, please," Matthew corrected, in the merry key of F major. "My brother is a world-renowned botanical scholar and an expert on the propagation of roses."

This was not teasing, but rather, the fraternal version of a smack to the back of the head. Part affection, part challenge, part gratuitous violence, because between loving brothers, gratuitous violence was a form of endearment.

"We can discuss my illustrious scientific undertakings some other time," Axel said, resuming his place behind the desk. "Abigail is contemplating a remove to Stoneleigh Manor while the murderer yet goes free. I find that situation untenable."

Matthew brought his lullaby—he'd been playing a damned lullaby—to a close. Nicholas topped up his drink, and they both took chairs facing the desk.

"One wondered if the gleaming spires of Oxford had so dazzled you that you'd forgotten about murder on the neighboring property," Matthew said.

Had a ton of oak not separated them, Axel would have kicked his brother for that taunt.

"Abby needs to go back to the scene of the crimes," Nicholas said, studying the condolences piled on Axel's left. "Needs to exorcise Stoneleigh's ghost from her heart, and she'll do that by airing out the house, so to speak."

Literally airing it out. "I noticed when I was a casual caller, that after a visit to Stoneleigh Manor, one came away reeking of pipe smoke, if the visit involved time spent in Gregory's domain. The study, the library, his apartment… they will bear the scent of his tobacco for some time."

Axel thought of Caroline's dresses, lovingly wrapped in tissue in the attic, a bottle of the fragrance he'd made only for her stored with them. How different, if the very scent of his entire house had brought on foul memories and fear rather than comfort and good associations.

"So Abby plans to redecorate Stoneleigh Manor?" Matthew asked. "New curtains, fresh wallpaper, out with the old, in with new?"

"She needs to," Nick said, picking up the franked epistle Abby had left on the corner of the desk. "Expensive, but she can apparently afford it. The property is attractive enough…. Why is my Abby corresponding with a duke's heir?"

Axel leaned over the desk to snatch the letter from Nick's grasp. "She's not your—what do you mean?"

"That's from the household of the Earl of Westhaven, heir to the Duke of Moreland," Nick said. "Decent sort, though somewhat lacking in humor. His countess is lovely, even if her taste in men leaves one puzzled."

Diverse scraps of information floated into a pattern in Axel's head, like a series of crosses sometimes assembled themselves when he sought to create a particular sort of rose.

"Abby mentioned distant cousins, whom she visited once in childhood. One of them has apparently married the earl." And wasn't that just grand? Abigail now included titles among her family, and a fortune that dwarfed Axel's not inconsiderable resources.

"The bachelors will swarm about her as soon as she puts off her widow's weeds," Nick said. "Fortunately, that won't be for some time."

Why did common parlance liken mourning attire to weeds? What was a weed, anyway, but a plant nobody had discovered a use for? Doubtless, to a hungry stag, roses were weeds.

"All of Abigail's wealth," Nicholas said, "her family connections, her determination, will not keep her safe if a killer is determined to do her harm. You could arrest her."

No, Axel could not. "I would not so abuse the trust placed in me by virtue of my position," he said, adding the London letter to the pile of condolences. His academic correspondence was nearly the same height. Botanists turned to correspondence in the colder months. In summer, they tended to haunt their gardens.

"Sir Dewey would object if you arrested Abby without cause," Matthew muttered. "Why don't you simply propose to her, for God's sake? She's a garden-variety widow in the eyes of the law. Nobody's succession is beclouded if she remarries shortly after her husband's death, and among us common folk, such remarriages are the norm."

Men remarried hastily. Some men.

"Ambers has given notice," Axel said. "In Abigail's mind, either he or Shreve are the most likely killers." Or possibly, the two working in concert.

"No motive," Matthew said, slouching. "Who the hell had both motive and opportunity?"

"And how the hell to keep Abby safe until we can solve that puzzle?" Nick mused.

"We know the killer gained access to the premises at least once," Axel said, "and might have been intimately acquainted with the schedules and routines of its occupants. Stoneleigh could have admitted the murderer to the study voluntarily, might have even given the scoundrel a key, though I'm having the locks changed. We know Stoneleigh had a hidden fortune, some of it stolen from Abby's family, some of it from importing erotica."

Axel's last, desperate theory of the case was that the money would lead to the answers.

Nick snorted. "Erotica? Was that what Sir Dewey told you? Why import erotica when so much is available domestically? Half of the bookshops in Bloomsbury are supported by what's sold in the back rooms and gentlemen's reading rooms. A great deal passes for foreign art, of course, but it's no more foreign than Southwark or Cambridge, and no more art than what I could sketch with my left hand."

Axel scowled at his academic correspondence, which he'd lately been neglecting.

"Nick's observation bothers you," Matthew said. "Why?"

Everything bothered Axel. Abigail's hasty departure from the room, her planned departure to Stoneleigh Manor, and if that weren't enough, Axel's own indifference to the news from the committee at Oxford.

He could choose between *two* fellowships, and end the year as an Oxford don... The invitation had the feel of a rose from which the thorns had been peeled, one by one. A rose rendered harmless by virtue of myriad small wounds and disfigurements. A beautiful specimen, easier to handle... but not as definitively a rose.

"Abigail is in possession of a dangerously large fortune," Axel said, tidying both stacks of mail. "More money than her family might have made from even shrewd management of a few commercial establishments in Oxford.

Stoneleigh was notably lacking discipline regarding business matters, at least to appearances, and we cannot interview the late Herr Brandenburg, who might have provided insights into why the import business thrived."

"So where did the money come from?" Matthew asked. "Back to that."

"I'd thought importing erotica might explain the mystery," Axel replied. "Nicholas intimates otherwise."

"I don't intimate. I'm telling you, as a man with dear friends in low, scandalous places, that nobody gets rich off salacious pictures alone, and those are certainly to be had on home shores in quantity without resorting to imports. Coin might accrue from association with naughty ladies, naughty men, the vices of excess, gambling, the smuggling trade, though less so than before the Corsican's defeat... "

"Blackmail?" Matthew suggested. "Naughty ladies and people who ought not to be in their company?"

A good suggestion. "Which means Abby is not safe, not if those people suspect she inherited whatever evidence Stoneleigh had amassed. I've questioned the staff as delicately as I can, and tapped on walls when I had the privacy to do so, but I wish we knew where the damned second safe was."

The final dinner bell sounded. Nobody moved.

"What will you do?" Matthew asked. "I confess I don't feel as if I've been of much help to you. The case is difficult, for many reasons."

Getting drunk appealed strongly.

"I have delayed Abigail's return to Stoneleigh Manor on the pretext that I need to interview Ambers again and look for that second safe. When I can no longer put her off, I will offer her the assistance of six of my stoutest footmen, who can move furniture, store paintings, beat rugs, and otherwise spy on my behalf. Nicholas, you will decamp for London to investigate the import business, most especially the particulars of Brandenburg's demise. You're not to be obvious about your tasks either."

"Who is Brandenburg?" Matthew asked.

"Gregory's late business factor in London," Axel said. "An older fellow who became involved in the business when Abby's grandfather still had a hand in matters."

"I shall be Viscount Discretion, as usual," Nick said.

"You'll do better than that," Axel said. "You will send me items gathered from Gregory's inventory of goods. I want a sample of whatever he trafficked in, from fans to shawls to feathers to bad art."

Nick crossed one ankle over his knee. "Thinking to add to your collection, Professor?"

"No, Nicholas. I'm thinking to solve a murder. Racketing about the shire, interviewing all and sundry, and reviewing records by the hour hasn't accomplished that objective. All else having failed, I'll do what a botanist does, and examine what specimens I can collect from the field."

"The footmen are a good idea," Matthew said, the comment clearly a sop to a frustrated investigator's dignity.

"Abby will accept the temporary loan of two, if I'm lucky." Lately, Axel had not felt lucky, though he'd felt well blessed—also worried as hell.

"You, Matthew, will call upon your capacity for charm," Axel went on. "You will visit the Weasel and chat up the yeomanry with your signature approachable style. You will talk hounds and horses with the local huntsmen, with intent to learn anything we can regarding the loyal, faithful Mr. Ambers."

Axel rose and gestured for the other two to precede him to the dining parlor, though a random thought popped into his mind: Sir Dewey had said that riding to hounds no longer appealed, and yet, Sir Dewey also accompanied Gregory to Melton for weeks at a time, ostensibly to enjoy the foxhunting.

He'd ask Ambers about those outings, and ask Sir Dewey as well—*again*.

Matthew slung an arm around Axel's shoulders and promenaded him toward to the door.

"Being a devoted older brother, I'll swill bitter winter ale by the hour, my favorite pastime in the world, while you do what?"

Axel shrugged free of Matthew's hold. "Further neglect my correspondence."

And somehow, acquire the ability to let the lady he loved go free.

* * *

"You could marry me," Nicholas said, giving his horse's girth a tug. He rode an enormous mare named Buttercup, and if any horse could make the journey to London despite threatening winter weather, she looked up for the task.

"Nicholas, you needn't flirt with me. I'll miss you," Abby replied. *Had* he been flirting, or had Nick for once been in earnest? "Must you go now? Hennessey's great-aunt's knees predict a snowstorm."

"Did your cousin invite you to visit her in London?" Nick asked, retying bulging saddlebags to the cantle. "You could not have more prestigious connections than the Duke of Moreland's family, Abby."

Abby's cousin—second or third cousin, with maybe a remove or two thrown in—had indeed invited her for a visit.

"I'm in first mourning. By rights, I shouldn't be visiting anybody."

A fraught silence fell while Nick moved to the mare's other side and retied the saddlebag there as well.

"You're visiting somebody now, dearest darling Abby mine. Somebody whom half the shire thinks you should marry. I could escort you to London. I can wait a day while you pack up your weeds, and send word ahead. I'm a fine escort—my sisters have trained me well."

Abby was not half tempted, not one-quarter tempted, which had probably been Nick's point. What rural widow with no family in the area would turn down a visit to a cousin well situated in London?

Family could visit family during mourning, particularly under Abby's circumstances.

Axel and Matthew came striding into the stable, bickering as they had through breakfast.

"Nicholas, you are daft," Matthew said. "If the clouds were any lower, you'd be riding to London through fog."

"It's too cold to snow, I tell you," Axel retorted. "Tomorrow perhaps, more likely the day following. This is Oxford, not the balmy fields of Sussex, and Nicholas has procrastinated long enough."

Abby did not want to see Nick leave. Did not want anything to change, in fact.

"I've offered to wait a day," Nick said, idly scratching his mare just above her tail. "Abby has been invited to visit her cousin in London—her titled cousin. This would allow the professor's investigation to continue, re-acquaint Abby with family, remove her from any possibility of danger, and provide me more time to woo her."

The mare's great head drooped with apparent horsey bliss, while Abby wanted to thrash Nicholas for making so much sense—except the wooing part, of course.

"Oh, that's a fine idea," Matthew snapped. "Give a grieving woman lung fever on the king's highway, then thrust her into the arms of near strangers, at a time when mourning prevents her from enjoying any of the blandishments of the capital. Subject her to your tedious company for the duration, and hope nobody comes to grief in an icy ditch along the way."

Lecturing was apparently a family trait.

"Would you like to visit this cousin, Abigail?" Axel asked, tucking Abby's scarf over her shoulder. "Nicholas's suggestion makes sense and would keep you safe. Your safety concerns me greatly."

Her safety, but not her future, not her heart.

"Buttercup, come," Nick said, walking the horse up the barn aisle. She was obviously a mare who held her breath as the girth was tightened. A prudent rider gave her a moment to adjust to the saddle, then fastened the girth more snugly.

"Abigail?" Axel pressed. "I'm off to speak to Ambers today, assuming the heavens don't open up. Unless that interview yields a confession, my investigation has yet to reach its conclusion. Nick will get you safely to London, and my traveling coach is at your disposal."

Now, Abby wanted to thrash Axel, though she'd hug Matthew at the first opportunity.

"Matthew has the right of it," she said. "I met this cousin once in childhood. I don't know the family she's married into at all. London coal smoke is notoriously unhealthy, and as a new widow, but for Sunday services, I could hardly set foot outside my cousin's home."

The clip-clop of hooves and the soughing of a bitter wind were the only sounds. Abby could not read Axel's expression.

"You should have buttoned your greatcoat, Professor," she went on. "Should have worn gloves, a scarf, a hat. This cold grows dangerous."

"I didn't want Nicholas to depart without a farewell. He hates good-byes."

Matthew had wandered down to the foaling stall, and Nick was fiddling with Buttercup's bridle at the other end of the barn.

"I hate good-byes too," Abby said. "I took a casual leave of my parents one fine spring evening, resentful that my mother made me wear my good bonnet instead of my straw hat—I was only humoring Grandpapa's former business associate after all—and by the time the colonel and I had strolled for an hour, my life had gone up in smoke."

Axel didn't even glance about, he simply took Abby in his arms. "I'm sorry, my dear. Memories ambush us, and it's a sign we're getting stronger, not weaker. Lately, my regard for my late wife has become more fond, less fraught. The anniversary of her death is in March, but I'm not dreading it as much this year."

As much. Abby knew exactly what he meant. "I'll return to Stoneleigh at week's end, weather permitting." This was the good-bye she truly dreaded, the one for which Nick's departure was merely a rehearsal.

"Please take six of my most able footmen and several of my maids. They grow bored looking after me without my sons underfoot, and you can use the help putting Stoneleigh Manor to rights."

Damn and blast, did he have to be so thoughtful? "I don't need six, Axel."

"I need to lend them to you. I will evaluate their progress regularly, Abigail, and I will not close the investigation until I have answers. I will also arm you with a gun if you like, and you cannot stop me from changing every lock on every door on the premises."

Warmth trickled through Abby, and relief. Why hadn't she ordered all the locks changed?

"You've already arranged for a locksmith?"

"Three locksmiths are at work as we speak. Once Ambers departs, I'll have him followed to ensure he's left the shire, and I'll confiscate every old key from every tweenie, boot boy, and goose girl on the property. The locksmiths might have some notion where a second safe could be secreted as well."

"At week's end, then. I'll thank my cousin for her kind wishes, and suggest a visit when my first mourning is complete."

Was Axel relieved at that pronouncement? How could he stand about in this cold, wearing only an open greatcoat for protection?

"A fine plan, madam. Let's see Nicholas on his way, and then I can repair to Stoneleigh Manor for an interview with Ambers."

"I'd like to go with you."

"Abigail, you've said it yourself. The weather grows dangerously cold. Send me with lists, instructions, and lectures, but do not needlessly inconvenience yourself for the sake of showing the flag."

The mare clip-clopped back up the aisle. Matthew left off pretending to be fascinated with the new foal.

"Kiss me good-bye, Abby dearest," Nick said. "I'll need the warmth of that memory to see me through the coming storms."

"Safe journey," Abby said, going to the very tips of her toes to kiss Nick's cheek. His arms swooped around her, a snug embrace that tucked her against a broad, warm chest. She was saying good-bye to the first new friend she'd made in years, and that... hurt.

And comforted too. If she ever did travel to London, she'd have a countess for a cousin and an earl's heir for a friend.

"You will write to me, Nicholas," Abby said, burrowing closer. "You will report all your exploits in naughty detail. You will relay gossip about people I don't even know, and leave a trail of scandal across the pages of your correspondence."

Axel gently extricated her from Nick's arms. "Failing that, Nicholas," he said, "find yourself a good woman, settle down to make fat, healthy babies with her, and get your younger siblings married off."

The men embraced as men did—quick, back-slapping hugs that nonetheless conveyed much affection.

Never once had Abby seen anybody hug her late husband. The realization was odd, and... gratifying. Gregory had been wealthy, snide, mean, dangerous, vile... and in some regard she didn't yet understand, also *pathetic*.

Then Nick was on his way, down the lane at a relaxed trot that took him from view all too quickly.

"Shall I accompany you to Stoneleigh?" Matthew asked as all three left the stable yard for the warmth of the manor house. "Two can look for a safe more effectively than one, and Abby can return home that much more quickly."

The squire, whom Abby would have pronounced quite steady on his feet, stumbled.

Axel righted his brother solicitously. "Watch the footing, old man. I'd rather you bided here, in case Sir Dewey calls again, or Abigail has need of good company. You might consider working on those duets, for I say with all kindness, you are far from being able to impress your lady wife with them, much less your children."

"We can't all be experts, baby brother. I beat you regularly at cribbage, and my skills over fences eclipse your own handily."

"I mix a better holiday punch, and always have."

They nattered back and forth, while Abby swallowed around the lump in her throat. She'd miss Nick, and having somebody to miss was... better than having nobody to miss.

"Madam, this will not serve," Axel said, linking his arm through Abby's. "Nicholas has upset you with his leave taking. Matthew, please have the kitchen send a tray with hot chocolate and scones to the glass house and find Mr. Pennington's journal to send along with it. Have a footman bring out a hassock and blankets, as well. Abigail will be enjoying some solitude among the roses, where all is peaceful, fragrant, and warm."

Matthew bowed and marched off toward the house.

While Axel produced a key from his watch pocket and curled Abby's cold fingers around metal that bore the warmth of his body heat.

* * *

All the way to Stoneleigh Manor, and all the way back to Candlewick, Axel contemplated the image Abigail had made in his glass house that morning. He'd left her swaddled in a soft wool blanket, her grandfather's journal open before her, a pot of chocolate at her elbow. Every lady deserved hours spent thus, and every gentleman deserved a lady upon whom to shower such devotion.

As a new husband, Axel had invited Caroline to his glass house, but he hadn't known how to *lure* her, hadn't known luring came into it—and neither had Caroline.

Ah, well. Oxford was now luring *him*, his last treatise having caught the notice of both the Regent and the Regent's personal physician. His correspondence with the late empress had somehow become known in academic circles, and his nephews had distinguished themselves for their diligent scholarship, or perhaps…

He turned Ivan onto the Candlewick lane, the manor house at the end cheerily abloom with lamplight. For a moment, he halted his horse, trying to name the emotion that suffused him.

Welcome was part of it, sanctuary another. This was his home, where he'd raised his children; said his earthly farewells to Caroline; written his scholarly works; and developed roses renowned for their beauty, hardiness, and fragrance.

That all mattered, but lately, what mattered more was that here, Abigail Stoneleigh had given him her trust. Surely a piece of her heart had come along as well?

Ivan stomped a hoof in the snow.

"You want your oats." Axel gave the horse permission to walk on. "I want… I wanted a position at the university. I wanted a thornless rose." Those were fine ambitions, ways to make meaningful contributions to posterity and even to present society. A thornless rose might lead to thornless raspberries, for example.

But those ambitions no longer had the feel of wishes, of cherished dreams.

The cold had acquired the profound stillness of deep winter, a good time for contemplation before a roaring fire. Axel turned his horse to the stable yard some moments later as a black-clad figure emerged.

"I lied to your brother," Abby said, marching up to Ivan's side. "I told him I'd left Grandpapa's journal in the glass house. I simply wanted to be out in the fresh air, and I wanted to wait for you here."

Which explained Wheeler's absence once more, also the warmth blooming in Axel's heart, where before all of him had been chilled.

He swung down and flipped the reins over Ivan's head. "Come into the barn, Abigail. You'll develop an ague in this cold. I suppose you're curious about my interview with Ambers."

She pitched into him so hard Axel nearly stumbled. He got an arm around her and tucked his chin over her crown.

"Madam, is something amiss?"

Now would be a fine time for her to confess she wasn't ready to return to Stoneleigh Manor, and she wasn't up to the task of dwelling there through the months of refurbishing the house.

"Mr. Weekes paid a call this afternoon."

Mrs. Weekes must have taken a day off from her baking. "I trust he did not give offense?"

"Matthew charmed him, of course. Strutted his magistrate's credentials, gossiped about mutual acquaintances from the university, but Mr. Weekes remarked pointedly about how much better I appeared to be doing—several times. He hopes to see me at services this Sunday."

Well, damn.

"I will be happy to escort you." Though if Axel escorted her to services, this quiet little repairing lease at the neighbor's became common knowledge, as did Abigail's greatly improved health. Courting couples went to services together.

Axel guided Abigail into the barn, but such was the weather that even the stable wasn't warm. He whistled for Wheeler, who came bustling in from the direction of the carriage house.

"A hot mash for my intrepid steed, Wheeler," Axel said, giving the horse's neck a pat, "and I'd bring over extra hay from the home farm, were I you. The cold will keep the horses hungry, and if the temperature warms up, snow is likely."

Wheeler touched his cap to the lady and led Ivan the Intrepid off to the cross-ties. Ice balls clung to the horse's fetlocks, and his hoofs left a wet trail in the dirt of the aisle.

"Why did Weekes come calling?" Abby asked, pacing away from Axel. "For years, he could not bestir himself to visit me at Stoneleigh Manor unless Gregory was in residence, and then no more than every few months. That presuming old man patted my knee."

The pastor had a latent wish to make the immediate acquaintance of his Maker. "Abigail, you are welcome here as long as you like, and my own peace of mind would be best served if you did not return to Stoneleigh Manor unless and until we know who killed Gregory."

Her shoulders sagged. "Then Ambers did not kill Gregory over a collection of smelly old pipes?"

"Likely not. The maid confirmed that Ambers had merely stepped out for a moment to smoke, as he often did at the end of the evening." Axel turned Abby toward the manor, when what he wanted was to take her to the glass house and make passionate love to her—which would, of course, solve nothing. "If we're fortunate, the weather will obviate the need for anybody to attend services this Sunday."

Though no wonder Weekes had remarked Abigail's improved health. Between rest, good nutrition, and her present blazing temper, she was positively thriving.

"I can't pray for a great storm," she said, stomping across the garden toward the back terrace, "because Nicholas is traveling. Matthew might soon be traveling too, and you had wanted to pay another call on the lawyers, if I recall."

"Nobody *wants* to pay a call on lawyers, Abigail. I shall though. Ambers's recollection matches Shreve's. He was never asked to witness your signature on any document, and like Shreve, he completed an affidavit to that effect for me."

Abby had mentioned once that Ambers had lovely handwriting. Having seen an example, Axel was gratified to think that its distinctiveness would go far toward making a case against Handstreet.

"So you'll be able to compare signatures with whatever the lawyers produce." Abby stopped at the top of the terrace steps, her breath puffing white before her. "I'd rather you tell me the rest of it now, instead of waiting until your brother is on hand to see me raging and fuming anew when you announce that Gregory was faithful to his mistress while he couldn't be bothered with me."

In her present mood, Axel knew not what to say, or do. He risked a kiss to her forehead.

"I am ever so glad Gregory did not *bother with you* in the sense you allude to. In my eyes, respecting your chastity was Stoneleigh's sole virtue."

Abby leaned against a lamp post, as if abruptly fatigued. "Are you angry with me because I was... without experience?"

"I am more flattered and bewildered by the gift of your virginity than I can convey, Abigail. Had I known—must we speak of this here and now?"

Speak of it at all? Axel longed to retreat to his roses rather than muddle on with this conversation, but more significantly, he wanted to muddle *through* whatever upset plagued Abigail.

She pushed away from the lamp and the circle of light it cast. "Had you known I was without experience, you would never have presumed, and there I'd be, the only widowed virgin in all of England."

Not for long. "You overestimate my gentlemanly self-restraint, and underestimate your own charms. Had I known, I would have taken infinitely more care with you."

She stopped mid-stomp across the terrace and turned, slowly. "*More* care? I don't see how you could possibly have taken *more*..." Her brow knit. "You are distracting me from the matter at hand, Mr. Belmont."

"None of that Mr. Belmont-ing, Abigail. Gregory did not have a mistress in the usual sense."

She resumed pacing at a brisk rate. "Oh, delightful. Now you'll tell me he paid some madam to beat his naked backside on the first Wednesday of each month without fail, or that he preferred boys. I shall be sick all over again before we find the end of Gregory Stoneleigh's dirty little secrets."

"How could you possibly know about erotic flagellation?" Much less bring it up in conversation with such marvelous bravado?

"I read, Mr. Belmont. So do you. I've inspected your library, including that shelf behind your desk."

If there had been any doubt of Axel's regard for this woman before, he was smitten past all recall now.

"Abigail, you peeked at my erotica."

"I did not peek. I read some of it and studied more. Your tastes are refined and eclectic. My grandfather would have approved."

Very few honest men disapproved of erotic art. "I didn't start that collection until I was widowed. Do *you* disapprove?"

Abby came to a halt before him. "One of your books looks... Japanese? I'd like to borrow it. The woodcuts are very graceful and... inventive."

Axel kissed her on the mouth, mostly because whenever he saw her, that's where he wanted the kissing to start, in the usual location, well rooted in tradition and experience. From there... he'd like to kiss her all the way to Japan, so to speak.

"I'll make a gift of it to you. Gregory did have a mistress, of a sort."

She kissed him back, then leaned against him, her forehead on his shoulder. "Tell me. I missed you today, and we must go in to dinner, and then we must endure your charming brother and pretend we aren't worried for Nicholas."

We, we, we... Smitten was not the half of it. "I'll come to you tonight, if you'll allow me to."

Oh, and he'd planned to be such a proper damned host. Then Weekes had stuck his oar in, and now Abby was upset, and the investigation might never come to a satisfactory conclusion.

But Axel could still show her what infinitely more care looked like.

"Please do come to me, and don't play an extra hour of cribbage with your brother first, merely to make me more eager. Whoever Gregory's mistress was, I want the woman to have a pension."

"Not a who, but possibly a what. The colonel's destination on his monthly sojourns to Oxford was a humble tobacconist's, though one apparently doing quite well. Ambers picked up and paid for the colonel's monthly order of tobacco and sundries for his pipe habit. Did you know Stoneleigh smoked substantial quantities of hashish?"

CHAPTER SEVENTEEN

"Hashish?" Matthew asked, crossing his knife and fork over an empty plate. "I haven't heard mention of it since I left university. Rather exotic vice, as I recall."

Axel looked tired, Abby agitated, and both of them for the duration of the meal had been looking anywhere but at each other.

"I tried it at university, purely in the interests of science, of course," Axel said. "Very pleasant effect, if one doesn't mind the whole business of drawing ash into the lungs."

"What does pleasant mean?" Abby asked.

The servants would not clear the table until summoned, and the dining room was kept warm by blazing fires in both hearths. Matthew had taken many a fine meal here, but without children underfoot, the room seemed too large... too quiet.

Too serious and sad.

"Pleasant," Axel said, as if stating the title of a lecture. "When smoking hashish and for a time afterward, one feels a peaceful lassitude, a general euphoria, a lessening of anxiety and ill will. The appetite can be stimulated at the same time agitation of the mind ebbs. Hard on the respiration, though casual use hasn't been noted to cause lasting damage."

Matthew reached for a pear, and Axel passed him a silver fruit knife. "If a man was having trouble with his temper," Matthew remarked, "with controlling impulses, with violent displays, such a soporific might be medicinal."

Abigail left off tracing a fingertip around the rim of her wine glass. "Shreve said Gregory was growing more difficult. In hindsight, I concur, but this... hashish. Is it foreign? Indian?"

Matthew would have had to consult his library, where he'd probably find nothing germane. The next step would be correspondence with his brother, but failing that, nothing short of a trip to consult the gardeners at Kew would have answered Abigail's question.

"The plant itself is usually grown in warmer climates," Axel said, "for rope making. My reading suggests the Tibetan mountains are home to the best medical specimens, but varieties are common now all over India. The Chinese are familiar with it, though opium has a much stronger effect and is a more lucrative business. Both are considered habit-forming, and hashish lacks opium's pain-relieving qualities. Opium has more dramatic flowers too."

Which Axel could doubtless have sketched for his lady.

"Will you interview the tobacconist?" Abigail asked.

"After I call upon the solicitors and explain to them that defrauding a young woman of her inheritance is a felony offense, as is conspiracy to commit fraud."

"I'd missed that," Matthew said, setting the plate of sliced pears beside a pot of violets in the center of the table. "The statute of limitations on the crime of conspiracy will not have tolled."

Abigail set a section of pear on her plate; Axel took none. He was doubtless feasting on his lady's mere appearance, though he'd given a good account of himself at supper.

As had Abigail, to Matthew's relief.

"I did almost nothing today," Abigail said, considering her pear. "And yet, I am fatigued. Gentlemen, I'll leave you to your port and take myself upstairs to cavort with Colonel Brandon. Perhaps we can discuss the solicitor's situation further at breakfast."

"Sweet dreams," Matthew said, getting to his feet.

Axel said nothing, but visually followed Abigail's progress to the door, then cocked his head as the door closed and her footsteps retreated.

"As I recall," Matthew said, resuming his seat, "Colonel Brandon wasn't the cavorting sort."

Axel sat and popped Abigail's uneaten slice of pear into his mouth. "Don't underestimate a fellow simply because he's quiet and gentlemanly. What did you learn at the Weasel?"

"Not much. Ambers is a competent horse-master though something of a dandy who dropped the occasional French curse when he first came to the shire. According to Miss Nairn, he fancies himself too good to marry a local woman, though he's not above importuning a pretty domestic. He doesn't speak ill of his employer except after a few too many brandies—brandy, not ale, mind you—and then mostly the usual mutterings."

Another slice of pear disappeared. "Mostly? The trip to the tobacconists was undertaken even in the foulest weather, according to Ambers. Even if the colonel was traveling, if Ambers remained behind at Stoneleigh Manor, he was to fetch the package from that shop upon pain of discharge."

The facts, in other words, were not adding up to a solution—again. "What sort of huntsman leaves his head groom at home in the middle of the foxhunting season?" Matthew mused. "Then too, a shopping excursion to a tobacconist seems an odd errand to discharge one's stable master for."

"Doesn't it? And I've yet to hear from Sir Dewey about the exact dates and destinations of all the colonel's travel. One wonders if those journeys were as imperative as this simple errand."

Another loose end Matthew hadn't thought to pursue. "What will you do with the lawyers? They colluded with a felon to bilk Abigail of her family's fortune, and probably profited handsomely."

Axel had a well-developed sense of justice. An older brother's heart was pleased to see that where Abigail Stoneleigh was concerned, Axel's protective instincts had also become razor sharp.

And as far as Matthew was concerned, Oxford fellowships should be tossed down the jakes.

"When it comes to the lawyers," Axel said, "with Abigail's approval, I will threaten and drip innuendo. She doesn't need a money settlement from them, but a substantial bank draft might give her satisfaction. A draft large enough to put the damned pestilential ciphers out of business. She wanted to establish a pension for any mistress who'd spared her Stoneleigh's attentions."

Which notion, the present magistrate seemed to heartily endorse.

"At the risk of finding myself face-down in some horse trough when I least expect it—or stoutly kicked halfway across the garden without warning—I will again venture the opinion that you and Mrs. Stoneleigh would suit."

Had Matthew not been watching his brother, he would have missed the expression that flickered through Axel's blue eyes.

"Nicholas, whose instincts regarding females are not to be dismissed, was correct, Matthew. Abigail has ghosts to exorcise at Stoneleigh Manor, and for me to proffer marriage now, when she's again grieving, at sixes and sevens, upset, reeling, and not even in the best of health, would be to take advantage as the colonel did."

Oh, right. Love made sensible people too noble for their own good. "The colonel sought to exploit your Abigail, and then end her existence. You seek to cherish her and give her the rest of your life."

That fleeting, hopeless, besotted, resolute expression came and went again. Martyrs wore such expressions. Matthew felt a long, frustrated letter to his wife coming on.

"I seek Abigail's well-being and her happiness," Axel said. "You will excuse me for abandoning you. I want to read up on hashish, on whether long-term use can lead to violent tendencies, or derange an otherwise sound mind."

"Love deranges an otherwise sound mind." Matthew braced for a brotherly blow to the back of the head.

Axel sliced another pear and added it to the silver plate in the center of the table. "And yet, love puts all to rights with the heart. How much longer can you stay?"

Matthew wanted to stay as long as Axel needed him, but the vagaries of winter travel prevented that, as did a new wife in a delicate condition.

"I should likely leave at the first of the week, weather permitting. Theresa reports all is well at Belmont House, but…"

Axel rose and patted Matthew's shoulder. "You miss your wife, and she torments you with cheery recountings of all going well and her spirits being sanguine. She's staying busy, in other words, and dreaming of you. Investigate the upper shelves behind the desk in the library if it helps, but it won't cure with what ails you. I predict a joyous reunion and, despite the state of the king's highways, a very swift journey home."

Axel kissed the top of Matthew's head, snatched up the plate of pears—and the violets—and sauntered off, likely to charm his lady through a long winter night.

A tug on the bell-pull would bring the servants to clear the table—something the master of the household had forgotten to tend to. Matthew picked up his wine glass and the half-full wine bottle, and headed off to the cozy solitude of the library.

Where he would write that letter to his wife, and that would help only a little.

* * *

Axel balanced the violets and pears in one hand and tapped at Abby's door, feeling… all manner of things. Hopeful, desperate, determined, worried. She had defended his botany in a stirring lecture to Nicholas, but she'd also defended her own intention to remain unattached—all for the best, surely.

And then she'd invited Axel to come to her bedroom once again.

The door opened, Axel stepped into Abby's room, and that was that. No discussion, no scowling glance into the corridor, no firming of her lips that might mean impatience, rejection, ire, anticipation… Before he could put down either the flowers or the fruit, Abby kissed his cheek.

"You gave me your key," she said. "I forgot to thank you for that."

"The key to the glass house?"

She took his offerings and set them on the bedside table. "To the glass house with all your experiments, the one with the cozy hearth, your most treasured records."

Axel's most treasured recent memories too. He'd had a day to consider the significance of giving Abigail his key, a gesture apparently not lost on her.

"I could think of no more pleasant, soothing, or solitudinous place for you to while away a morning." Amid his hopes and dreams, his best work, his greatest acts of patience and faith.

His treasured failures, many of which had been more illuminating and inspiring than his successes. As Axel slipped his arms around Abigail, he pushed aside the notion that she would be one of his failures, or he one of hers.

She gave him her weight, fatigue evident in her surrender. "Make love with me, please?"

"If you'd rather rest tonight, you should rest," Axel said, nuzzling the curls at her temple. "You need not make any hasty plans, just because that knee-patting disgrace from the manse has decided to turn up puritanical, meddling, and bothersome. Your safety must come before all else, Abigail, and I will cheerfully remind the good pastor that 'thou shalt not kill' trumps the rest of the list handily. Putting a parishioner in the path of harm, merely because some committee of clucking, matchmaking biddies has—"

Abigail sighed, which meant she pressed closer, and that purely deprived a man of spontaneous lectures regarding moral taxonomies.

And imbued him with a pressing need to get his clothes off.

"Help me with my cuffs," Axel said, stepping back and holding out both wrists, as a prisoner obliges one putting on shackles. "Did you enjoy your morning?"

Abby undid his cuff-links and passed them to him for stashing in his watch pocket.

"Your glass house is magic, Axel. I was fretful and upset when I sat down with Grandpapa's journal, but I dozed off before I'd finished my first cup of chocolate. The roses form a sort of guard, with their greenery and their scent. I'm even comforted by the thought of their thorns."

"Interesting theory, that we value them for those thorns." Axel's waistcoat came next, then his cravat, and half-unbuttoned shirt.

"Every image I've seen of a princess in a fairy tale has her tower guarded by thorny roses. Give me your clothes, sir."

Wives spoke thus. *Do this. Stop that. Here, now. You mustn't.* Husbands complied, usually. Axel passed over his shirt, which Abby folded up on the chest at the foot of the bed. He might, in six attempts, have managed the same tidy result she achieved on a casual first go, such was the mystery of feminine domestic expertise.

"Shall I take down your hair, Abigail?" She hadn't had time to tend to that, apparently more focused on getting into her nightclothes.

Those brisk, competent hands paused with Axel's cravat stretched between them. "I'd like that."

Axel tugged off his boots and stockings, set them near the door, and took up a post by the vanity.

"You did this for your Caroline?"

"Occasionally, when she was weary. Like many couples, we had neither lady's maid nor valet. Finances early in the marriage were occasionally constrained." And always, Caroline's first suggestion had been to spend less on the roses, though they'd quickly become a reliable source of income.

Abigail took a seat on the vanity stool. "I am weary, but not as tired as I was when you kidnapped me from Stoneleigh Manor. The longer I'm here, the more I can see how unwell I'd become."

Axel extracted the first pin from the back of Abby's coiffure. In his passing liaisons, this tending to a lover hadn't come into it. Of course, he'd laced up the occasional corset, lent a lady his comb, and otherwise observed bedroom civilities. God help him now, he was positively wallowing in the pleasure of strutting about Abigail's bedroom without his shirt.

For she was *admiring* him in the mirror, tired though she was.

"Sorry." He had tugged a pin loose, and inadvertently tugged at a dark curl too.

Abby leaned forward, resting her head on her folded arms. "To be tended like this… you can't know, Axel Belmont. You have no earthly, heavenly, inkling of an idea how lovely your generosity is."

He had a wealth of ideas where Abigail was concerned, an herbal full of them. "I'll send Hennessey with you to Stoneleigh Manor. She fancies herself a lady's maid now, and Candlewick simply hasn't need of same."

Drat the dratted damned dratting luck.

Axel worked in comfortable silence, piling pins in a ceramic dish with cabbage roses painted into the bowl. When he'd finished taking down Abby's hair, she sat up.

"Does madam prefer a hundred strokes?" Axel asked.

She studied his bare torso in the mirror, a frank and female perusal. "Fifty, please."

He made it to seven-and-thirty, possibly. "That ought to suffice. One braid or two?"

"I'll braid it. You can use the wash water."

And no need for anybody to warm up the sheets, for Axel's breeding organs were already anticipating what would happen in that bed. He strolled behind the privacy screen when everything in him clamored for a mad dash.

Abby's voice floated through the shadows. "I'll miss you, Axel Belmont."

He braced himself with both hands on the sturdy porcelain washstand—more cabbage roses. Now would be a fine time to make further impassioned arguments against her leaving and in favor of holy matrimony to the nearest handy botanist.

He dipped a cloth in the cool wash-water and wrung it within an inch of its life.

"I'll worry about you, madam."

Silence, then the sound of Abby flipping covers back and batting at the bedclothes.

Axel tried again. "I'll lecture your staff at length on the matter of your safety. You will eschew solitude, please, until my investigation has concluded. You will rest frequently, napping in the middle of the day if you so choose, and fashioning menus with your cook that appeal to your tastes, however eccentric or unusual those might be."

He added toothpowder to Abby's toothbrush, and regarded the desperate, besotted fool in the mirror who silently pleaded with him to shut his stupid mouth.

When his teeth were quite clean, the fool recommenced lecturing. "You will do with Stoneleigh Manor as you please, and I will provide you detailed sketches of some ideas I've been cultivating for your conservatory. The space has potential, despite the neglect of its previous owner."

A shadow moved behind him. When he turned, Abigail stood to his left, her arms crossed, a single braid over her shoulder.

"Even your back is beautiful, Axel Belmont. I'd love to sketch you without clothes. Start my own erotic collection."

She broke his heart, over and over. "I would not object, provided you allowed me the same privilege."

Axel expected her to flounce off to bed, though he wasn't teasing. He did not know how to tease.

Abigail held out her hand. "Before I leave, we'll lock ourselves in the glass house, and have a sketching session."

He'd move a bed in there first. "I am your servant in all things."

Her aroused servant, though Abigail wasn't shy about her desire. She stopped Axel halfway to the bed and kissed him free of what few wits he still possessed. When he peeled out of his breeches, she unbelted her robe and shrugged— what an elegant, devilish movement—out of her nightgown.

"You jeopardize your health and my sanity," Axel said, lifting her onto the bed. "But how lovely, to be naked with you."

That last part just slipped out, and got him Abby's hand fisted in his hair, holding him still for another kiss as he bent over the bed.

The lovemaking did not go according to Axel's plan. He'd intended gentle, measured, respectful intimacies with a woman new to passion. He'd been determined to savor and cherish, to add a warm and sweet memory to their small store of shared encounters.

He'd not intended to *be* cherished, to close his eyes the better to feel Abigail's hands mapping his back, his shoulders, his chest. He'd not planned on her touch reorganizing his awareness of his own body, so he became a creature confused by lust and tenderness in equal abundance.

And she touched him everywhere. Put him on his back and got friendly with his stones, his cock, his thighs and belly. Then the nuzzling began, and Axel nearly spent from the feel of her braid teasing about his parts.

"You have been at my books," he said. "The ones behind the desk."

Oh, what a woman could do with the tip of her braid and two inquisitive lips. "I love books. I want to be on top."

Axel loved books passionately right about then too. "I'm the academic sort, you will have noticed. I esteem a liberal education." He guided her to her chosen perch, then endured the mortal pleasure of Abigail Stoneleigh learning how to indulge herself with a man so willing to accommodate her, he nearly lost consciousness restraining his own passion.

She leaned forward, flushed and disheveled from her exertions. "When do you have a turn?"

"Any more of a turn, madam, and I'll be the one needing to nap in the safety of the glass house."

She swooped in for some more kissing, a skill for which she had a precocious aptitude, particularly when her tongue and her hips synchronized.

"I want you to spend this time," she said, pinning Axel's wrists to the pillow. "You said it yourself. The law provides a period of grace, when a new widow is not accountable for sharing her favors. I want that grace."

She wanted his soul. "Abigail, that is not wise."

"I will not entrap you. I've read the draft of your women's herbal, and certain tisanes…"

He rolled them rather than roar out that any child of theirs would be his greatest treasure, conceived in love and reared with every advantage—including legitimacy, by thunder.

"You ask too much," Axel said. "And yet, you ask not nearly enough."

Abigail was primed to fly, fast and high, and he took advantage of her arousal. When she was keening against his shoulder for the third time, her teeth scoring his flesh, Axel withdrew and spent in a great, shuddering mess on her belly.

That much, he had planned, more or less.

As he hung over her, panting, mind for once without an opening thesis, supporting statement, or even a single corroborative detail, Abby brushed his hair back from his brow.

"I have something to say to you, Axel Belmont."

Tell me you can't leave, tell me you want to stay. "I'm not in any condition to take myself out of earshot."

"I am proud of you. Proud that Oxford would offer you your pick of the fellowships. Grateful to you for your generous hospitality, and your efforts on my behalf. You have done nothing less than save my life, and I will miss you for the rest of my days and nights. When you grow that thornless rose, nobody will toast your success more sincerely than I."

He buried his face against her shoulder, lest she watch a grown man struggle with tears. Her fingers winnowed through his hair, her words scraped across his soul.

Gratitude, pride, good wishes… all very lovely. Very precious. For years, he'd longed to have an intimate companion who appreciated what his science meant to him.

God damn the timing, the thorns, the fellowships, all of it.

"Thank you for those kind sentiments," he said, pushing up onto his arms some moments later. "Stay as you are, and I'll tend to the mess I've created."

Axel left the bed, but as he twisted a wet flannel halfway to oblivion, he also began composing a reply to the Oxford committee's offer. Only a draft of course, for a man who'd advised an empress regarding one of the most renowned botanical collections in the world, knew that each cut of the drafting knife had to count, and with all his hopes and dreams hanging in the balance, each stroke of the pen had to count too.

CHAPTER EIGHTEEN

"Be careful," Abby said, making no effort to keep her voice down. "They are lawyers, and you are confronting them with irrefutable evidence of wrongdoing."

Axel drew on riding gloves that Abby suspected would do little to keep his hands warm.

"I will get answers from them, then put them out of business, madam. They will be relieved I stop there, considering the harm their mischief caused you."

She loved it when he called her madam. "If it starts to snow, you come straight home. Ivan can slip, the same as any other horse."

Around them, grooms put three horses under saddle, else Abby might have kissed her love on his way.

"Take the key," Axel said, passing Abby a small, familiar object. "You are not to spend the entire day at Stoneleigh Manor. Face down a few demons, let Matthew have a look around the place, confer with your staff and plan your renovations. Collect up the pipes for Ambers in case he takes a notion to leave before April, but don't tire yourself out."

Axel had slept with her previous night, the most glorious, restful, sweet, hours Abby had spent in a bed, ever. She twitched at his scarf, simply as an excuse to touch him.

"You have a clear aptitude for sharing a bed, Professor. I am well rested."

She was ruined, having learned just how delightful a night spent with an affectionate man could be. Axel had wrapped her in a warm embrace. He'd rubbed her back, massaged her scalp, tucked covers around her just so when her shoulder might have taken a chill.

He'd also awoken ready to pleasure her with a leisurely loving, her back to his front, before he'd stolen away into the pre-dawn darkness.

"You are… You be careful too, Abigail. No disappearing up to the attics unescorted, no investigating the cellars without Matthew. I've told him not to let you out of his sight, and I expect your cooperation."

And yet, Axel would not stop her from taking yet another step in the direction of returning to Stoneleigh Manor, nor did Abby entirely want him to.

She saw Axel to the mounting block—no good-bye kisses with Matthew standing at her side—and settled aboard her mount, determined to make a start on turning Stoneleigh Manor into her home.

"I want to change the name of my property," she told Matthew, as he climbed on his gray. "I'm open to suggestions."

"We must ponder possibilities, of course. A few bottles of wine might aid our endeavors. Will you marry my brother?"

This much Abigail knew: If Axel asked, she'd be tempted to say yes, and that would not be fair.

"He has waited years for the letter sitting folded on the desk in the library, Mr. Belmont. He has worked endlessly, earned the respect of his peers across the realm and across the world. A university appointment would be acknowledgment of academic achievements most men could not attain in three lifetimes."

"All true. My brother is brilliant in his way."

In the *way* of siblings, Matthew had implied his brother was also somehow not brilliant.

"Axel would not thank you for meddling." That Matthew Belmont might welcome Abby into the family was a comfort though. Axel might offer, if the alternative was to destroy Abby's reputation, or put her in harm's way. "One marriage of expedience was more than sufficient for me. I would not ask a man I care for to undertake another, particularly when the result would be to deny his heart's desire."

That comfort, of knowing Axel could have the recognition he deserved, was rich. A rose with thorns, but beautiful and fragrant, nonetheless.

"So expedience sent the professor straight up the stairs last night," Matthew mused, "when he'd claimed to be intent on consulting his references regarding the long-term effects of smoking hashish? Interesting."

"*Straight* up the stairs?"

"Bearing gifts of fruit and flowers, and looking mightily determined. Warms a brother's heart, to see such a devotion to scholarship in a younger sibling."

Abby knew not what to say to that, so she cued her mount into a canter, and left the observant Mr. Belmont laughing in her wake.

* * *

"Your retirement has just become imminent," Axel said, jabbing a finger at the papers on the ornate oak table in Handstreet's conference room. He'd laid Ambers's and Shreve's affidavits and a copy of Abigail's signature next to

Handstreet's so-called power of attorney.

The evidence spoke for itself.

"You purport to have dealt honestly with Mrs. Stoneleigh prior to her marriage," he went on, "but you did not observe her creating this power of attorney, or even compare her signature with any known examples. You accepted Stoneleigh's word that these signatures were valid and cheated a young woman out of her fortune."

Handstreet rose, a bad move from a histrionic standpoint, because he was several inches shorter than Axel.

"You take great liberties with the facts, Mr. Belmont. Mrs. Stoneleigh was grieving, barely an adult, without a friend in the world, depending on shops that teetered on the brink of ruin, and Colonel Stoneleigh took her entire situation in hand. You were not present, he was, and that woman desperately needed his good offices."

Kicking, even in a choice location, was too good for such a maggot.

"Now you compound your fraud with mendacity, Handstreet. Cassius Pettiflower, who prospers in the book trade to this day, says the businesses were doing well, and always had. He investigated the Pennington family finances in anticipation of offering for Abigail, but was repeatedly turned away by Stoneleigh when he came bearing condolences. He has no reason to dissemble, while you wouldn't know the truth if it delivered a stout blow to what passes for your cods."

"You speak ill of the dead," Handstreet sniffed. "The king's man, insulting a respected military—"

Axel leaned across the table, treating Handstreet to his best professorial glower.

"I speak the truth regarding the living. You colluded in Stoneleigh's fraud. You mispresented a young woman's situation and delivered her into the hands of a scheming, vile, greedy, sick, murderous old man. The statute of limitations has not run, Handstreet, not on the fraud, not on conspiracy to commit fraud, not on conspiracy to commit murder."

A beat of silence went by, while Handstreet's gaze dropped to documents which proved his wrongdoing three time over.

The solicitor crumpled into a chair, a legal hot-air balloon losing its wind. "Murder, Mr. Belmont?" Handstreet tugged at his cravat, as if somebody had tightened a noose around his fat neck.

Axel stuffed the documents—including the fraudulent power of attorney—into his saddlebag.

"Mrs. Stoneleigh is recovering from poison administered repeatedly by her husband's hand. You put her in the colonel's care, knowing he'd cheat, lie, steal, and otherwise break the law for his own purposes. How long did you think he'd wait before conveniently assuming the role of sole heir to the Pennington fortune?"

Handstreet turned a mottled red. "Murder, you say?"

"Murder, from a proximity and position of trust you alone made possible."

Handstreet filled the chair with his prosperous figure. Oxford boasted excellent tailors, fine bootmakers, skilled jewelers, all of whom he apparently patronized. No less than three watch chains stretched across his belly, and a gold ring winked on the smallest finger of his left hand.

Crime paid, as Matthew often observed. Crime could pay very well.

"Despite what you might think," Handstreet said, "somebody needed to deal with that young woman's situation, Mr. Belmont."

"And no one in the business community was a close enough friend of the family to do that? Her late grandfather had no trustworthy connections left from his years in the military? Her cousin—now a countess and married to a duke's heir—could not be prevailed upon to solicit the assistance of titled relations?"

Axel had no idea what the cousin's situation might have been years ago, but next of kin still meant something under the law, and Handstreet had done nothing to put Abby in touch with what little family she had.

All the mendacious bluster deserted Handstreet, leaving a frightened, fat, aging disgrace to the legal profession.

"My wife will not survive the scandal," Handstreet rasped. "I beg you to think of my wife. Her nerves are delicate, the physician's bills alone beggar me, and then she's off taking the waters in the north for months… The colonel came across her at Harrogate…"

Stoneleigh, doubtless, had learned of Handstreet's financial woes and the wife's mental instability and had taken advantage.

Though what had Stoneleigh been doing in a venerable, stodgy spa town?

"You will leave the profession," Axel said. "You will tidy up your affairs, close this office, and either live so quietly that Abigail Stoneleigh never hears your name again, or you will leave this county and not return. If the shingle outside your door is not taken down by the first of next month, I will file charges. Your best effort at reparation to the wronged party will be in Mrs. Stoneleigh's hands by that date, or your wife's ill health—or tippling—will be the least of your worries. When information is laid, I can assure you, the signatures will be valid. Good day."

Leaving Handstreet's office for the chilly air of a quiet street was a relief, though Axel was still fuming when two streets over, he opened the door to a nondescript establishment trading as "F. Farleyer, Tobacconist."

Tobacco itself was considered a sacred herb among many indigenous peoples. Axel, however, inherently mistrusted anything—gambling, drink, tobacco, hashish—that lent itself to compulsive consumption.

Witness his tantrum regarding Abigail's medical use of laudanum.

The scent of the tobacconist's shop was pleasant, richly botanical, with smoky overtones of cherry, vanilla, citrus, and spices.

"Good day, sir. May I be of assistance?" A dapper, graying fellow stood behind a marble-topped counter, his spare frame putting Axel in mind of an apothecary.

Axel passed over a card. "I come on the king's business, if you're Mr. Farleyer?"

"Marie Farleyer was my grandmother," the fellow said, studying the card. "She supported herself with this shop through a long widowhood. How might I be of assistance, Mr. Belmont?"

"I'm investigating the death of Colonel Gregory Stoneleigh, whom I understand to have been a devoted patron of your shop."

Farleyer's posture and expression remained unchanged—carefully so. "A pity about the colonel's passing. He was a customer of long standing, and he and his patronage will be missed."

Axel pretended to study the jars lining the shop's shelves, which again put him in mind of an apothecary's or herbalist's establishment.

"I'll pass along your condolences to his widow, but what exactly, was his custom?"

Farleyer tucked the card under the counter. "Why, tobacco, of course."

Today must be Lie to the Magistrate Day in Oxford. "Stoneleigh had no less than twenty different pipes that we've located so far. One expects he'd buy tobacco from a tobacconist. What sort of tobacco?"

"Lately, he favored that blend there to your right, which is mostly Virginian, with a bit of this and that thrown in."

Axel lifted the lid of a large glass jar and took a sniff. "Very appealing." Rich, nutty, a hint of apples, nothing remarkable. Also nothing at all like the blend Stoneleigh had kept in the pouches in his desk drawer.

Farleyer remained behind his counter, his expression bland, his gaze... uneasy.

"If you were out of this blend," Axel asked, "did he have a secondary preference, as some people will alternate between black tea and gunpowder?"

"The jar on the corner of the center table, almost empty. It's popular and relatively inexpensive. The university fellows favor it, and the colonel occasionally did too."

Axel sniffed, and again, other than a general tobacco odor, nothing in the jar fit with his recollection of the tobacco in Stoneleigh's pouch.

"Interesting blend. What's in it?"

Farleyer prattled on from behind his mercantile pulpit as Axel wandered about the little shop, stopping before a shelf of pipes and pamphlets. The paraphernalia of the tobacco habit was arrayed in a manner intended to separate patron from coin—all gleaming brass, shining wood finishes, elegant boxes, and delicate brushes.

And an elegant brass water pipe.

"Do you smoke, Mr. Farleyer?"

"No sir, I do not." No diffidence or hesitation about that reply.

"Neither do I," Axel said. "Hard on the lungs, I think, despite what the physicians say. Then there's the fact that tobacco can become a habit."

A minute pause ensued as Farleyer studied a patron outside the door. The fellow had a hand on the latch, but as Axel approached the counter, the prospective customer went hustling up the walkway.

"A harmless habit, I'm sure, Mr. Belmont, and physicians do assure us it's quite healthful and relaxing. Had you specific inquiries to put to me?"

"Can you tell me anything that might be of interest regarding Colonel Stoneleigh's personal habits? His death does not appear to have been a simple accident."

Farleyer stared past Axel's left shoulder, as if scouring memory for something helpful—or as if concocting a falsehood.

"You already know the colonel smoked, and smoked a fair amount. You know he favored certain blends. I'm not sure what sort of information I could convey that would benefit your inquiry."

Another customer nearly came into the shop and went so far as to touch his hat brim to Farleyer before retreating from the door. Young fellows, both of them, likely university scholars indulging their gentlemanly habits.

Or needlessly running up their accounts.

"Here is what I know," Axel said, coming face-to-face with Farleyer across the marble counter. "You have lied to a magistrate on the king's business not once but three times. Somewhere on these premises you likely stock hashish, and the cannabis from which it is derived. Stoneleigh bought his supply from you. You also lied to me twice regarding the colonel's preferred blends of tobacco, confirming that you have something to hide, though you're not very adept at hiding it. What I don't know, is whether I must arrest you for obstructing my investigation. That matter—for now—remains in your hands."

Farleyer extracted a handkerchief from an interior coat pocket and mopped first his brow, then the corners of his thin lips.

"The colonel's demise had some irregularity about it?"

"No, Mr. Farleyer, it did not. The colonel's demise had *a great deal* of irregularity about it. I'm guessing that the merchandise he or his stable master picked up without fail on the first Wednesday of each month had some irregularity about it too."

The scent of the place was making Axel queasy, and that put him in mind of Abigail, whom he hoped to find napping peacefully in the glass house rocking chair when he returned to Candlewick.

Farleyer tucked his handkerchief away. "The colonel's preferences weren't that unusual, though they ran closer to the fancies of a young man. He liked a bit of cannabis mixed with his tobacco."

The combination wasn't unusual. "Anything else?"

"One doesn't like to speak ill of the—"

Axel slapped both palms down on the marble counter top. "Of the *murdered*. Not simply dead, murdered. His widow has no explanation, no idea who would wish the colonel ill, why, or whether she's safe in her own bed, on the very same premises where her husband lost his life. Relieve yourself of any excesses of discretion, for *I* suffer an excess of zeal when it comes to finding justice for all concerned."

Threats apparently had a greater impact than lectures. Farleyer wilted, much as Handstreet had.

"All right, then, but you must not linger here, Mr. Belmont. You're driving away my regulars, and they are not a patient lot. The colonel, like many who return from India, like many of the university scholars, enjoyed the occasional pipe laced with opium."

Goddamned opium. "How occasional?"

"I cannot say, and not because I want to prolong our conversation. Everybody's sensitivity to opium is different—ask the apothecary across the way if you don't believe me. Some people can use the drug for years with no ill effects. Some people can't function without it and must have increasing quantities or all manner of medical difficulty results. I've rarely seen a tobacco enthusiast become dependent on opium, but then, one wouldn't see such a thing, would one? Nobody advertises an addiction if they can help it."

Axel spared a thought for Handstreet's wife and her delicate nerves, which might well be nothing more than an over-fondness for Madeira, Godfrey's Cordial, or some other patent remedy.

"How much, relatively, did the colonel buy each month?"

"A good amount, but he was a devoted pipe smoker, and enough to send you into endless pipe dreams might have had a barely discernible effect on him."

Outside, a few fat snowflakes drifted down, lazy white harbingers of a miserable ride back to Candlewick. So much for a mug of coffee and plate of rum buns with Axel's nephews.

"I'd like a record of all of the colonel's purchases for the last year, amounts, dates, items, and details, sent out to my residence within the week. Is there anything else you can tell me that might give me insight into the colonel's death?"

Farleyer's mouth twitched. "I didn't like him."

Axel purely and passionately hated the late colonel, on Abigail's behalf if not on general principles.

"Meaning?"

"The college boys smoke their fancy pipes, get behind on their accounts, and are a general bother, but they're college boys. The professors, fellows, and deans, they're a bunch of self-important buffoons, but largely harmless. I like them all. Their custom is steady, and they mean nobody any harm. The colonel and even the dandy he sent 'round to fetch his order acted as if having his custom was a great privilege, but I sensed... desperation. If I forgot to wrap his order before he arrived, or I had too many customers to see to him immediately, he'd fly nearly into a rage. The man of business he sent in his stead wasn't much better."

Another dispassionate observer commenting on Stoneleigh's foul temper.

"Do customers typically use both hashish and opium?"

"Some... the more adventurous, but I don't favor it. Both hashish and opium dull the senses, and the opium can become a habit quickly. One likes to think one is selling a mere recreation to those who can enjoy it. In the colonel's case... he was not my favorite customer."

"If you recall anything else, please drop me a note."

Axel left the premises and on instinct, crossed the street as if heading for the pub three doors up. Before he even reached his destination, three customers had passed through Farleyer's door, suggesting...

Suggesting that procuring their regular supply of tobacco was for those three urgent, and something they'd not undertake with a stranger in the shop. Perhaps Farleyer specialized in certain adulterations of the product. Axel made a note to ask his nephews about that, if he ever got to see them again.

His backside was taking a decided chill from the stone bench he'd appropriated, when the first of Farleyer's customers emerged from the tobacconist's and marched directly across the street to the apothecary.

The second did likewise five minutes later.

A tobacconist adulterating his product with opium had to obtain that opium from somewhere, and the apothecary was the logical source. Nothing unusual about that.

And yet, the cold prickle down the back of Axel's neck had nothing to do with the thickening snow, and everything to do with the apothecary right down the street.

Farleyer needed a reliable supply of high-quality opium to add to his tobacco, and a man bent on poisoning his wife needed a reliable supply of poison to accomplish his goal.

Axel rose and marched straight for the apothecary's door.

* * *

"Well, there is good news," Matthew said, leaning down to sight along his cue stick. "The snow means nobody will be expected to attend services tomorrow."

Abby hadn't thought of that, though it was good news. "And we know Gregory was consuming both hashish and opium, which might explain his foul tempers. One wonders if Sir Dewey knew."

Axel remained by the sideboard, his cue stick in hand. "How could he not? He traveled with Gregory, but either he didn't consider aberrations from regular tobacco use remarkable, or he hoped we'd not consider them noteworthy. Matthew, spring will arrive before you take your shot."

"Genius cannot be hurried. My daughter Priscilla reminds of this regularly."

How easily he spoke of the child, whom Axel had described as a right terror, about eight years of age, devoted to her stories, her pony, and managing her newly acquired older step-siblings.

Matthew took a shot, balls careening about the billiards table, though none sank.

"Abigail, your turn," Axel said. "How is the fair Priscilla? I should ask her for a story of my own."

Such affection he had for a step-niece of recent acquaintance.

"You will wait your proper turn for a story, Professor," Matthew replied, sounding quite fierce. "The boys have already asked for stories, while you rode off in a great pout because I am Priscilla's dragon-slaying, sea monster-taming hero, and she casts you only as the hero's faithful, if somewhat pontifical, brother."

"Abigail, Matthew has been up past his bedtime. Show some pity for an old man grown fanciful and take your shot."

Abby finished her perambulation about the billiards table, seeing that Matthew's strategy had been not to sink anything, but simply to leave her without good options. A metaphor for her current situation, surely.

"Priscilla might trade her uncle a story for a sketch," Abby said, spotting a possible angle. "Or a story in exchange for naming a rose after her." Abby drew aim, as Axel had shown her to do, then had to straighten and yawn behind her hand.

"Matthew let you wear yourself out," Axel groused, taking her cue stick from her. "I cannot trust my own brother to provide a responsible escort to a lady in delicate health. Some hero he is."

"You're the one who traveled to Oxford and back," Abby retorted, though the effect was spoiled by another yawn. "And you brought a snowstorm on your heels."

How she longed to lean into his embrace, to cup his cheek and invite him to rest against her.

That arduous trip to and from Oxford had revealed that Gregory's pipes had been more significant than she'd known, possibly accounting for his increasingly rotten temper. A small answer, but better than no answer at all.

"I will concede a draw," Matthew said, replacing his cue stick on the rack opposite the sideboard. "Abigail is yawning, and my own fatigue has caught up with me. I don't know that a single hunt scene—a single painting—remains on the walls at Stoneleigh Manor, though nobody warns a fellow that art can be heavy."

Heartache weighed more, but Abby had rejoiced to see those damned paintings coming down, one by one.

"I'll bid you good night, Matthew," Axel said, putting the other two cue sticks on the rack. "My thanks for accompanying Abigail on her errand today."

"Mine too," Abby said. "I felt safer with you along."

"While I felt useful. Good night to you both."

Matthew kissed Abby's cheek and took himself off. Abby waited until the sound of his boot steps in the corridor had faded to slip her arms around Axel's waist.

"I worried for you so when the snow started coming down in earnest."

Axel's embrace was snug and already dear. His scent was familiar, as were his lean, muscular contours, and even the small silences preceding much of his speech. Abby mentally pictured him behind a podium, arranging note-cards before embarking on the spoken word.

"You told me to leave town at the first sign of snow."

Which he must have done. "You wanted to kill Handstreet, didn't you?"

"Yes." No hesitation there. "Abigail, I didn't come straight home after leaving the tobacconist's."

"I won't like this, will I?" She loved holding him and being held by him, though.

"You would like this less if I kept it to myself. Across the street from the tobacconist's is an apothecary. On the first Wednesday morning of the month, without fail, the apothecary sent goods across the street to Farleyer's for inclusion in the colonel's regular order. The apothecary's inventory was extensive, and I was assured he has connections to London, as well as several port cities."

"I can't hate Gregory any more than I do. What was he procuring at the apothecary?"

Axel's hand settled on Abby's nape, and the upset stirring to life inside her calmed. In the course of one shared night, he'd learned how to soothe her with the sweetest, unhurried caress to the back of her neck.

"The colonel bought a number of items, such as I might buy if I wanted to create the illusion that my wife enjoyed dithering over her toilette. Powders, salves, a bottle of scent, cosmetics."

"I have one bottle of scent," Abby said. "Lavinia sent it to me almost a year ago. Was there a mistress after all?"

A sigh breezed past her cheek. "I doubt, given recent developments, that Gregory was able to entertain a mistress."

Abby's mind groped for connections and found only dread. "Tell me."

"The goods Gregory ordered from the apothecary varied from month to month, and many I know to be harmless. Decoys perhaps. Others contained substances, arsenic, for example, that are considered safe in moderation, but not when used in quantity or for long periods. The result is that somewhere, likely in the second safe at Stoneleigh Manor, is a supply of sundries from a well-stocked apothecary, and Stoneleigh was using them to poison you."

Axel was not lecturing her. Each word was a labored admission, part confession, part curse. She'd accepted that Gregory had been poisoning her, but further proof only made the reality upsetting all over again.

"I don't use cosmetics."

"We suspect the demented fiend stirred the poison into your tea, my dear, at least. What remains might be in a sugar bowl, mixed into a jar of your bath soap, sprinkled into the drawer that holds your favorite tea, anywhere. You could poison yourself inadvertently, to say nothing of what might befall your staff. I have no way of knowing where on the premises the poison might be, but a cache of deadly mischief secreted where you live is the stuff of my worst nightmares, Abigail."

CHAPTER NINETEEN

Axel's concern was precious to Abby, his love would have been... Well. Abby had his affection, his protectiveness, and for the moment, his company. His very worried, weary company.

"We are both too tired to think this through, and Matthew will want to add his observations. Nobody on my staff is sickening, nor have they since I started to feel poorly over the summer."

Axel peered down at her, and Abby could almost see the gears of his mind whirring to life, and worry ebbing as logic seized hold of him.

"An interesting point. You also enjoyed better health when Gregory was not on the premises. Nobody has sickened? Not a chambermaid or an underfootman?"

A clock struck eleven, the hour at which Gregory had been killed. Abby bundled closer, and Axel likely knew exactly why.

"Mrs. Jensen would have told me if anybody's health was fading," Abby said. "Now that they know I'm coming back, the staff has been busy putting the place to rights. Every tweenie, footman, and scullery maid is putting in long hours."

Axel turned her under his arm and began walking with her toward the door. "Apparently there was great effort today. You've started removing the paintings?"

"Every one of those blasted hunt scenes. The only paintings remaining are the ones I colluded with Lavinia to procure. Two in my sitting room, one is in my office, one is immediately outside Gregory's apartments. I'm particularly proud of that one—a cat napping in the sun—because he admired it enough to hang it where he'd see it every day."

"What comes next?"

Abby allowed Axel to steer the conversation from poison and murder to domestic renovations, lists, and schedules, though she well knew he was distracting her on purpose.

"Gregory's apartment still bears the scent of his habits," Abby said. "I've directed that the windows be kept open indefinitely. The snow can ruin his carpets for all I care. I want the stink of him out of my house."

They wandered down the corridor toward the family wing, arm in arm, as any couple might have. The sheer comfort of that, the casual familiarity that had sprung up where loneliness and awkwardness had been… stole Abby's heart all over.

"Will you stay with me tonight?" Abby asked as Axel opened her door and ushered her into the warmth of the bedroom.

"If you're sure, Abigail, but only if—"

Abby plastered herself to him. "I don't want to go back to Stoneleigh Manor, do you understand that? I don't *want* to go. I don't want to set foot on that property, but part of me needs to go. I don't want to introduce myself ever again as Abigail *Stoneleigh*, when by rights I ought to be Abigail Pennington."

"Or Abigail Pettiflower?"

She stepped back and locked the door. "Don't be daft. Help me with my dress hooks, please."

Axel slipped his arms around her from behind and pulled her back against his chest. He wasn't aroused, and that made his embrace all the more dear.

"Tell me again why are you returning to Stoneleigh Manor?"

"I'm changing the name of the place. I don't know to what, but every hint of a mention that Gregory Stoneleigh once dwelled there will be eradicated. That's part of why I'm going back—to kick him out, of the house, of my life, of the lives of my staff. He was a pestilence of a human being, and in many regards, that house requires fumigation."

Axel kissed the side of her neck. "So fierce, and I've every faith you'll accomplish this task in short order. What's the other part?"

The other part was because imposing on the hospitality of a man who'd become friend and lover, champion and companion, was not… not honorable. Abby could eke out a few more weeks at Candlewick, convalescing in one sense, malingering in another, but that simply delayed the inevitable.

Leaving Axel would be awful. Terrifying, heart-wrenching, difficult… but she was his friend too, his lover, his champion. The way forward required fortitude and courage, but what was love, if not fortitude and courage in service to one's beloved?

She turned in his embrace, so they were face-to-face. "I want you to promise me something."

"Anything reasonable. I gave the staff direction to move a daybed out to the glass house tomorrow if the weather permits."

A daybed, upon which Abby might sketch the master cultivator of roses and impossible dreams.

"I want you to promise me, Axel Belmont, that when you create that thornless rose, that perfect specimen of fragrance and beauty without any nasty prickles, that I'll be the first person you share it with. I don't care if it's five years from now, and you are the most celebrated botanist ever to grace the halls of Oxford. I don't care how many empresses and royal gardeners are currying your favor. I want to be the first to congratulate you on making that dream come true."

"Abigail…"

Abigail, *what?* Axel was tired, clearly, and much in need of sleep. Abby needed to feel his arms around her, to listen to his breathing change as he succumbed to slumber, to reach out her foot in the middle of the night and trace the contour of his muscular calf.

She also needed this one, small connection to him, saved for her and her alone.

"Please, Axel. Oxford gets you and your brilliant science for the rest of your days. I have a handful of nights left with you, but I want to share that special rose with you too."

He kissed her forehead. "Such faith you have in me… of course you have my promise. You ask far too little, though, for a woman from whom much has been taken. Should I succeed in cultivating a thornless rose, I will tell no other until I have told you."

A promise from Axel Belmont was no small boon, and he would succeed where so many others had failed. He'd keep his promise, and Abby would be proud of him, even if it killed her.

* * *

Loving Abigail Stoneleigh was killing him.

While Matthew obligingly lolled about the library, practicing his piano, penning letters to family in Sussex, and eating nearly incessantly, Axel hid in the attics with Abigail, sorting through paintings and sketches he could lend her until she'd bought out the shops in London or Oxford.

Or Paris, or Lisbon, may God have mercy on his soul.

He played the violin for her before luncheon, and when the snow stopped, had the footmen shovel a path to the glass house. He took up a shovel himself in defense of his sanity, while Matthew waved and smirked from the library window.

When the way was clear to the glass house—and a daybed had been moved out and somehow wedged through the door—Axel endured the pleasure of modeling for his beloved such parts of himself as she was pleased to sketch.

Abigail was pleased to sketch *all* of him. She was pleased to model all of herself, the fiend, and had she not been a fascinating subject, Axel might have tossed his sketchbook into the fire. He wanted these sketches though, wanted to have them for the rest of his days, like a rare, preserved blossom pressed in an ancient tome.

"Let's visit the hopes and dreams," Abigail said, when Axel had, by virtue of superhuman self-restraint, buttoned her back into her dress. "You've doubtless neglected them in the past few days."

Oddly enough, Axel had. He'd been nagged by a longing for the glass house, but not the grinding impatience he usually suffered after a day or two away from his roses.

"Wouldn't you rather return to the house, Abigail? I can't imagine your lists are complete, or that you don't have letters of condolence to reply to."

Axel had a letter to re-copy, one to the committee at Oxford.

"The condolences have finally slowed down," she said, slipping her arm through his and tugging him toward the first row of roses. "This is a cross, as I recall. You will explain what you're trying to achieve with it."

Axel obliged with botanical blather until they reached the end of the table. Desire was a constant ache low in his gut, and getting through dinner would be a forced march indeed.

Then he spotted the young specimen in the plain green crockery pot.

"What have we here?" He hunkered beside the pot, which held an afterthought of an experiment, two crosses subsequently crossed with each other. The result had as much chance of being a prickly, stinking, weakling as it did of being something else entirely.

"An experiment bearing fruit?" Abigail asked.

"Something." The pale green stem emerging from the soil was... vigorous, and a leaf shoot or two would soon bear its tiny reddish foliage. "No prickles yet, but they sometimes wait for more height before they reveal themselves."

"Such patience." Abby sniffed a bright red neighbor who had no business blooming at this time of year.

The roses did that. Had minds of their own, a sense of humor even, about when they would and would not conform to expectations. Children did too.

"I miss my boys," Axel said, though what wayward paternal sentiment had sprouted that admission, he could not say. He was soon to miss his brother too. He was already missing Abigail. "I have more sympathy for Matthew, who has two sons nearly a hundred miles away when they're off at university, while my children will simply be a short way from home when they matriculate."

Abby kissed his cheek. "You will be there with them, Professor. Have you forgotten your fellowships? Truly, Matthew will need his wife, daughter, and newborn to console him, because every other Belmont will be at Oxford by autumn."

Well, *possibly*.

They moved down through the rows of plants, Axel's chest aching queerly, perhaps due to the odd weather. By the time they emerged from the glass house, the air was nearly mild, the eaves dripping, and the sunshine in the snowy garden blindingly bright.

Or perhaps that ache was due to the fact that Matthew would soon leave, Abigail would soon leave, and Axel could complete his herbal in plenty of time to organize a remove to Oxford for the coming academic year, if need be.

Though for two hours sketching with Abigail in the glass house, he had, indeed forgotten all about the damned fellowships, about the investigation, about everything.

Except the sheer joy of being with her, and the heartache that was sure to follow.

* * *

The fickle weather gave Abby one more night sharing a roof with her beloved. The snow was melting apace, and the result was mud everywhere. Matthew Belmont departed for Oxford, where he'd spend a few days with his sons before trying his luck on the highway.

Abby left the professor in solitude for most of the day after his brother's departure, trusting that the roses would soothe the ache of parting. She packed up her dresses and sent them back to Stoneleigh Manor, reread some of her grandfather's journal, and took herself to the Candlewick library intent on responding to the last of the notes of condolence.

"The calls will start as soon as you're back at Stoneleigh Manor," Hennessey said, setting down a tea tray by Abby's elbow. "You're a pretty widow, and the neighborhood will beat a path to your door. That handsome Sir Dewey will be among them, I'll warrant."

"Thank you for the tea, Hennessey. It's too soon for the calls to properly start, and the roads are a mess. I hope we're spared visitors for a short while at least."

Or maybe the calls would help Abby stay busy while she tried not to wonder how Axel went on. That question had at some point eclipsed the matter of who had killed Gregory Stoneleigh.

Hennessey departed in diplomatic silence, and Abby moved aside Axel's latest pile of letters rather than risk a spill on the lot. On the top of the stack was a single unfolded sheet of vellum, the handwriting elegant and bold.

My Dear Dean Clemson,

The undersigned is in receipt of, and humbly thanks you and the committee for, your kind offers of Thursday last. Upon reflection, I find that my circumstances are now such that either a deanship or continued service in a purely professorial role are the—

Abby set Axel's reply from her as if the paper might burst into flames. Of course, she wanted to respect his privacy. She also wanted that letter to say that nothing Oxford had to offer, not international respect, brilliant scholars, intellectual challenge, nothing, could compare with the love of an upset, almost-virgin widow who was only now learning how to kiss.

"My timing, as usual, is impeccable," Axel said, marching into the library. "That tray needs at least another three sandwiches and a decent pear or two. Cook always goes into a pet when Matthew departs. I should threaten to turn her off without a character and cheer the poor soul up."

"Ask her for a batch scones," Abby said, "but insist she use her own recipe." Axel took the tray to the low table before the sofa. "Come sit with me, Abigail. How did you know I'd finish up in the glass house before dark? You left me all the chocolate tea cakes, which I cannot possible eat myself."

"One can hope," Abby said, abandoning the desk. "It's a wonder my dresses still fit, the way your kitchen feeds me."

He bit into a tea cake and settled beside Abby on the sofa. "If your dresses no longer fit, you must leave them off. Are you ready for tomorrow's journey home?"

No, Abby was not, and the journey was not homeward. She'd simply return to the place she'd lived before being widowed.

"I'm not afraid the killer will return." Not as afraid. "What we've learned about Gregory suggests he could have made enemies with reason to do him bodily harm. I don't condone murder, but neither do I think those enemies have a motivation to harm me."

Axel's arm rested along the back of the sofa, and he had to lean partway across Abby to choose a raspberry tea cake.

"You attribute rational processes to somebody capable of taking a life, madam. I'm worried about you leaving Candlewick, and wish you'd reconsider."

This wasn't what they needed to discuss. "You are sending no less than six footmen, four maids, and Hennessey to guard my well-being. You've lectured my staff at length, inspected the premises, changed the locks on every door, including the larders and pantries, found one safe, and doubtless set the staff to searching out the other—if it exists. What more could you possibly do?"

Besides offer the protection of marriage, which Abby would be honor-bound to reject.

Axel held the raspberry cake up for her to take a bite, then finished it off himself.

The silence became thoughtful, then, for Abby, sad. They would likely not sit thus, companionably enjoying a tea tray, ever again.

"I will miss you, Abigail, and will, as you suggest, continue my investigation as unobtrusively as I can. I expect word from Nicholas any day regarding the import business, and I will start reading your grandfather's journal tomorrow. Your turn to choose a tea cake."

He did this. Made up intimacy out of nothing, so that in the course of the day's least remarkable moments, vines of shared memory wrapped around Abby's heart.

"Bother the tea tray, Axel. What happens when I go back to the manor?" Not Stoneleigh Manor. She'd find another name for it.

He sat back and took her hand in his. "You will have a discussion of this? Very well, we'll discuss it. You shall return to your property, and at the Weasel, some money will exchange hands, for our prospects are doubtless the subject of vulgar wagers. I will finish my herbal, find a comfortable set of rooms in Oxford, and prepare to enjoy the life of a much respected academic. You will become the most visited widow in the shire."

Axel kissed her knuckles and gave her the saddest specimen of a smile she'd ever seen.

"You will not be among those visitors?"

"The talk must die down, Abigail, and you must make a dispassionate appraisal of all the options before you. You are among the wealthiest landowners in the area, if not the shire. I have created certain expectations that mean I cannot offer you matrimony at present, but you well deserve to remarry if you so choose."

The ache in Abby's heart had dulled her brain. "You think I should remarry— you who has had years to remarry and declined the pleasure?"

He patted her hand, for which Abby wanted to smack him. "I think you are lovely, and deserve the devoted appreciation of a man who can stand beside you as a spouse, if that's what you desire."

"What if you're what I desire?"

"Then we should retire early tonight, for tomorrow will be a full and fraught day."

Abby was about to ask him what in the perishing perdition that meant when Hennessey returned with enough sandwiches to satisfy an entire university college.

Rather attempt to eat, Abby rose and paced across the room, which at midafternoon was full of the sunlight reflecting off the snow.

"You are denying me a continuance of our liaison?" she asked, her back to the man who'd promised her much, but not what she needed.

"I'm suggesting that you take time to consider options, Abigail. That right was wrenched away by a scoundrel when your parents died. You were harried, misinformed, taken advantage of, and victimized."

"I hate that word."

"I hate that you suffered."

Blast him and his honorable heart. "Thank you. I understand what you're about." Abby's mind did, the part of her that could puzzle out what the woodcuts in Axel's books depicted, outlandish though they might be. Her heart was like a potted rosebush dropped to the floor of the glass house—torn leaves, exposed roots, shattered crockery, dirt everywhere, blossoms trampled into unrecognizability.

"What am I about, Abigail?"

"You are easing me away, gently, for my own good. You presume to know what my good is."

Abby turned to see him getting to his feet, and for a moment, she expected him to leave the room. She was being… ungrateful, selfish, shrewish.

Also honest. Who was Axel Belmont to say what she needed from whom, or when?

"I am presuming to respect you," Axel said, enfolding her in his arms.

They were before a window, visible from the stable, and Abby cared not one whit. Widows needed comforting, by God, and so did a woman saying good-bye to the man to whom she'd given her heart.

"I'm being cross," Abby said. "Maybe I am afraid after all." Terrified, more like, but not of somebody who'd born a grudge against Gregory Stoneleigh.

"If you need me, Abigail, a note will suffice. I'm still your closest neighbor, and I'm your friend too, and always will be at least that. Turn Stoneleigh Manor upside down, turn every bachelor in the shire upside down, but mostly, be happy. You deserve to be happy, and your happiness matters to me a very great deal."

Abby wanted to run out to the sanctuary of the glass house and weep until sunset.

She settled for making love with Axel on the sofa, then ruining her supper by helping him demolish what remained of the offerings on the tea tray.

* * *

Madeline Hennessey had been half in love with Axel Belmont since she'd joined his household at the age of sixteen. He'd been a few years older than she, but decades wiser, and had ignored or convincingly misinterpreted every inexpert lure she'd cast.

The Belmonts had not been the most cheerful couple, but the young master of the household had been sensible, and devoted to his wife even when not quite enthralled with her. Eventually, Hennessey's respect for Mr. Belmont had eclipsed her infatuation.

As he and Hennessey waited for Mrs. Stoneleigh to emerge from the Candlewick manor house, Hennessey felt neither respectful of, nor devoted to, the professor.

Though she *liked* the poor wretch more than ever.

"So I'm to watch over Mrs. Stoneleigh, see to her welfare, and insinuate myself into her confidences?" Hennessey asked, as Mr. Belmont paced before the mounting block.

They were taking the coach over to Stoneleigh Manor, for a closed conveyance was fitting when a widow was in first mourning. Then too, Mr.

Belmont had spent most of the day in the glass house with Mrs. Stoneleigh. Somebody had muttered about "letting the lanes dry out," though that would take until April.

And now, darkness was falling, and not only in the literal sense.

"You are to *earn* her confidences," Mr. Belmont said, turning to pace the distance between the mounting block and the lamp post. "You are to keep those confidences, from me, from the rest of the staff, from any who would pry. You are to protect her with your life, and bring to bear all the common sense I know you to possess. Abigail—Mrs. Stoneleigh, that is—appreciates common sense.

"Draw upon the second sight you claim to have inherited from your great-grandmother," Mr. Belmont went on, "upon the charm the footmen attribute to you without limit, Hennessey. Abigail Stoneleigh deserves to be happy, to make friends, to entertain those friends, and have them about her. She needs books and beautiful flowers, complicated projects and simple joys. She should take her conservatory in hand—you might suggest that to her, there being a botanist in the neighborhood who has some helpful ideas—and she's to discard mourning if she'd rather ignore convention. Above all things, she should be—"

"She should be with the man who loves her," Hennessey interjected.

Mr. Belmont came to a halt facing the lamp post. Hennessey would not have been surprised to see him smack his forehead against it, repeatedly.

"Many people have supported my cause at the university, Hennessey. I have created obligations there I cannot extricate myself from easily. My own children expect me to be on hand when they matriculate. As for Mrs. Stoneleigh…"

His gaze went from the mud and snow along the main drive to Candlewick's front door. The look in his eyes was wrenching—love, determination, and heartache, blended with the noble bewilderment of a man incapable of acting on a selfish impulse.

"She loves you too," Hennessey said. "You do her no favors by abandoning her this way."

He braced himself with a hand on the lamp post. "Hennessey, you forget your station."

"So turn me off without a character," she shot back. "I'm a woman, I know what it is to love a man beyond reason. She thinks you don't want her, that your infernal roses are more important to you than she is. I must say, for a man of science, you are not very intelligent, sir. I'm glad I no longer work for you. Mrs. Stoneleigh and I will be fine."

The hint of a ghost of a suspicion of a smile that Mrs. Turnbull and Cook watched for and discussed and treasured upon each sighting flickered over Mr. Belmont's features.

"Hennessey, that was a lecture. I'm quite sure the ability to lecture has been grafted onto my very staff."

"I'm not your staff anymore," Hennessey retorted, though in some sense, she wanted to be the professor's friend. His ally, for she did owe him. "Mrs. Stoneleigh will worry about you. Mourning means she can't call on you, and thus you consign her to that stinking house, like a princess locked in a tower. She'll miss you, and her heart will *break* for want of your company when she needs you most. You encourage her affections, and then you turn her out. You are being a dunderhead, sir. A complete, hopeless dunderhead."

He leaned against the lamp post, crossed his arms, and regarded her with such a ferocious scowl, Hennessey was glad she was no longer in his employ.

"I will explain myself to you, Hennessey, out of respect for your years of service to me and my household, though I ought instead to arrest you for some damned thing or other. When a man's regard for a woman exceeds a certain limit, his own needs cease to matter. Above all—above *all*—Abigail Stoneleigh needs to know that she is the sole authority operative in her life. *She chooses* with whom she associates now. *She chooses* the art hanging in her stairwells, the amount of sugar in her every cup of tea, whether her front door is manned by a butler, footman, or porter.

"*She chooses* whether she rides a mare or a gelding, whether her boudoir is done up in green or blue or peacock or cloth of gold, do you hear me? I'll not have it said she was taken advantage of again, that she exercised poor judgment in a weak moment, that her grief clouded her reason. *She chooses*, from a position of unassailable independence, which she has earned very nearly at the cost of her life, and the rest of the world accommodates her choices."

The professor's words rang through the late afternoon air with the conviction of an impassioned sermon. He believed what he said, and he had a point.

Colonel Stoneleigh had been gone only a handful of weeks, and Mrs. Stoneleigh's remarriage now would be seen as hasty. A prudent widow caught her breath after her first dalliance rather than leap straight into remarriage, especially a prudent widow who'd inherited significant wealth.

And yet, there stood Axel Belmont, gaze fixed on the front door like some Romeo beneath his beloved's balcony, his roses very likely all but forgotten.

About damned time.

The door opened, and his expression became that of a man beholding a wish come true. Mrs. Stoneleigh was all in black, though she looked... hale. Healthy, if a bit pale, but black made everybody appear washed out. She moved down the steps with good energy, her gaze clear-eyed and calm.

"Mr. Belmont," she said. "Take me back from whence I came. There's a great deal to be done to set my estate to rights, and I'm sure you'd like to get to your glass houses on such a temperate evening."

He looked puzzled, as if he could not recall which glass houses she referred to, but he handed the lady into the coach, provided Hennessey the same courtesy, and climbed in afterward.

The journey was silent and sad, but as Hennessey watched two people who ought to be together pretend to ignore the brush of the lady's hems over the gentleman's boots, a thought intruded.

For Mrs. Stoneleigh to assume control of her life was important. The slight trepidation in the widow's gaze, the pensiveness of her expression as she pretended to read her correspondence, vindicated the professor's judgment on that point. A wealthy widow needed confidence in life, and confidence did not result from sticking exclusively to the paths others mapped for her.

But men needed confidence too. Mrs. Stoneleigh needed to take charge of the choices in her life, and Mr. Belmont craved—longed—to be chosen for himself, and for himself alone, roses, thorns and all.

CHAPTER TWENTY

Unless Axel immediately concocted a convincing lecture on the inadvisability of breaking a man's heart, he and Abigail would spend their last moments together in silence. She sat across from him in the coach, apparently engrossed in a yet another note of condolence.

"Sir Dewey is leaving for some foxhunting in Leicestershire," she murmured. "He says winter has gone on too long, and hunt season has all but fled. He promises to call upon me when he returns, and has given me his direction. I'm to send to him if I have need."

Would that Sir Dewey had been of a mind to hunt foxes in darkest Peru. "You will send to me, Abigail, if you need anything at all."

Abby stashed the note into her reticule and jerked the strings closed. Hennessey, sitting beside her on the forward facing seat, took to studying the darkening landscape beyond the window.

"I will send to whomever I please, Mr. Belmont."

What imbecile had been ranting—not lecturing, *ranting*—about the necessity of according Abigail Stoneleigh despotic authority over every aspect of her life?

"I beg your pardon, Abigail. I beg—I'm ready to help, if aid is required." Fat lot of help he'd been so far. His almighty aid, over a period of weeks, had failed to solve the mystery of Stoneleigh's murder.

His apology had Abigail staring out the window too. The sun had nearly set, meaning there was nothing for either woman to see outside the coach but dormant trees, snow, and the occasional slash of dead grass or mud. The coach lamps afforded Axel one more opportunity to memorize the curve of Abby's cheek, the slope of her nose, the exact contour of an ear he'd whispered outlandish suggestions into only hours earlier.

"Why is Sir Dewey going hunting?" Abigail murmured.

"Most gentlemen ride to hounds because they like to get tipsy and go for a good gallop." The tipsy part was appealing more strongly by the moment.

"But Sir Dewey doesn't foxhunt. I thought he accompanied Gregory on various jaunts about the countryside because men are social that way, but… maybe it's nothing. With Gregory gone, I expected Sir Dewey might be less inclined to travel."

Did she *want* Sir Dewey to remain consistently in the area? That useless inquiry came to a halt as Axel recalled Sir Dewey himself stating that he had no interest in foxhunting.

A prickle of unease shivered over Axel's nape. "Do you know if Sir Dewey enjoyed shooting?" Sir Dewey's elegant, exotic library came to mind. Not a weapon in sight, not a weapon on display anywhere on the premises.

Premises owned by a bachelor knight with a long and distinguished military career.

"I don't know if he enjoyed shooting," Abby said, gaze swiveling to Axel's. "Now that you mention it, when he and Gregory went off to the grouse moors, they never packed any guns. Gregory had no fowling pieces other than the antiques on display in the library. Don't most men like to use their own firearms when they hunt?"

"My brother certainly claims that familiarity with a trusted piece increases the likelihood of a successful outing." Matthew had said something else, about a case often breaking right after the investigator had given up hope of ever solving it.

The coach turned up the drive to Stoneleigh Manor, while a sense of dread coalesced in Axel's chest.

"I don't want to leave you here, Abigail. I have failed to find the person who killed the colonel, failed to locate the second safe, failed to—"

Failed to tell her he loved her, though that sentiment was not for Hennessey's ears.

Abigail held up a black gloved hand, a gesture clearly intent on silencing the great lecturer.

"I wrote to Gregory on several occasions," she said, "when he'd told me he'd be in London, meeting with Mr. Brandenburg, dealing with matters related to the import business. I suspected he was merely socializing, renewing army acquaintances, doing whatever gentlemen do in London, but he seldom responded to my letters."

"Not every man is a reliable correspondent."

"That's not what I mean," she said, as the coach slowed. "I mean it's as if he never got my letters. I'd send along word that one of his mares had foaled early, and he'd be surprised to see the foal upon his return. I'd pass along a notice that one of his army acquaintances had died, and when I'd condole him on the loss, he be taken aback to hear the news. I didn't confront him about this, but then,

I never confronted him about much of anything."

The prickle of unease came again, more strongly. "You're suggesting Gregory wasn't in London when he said he'd be there, and wasn't off shooting when he was supposed to be on some grouse moor. Now we learn that Sir Dewey, who's never been to a local meet and doesn't own a single hunter, has a sudden compulsion to spend the last weeks of winter chasing foxes far to the north."

The coach came to a halt, and the moment for solving riddles was abruptly overtaken by the moment for saying good-bye. Unease turned to dread, then oddly, to… certainty.

Axel had promised his lady answers. The good-bye would have to wait.

"Hennessey," Axel said, "you will excuse us. Let the staff know Mrs. Stoneleigh will return later this evening, and please be sure all is in readiness for her."

Abigail's expression was wary and curious. "Mr. Belmont, what are you about?"

"I'm kidnapping you, madam. One doesn't like to make a habit of felonious behavior, but we must pay a call on Sir Dewey Fanning. You raise questions to which only he will have the answers."

"Ma'am?" Hennessey said, as the coach door swung open.

Abby didn't spare the open door so much as a glance. "You will excuse us, Hennessey."

Cold air wafted in, and for an instant, Axel was tempted, truly tempted, to kidnap the woman he loved. He'd wanted to see Abigail become independent, self-determined, and confident, but at the same time, he needed to know she was safe.

"I've had enough of being kidnapped, Mr. Belmont," Abby said, when Hennessey had stepped down.

Well, damn. Probably for the best. "I understand. If Sir Dewey is hiding secrets, confronting him might be dangerous. I'll call on him myself. If I learn of anything—"

Abigail pulled the door closed and secured the latch. "Axel, you need not kidnap anybody. We'll go together, and I agree, we need to go now. Sir Dewey's note said he'd be leaving in the morning. Please tell John Coachman to drive on, or we'll lose all the light."

No kidnapping then, *and no saying good-bye*. Not just yet. They'd carry on together. Like a good, healthy graft, or a robust cross. Together was a fine concept, as was anything that delayed the moment Axel had to bid his lady farewell.

* * *

Two sentiments blended for Abby as the coach rattled down the drive and Axel took an elegant, business-like pistol from beneath the seat. First, she admitted to a ferocious protectiveness toward Axel Belmont. Not simply attraction, respect, affection, or admiration…

She'd slay dragons for him, without question, because he'd already slain dragons for her. Her fears, doubts, poor health, insecurities, and not a little ignorance had gone down to defeat at the professor's capable hands.

The second emotion was nowhere near as fine and noble—sheer relief, to put off the moment of parting. The staff had worked hard to scrub, clean, reorganize and re-arrange Stoneleigh Manor's interior, but nothing could change the memories Abby had of the place.

Nor make her memories of Candlewick any less dear.

"Sir Dewey told me he occasionally called on Gregory at the odd hour," Axel said, switching to the forward facing seat and taking Abby's hand. "I thought that meant calling in the middle of a morning ride, but I'm guessing you might have occasionally found Sir Dewey in Gregory's study sharing a nightcap."

Oh, how lovely, to hold Axel's hand again. They'd spent most of the afternoon intimately entwined, but the simple clasp of hands was precious too.

"Now that you bring it up, yes. In years past, I'd find Sir Dewey with Gregory in his study at a late hour. I assumed he'd come in the front door, but I suppose…"

"Sir Dewey might have used the French doors. I would have an easier time viewing him as a killer if more of what he'd said had rung false."

Honest men did not easily see perfidy in others—neither did honest women. "He told you Gregory had been importing erotica, didn't he?"

"Sir Dewey spoke in delicacies and innuendo, and as if his knowledge was from years past. Nicholas cast doubt on the profitability of importing erotica, there being a surfeit of prurient material available domestically."

Darkness overtook daylight while the horses trotted on, until the lamps of Sir Dewey's gateposts came into view.

"You don't want Sir Dewey to be a murderer," Abby said. "Neither do I."

"He was kind to his dog, Abigail. Indulgent toward his staff, decorated for bravery. He was protective of you. I nearly hated him for that, but I respected him too. What the hell?"

The coach had slowed to make the turn and then pulled to a jostling halt. The way was narrowed by banks of snow on either side of the drive, and thus the path forward afforded space for only one coach to pass at a time.

Which meant Sir Dewey's coach, traveling in the opposite direction, had also come to a bouncing, swaying stop.

* * *

Axel stepped down from the coach, the pistol at his side. Abigail climbed out unassisted and took up a place behind him.

"Sir Dewey," Axel called, "you will come out with your hands in the air, and you will explain why you're leaving the shire at an hour when the roads grow treacherous."

"Mr. Belmont has a lovely gun," Abigail added, her voice colder than the winter night. "Do as he says."

The coach door opened, and Sir Dewey emerged, two gloved hands held aloft. The lamps cast lurid shadows over his features, and yet, his expression was not that of a murdering madman.

"The gun isn't necessary," Sir Dewey said, sounding weary. "I have a mortal dislike for guns and stand before you unarmed."

"You stand before us untruthful," Abigail retorted, sidling out from behind Axel. "What in the perishing damnation is going on, Sir Dewey? You have prevaricated if not lied outright, and denied the king's man the answers he's been diligently seeking. Did you kill Gregory?"

Right to the point, and she was staying clear of Axel's line of fire.

"I did," Sir Dewey said. "I shot the colonel, and will sign any document you please to that effect, but I must ask again that the gun be put aside."

A trickle of perspiration ran down the side of his face, despite the cold.

Axel should have been relieved to have found an answer to the riddle of Gregory Stoneleigh's death. He felt instead a staggering sense of self-castigation.

Of course, Sir Dewey had killed Gregory Stoneleigh. *Of course.*

"If you attempt to flee, I will shoot you," Axel said. "My aim is excellent, and I am vexed enough to put a bullet in your handsome arse." The entire investigation lay before Axel like a series of misguided crosses, aiming to strengthen one set of characteristics, while concentrating weakness in another.

"You have my word, I will not attempt to flee," Sir Dewey said. "Perhaps we might continue this discussion indoors, for I would do nothing to put Mrs. Stoneleigh at risk of harm."

"Spare me your chivalry," Abigail spat. "And start walking."

Axel lowered the gun, but remained behind Sir Dewey for the duration of the march up the drive. Only when they were ensconced before a blazing fire in the elegant library did Axel set the pistol aside.

"The most common motives for murder," he said, "are passion, greed, and revenge. I looked for somebody with a proper motive for murder, when I should have been looking, not for the person with a motive to kill Gregory Stoneleigh, but for the person Stoneleigh was most likely to have been aiming for when he died. You killed Stoneleigh in self-defense."

Sir Dewey had taken up a place near the fire, one hand propped on the mantel. At Axel's statement, he didn't nod, so much as he bowed his head.

Abigail remained by Axel's side, exactly where he preferred she be.

"You shot in self-defense," she said, "confirming Gregory was a menace to all in his ambit save his blighted dogs and hunters. Nonetheless, when you had every opportunity to explain the situation to one of the most rational, intelligent, diligent magistrates in the realm, you withheld that information.

Why?"

"Might we put the gun out of sight?" Sir Dewey asked. He gaze was on the fire, but with a studied detachment, such as a person terrified of dogs might employ when confronted with the realization that a mastiff gnawed a bone across the room.

"Abigail, what say you?"

She set the gun on the sideboard and came back to Axel's side, while a large, long-haired black cat stropped itself against Sir Dewey's boots.

"I am uneasy around guns," Sir Dewey said. "I'll not provoke anybody to firing one if I can help it."

"You can help," Abigail snapped, "by telling the truth. You and Gregory went haring all over the realm, and you weren't pursuing any kind of gentlemanly sport. What were you about?"

A snippet of conversation emerged from Axel's memory. "Explain what the colonel might have been doing in Harrogate, for example. Foxes and grouse do not frequent spa towns, as best I recollect."

The fire popped, and Sir Dewey started. Abby, by contrast, remained calm. The shire should start appointing widows to serve as magistrate, so steady were her nerves.

"Gregory was addicted to the opium," Sir Dewey said. "Addicted and growing worse. All those so-called shooting trips to the north, the removes to Melton in hunt season, the weeks spent allegedly in London, were Gregory's attempts to get free of the opium. He failed. Inevitably, he failed."

Axel endured another spike of self-castigation, for evidence of Stoneleigh's dependence—the twenty pipes, the mandatory trips to Farleyer's, the erratic moods—was obvious only in hindsight.

"Opium?" Abigail murmured. "Why should that matter? Many people rely on a regular dose, and few are the worse for it."

"Might we be seated?" Sir Dewey asked.

"Take the arm chair," Abby said. "Mr. Belmont, if you'd join me on the sofa?"

Sir Dewey threw himself into the chair nearest the hearth. Gone was the witty, urbane veteran, and in his place was an exhausted man burdened by a sad tale.

"Mrs. Stoneleigh asks why Gregory Stoneleigh, of all His Majesty's subjects, could not manage a cordial relationship with a medicinal commonplace," Sir Dewey began. "I don't know the answer to that, but I can tell you the sheer humiliation of addiction drove the colonel. He could not abide what the cravings did to him, could not stand to be vulnerable to a white powder obtained from half way around the world at significant cost."

"Why not simply tell Stoneleigh to get help from some obliging physician?" Axel asked. "Why involve yourself in the situation at all? Were you still entangled in the business?"

The cat hopped into Sir Dewey's lap. Purring commenced, loud enough to be heard across the room.

"I'm knighted for bravery," Sir Dewey said, "but my ability to form coherent sentences is jeopardized by the presence of a gun. There's more to the tale, though the retelling is difficult."

He stroked the cat gently, and the creature settled in his lap. Axel did not want to hear this difficult tale, and yet, he'd promised his lady that he'd find her the truth.

"Say on, Sir Dewey. I've an investigation to conclude, and I'm sure Mrs. Stoneleigh is interested in what you have to tell us."

* * *

Sir Dewey had nearly been one of Gregory's victims too. This thought tolled through Abby with the clarity of a bell, and the solemnity too. This soldier, a man in his prime, had also been in some regard tainted by Gregory Stoneleigh's lies and schemes. If a wealthy officer, a knight of the realm in full control of his situation, had fallen prey to Gregory's machinations, what chance had a grieving shop girl had?

"Tell us your story, Sir Dewey," Abby said. "Don't consider it a confession. Consider it an explanation."

Axel's gaze was approving. Despite the circumstances, Abby kissed him, and a ghost of a smile curved his lips. The brave knight was pale, nervous, and exhausted, while Axel looked good. The sight of him, the simple sight of him, fortified Abby as nothing else could.

She went to the sideboard and poured Sir Dewey a finger of brandy.

When he accepted the glass, his hand trembled minutely. "My sincere thanks." He downed the brandy in a single toss, and passed back the glass.

"I am not nervous of guns," Sir Dewey said. "I am entirely undone by them. I was taken captive in India, and day after day, the guards would play a game with me. They would lay out eight pistols, put a bullet in one of them, and then rearrange the guns, very rapidly while I watched. I was to choose a succession of pistols. Each one I chose was then fired against my temple. By the time I escaped, even saying certain words caused me to shake uncontrollably."

Axel got up and poured a second serving of brandy. He offered it first to Sir Dewey, who declined, then to Abigail. She took a sip and passed the remainder back to him before he resumed his place beside her, drink in hand.

"You have suffered much," Axel said, "and some of the damage was permanent."

"I hope not," Sir Dewey replied. "But years later, I am still not... I can hold a gun. I can even fire a gun, apparently. A relief, that, as awful as the admission is. Shall you see me hanged, Belmont?"

Despite Sir Dewey's casual tone, despite even Abby's anger at him, her heart hurt for him too. He had been brave, he was brave still—also broken.

"Gregory's gun was loaded," Abby said. "Both chambers. That's how we knew he didn't take his own life."

Sir Dewey looked away, into the fire. "Belmont had said only that Gregory's gun was not the one that had killed him. I hadn't been... I hadn't been sure. My mental faculties have... I've vacillated between an urge to confess, which will bring scandal down on my siblings if I'm convicted of murder, and silence, which brought dishonor to me, and left Mrs. Stoneleigh without answers."

"You truly did fire in self-defense," Axel said. "Why didn't you simply sever all ties with Stoneleigh and warn Abigail of his problems?"

"Mrs. Stoneleigh was not well," Sir Dewey said, "and a wife would have no authority to deal with a husband's addiction. Stoneleigh had brought his habit home with him from India. I know this, you see, because I am the person who introduced him to the sedative qualities of opium."

Sir Dewey's hand paused on the cat's back, as if the past had become more real to him than the present.

"The patent remedies are a pale imitation of the relief the pure product can yield," he said, "and when I escaped from my captors, I became dependent on the drug. Guns are a fact of military life, and there I was, dreading every morning inspection."

Abby knew how that felt. Dreading every breakfast meal, praying for hunt season to start early, praying for a late spring, regardless of the impact on the crops, because a late spring would have meant Gregory tarried at Melton.

Or wherever Sir Dewey had taken him.

Axel was sitting too close to her for propriety, thigh to thigh. She took comfort from his nearness and hoped he took comfort from hers.

"Are you addicted now?" she asked.

"Mercifully, no," Sir Dewey said. "I weaned myself, I left India, I let time work what healing it could. I surrounded myself with people I trust, I allowed myself only moderate use of spirits, and I forced myself into increasing proximity with guns, by the most gradual degrees. I started with a painting that included a gun as a detail and made myself study it from across the room."

"All very commendable," Axel said, "but what has this to do with Gregory Stoneleigh?"

Sir Dewey seemed calmer now, but also infinitely sad. As if all the charm and manners he wore so consistently had weighed as much as armor, which for the first time, Abby was seeing him without.

"Stoneleigh learned his opium habit from me, sent his servants to buy it where mine bought my supply. I eventually explained to him why I'd begun using the drug, hoping I could prevent him from growing dependent. He was at first scornful of my weakness, then he blamed me for his inability to control his habit."

"He ridiculed your honor," Abby said. "He ridiculed my intellect, my innocence, my grief, my reading, my music, and made sure everybody in the neighborhood had reason to suspect me of mental incompetence."

Sir Dewey sat up straighter at Abby's recitation. "I kept telling myself—and Gregory told me too—that a once honorable officer had been ruined because of me, because of a comment I'd made over tea that an occasional pipe could make life more bearable."

Abby shared a look with Sir Dewey, an acknowledgment of both victimhood and survivorship.

"Disabuse yourself of the notion that you ruined a competent officer," Axel said. "I've corresponded with some of Stoneleigh's military acquaintances. He was a harsh commanding officer, at best."

"Commanded from the rear," Sir Dewey muttered. "He was liberal with the lash, and parsimonious with commendations."

"You didn't ruin him," Abby said. "And he didn't ruin you." Damn Gregory Stoneleigh to the blackest pit, for he'd surely condemned Sir Dewey to endless suffering.

"You are generous," Sir Dewey said. "I had to try though, to free the colonel from the drug. He demanded it of me, blamed me for his situation, and threatened to reveal my cowardice to all and sundry. I did try repeatedly, Mrs. Stoneleigh, but the measures that had proven effective for me had taken years, with false starts and false dawns. The colonel wanted instant resolution of his cravings. All issues of dependence aside, I fear he was losing his reason."

The cat rubbed its head against Sir Dewey's chin, and Abby swallowed past a lump in her throat. Gregory had denied her even a pet of her own. At least Sir Dewey had had the comfort of the mute beasts.

"Stoneleigh had certainly lost his moral compass," Axel said, "if ever he possessed one. You might have weaned him from the drug, you could not have repaired his integrity. One wonders if the drugs were to assuage his guilty conscience, assuming he had any conscience at all."

Abby resisted the urge to lay her head on Axel's shoulder. She'd been aware of Gregory's true nature for a handful of weeks, while Sir Dewey had been in Gregory's confidence for years.

"Tell us about the night Stoneleigh tried to kill you," Axel said.

CHAPTER TWENTY-ONE

Oh, what relief Abby felt, when Axel recast the facts for Sir Dewey into the posture of a life saved rather than a life taken. No longer the night of the murder, but the night Gregory had tried to take another victim's life and failed.

"Gregory sent Ambers with a note earlier in the day," Sir Dewey said, "summoning me for a late-night chat, which was not unusual. I'd been trying to tempt him into some time away, but he did not oblige me. His manner was gloating and secretive, and he hinted that soon, all of our racketing about would be unnecessary. I had noticed that Mrs. Stoneleigh was increasingly ill, and when I asked Gregory if he feared for his wife's well-being, he laughed.

"That laugh," Sir Dewey went on, "wasn't maniacal or forced. Gregory's laughter was friendly, sad, regretful… that laugh said he was utterly lost, beyond decency. He'd been cleaning his pistols when I arrived, and instinct told me to remove them from his grasp. I put one out of the colonel's reach on the sideboard, as if making a place to set Stoneleigh's brandy down among the items on his desk. I never supposed the gun was loaded, and even touching it made me uneasy."

"Stoneleigh doubtless noted your disquiet," Axel said.

"He taunted me, of course. Asked when I'd get over my cowardice, asked if the knighthood weighed on my conscience when I couldn't even trust myself to shoot a damned pheasant. I can't, by the way. Hadn't killed another living creature since I came home, until Gregory drew his pistol on me."

"Do you doubt that Gregory was planning to kill you?" Abby asked. "He had loaded two guns, Sir Dewey. Four shots is more than enough to end any life."

"I know when I turned from the sideboard, to tell the colonel to shut his damned mouth, he was holding one of those guns on me, smiling a genial, condescending smile, his nightcap at his elbow, his wife asleep upstairs, possibly losing ground day by day to either neglect or worse at his hands.

"I hated him then," Sir Dewey said. "I hated him with everything in me, and I do not apologize for that. He was confident I would not defend myself in any fashion."

"Stoneleigh ridiculed you," Axel said. "He made implied threats on his spouse's life, and he held a gun on you when you were unarmed. Then what happened?"

Sir Dewey's countenance grew thoughtful at Axel's summation. "Stoneleigh leveled the gun at me, told me I'd become a nuisance, and commended me to the company of the angels, where his wife would soon join me. He regretted that a knight of the realm who struggled with terrible memories was about to become aggressively violent—meaning myself, of course—and to require the same mercy as a rabid dog would."

"With no one to gainsay him," Axel said, "Stoneleigh's claim to have fired in self defense would likely have stood. You would be dead, and Mrs. Stoneleigh still very much in harm's way."

Sir Dewey remained silent for a moment, perhaps absorbing the absolution in Axel's words.

Abby remained silent as well, though this recitation relieved the last of the fears she'd carried with her from Candlewick. She was safe in her own home. The remaining challenge was to fashion her future according to the dictates of her own heart.

"I do not recall picking up the gun I'd set on the sideboard," Sir Dewey said. "I recall the kick of the recoil in my grasp. I was out the French doors in the next instant, running through the darkness like the hounds of hell were after me, the gun still in my hand. Had there been a cliff at the edge of Stoneleigh's property, I would have run straight off it. I don't expect anybody to understand, but in an odd way, Stoneleigh gave me a parting gift, for I learned that night that I do not want die—not with Stoneleigh's bullet in my heart, and not with a noose about my neck either."

"There is a precipice," Axel said. "Please consider carefully whether you leap off of it after all the effort you've put forth to regain safety. Stoneleigh tormented you with guilt for years, used you as his personal nursemaid, put you into proximity with guns and drugs knowing your aversion to both, and ultimately sought to kill you. Your crime, if any, is a misguided excess of honor. I suggest you forgive yourself for it."

Oh, what a brilliant lecture. Abby nearly applauded, but that would have meant turning loose of Axel's hand.

"And yet," Sir Dewey said, setting the cat down and rising, "I will apologize to Mrs. Stoneleigh. I allowed her to suffer groundless fears, when I should have come forward and trusted to the king's justice. Had I been a better friend to her, she might be in more robust health. Had I been more willing to see the evidence of my own eyes, her husband's poor treatment of her might have ended... I'm rambling. I'm sorry. I wish I'd killed him sooner. I should apologize for that, but I'm... Forgive me."

Sir Dewey was a dignified figure, a portrait of weary honor by the crackling fire, and yet Abigail had a sense he had not yet found... peace. Years and years of struggling, and part of him was yet held captive by savages.

"I wish the colonel had suffered the fate you did," Abby said. "In India. I wish those demented, vile, ingenious guards with their loaded guns had captured Gregory instead of you. Justice would have been better served all around."

The man knighted for bravery went entirely still, not simply motionless. He stared into the fire for a long moment, while the flames crackled and the clock ticked. Axel raised Abby's hand and kissed her knuckles, though he too remained quiet, as if waiting for a promising scholar to mentally thrash his way to a correct answer.

"*Yes,*" Sir Dewey said, smacking the mantel with his fist. "Yes, exactly. That is... that is brilliant, Mrs. Stoneleigh. I thank you."

"I quite agree," Axel said, standing and drawing Abby to her feet. "Such a fate for Stoneleigh has a pleasing symmetry, and we can comfort ourselves with the possibility that in the hereafter, he's enduring exactly such torment. Sir Dewey, we will take our leave of you. I have a report to write and an investigation to conclude. In future, I hope you'll call at Candlewick, even if Mrs. Stoneleigh no longer bides there."

How kind Axel was, and how bewildered Sir Dewey appeared.

"Call often," Abby said. "I owe you much. Hospitality is the least I can offer in return."

Sir Dewey saw them out, looking all the while as if he were translating parting civilities from an obscure foreign language.

"I'll bid you both good night," he said, "and thank you for the compliment of your continuing regard."

He bowed them on their way, and Abby went into the cold, night air with a sense of enormous relief.

"He'd make a decent magistrate," Axel said, escorting Abby down the steps and into the waiting coach. "The poor wretch is ready to collapse with relief though. As am I."

While Abby was ready to collapse with... love? Frustration? She kissed Axel's cheek.

"You handled that beautifully. I doubt Sir Dewey has told another soul that awful tale, not the whole of it. Confession is good for the soul, and he'll make a brilliant magistrate." He'd make somebody a lovely husband too, the right somebody.

Axel handed Abby into the coach, took the place beside her, wrapped an arm around her shoulders, and rested his chin against her temple.

An "all's right with the world" feeling settled around her heart. All was not right, though. The daft man holding her thought his sole calling was to fill the world with perfect roses.

"Sir Dewey might come to enjoy the magistrate's job," Axel said, as the horses trotted on. "How my brother held the position for years is beyond me. Damned lot of haring about and wrestling with riddles. Now, I suspect there was only the one safe, though I still haven't brought you an explanation for all of Stoneleigh's wealth."

Axel had brought her the truth, and Abby purely loved being close to him. She kissed him again, in gratitude and relief, and simply because she could.

"Abigail." For a man who prided himself on his lectures, he could put a wealth of forbearance and affection in the mere utterance of a name.

"Axel Belmont, come home with me and take me to bed. In the morning, we'll have much to discuss, but for now, I want your arms around me and the feel of you near me as I fall asleep."

She feared he'd resist, and blather on about propriety, a widow's good name, the late hour… Instead, he went uncomplaining to his fate, almost as if the thought of returning to Candlewick without her held no appeal.

When they'd made the journey to Stoneleigh Manor, and he'd escorted her to her bedroom, the disrobing was relaxed and unhurried, the climbing into bed the most mundane, profound comfort imaginable.

Axel took Abby in his arms, spooned himself around her, and then she was dreaming of gleaming spires, and of a gallant botanist, who galloped through golden snow to toss perfect roses at her balcony.

When she awoke in the morning, she was alone in the bed and had no evidence that she'd passed the entire night in Axel's tender embrace.

* * *

Clemson's epistle delicately suggested that a deanship for Axel was a strong possibility, provided the contents of Candlewick's botanical library were entrusted to academic hands—preferably Clemson's.

A few months ago, Axel would have been packing up his treasured books, thanking his lucky stars, and marveling at what a few letters from a deceased empress could do for a fellow's academic aspirations.

Now, he simply missed Abigail. He'd written his report, though the gaps in it bothered him—was there a second safe? If so, what was in it? How had Stoneleigh amassed all that wealth—lucky investments? Chance wagers? Inherited wealth of which he'd kept Abigail in ignorance?

In the space of a week, pondering these questions had given Axel the ability to nearly stop time. The library clock had moved only twenty minutes past the hour of ten in the evening since he'd sat down to deal with correspondence that had been piling up for days.

Twenty-two minutes past the hour saw him sorting through letters, though only one caught his attention, from Nicholas, who'd taken up residence in London in anticipation of the Season.

If Nick had found a bride already…

Axel sat for a moment in a library into which he no longer bothered bringing cut roses. He's sent a bouquet to Abigail days ago, after Sir Dewey's difficult disclosures had been shared.

Axel had risen from a night of rest in Abigail's arms, grateful that she was safe, but even more determined that her future remain her own to command. Since then, he'd had one note from her, thanking him for the flowers. She'd sent back all but two of the footmen, though every male on Axel's staff was in a decline due to Hennessey's departure.

"I am in a decline," Axel informed the pile of correspondence.

He tended his roses, he made notes for his herbal, he dutifully corresponded with his sons, and had taken his nephews out for a meal. He'd even gone to services hoping to see Abigail, but she was trading on her bereavement—or out of charity with Weekes—and eschewing church.

Perhaps she'd been resting… or avoiding a man whose ambitions she'd greatly admired.

"Dratted ambition. May a blight, a smut, and black spot plague all academic ambitions."

Though why shouldn't Abigail admire Axel's ambitions? He'd fed, watered, and tended as if they were the last roses in his possession, though now, he'd give anything to be the blossom Abigail chose to take up to her bedroom at night.

"I'm growing daft." Also lonely. Axel slit open Nick's letter.

Greetings, Professor,

The accompanying parcel includes a sample of the goods Gregory Stoneleigh was importing for distribution to various establishments in London, some of those establishments quite disreputable. One understands why the estimable Sir Dewey would eschew such trade. You will please dissuade my Abigail from marrying such an honorable prig, by the way. If I'm to lose her to anybody, it had better be you.

Those responsible for handling Stoneleigh's goods have become curiously unavailable for interviewing, and Gervaise Stoneleigh has no intention of continuing his late father's commercial enterprise.

When you've realized that Oxford celibacy will be a curse compared to what you could have with Abigail, please do bring your new wife to visit the capital. My flirting skills grow apace, though I have only dear Buttercup's company upon which to practice them. She, alas, is difficult to impress, but at least she has no designs on my freedom.

I remain, as ever, your very dearest,

Wee Nick

"Nicholas, I love you like a brother, but you are fool." A fine opening statement for a long overdue lecture.

Axel uncapped the ink sitting on the standish, took out a sheet of paper, and trimmed the quill pen, for Nick's note wanted answering.

Nick feared that any wife he chose would kidnap his every hour, commandeer his every moment, and begrudge him a quiet morning on horseback. As Matthew had pointed out, the right female, a sensible woman with a good heart and her own affairs to tend to, would never—

A queerish feeling settled over Axel. Not foreboding, and not the warm shivers, either. More of a dawning awareness, like prescience. An image came to his mind, of himself, pacing back and forth before the mounting block, insisting to a mulish Hennessey that Abigail Stoneleigh be given control over every detail over her life, every moment of her day.

"I am an idiot," Axel announced to the room at large. "Abigail did not need anybody to vindicate her right to fashion a life of her own choosing. Abigail has a fine, if recently acquired, sense of her own preferences. I am the one who must work at both divining and expressing my needs and desires."

Insight tumbled upon insight, as Axel recalled himself as the younger Belmont son, largely overlooked in the midst of his mother's drama. He'd sought the quiet of the woods, where he'd wandered for hours, ostensibly collecting botanical specimens while he'd in truth searched for a sense of self-possession.

Then he'd been the youthful husband, nonplussed by his wife's demanding personality. Then he'd become a widowed father with two boys to raise and every eligible woman in the shire determined to supervise him in that undertaking.

"I needed better thorns where the ladies were concerned," he said, setting the quill down. "I needed better judgment... I needed..." All manner of metaphors came to mind, but they all pointed to the same conclusion—one Matthew had tried to drive home.

Abigail saw the real man and supported his dreams.

"I need Abigail."

This admission lifted a great weight from Axel's heart, and replaced it with a hope. His need for her was adult, measured, reasonable, and only slightly tinged with desperation. He would not fall to pieces without Abigail—she hadn't fallen to pieces with him, clearly—but he'd be less than entirely happy without her.

Now *there* was an opening statement upon which a learned and smitten fellow might build the most important lecture he ever presented. Axel crossed to the sideboard, thinking to fortify himself with a tot of courage, when he noticed the parcel Nick had sent up from London.

Crafting a diatribe that would be part marriage proposal, part explanation, and part apology would require many drafts, and Nick's parcel was a loose end, like botanical specimens yet to be catalogued and preserved.

Brown paper and plain twine wrapped about a box about two feet square.

"Best have a look."

Axel used the penknife to slit the twine, tossed the twine into the fire, and did likewise with the paper. The box held a lovely peacock blue silk shawl, a pair of worked brass candlesticks, a fan bearing a painting of a crouching tiger, several unremarkable books of naughty sketches, and a sandalwood box.

That smaller box appeared at first to be filled with chopped straw, more fodder for the fire, until a length of cool, green jade fell into Axel's hand.

"Hilarious, Nicholas. Disreputable establishments, indeed."

The jade was shaped to emulate the erect phallus, its surface scored with a pattern of leaves, lotus blossoms, and vines. Axel set the box on the sideboard and brought the jade to the desk.

The carving was intricate, raising the piece to the level of erotic art. And yet, to a botanist's eye, something was... off. The pattern was stylized, of course, but the weight... Jade was heavy, and this...

Axel took up a quizzing glass, peering at the looping, curving design, until he could make out one line scored more heavily than the others. That single carved line disrupted an otherwise consistent pattern of opposite, alternating leaves, and suggested...

A stout twist opened the jade into top and bottom, and a heap of fine white powder poured onto Axel's desk blotter. He touched a finger to the powder, then to the tip of his tongue.

Bitterness came first, followed by a cool sensation that turned hot, then numb.

"God in heaven."

The clock struck the half hour as Axel yanked the bell-pull.

"Have Ivan saddled," he informed the footman who showed up with two buttons undone on his jacket. "And tell Wheeler to please hurry."

Somewhere in Abigail's house, Stoneleigh had very likely secreted a king's ransom in opium. He'd not only been addicted to the stuff, he'd been *trafficking* in it, and the man who'd abetted the colonel's smuggling was still in Abigail's employment.

* * *

Colonel Brandon was not the stuff of a restless widow's dreams. Mr. Darcy hadn't been worth a second read, and Mrs. Radcliffe lacked... credibility. If only Abby had thought to ask for the loan of some of Axel's herbals and treatises, she might be whiling away her evening tormenting herself in earnest.

A week had gone by, and she'd had... a polite note thanking her for the loan of Grandpapa's journal. She'd all but run out of tasks for the Candlewick footmen to do. Gregory's bedroom had been reduced to a cold empty space, the windows yet open because Abigail could order they be kept so.

Axel might have some ideas for what to do with that apartment, but the professor was apparently busy with his herbal and his roses. Hennessey had shared that much servants' gossip from Candlewick, before Abby's dignity had asserted itself.

Abby also refused to permit herself a few drops of the poppy to ease sleep nearer, because... just because. Another book would have to do until she could order Axel's treatises by mail from one of the shops in town.

She'd spent fruitless hours searching for the second safe Gregory had secreted somewhere on the premises, though her sense of urgency about that task had ebbed given Sir Dewey's explanations.

Not a confession, never that.

"I've thought about Mr. Belmont," she informed her cat. She'd limited herself to two feline companions, for starters. Eros sat at the foot of her bed, looking white, fluffy, and inscrutable. "For an entire week I've thought about him. Pride be damned, I know what and who I want. If Axel Belmont must have his fellowships, then I'll wish him the joy of them, provided he also makes me the merriest widow in the shire."

Psyche hopped onto the bed, already purring. Abby had promoted them from the home farm because they resembled the cats in the paintings she'd slipped past Gregory's guard all those years ago. Confident, dignified, luxuriously healthy, proud... everything Abigail had not been when she'd married Gregory. She loved these cats, loved allowing them onto her bed, or wherever she pleased to settle herself throughout the day.

A thought caught in the gears of her imagination, and insight flared up like a vigorous green shoot in a pot of rich earth.

"I know where that damned safe is," Abby said, pushing off the bed and grabbing a night-robe. Her room was toasty—at all hours, her room was toasty—but the corridors were chilly, and Gregory's apartments were downright frigid.

"I know where that safe is, and may Gregory burn in hell for abusing my sensibilities yet again."

She was out the door, past the exhausted footman slumped in his chair at the end of the corridor, and crossing to the family wing when the recollection of her last encounter with Axel Belmont stopped her.

She knew where the safe was, but she also knew that even at this late hour, her surest ally and champion would come if she sought his aid. Abby roused the footman, gave him quiet instructions, then turned her steps toward the coldest corridor in the house.

* * *

All Axel could think as he rounded the top of the Stoneleigh Manor main stairs, was that Abigail had best be whole and hale, or more murder would be done under this roof. On the heels of that sentiment, he caught sight of something pale whipping around the first turning of the corridor to his right.

The hem of a nightgown? Stoneleigh's ghost? In Axel's present mood, he wasn't above shooting a ghost, nor lecturing one right back to eternal perdition. He pursued as quickly as silence allowed, making the next turn only to see nightmares come back to life.

Abigail stood motionless, this time before the alcove outside Gregory's apartments. A painting of a white cat asleep in the sun rested against the floor, while a man with his back to her once again emptied the contents of a safe.

Axel crept up behind Abigail, just as she took a noiseless step away from the intruder. She nearly bumped into Axel, but something—his scent perhaps?—warned her to look behind her. She stepped aside—the lady had the most wonderful inclination to common sense—and gave Axel a clear shot.

"Turn around, Mr. Ambers," Axel said, "and explain yourself."

Ambers complied slowly, his expression disdainful. "Well, if it isn't the king's buffoon and the charming widow. You can put the gun down, Mr. Belmont. I haven't killed anybody, and you'll never be able to prove otherwise."

Axel brought the gun up. "A buffoon I may be, but you insult the lady at your peril. The use of force to apprehend a fleeing felon is well within my authority—deadly force, as it happens."

"What a cheering thought," Abigail said. "You're trespassing, Mr. Ambers. I'd be very surprised if that safe doesn't hold valuables, suggesting theft is also among your accomplishments. Insulting the man who will decide what you're charged with doesn't strike me as a very smart."

Insulting the lady of the house in Axel's hearing would be downright imbecilic.

"Careful Ambers," Axel said. "If your temper is troubling you, please recall my gun is loaded. I can also charge you with conspiracy to commit murder."

Ambers yanked down his waistcoat. "I have done nothing wrong, and when my father hears of this, you'll regret it, Belmont."

"This would be some fellow with a title?" Axel suggested. "A man who apparently paid for you to have a gentleman's education? For you are well spoken, literate, can curse in French, have passable taste in clothing, and fine penmanship, all of which made you an ideal accomplice in smuggling endeavors. Oh, and I forgot—you also bother the maids, proof positive of titled antecedents."

Axel had the fool's attention now, and Abigail was looking positively impressed. Also a tad chilly, which meant the discussion needed to be brief.

"See here, Belmont. I am the son of no less person than Henry Ambers, eleventh Baron of—"

"Now, Ambers," Axel chided. "His lordship will be very disappointed to learn that his son was involved in trafficking opium... smuggling being a hanging felony, of course. Though perhaps his lordship would be more upset to learn that you were procuring the poison that very nearly brought Mrs.

Stoneleigh to her eternal reward. Accessory before the fact, or conspiracy, that is the question."

Ambers's air of bravado faltered, but Axel's discourse wasn't nearly concluded.

"Farleyer referred to you as a man of business," he went on, "which I took for a reasonable error, given your airs and graces. I wondered why Stoneleigh granted his head groom the use of a lovely cottage. I should also have wondered why a glorified stable boy rode prime horseflesh, dressed to the nines, and swilled brandy at the Weasel rather than good English ale."

"Excellent points," Abigail said. "What I note now is that Ambers needs to be removed from the premises, Mr. Belmont."

Hennessey, flanked by Mrs. Jensen, Heath, and Jeffries, all in evening dishabille, came up on Axel's right.

"Reinforcements," Axel said. "My thanks, Mrs. Stoneleigh."

"Madam sent a summons below stairs," Jeffries said. "Miss Hennessey grasped the situation when madam was not in her apartment. Heath and I are happy to assist, Mr. Belmont."

"As am I," Mrs. Jensen added, brandishing a skillet.

Hennessey said nothing, but her eyes promised a slow, painful demise to Stoneleigh's familiar.

"Lock Mr. Ambers in a loose box stall," Axel said. "Give him a blanket or two, water if he asks for it. Tomorrow, take him to the Weasel and he'll be bound over for the assizes at the next parlor session."

"You can't prove anything," Ambers said, taking a step back and bumping into the safe's open door. "I wasn't even in the house when Stoneleigh died. I can hardly pass over the threshold here without Mrs. Jensen having me followed by a footman, else I might have found this safe sooner. All I want is the sum Stoneleigh promised me for years of loyal service."

Oh, right. Years of loyal service disregarding the law, the Commandments, and common decency.

"Heath, Jeffries, be careful," Axel cautioned. "Ambers go peacefully, and consider writing a confession. You're guilty of trespassing, attempted theft, possibly embezzlement, smuggling, collusion, obstructing a magistrate in the prosecution of his lawful duties... I might suggest the courts sentence you to transportation if you show remorse."

That silenced the culprit, for when transportation loomed as a man's best hope, the situation was dire indeed.

Heath and Jeffries escorted Ambers down the steps, Mrs. Jensen sniffing indignantly as they passed.

"I wondered why he was always in the house during madam's absence," Mrs. Jensen said. "For years, he took his meals at his own table, but once Shreve left, there's Ambers, bothering my maids, and turning up at all hours where he ought not to be."

"Doubtless looking for the safe and any evidence that would tie him to Gregory's crimes," Abigail said. "And like a fool, I ordered that Gregory's balcony doors remain wide open. If Mr. Belmont hadn't shown up—"

She wrapped her arms about her middle.

"You rang for your staff," Axel said. "Ambers was unarmed, and my guess is, he was looking to get the poison and any evidence of smuggling off the premises before he took his leave in April. Perhaps the safe holds records, perhaps there's also cash in there, but we need not discuss this now."

"Come along, Mrs. Stoneleigh," Hennessey said, offering Abigail her shawl. "You'll catch your death in this corridor, and I'm sure Mrs. Jensen can have the kitchen make you up a posset."

That should have been Axel's cue to withdraw, to get back into his cold saddle and ride through the darkness to his own bed. He remained right where he was, close by Abigail's side.

"Thank you, no, Hennessey," she said. "You and Mrs. Jensen have my thanks, for your quick thinking and your bravery. For the present, Mr. Belmont and I have more to discuss. I'll see you both in the morning."

Discussion was encouraging. A fellow engaged in a discussion might slip in a small lecture about true love, dunderheaded tendencies, and undying devotion, with a passing mention of wild passion. Perhaps an entire digression on the topic of wild passion.

Mrs. Jensen sniffed and harrumphed some more, but Hennessey declared that *she* was in need of a posset, and got Mrs. Jensen by the elbow. Before those good ladies were halfway down the stairs, Abigail was in Axel's arms.

And he could not think of one damned useful thing to say.

* * *

The goddamned rose bit Axel on his right index finger, which would pain him when next he took up his quill pen. Such injuries were to be expected when harvesting blooms from the Dragon.

"Perishing lot of thorns," Axel muttered, wrapping his bouquet in chamois. The day was moderate, a foretaste of spring. The same temperature in October would have been brisk, in March it was reassuring.

Axel had spent half the morning bathing, changing his clothing, and searching out fresh blooms and fresh courage. A note from the Weasel confirmed that Ambers was under lock and key, and for once not criticizing the fare he'd been offered.

After cutting a profusion of roses, Axel climbed upon Ivan the Inconveniently Frisky and made for Stoneleigh Manor at a trot, flowers at the ready.

He had a key—thank God he'd thought to keep a key to the front door— but waited like an anxious suitor for Jeffries to admit him.

"Good morning, Mr. Belmont. Mrs. Stoneleigh was preparing to go out.

Shall I see if she's receiving?"

Go out? Abby was a grieving widow. Where would she go out *to?*

"I'll await her,"—where?—"in the conservatory."

"The conservatory is largely unused, sir."

"Never trust a man with an unused conservatory. First rule of amateur botany. I'll be in the conservatory."

Rather than surrender his roses, Axel took them to the dusty, chilly cavern at the back of the house. The southern exposure and the morning hour made the place sunny, at least, and it had...potential.

The few ferns struggling by the door had noticed the lengthening days and weren't struggling quite as miserably, though their air was neglected.

Axel took off a glove and tested the soil, finding it adequately moist for ferns.

"Professor? Have you come to inspect my plants?"

Abigail, in a fetching brown velvet riding habit, stood framed in the doorway. Not a typical half-mourning color, but subdued and dignified nonetheless. The color suited her complexion and hair nicely, and the cut...

Axel did not allow himself to admire how the cut of the outfit flattered the figure she sported now.

He thrust his bouquet at her. "These will need water." The dozen or so blooms had made the journey well. "Be careful, for they've a devil of a lot of thorns. If the stems are trimmed under water, the blossoms seem to last longer."

Abigail leaned in for a whiff. "Marvelous fragrance. Do they have names?"

"Abigail, I care not what names they have. I care what name *you* have."

She took the roses, leather wrapping and all, and set them in a fern pot. "Have you a lecture to deliver, Professor? I had hoped to waken to one of your lectures, but once again, I found you'd stolen away in the night. I was on my way to Candlewick to deliver a lecture of my own."

Contagious, then. Lecturing was contagious after all. "Doubtless, I had a lecture prepared when I left Candlewick, Abigail, though I'm so glad to see you I can't recall a word of it. I went home to fetch you some flowers."

For a moment Axel simply admired her, this woman who'd endured so much and who made love so generously. He'd fallen asleep rearranging supporting statements, sub-theses, propositions, and phrases.

And once again holding on to Abigail for dear life.

She stepped closer and, without touching him anywhere else, kissed him on the mouth.

"Does that aid your recall, sir? Perhaps you'd like to hear my lecture now."

Axel's heart did an odd hop. "I had best bumble onward first, lest your diatribe cause me to lose all heart and hope. I am at present a bit rootless, you see, in need of transplanting."

"I don't want your roses," Abigail said, stepping back. "I would never take them from you. You need not retreat to the tower at Oxford to protect your roses, you daft man."

Daft, well yes. "We are in agreement, then, because I find I don't particularly want my roses either."

"And yet, you came here this morning, bearing flowers. I was sending for you last night, you know. I'd realized that the second safe had to be immediately outside Gregory's rooms. I was so pleased when he admired the last of the four paintings I'd chosen, that I asked if he'd like to hang it in his wing of the house. Nonetheless, I did not want to investigate further without your steadying presence."

The safe had held the colonel's opium, various records, and an appalling quantity of a sweetish, powdery concoction that had to be responsible for Abigail's former decline.

Her words now fortified Axel against that recollection—a little.

"You were sending for me, and here I am, bearing roses, several of which were cut from the thorniest grafting stock in my glass house. I can put any puny specimen in the care of the Dragon, and the next season, the flowers are magnificent. The Dragon never refuses a graft either. The thorns are awful, though. He's a right terror."

And Axel was babbling.

Abby spared the roses a glance. "I'm more than passing fond of the only right terror I know."

That peculiar hop, which Axel suspected might be hope, befell him again. "I thought I'd done it, you know—developed a rose without thorns. Damned little trickster was merely saving them up, but yesterday afternoon, when I realized I'd failed again, all I wanted was to tell you about it. To tell you I might have come a little closer, might have eliminated one more wrong turn. I wanted to show you the results, however the experiment turned out, wanted to discuss them with you."

"You came close? Won't the fellowship—?"

"Abigail, I've refused the fellowships, both of them. Professors can marry, deans can marry, and if Oxford offers me a deanship, I'll discuss that with you too, though I suspect the thieving miscreants only want the contents of my library."

She ran a finger over the petal of the palest rose in the bunch, another of the fragrant white flowers she'd so enjoyed in that same library.

"Deans can marry." This fact inspired her to smile. "You turned down the fellowships, and I think you did this even before I'd left Candlewick. Was that wise, Professor?"

"I don't care if it was wise. Remove the thorns and the result is somehow less of a rose. I can't put it any better than that. Please marry me. My hands are frequently dirty, I forget what time it is when I'm in the glass house, I will pester you without ceasing in bed, and probably any place else with a door that locks, but please marry me, Abigail. The academics, the glass houses, the treatises… they are no substitute for your company, and I would trade them all to walk beside you, to dream beside you, to love you as I have these past few weeks."

That was no sort of lecture, with the main thesis hidden in the undergrowth at the end, no care given to the rhetoric, not a pause for emphasis in the lot. Axel's heart was hammering against his ribs, and he couldn't get a decent breath either.

He snatched up the flowers and thrust them at her. "Please, Abigail."

Gently, she cupped her hands around his, so they both held the bouquet, Axel's grasp protecting her palms from stray thorns.

"I need transplanting too, Axel Belmont. I've aired out this house, beaten every rug, replaced every objectionable painting. I've made lists and schedules, for changing the draperies in this room, the carpets in that one. This will never be my home."

Axel took a step closer, though that crowded the flowers between them. "This could be a handsome property, Abigail. The estate has thrived in your care."

"This estate will never bear the scent of a one-of-a-kind bloom, Axel. All the airing in the world won't change the fact that the library here was assembled to impress with appearances, while boring with its substance. All the—"

This time she snatched a kiss.

"Go on, Abigail."

"I need to know you're happy out in your glass house, while I peek at our collection of erotic books and plan our evening. I want a household where the footmen and the maids flirt madly, where family comes to visit uninvited, sure of a warm welcome. Where friends come for sanctuary and to flirt. Keep your roses, your treatises, your dreams and hopes, but keep me too, Axel Belmont. Please, keep me too."

"All failures," Axel said, kissing her cheek, the roses catching at his cravat. "All of it so much treasured failure without you, Abigail. Come bloom with me, and I shall bloom with you."

The roses got the worst of that kiss, for Abigail grew enthusiastic, lecturing Axel with lips, embrace, hands…everything. The door to the conservatory did *not* lock, and thus after a frustratingly brief period of enjoying Abigail's acceptance of his proposal, Axel allowed her to lead him into the house.

Axel's bouquet soon graced Abigail's bedroom, as did Axel.

In the years that followed, he graced the bedroom with her rather a lot, and the glass house, and a few follies, the occasional picnic blanket, the odd hammock—a renowned professor of botany might be expected to enjoy natural settings—but also the library, the stillroom, a parlor or two, and nearly every room at Candlewick.

Wherever Abigail transplanted him, Axel Belmont thrived, though he left pursuit of the thornless rose to those of more modest dreams and hopes than he enjoyed with his beloved Abigail.

For he'd scaled the tower, earned the love of the lady, and—thorns, roses, and all—earned the happily ever after reserved for only the most intrepid of damsels and bravest of botanists.

-THE END-

To my dear readers!

I hope you enjoyed Axel and Abigail's story, the third in the *Jaded Gentlemen* trilogy (after **Thomas** and **Matthew**), and yes, I expect Sir Dewey will make somebody a lovely husband… I just haven't figured out yet who the somebody should be.

While I ponder that challenge, if you're in the mood for more Regency romance, **Will's True Wish** is available for pre-order. If you've already ordered your copy of the last of the *True Gentlemen* (Will Dorning told me to write that) then you can stay up to date on all my illustrious doin's by signing up for my newsletter at **GraceBurrowes.com/contact.php**. Next year will be busy but loads of fun, too!

And in case you haven't heard… I'm undertaking a very special project in September 2016, which I've called **Scotland With Grace**. For ten days, I'll tour various sights in Scotland with a small group of aspiring writers and avid romance readers. Details on that adventure can be found at **GraceBurrowes. com/retreat.php**, if you'd like to join us. No, you will not have to eat haggis, but yes, you will have a great time and learn a little something about how I write my romances.

As always, you can contact me through my website at **graceburrowes.com**, and I love to hear from my readers.

Happy reading!
Grace Burrowes (who's included a little sneak peek from **Will's True Wish**….)

CHAPTER ONE

"We were having a perfectly well-behaved outing," Cam said, though Cam Dorning and perfect behavior enjoyed only a distant acquaintance. "Just another pleasant stroll in the pleasant park on a pleasant spring morning, until George pissed on her ladyship's parasol."

The culprit sat in the middle of the room, silent and stoic as mastiffs tended to be, tail thumping gently against the carpet.

"Georgette did not insult Lady Susannah's parasol all on her own initiative," Will Dorning retorted. "Somebody let her off the leash." Somebody whom Will had warned repeatedly against allowing the dog to be loose in public unless Will was also present.

"Lady Susannah wasn't on a leash," Cam shot back. "She was taking the air with her sister and Viscount Effington, and his lordship was carrying the lady's parasol—being gallant, or eccentric. I swear Georgette was sniffing the bushes one moment and aiming for Effington's knee the next. Nearly got him too, which is probably what the man deserves for carrying a parasol in public."

Across the earl of Casriel's private study, Ash dissolved into whoops that became pantomimes of a dog raising her leg on various articles of furniture. Cam had to retaliate by shoving at his older brother, which of course necessitated reciprocal shoving from Ash, which caused the dog to whine fretfully.

"I should let Georgette use the pair of you as a canine convenience," Will muttered, stroking her silky, brindle head. She was big, even for a mastiff, and prone to lifting her leg in the fashion of a male dog when annoyed or worried.

"I thought I'd let her gambol about a bit," Cam said. "There I was, a devoted brother trying to be considerate of *your* dog, when the smallest mishap occurs, and you scowl at me as if I farted during grace."

"You do fart during grace," Ash observed. "During breakfast too. You're a farting prodigy, Sycamore Dorning. Wellington could have used you at Waterloo, His Majesty's one-man foul miasma, and the French would still be—"

"Enough," Will muttered. Georgette's tail went still, for the quieter Will became, the harder he was struggling not to kill his younger brothers, and Georgette was a perceptive creature. "Where is the parasol?"

"Left it in the mews," Cam said. "A trifle damp and odiferous, if you know what I mean."

"Stinking, like you," Ash said, sashaying around the study with one hand on his hip and the other pinching his nose. "Perhaps we ought to get you a pretty parasol to distract from your many unfortunate shortcomings."

Casriel would be back from his meeting with the solicitors by supper, and the last thing the earl needed was aggravation from the lower primates masquerading as his younger siblings.

More aggravation, for they'd been blighting the family escutcheon and the family exchequer since birth, the lot of them.

"Sycamore, you have two hours to draft a note of apology to the lady," Will said. "I will review your epistle before you seal it. No blotting, no crossing out, no misspellings."

"An apology!" Cam sputtered, seating himself on the earl's desk. "I'm to apologize on behalf of your dog?! I didn't piss on anybody."

At seventeen years of age, Cam was still growing into his height, still a collection of long limbs and restless movement that hadn't resolved into manly grace. He had the Dorning dark hair and the famous Dorning gentian eyes, though.

Also the Dorning penchant for mischief. Will snatched the leash from Cam's hand and smacked Cam once, gently, for violence upset Georgette and was repellent to Will's instincts as a trainer of dumb beasts.

"Neither of you will take Georgette to the park until further notice," Will said. "If you want to attract the interest of the ladies, I suggest you either polish your limited stores of charm or take in a stray puppy."

"A puppy?" Cam asked, opening a drawer into which he had no business poking his nose. "Puppies are very dear."

Nature had intended that puppies of any species be very dear, for they were an endless bother. Ash, having attained his majority, occasionally impersonated a responsible adult. He ceased his dramatics and perched beside Cam on the desk.

"Shall you apologize to Lady Shakespeare or to Effington's knees?" Ash asked. "At length, or go for the pithy, sincere approach? Headmaster says no blotting, no crossing out, no misspellings. I'm happy to write this apology on your behalf for a sum certain."

Ash had an instinct for business—he had read law—but he lacked the cunning Cam had in abundance.

"Ash makes you a generous offer, Cam," Will said, stowing the leash on the mantel and enduring Georgette's But-I'll-Die-If-We-Remain-Indoors look. "Alas, for your finances, Ash, you'll be too busy procuring an exact replica of the lady's abused accessory, from your own funds."

"My own funds?"

Ash hadn't any funds to speak of. What little money Casriel could spare his younger siblings, they spent on drink and other Town vices.

"An exact replica," Will said. "Not a cheap imitation. I will expect your purchase to be complete by the time Cam has drafted an apology. Away with you both, for I must change into clothing suitable for a call upon an earl's daughter."

Into Town attire, a silly, frilly extravagance that on a man of Will's proportions was a significant waste of fabric. He was a frustrated sheep farmer, not some dandy on the stroll, though he was also, for the present, the Earl of Casriel's heir.

So into his finery he would go.

And upon Lady Susannah Haddonfield, of all ladies, he would call.

* * *

"A big, well-dressed fellow is sauntering up our walk," Lady Della Haddonfield announced. "He's carrying a lovely purple parasol. The dog looks familiar."

Though dogs occasionally accompanied their owners on social calls, men did not typically carry parasols, so Lady Susannah Haddonfield joined Della at the window.

"That's the mastiff we met in the park," Susannah said. "The Dorning boys were with her." A trio of overgrown puppies, really, though the Dorning fellows were growing into the good looks for which the family was well known.

"Effington said that mastiff was the largest dog he'd ever seen," Della replied, nudging the drapery aside. "The viscount does adore his canines. Who can that man be? He's taller than the two we met in the park."

Taller and more conservatively dressed. "The earl, possibly," Susannah said, picking up her volume of Shakespeare's sonnets and resuming her seat. "He and Nicholas are doubtless acquainted. Please don't stand in my light, Della."

Della, being a younger sister, only peered more closely over Susannah's shoulder. "You're poring over the sonnets again. Don't you have them all memorized by now?"

The genteel murmur of the butler admitting a visitor drifted up the stairs, along with a curious clicking sound, and then…

"That was a woof," Susannah said. "From inside this house."

"She seemed a friendly enough dog," Della replied, taking a seat on the sofa. Della was the Haddonfield changeling, small and dark compared to her tall, blond siblings, and she made a pretty picture on the red velvet sofa, her green skirts arranged about her.

"She's an ill-mannered canine," Susannah said, "if my parasol's fate is any indication."

Though the dog was a fair judge of character. Lord Effington fawned over all dogs and occasionally over Della, but Susannah found him tedious. The Dornings' mastiff had lifted her leg upon Lord Effington's knee, and Susannah's parasol had been sacrificed in defense of his lordship's tailoring.

Barrisford tapped on the open door. One never heard Barrisford coming or going, and he seemed to be everywhere in the household at once.

"My ladies, a gentleman has come to call and claims acquaintance with the family."

The butler passed Susannah a card, plain black ink on cream stock, though Della snatched it away before Susannah could read the print.

"Shall I say your ladyships are not at home?" Barrisford asked.

"We're at home," Della said, just as Susannah murmured, "That will suit, Barrisford."

She was coming up on the seventy-third sonnet, her favorite.

"We can receive him together," Della said. "If Nicholas knows the Earl of Casriel, he very likely knows the spares, and Effington fancied that dog most rapturously."

"Effington fancies all dogs." The viscount fancied himself most of all. "You'll give me no peace if I turn our caller away, so show him up, Barrisford, and send along the requisite tray."

"I've never drunk so much tea in all my life as I have this spring," Della said. "No wonder people waltz until all hours and stay up half the night gossiping."

Gossiping, when they might instead be reading. Was any trial on earth more tedious than a London Season?

"Mr. Will Dorning, and Georgette," Barrisford said a moment later. He stepped aside from the parlor door to reveal a large gentleman and an equally outsized dog. Susannah hadn't taken much note of the dog in the park, for she'd been too busy trying not to laugh at Effington. The viscount prided himself on his love of canines, though he was apparently fonder of his riding breeches, for he'd smacked the dog more than once with Susannah's abused parasol.

Barrisford's introduction registered only as the visitor bowed to Susannah.

Will Dorning, not the Earl of Casriel, not one of the younger brothers. Willow Grove Dorning himself. Susannah had both looked for and avoided him for years.

"My Lady Susannah, good day," he said. "A pleasure to see you again. Won't you introduce me to your sister?"

Barrisford melted away, while Della rose from the sofa on a rustle of velvet skirts. "Please do introduce us, Suze."

Della's expression said she'd introduce herself if Susannah failed to oblige.

The dog had more decorum than Della, at least for the moment.

"Lady Delilah Haddonfield," Susannah began, "may I make known to you Mr. Will Dorning, late of Dorset?" Susannah was not about to make introductions for the mastiff. "Mr. Dorning, my sister, Lady Delilah, though she prefers Lady Della."

"My lady." Mr. Dorning bowed correctly over Della's hand, while the dog sat panting at his feet. Like most men, he'd probably be smitten with Della before he took a seat beside her on the sofa. Only Effington's interest had survived the rumors of Della's modest settlements, however.

"Your dog wants something, Mr. Dorning," Susannah said, retreating to her seat by the window.

Mr. Dorning peered at his beast, who was gazing at Della and holding up a large paw.

"Oh, she wants to shake," Della said, taking that paw in her hand and shaking gently. "Good doggy, Georgette. Very pleased to make your acquaintance."

"Georgette, behave," Mr. Dorning muttered, before Susannah was faced with the riddle of whether manners required her to shake the dog's paw.

Georgette turned an innocent expression on her owner, crossed the room, and took a seat at Susannah's knee.

Presuming beast, though Georgette at least didn't stink of dog. Effington's endless canine adornments were the smelliest little creatures.

"My ladies, I'm here to apologize," Mr. Dorning said. "Georgette was in want of manners earlier today. We've come to make restitution for her bad behavior and pass along my brother Sycamore's note of apology."

"Do have a seat, Mr. Dorning," Della said, accepting a sealed missive from their guest. "At least you haven't come to blather on about the weather or to compliment our bonnets."

Bless Della and her gift for small talk, because Susannah was having difficulty thinking.

This was not the version of Will Dorning she'd endured dances with in her adolescence. He'd filled out and settled down, like a horse rising seven. Where a handsome colt had been, a war horse had emerged. Mr. Dorning's boots gleamed, the lace of his cravat fell in soft, tasteful abundance from his throat. His clothing *fit* him, in the sense of being appropriate to his demeanor, accentuating abundant height, muscle, and self-possession.

Even as he sat on the delicate red velvet sofa with a frilly purple parasol across his knees.

"This is for you, my lady," he said, passing Susannah the parasol. "We didn't get the color exactly right, but I hope this will suffice to replace the article that came to grief in the park."

Susannah's parasol had been blue, a stupid confection that had done little to shield a lady's complexion. That parasol hadn't made a very effective bludgeon when turned on the dog.

"The color is lovely," Susannah said, "and the design very similar to the one I carried earlier."

Susannah made the mistake of looking up at that moment, of gazing fully into eyes of such an unusual color, poetry had been written about them. Mr. Dorning's eyes were the purest form of the Dorning heritage, nearly the color of the parasol Susannah accepted from his gloved hands.

Willow Dorning's eyes were not pretty, though. His eyes were the hue of a sunset that had given up the battle with night, such that angry reds and passionate oranges had faded to indigo memories and violet dreams. Seven years ago, his violet eyes had been merely different, part of the Dorning legacy, and he'd been another tall fellow forced to bear his friend's sisters company. In those seven years, his voice had acquired night-sky depths, his grace was now bounded with self-possession.

Though he still apparently loved dogs.

"My thanks for the parasol," Susannah said, possibly repeating herself. "You really need not have bothered. Ah, and here's the tea tray. Della, will you pour?"

Della was effortlessly social. Not the reserved paragon their old sister Nita was, and not as politically astute as their sister Kirsten. Both of those ladies yet bided in Kent, either recently married or anticipating that happy state.

Leaving Susannah unmarried and abandoned as the Season gathered momentum.

Exactly as she'd felt seven years ago.

"Georgette likes you, Susannah," Della said, pouring Mr. Dorning's tea. "Or she likes that parasol."

The dog had not moved from Susannah's knee, though she was ignoring the parasol and sniffing at the sonnets on the side table.

"Georgette is shy," Mr. Dorning said, "and she's usually well mannered, save for occasionally snacking on an old book. Her mischief in the park was an aberration, I assure you. Lady Della, are you enjoying your first London Season?"

For the requisite fifteen minutes, Della and Mr. Dorning made idle talk, while Susannah discreetly nudged the sonnets away from the dog, sipped tea, and felt agreeably ancient. Without Nita or Kirsten on hand, Susannah had become the older sister suited to serving as a chaperone at a social call.

And upon reflection, she didn't feel abandoned by her older sisters. She was simply taking her turn as the spinster in training before becoming a spinster in earnest.

Thank God.

"I'll bid you ladies good day," Mr. Dorning said, rising.

"I'll see you out," Susannah replied, because that was her role, as quasi-chaperone, and having Barrisford tend to that task would have been marginally unfriendly. Mr. Dorning, as the son of an earl, was her social equal, after all.

"Georgette, come." Mr. Dorning did not snap his fingers, though Effington, the only other dog lover in Susannah's acquaintance, snapped his fingers constantly—at dogs and at servants. He'd snapped his fingers at Della once, and Susannah had treated Effington to a glower worthy of her late papa in a taking.

Georgette padded over to her master's side, and Susannah quit the parlor with them, leaving Della to attack the biscuits remaining on the tea tray.

"You didn't used to like dogs," Mr. Dorning observed.

"I still don't like dogs," Susannah replied, though she didn't *dislike* them. Neither did she like cats, birds, silly bonnets, London Seasons, or most people. Horses were at least useful, and sisters could be very dear. Brothers fell somewhere between horses and sisters.

"Georgette begs to differ," Mr. Dorning said as they reached the bottom of the steps. "Or perhaps she was making amends for her trespasses against your parasol by allowing you to pat her for fifteen straight minutes."

Susannah took Mr. Dorning's top hat from the sideboard. "Georgette ignored the new parasol. I think my wardrobe is safe from her lapses in manners, though the day your dog snacks on one of my books will be a sorry day for Georgette, Mr. Dorning."

Despite Susannah's stern words, she and Mr. Dorning were *managing*, getting through the awkwardness of being more or less alone together.

"You're still fond of Shakespeare?" Mr. Dorning asked as he tapped his hat onto his head.

A glancing reference to the past, also to the present. "Of all good literature. You're still waiting for your brother to produce an heir?"

Another reference to their past, for Mr. Dorning had confided this much to Susannah during one of their interminable turns about Lady March's music parlor. Until the Earl of Casriel had an heir in the nursery, Will Dorning's self-appointed lot in life was to be his brother's second-in-command.

"Casriel is as yet unmarried," Mr. Dorning said, "and now my younger brothers strain at the leash to conquer London."

He exchanged his social gloves for riding gloves, giving Susannah a glimpse of masculine hands. Those hands could be kind, she hadn't forgotten that. They'd also apparently learned how to give the dog silent commands, for at Mr. Dorning's gesture, Georgette seated herself near the front door.

"I'm much absorbed keeping Cam and Ash out of trouble," he went on, "while allowing them the latitude to learn self-restraint. Apparently, I must add my loyal hound to the list of parties in need of supervision."

The dog thumped her tail.

Did Will Dorning allow himself any latitude? Any unrestrained moments? He'd been a serious young man. He was formidable now.

"We'll doubtless cross paths with your brothers, then," Susannah said, "for

Della is also determined to storm the social citadels." Once Della was safely wed, Susannah could luxuriate in literary projects, a consummation devoutly to be wished, indeed.

"You have ever had the most intriguing smile," Mr. Dorning observed, apropos of nothing Susannah could divine. "Thank you for accepting my apology, my lady. I look forward to renewing our acquaintance further under happier circumstances."

Having dispensed such effusions as the situation required, he bowed over Susannah's hand and was out the door, his dog trotting at his heels.

An *intriguing* smile? Susannah regarded herself in the mirror over the sideboard. Her reflection was tall, blond, blue-eyed, as unremarkable as an earl's daughter could be amid London's spring crop of beauties. She *was* smiling, though...

And her hands smelled faintly of Georgette. Perhaps she *had* stroked the dog's silky ears a time or two. Or three.

"Though I don't even *like* dogs."

Will's True Wish is now available for pre-order.

Made in the USA
Middletown, DE
20 July 2016